About the Authors

Brenda Harlen is a former attorney who once had the privilege of appearing before the Supreme Court of Canada. The practice of law taught her a lot about the world and reinforced her determination to become a writer – because in fiction, she could promise a happy ending! Now she is an award-winning, RITA® Award–nominated nationally bestselling author of more than thirty titles for Mills & Boon. You can keep up-to-date with Brenda on Facebook and Twitter, or through her website, brendaharlen.com

Sara Orwig lives in Oklahoma and has a deep love of Texas. With a master's degree in English, Sara taught high school English, was Writer-in-Residence at the University of Central Oklahoma and was one of the first inductees into the Oklahoma Professional Writers Hall of Fame. Sara has written mainstream fiction, historical and contemporary romance. Books are beloved treasures that take Sara to magical worlds. She loves both reading and writing them.

USA TODAY bestselling author **Day Leclaire** is described by Mills & Boon as 'one of our most popular vriters ever!' Day's passionate stories warm the heart, which may explain the impressive eleven nominations he's received for the prestigious Romance Writers of \merica RITA® Award. 'There's no better way to spend ach day than writing romances.' Visit www.dayleclaire. com

American Affairs

COLLECTION

American Affairs: Rocky Mountain Rumours

BRENDA HARLEN

SARA ORWIG

DAY LECLAIRE

MILLS & BOON

First Published in Great Britain 2020
By Mills & Boon, an imprint of HarperCollins*Publishers*
1 London Bridge Street, London, SE1 9GF

AMERICAN AFFAIRS: ROCKY MOUNTAIN RUMOURS
© 2020 Harlequin Books S.A.

The Maverick's Thanksgiving Baby © 2014 Harlequin Books S.A.
The Reluctant Heiress © 2012 Sara Orwig
Nothing Short of Perfect © 2011 Day Totton Smith

Special thanks and acknowledgement to Brenda Harlen for her contribution to the *Montana Mavericks: 20 Years in the Saddle!* continuity.

ISBN: 978-0-263-29832-1

For more information visit: www.harpercollins.co.uk/green

Printed and bound in Spain
by CPI, Barcelona

THE MAVERICK'S THANKSGIVING BABY

BRENDA HARLEN

For Leanne Banks,

Who shared some honest truths about
cowboys . . . and other subjects :)

XO

Chapter One

July

Jesse Crawford was an idiot. A completely smitten and tongue-tied idiot.

But far worse than that indisputable fact was that Maggie Roarke now knew it, too.

What had ever possessed him to approach her? What had made him think he could introduce himself and have an actual conversation with a woman like her?

While he'd never been as smooth with women as any of his three brothers, he'd never been so embarrassingly inept, either. But being in close proximity to Maggie seemed to rattle his brain as completely as if he'd been thrown from the back of a horse—and that hadn't happened to him in more than fifteen years.

The first time he saw her, even before he knew her name, he'd been mesmerized. She was tall and willowy with subtle but distinctly feminine curves. Her blond hair spilled onto her shoulders like golden silk and her deep brown eyes could shine with humor or warm with compassion. And her smile—there was just something about her smile that seemed to reach right inside his chest and wrap around his heart. A ridiculously fanciful and foolish idea, of course, and one that he wouldn't dare acknowledge to anyone else.

It was no mystery to Jesse why a man would be attracted to her, but he was still a little mystified by the intensity of *his* reaction to her—especially when he didn't know the first thing about her. The discovery that she was a successful attorney in Los Angeles should have put an end to his ridiculous crush. Experience had proven to him that city girls didn't adapt well to the country, and there was no way a lawyer—from Hollywood of all places—would be interested in a small-town rancher. But still his long-guarded heart refused to be dissuaded.

He'd come to the official opening of the Grace Traub Community Center today because he knew she would be there, because he couldn't resist the opportunity to see her again, even from a distance. It had taken the better part of an hour for him to finally summon the courage to introduce himself. And when he did, without muttering or stumbling over words, he felt reassured that things weren't going too badly.

She offered her hand and, in that brief moment of contact, he'd been certain that he felt a real connection with her. And then she smiled at him, and all his carefully rehearsed words slid back down his throat, leaving him awe-struck and tongue-tied and destroying any hope he had of making a good first impression.

He'd almost been grateful that Arthur Swinton intruded on the moment, whisking her away for a private word. Jesse had stood there for another minute, watching her with the older man and wondering if she might come back to finish the conversation they hadn't even started. But Arthur had no sooner turned away when another man stepped into her path: Jared Winfree—also known as the Romeo of Rust Creek Falls.

The cowboy tipped his head down to talk to her. Maggie smiled at him, though Jesse noticed that her smile didn't seem to have the same debilitating effect on the other man, who leaned closer for a more intimate discussion. Jesse finally unglued his feet from the floor and walked out of the community center, berating himself for his awkwardness.

His cell phone started ringing before he'd hit the bottom step, and he pulled it out to answer the call. At this point, he didn't even care who was on the other end of the line—he was grateful for any distraction.

After a brief conversation with Brett Gable, he was feeling marginally better. The local rancher was having trouble with an ornery stallion and wondered if Jesse could take a look at him and let the owner know if he was wasting his time trying to tame the animal or if he just needed to adjust his tactics. Jesse promised that he'd go out to the Gable ranch the next day.

As he tucked his phone away again, he resolved to keep his focus on four-legged creatures and forget about women. Because while horses might not look as good or smell as pretty, they were a lot easier to understand and a lot less likely to trample all over his heart.

Or throw themselves into his arms?

"Whoa." Jesse caught her gently as she bounced off his chest.

Maggie's wide, startled gaze locked with his. "I'm so sorry," she said breathlessly.

"Everything okay?"

She shook her head, an introspective look now competing with the panic in her dark chocolate-colored eyes. "Are you married?"

"What?" He had no idea what thought process had precipitated the question, but he immediately shook his head. "No."

"Engaged? Involved?"

"No and no," he said, just a little warily.

"Then I'll apologize now and explain later," she told him.

"Apol—"

He'd intended to ask what she thought she needed to apologize for, but that was as far as he got before she lifted her hands to his shoulders and pressed her lips to his.

To say that he was stunned would have been an understatement. But the initial shock was quickly supplanted by other stronger emotions: pleasure, happiness, desire.

He wanted this. He wanted *her*. As if of their own volition, his arms wrapped around her, pulling her against him as he kissed her back.

Somewhere in a part of his brain that was still capable of registering anything beyond the heavenly feel of this woman in his arms, he heard the crunch of gravel beneath heavy, impatient footsteps and a frustrated voice muttering, "Where on earth could she have… Maggie?"

The woman in question eased her mouth from his.

There was desire in her eyes—he wasn't mistaken in that. But there was something else, too—a silent plea?

A plea for what, he didn't know and didn't care. Right now, he would have promised her anything. Everything.

She finally turned to look at the other man, and Jesse did the same.

Jared Winfree's brows were drawn together, his expression dark as he glanced from Maggie to Jesse. "Are you making a move on my woman?"

Since Jesse had no idea how to respond to that question, he was glad that Maggie spoke up.

"I'm not—and never have been—your woman," she told the Romeo.

But Jared continued to scowl. "We were supposed to be going to grab a bite to eat."

"No—you offered to take me for a bite to eat and I told you that I already had plans."

"With this guy?" His tone was skeptical.

She took Jesse's hand and lied without compunction. "We've been dating for the past several months."

"Then how come I've never seen you with him before?" Jared challenged.

"We've been trying to keep a low profile and avoid being the topic of gossip," she said easily.

It was obvious by the stormy look in the other guy's eyes that he wanted to challenge the claim, but with Maggie's hand linked with Jesse's and her lipstick on his mouth, the evidence was pretty convincing.

"When you decide you want a real cowboy, give me a call," Jared told her, and stormed off in the direction from which he'd come.

Maggie blew out a breath. "Thank goodness." She released the hand that she'd been holding on to as if it was a lifeline and turned to him. "And thank *you*."

"No need to thank me for something that was very much my pleasure," he assured her.

And the big-city lawyer with the razor-sharp mind and persuasive tongue actually blushed when his gaze dropped to linger on the sweet curve of her lips.

"Do you want me to explain now?" she asked.

"Only if you want to."

"I feel as if I owe you at least that much."

Half an hour earlier, he'd barely been able to say two words to her, but locking lips seemed to have loosened his, and he couldn't resist teasing her a little. "Or you could just kiss me again and we'll call it even."

Her mouth curved as she held his gaze, and he knew she was giving his offer serious consideration. "I think, for now, we'll go with the explanation."

"Your choice," he said.

"I met him at the Ace in the Hole a few months back,"

she began. "I was there to have lunch with my cousin, Lissa, but before we even had a chance to order, Lissa got called away. I decided to stay and at least finish my coffee, and he slid into the empty seat and introduced himself. He seemed friendly and we chatted for a while, but when he asked for my number, I told him I wasn't interested in starting anything up with someone in Rust Creek Falls because my life was in Los Angeles."

Which, Jesse reminded himself, was a fact he'd be wise to remember.

"He seemed to accept that easily enough and said maybe he'd see me around the next time I was in town. And I know Rust Creek Falls isn't a big city, but every single time I've been back since then, I've run into him. And every single time, he asks me to go out with him."

"So why didn't you just tell him you had a boyfriend in Los Angeles? I got the impression he would have believed that more readily than he believed you were with me."

"I don't think he would've believed anything without proof—which you're still wearing," she said, and lifted a hand to rub her lipstick off the corner of his mouth with her thumb.

And he felt it again—the sizzle and crackle of awareness when she touched him. And when her gaze locked on his, he knew that he wasn't the only one who had felt it.

"He hit on Lissa, too, when she first came to Rust Creek Falls," Maggie told him. "Apparently he even started a bar fight with some other guy who asked her to dance."

"I don't pay much attention to the gossip around town," Jesse said. "But I remember hearing about that—both the sheriff and his deputy got punched and two guys got arrested."

Maggie smiled. "Lissa insisted it wasn't her fault, but

Gage said something about beautiful women being the cause of most trouble at the Ace in the Hole."

"Then you better stay away from the bar or you might incite a riot."

Her cheeks colored prettily, as if she hadn't heard the same thing a thousand times before. And if she hadn't, he figured there was something seriously wrong with the guys in LA, because Maggie Roarke was a definite knockout.

"So why aren't you involved with anyone back home?" he asked now.

"How do you know I'm not?" she asked.

"You didn't kiss me until you'd confirmed that I wasn't seeing anyone, and I can't imagine you'd be any less respectful of your own relationship."

"You're right," she acknowledged. "As for not being involved—I guess I've just been too busy to do much dating."

"Until me," he teased.

She laughed. "Until you."

The magical sound of her soft laughter filled his heart, and the sparkle in her eyes took his breath away. He didn't know what else to say—or if he should say anything else at all. Maybe he should just walk away while she was smiling and hopefully not thinking that he was an idiot.

"I really do appreciate your cooperation," she told him. "If there's anything I can do to possibly repay the favor, I hope you'll ask."

"Well, I was planning to grab a burger at the Ace in the Hole," he admitted. "And despite the sheriff's warning to your cousin, I'd be willing to take the risk if you wanted to join me."

"Are you inviting me to have dinner with you?"

"It would substantiate your claim that we're dating."

"The Ace in the Hole?" she said dubiously.

He shrugged. "Since this isn't your first visit to Rust Creek Falls, you know that our options here are limited."

Still she hesitated, and Jesse began to suspect that her gratitude didn't actually extend to the point where she wanted to be seen in public with him. And that was okay. He understood what she'd been saying about small-town gossip, and he really didn't want to be put under the microscope any more than she did. But damn, he really did want to spend more time with her.

"I could do better than a burger," she finally said. "I could make dinner."

"You'd cook for me?"

"Which part surprises you the most—that I *can* cook or that I'm offering to cook for you?"

"I'm not sure," he admitted.

She laughed again. "At least you're honest."

"I guess I just thought, with you being a busy lawyer and all..."

"Lawyers have to eat on occasion, too," she said, when his explanation ran out.

"Yeah, but I would figure you've got a lot of dining options in LA."

"We do," she agreed. "But as it turns out, I like to cook. It helps me unwind at the end of the day. So what do you say—are you going to let me make you dinner?"

He was beginning to suspect that he would let Maggie Roarke do absolutely anything she wanted, but he figured dinner was a good start.

"An offer I can't refuse," he told her.

Maggie prided herself on the fact that she was an intelligent, educated woman. She'd graduated summa cum laude from Stanford Law School and was establishing a reputation for herself at Alliston & Blake—a prominent

Los Angeles law firm. She'd gone toe-to-toe with formidable opponents in the courtroom, she'd held her ground in front of arrogant judges and she'd refused to be impressed or intimidated by powerful clients. One of her greatest assets was her ability to remain calm and cool whatever the circumstances. She simply didn't get flustered.

But as Jesse followed her into Gage and Lissa's kitchen, she was definitely feeling flustered. There was just something about this shy, sexy cowboy that had her heart jumping around in her chest. She opened the refrigerator, peered inside.

"What do you like?" she asked.

He looked at her blankly.

"For dinner," she clarified.

He flashed a quick smile. "Sorry, I guess my mind wandered. As for food—I'm not fussy. I'll eat whatever you want to make."

"Chicken and pasta okay?" she asked him.

"Sure."

She took a package of chicken breasts out of the fridge, then rummaged for some other ingredients. She found green peppers in the crisper, onions in the pantry and a bowl of ripe tomatoes on the counter. But what she really needed was fresh basil, and Lissa didn't have any.

"Do you know if they carry fresh herbs at the General Store?"

"I doubt it," Jesse said. "You'd probably have to go into Kalispell for something like that."

"I can use dried," she admitted. "But fresh basil leaves would add a lot more visual appeal to the dish."

"I'm going to have dinner with a beautiful woman," he said. "That's enough visual appeal that I wouldn't mind if you made macaroni and cheese from a box."

She felt her cheeks heat. She'd received more effusive

compliments, but none had ever sounded as sincere. No one had looked at her the way he looked at her.

"Even without fresh basil, I do think this will be a step up from boxed mac and cheese."

She filled a pot with water and set it on the back burner, then drizzled some oil into a deep frying pan. While the oil heated, she sliced the chicken into strips and tossed them into the pan. As the chicken was cooking, she chopped up peppers and onions, then added those, too.

"Can I do anything to help?"

"You could open the wine," she suggested. "There's a bottle of Riesling in the fridge and glasses in the cupboard above."

He uncorked the bottle and poured the wine into two crystal goblets.

She dumped the pasta into the boiling water and set the timer, then took the glass he offered.

"To new friendships," he said, lifting his glass in a toast.

"To new friendships," she agreed. "And first dates."

"Is this a date?"

"Of course. Otherwise, I would have lied to Jared."

"We wouldn't want that," he teased.

She added the tomatoes to the frying pan, sprinkled in some of this and that, gave it a stir. Her movements were smooth and effortless, confirming her claim that she enjoyed cooking. Which was convenient, because he enjoyed eating.

Ten minutes later, he was sitting down to a steaming plate of penne pasta with chicken and peppers.

"This is really good," he told her.

"Better than mac and cheese from a box?"

"Much better."

They chatted while they ate, about anything and everything. She learned that he worked at his family's ranch, The

Shooting Star, but had his own house on the property, and that he was close to his siblings but was frequently baffled and frustrated by them. She confided that she sometimes felt smothered by her brothers, who tended to be a little overprotective, and admitted that she could have gone to work at Roarke & Associates—her parents' law firm—but wanted to establish her own reputation in the field.

She had a second glass of wine while he had a second serving of pasta, and they lingered at the table. He was easy to talk to, and he actually listened to what she was saying. As a result, she found herself telling him things she'd never told anyone else, such as her concern that she'd been so focused on her career that she hadn't given much thought to anything else, and she was starting to wonder if she'd ever find the time to get married and have a family.

Not that she was in any hurry to do so, she hastened to explain. After all, she was only twenty-eight years old. But she was admittedly worried that if she continued on the same course, she might be so focused on her billable hours that she wouldn't even hear her biological clock when it started ticking.

Jesse told her that he'd gone to Montana State University to study Animal Science, graduating with a four-year degree. As for dating, he confided that he hadn't done much of that, either, claiming that most of the women in town had gone out with one or more of his brothers and he had no intention of trying to live up to their reputations.

After the meal was finished, he insisted on helping with the cleanup. While she put the dishes into the dishwasher, he washed the pans.

She'd enjoyed spending time with Jesse, and she wasn't eager for the night to end. He was smart and interesting and definitely easy to look at, and despite the underlying hum of attraction, she felt comfortable with him—or at least she did until he turned to reach for a towel at the same moment that she straightened up to close the door of the dishwasher and the back of his hand inadvertently brushed the side of her breast.

She sucked in a breath; he snatched his hand back.

"I'm so sorry."

"No, it was my fault."

But fault was irrelevant. What mattered was that the air was fairly crackling and sizzling with awareness now. And the way he looked at her—his gaze heated and focused— she was certain he felt it, too.

She barely knew him. But she knew she'd never felt the same immediacy and intensity of connection that she felt the minute he'd taken her hand inside the community center only a few hours earlier. But she was a Los Angeles attorney and he was a Rust Creek cowboy, and she knew that chemistry—as compelling as it might be—could not bridge the gap between them.

And Jesse had obviously come to the same conclusion, because he took a deliberate step back, breaking the threads of the seductive web that had spun around them. "I should probably be on my way."

"Oh." She forced a smile and tried to ignore the sense of disappointment that spread through her. "Okay."

She followed him to the door.

He paused against the open portal. "Thanks again for dinner."

"You're welcome," she said. "And if you ever need a fictional girlfriend to get you out of a tight spot, feel free to give me a call."

He lifted a hand and touched her cheek, the stroke of his fingertips over her skin making her shiver. "I don't want a fictional girlfriend, but I do want to kiss you for real."

She wasn't sure if he was stating a fact or asking permission, but before she could respond, he'd lowered his head and covered her mouth with his.

She might have caught him off guard when she'd pressed her lips to his outside of the community center, but it hadn't taken him long to respond, to take control of the kiss. This time, he was in control right from the beginning—she didn't have a chance to think about what he was doing or brace herself against the wave of emotions that washed over her.

For a man who claimed he didn't do a lot of dating, he sure knew how to kiss. His mouth was warm and firm as it moved over hers, masterfully persuasive and seductive. Never before had she been kissed with such patient thoroughness. His hands were big and strong, but infinitely gentle as they slid up her back, burning her skin through the silky fabric of her blouse as he urged her closer. Her breasts were crushed against the solid wall of his chest, and her nipples immediately responded to the contact, tightening into rigid peaks.

She wanted him to touch her—she wanted those callused hands on her bare skin, and the fierceness of the want was shocking. Equally strong was the desire to touch him—to let her hands roam over his rock-hard body, exploring and savoring every inch of him. He was so completely and undeniably male, and he made everything that was female inside of her quiver with excitement.

Eventually, reluctantly, he eased his mouth from hers. But he kept his arms around her, as if he couldn't bear to let her go. "I should probably be on my way before the sheriff gets home."

"He won't be home tonight," she admitted. "He and Lissa went to Bozeman for the weekend."

He frowned at that. "You're going to be alone here to-night?"

She held his gaze steadily. "I hope not."

He closed the door and turned the lock.

Chapter Two

November

Jesse had tossed the last bag of broodmare supplement into the back of his truck when he saw a pair of shiny, high-heeled boots stop beside the vehicle. He wiped the back of his hand over his brow and lifted his head to find Lissa Christensen, Maggie's cousin and also the sheriff's wife, standing there.

He touched a hand to the brim of his hat. "Mrs. Christensen," he said politely.

"It's Lissa," she told him, and offered a smile that was both warm and apologetic.

He wondered what she felt she had to apologize for. Maggie had told him that Lissa wasn't just her cousin— she was her best friend—and he would bet that whatever Maggie's reasons for ending their relationship before it had really even begun, she would have confided in the other woman. No doubt Lissa knew more than he wanted her to, but she didn't need to know—he wouldn't let her see—how hurt he'd been by Maggie's decision.

"Is there something I can help you with, ma'am?"

"Actually, I'm here to help you."

"While I appreciate the offer, I'm already finished," he said, deliberately misunderstanding her.

She shook her head, clearly exasperated with him. "Have you talked to Maggie recently?"

"Can't say that I have," he said, his tone carefully neutral.

"You need to talk to her," Lissa insisted. "Sooner rather than later."

And though Jesse's heart urged him to reach out to her once again, Maggie had trampled on it once already and he wasn't eager to give her another chance. Maybe pride was cold comfort without the warmth of the woman in his arms, but it was all he had left, and that pride wouldn't let him continue to chase after a woman who had made it clear she wasn't interested.

"If your cousin wants to talk, she knows where to find me," he countered.

Lissa huffed out a breath. "If nothing else, the two of you have obstinacy in common."

He closed the tailgate of his truck. "If that's all you wanted to say, I need to get back to Traub Stables."

"There's plenty more to say," she told him. "But it's not for me to say it."

He lifted his brows in response to that cryptic comment as he moved to the driver's-side door.

"Please talk to her," Lissa urged again.

He slid behind the wheel and drove away, but her insistence nagged at the back of his mind all the way back to Traub Stables. Lissa had to know that he'd been out of touch with her cousin for a while, so why was she all fired up about him needing to talk to Maggie? Why now?

Oddly enough, he'd got a phone call—out of the blue—just a few days earlier from his former fiancée. Shaelyn had said she wanted to talk, so he'd told her to talk. Then she'd said she wanted to see him, but he hadn't thought there was any point in that. Now he was wondering why the women from his past, who had already tossed him aside, had suddenly decided he was worthy of their attention.

He continued to puzzle over his recent conversation with Lissa as he worked with a spirited yearling. And because he was thinking about her cousin, when he got the feeling that someone was watching him, he instinctively knew that someone was Maggie.

He hadn't seen her since July, and the passing of time was evidenced by the changing of the season. When he'd met her the day of the community center opening, she'd been wearing a slim-fitting skirt and high-heeled sandals that showed her long, slender legs to full advantage along with a sleeveless silky blouse that highlighted her feminine curves. Today she was bundled up in a long winter coat that he'd bet she'd borrowed from her cousin since she wouldn't have much use for one in Los Angeles. In addition to the coat, she was wearing a red knitted hat with a pom-pom and matching red mittens, and even from a distance, he could see that her cheeks were pink from the cold.

Her choice to stand outside, he decided. And though it was obvious to both of them that she was waiting for him, he refused to cut the yearling's workout short. He wasn't being paid to slack off, and he wasn't going to let her distract him from his job. Even when she hadn't been there, she'd been too much of a distraction over the past several months.

While he continued to work with the filly, he cautioned himself against speculating on the purpose of her visit. He didn't know why she was there or how long she planned to stay this time, but he knew it would be foolish to expect anything from her. He finished running the young horse through her exercises before he passed her off to one of

the stable hands for cooldown and grooming and finally
turned his attention to Maggie.

"Hello, Jesse."

She looked good. Better than good. She looked like
everything he'd ever wanted in a woman, and he knew
that she was. He also knew that she was definitely out of
his reach.

He nodded in acknowledgment of her greeting. "When
did you get back into town?" he asked, his tone polite but
cool.

"Last night."

Which confirmed that she'd already been in Rust Creek
Falls when he ran into her cousin at the feed store—
suggesting that Lissa's appearance there had not been a
coincidence. "More of Arthur Swinton's business?"

She shook her head. "I came to see you."

And damn if his heart didn't kick against his ribs like
an ornery stallion trying to break out of its stall. Because
he was feeling more than he wanted to feel, more than
he intended to admit, the single word was harsh when he
asked, "Why?"

"I need to talk to you."

"Isn't that what we're doing now?"

"Please, Jesse. Can we go somewhere a little more private?"

He wanted to refuse. He definitely didn't want to be
alone with her, because that would undoubtedly remind
him of the last time he'd been alone with her—the night
they'd made love.

"I wouldn't be asking if it wasn't important," she said.

"Do you know where The Shooting Star is?" he asked,
naming his family's ranch.

She nodded.

"My house is the first one on the left, after the driveway splits. Can you meet me there in an hour?"

She nodded without hesitation. "That would be good."

No, good would've been if she'd come back three months sooner and asked to be alone with him. Then he would have been sure that they both wanted the same thing. Now, after so much time had passed, he had no idea what she wanted, what she thought they needed to talk about.

But he knew she'd been gone 119 days, and wasn't that pathetic? He'd actually been counting the days. At first, he'd been counting in anticipation of her return. More recently, he'd been counting in the hope that with each day that passed he would be one day closer to forgetting about her.

And he'd been certain he was getting there—but only five minutes in her company had him all churned up inside again, wanting what he knew he couldn't have.

What was she going to do for an hour?

She slid behind the wheel of her rental car and considered her options. She was less than five minutes away from Gage and Lissa's house, but she didn't want to go back there. Her cousin hadn't stopped nagging her since she'd got into town the night before. Not that Lissa had said anything Maggie hadn't already thought herself.

She pulled out of the parking lot and back onto the road, heading toward town. She drove down Falls Street, turned onto Sawmill, crossing over the bridge without any destination in mind. She was only killing time, watching the minutes tick away until the allotted hour had passed.

Her phone buzzed to indicate receipt of a text message, so she turned onto Main and pulled into an empty park-

ing spot by Crawford's General Store to dig her phone out
of her purse.

Have you seen him yet?

The message, not surprisingly, was from Lissa.

Mtg him at SS @ 4, she texted back.

Good luck! her cousin replied.

Maggie was afraid she was going to need it.

Since she had her phone in hand, she decided to check
her email from work. There wasn't anything urgent, but responding to the messages helped her kill some more time.

She knew that she was stalling, thinking about anything
but the imminent conversation with Jesse. Now that there
were less than twenty minutes before their scheduled meeting, she should be focused on that, thinking about what
she was going to say, how to share her news.

She'd hoped to take her cue from him—but the few
words that they'd exchanged at Traub Stables hadn't given
her a hint about what he was thinking. His gaze had been
shuttered, but the coolness of his tone had been a strong
indication that he was finished with her. It wasn't even that
he was over her—it was as if they'd never been.

Maybe she shouldn't have come back. Maybe this was
a monumental mistake. It was obvious that he felt nothing for her—maybe he never had. Maybe the magic of that
night had only ever existed in her imagination.

But she didn't really believe that. She certainly hadn't
imagined the numerous phone calls, text messages and
emails they'd exchanged every single day for the first couple of weeks. And during those early weeks, he'd seemed
eager for her to come back to Rust Creek Falls, as anxious
to be with her again as she was to be with him.

She'd originally planned to return in the middle of August, but only two days before her scheduled trip one of the senior partners had asked for her help with an emergency injunction for an important client threatened by a hostile takeover. Of course, that injunction had only been the first step in a long process of corporate restructuring, and Maggie had been tapped for assistance every step of the way.

She'd enjoyed the challenge and the work and knew it had been good for her career. Unfortunately, it had consumed almost every waking minute and had signaled the beginning of the end of her relationship with Jesse. Four months was a long time to be apart, and he'd obviously moved on.

She rubbed a hand over her chest, where her heart was beating dully against her breastbone. The possibility that their passionate lovemaking could have been so readily forgotten cut her to the quick. Maybe it was irrational and unreasonable, but she'd started to fall in love with him that night. Even when she'd said goodbye to him the next day, she didn't think it was the end of their relationship but only the beginning.

Of course, her emotions were her responsibility. He'd never made her any promises; he'd certainly never said that he was in love with her. But the way he'd kissed her and touched her and loved her—with his body if not his heart—she'd been certain there was something special between them, something more than a one-night affair. She didn't think she'd imagined that, but even if the connection had been real, it was obviously gone now, and the pain of that loss made her eyes fill with tears.

Blinking them away, she pulled from the curb and headed toward The Shooting Star.

Jesse's house was a beautiful if modest two-story with white siding, a wide front porch and lots of windows flanked by deep green shutters.

His truck in the driveway confirmed that he was home, and he opened the door before she even had a chance to knock.

"You're punctual," he said, stepping back so that she could enter.

"I appreciate you making the time to see me."

He shrugged. "You said it was important."

"It is," she confirmed.

She continued to stand just inside the door, looking at him, wanting to memorize all the little details she was afraid she might have forgotten over the past four months.

The breadth of his shoulders beneath the flannel shirt he wore, the rippling strength of his abdominal muscles, the strength of those wide-palmed hands. The way his mouth curved just a little higher on the left side when he smiled; the almost-imperceptible scar on his chin, the result of a misstep as he'd climbed over a fence when he was eight years old. His hair was damp, as if he'd recently stepped out of the shower, and his jaw was freshly shaven, tempting her to reach up and touch the smooth skin.

"Do you want to take your coat off?"

"Sure." But she pulled off her mittens and hat first, tucking them into the pockets of the long coat she'd borrowed from her cousin. When she finally stripped off the heavy garment, he took it from her, hanging it on a hook by the door, beside his Sherpa-lined leather jacket.

"Keep your boots on," he said when she reached down to untie them. "The floor's probably cold."

It might have been true, but the abruptness of his tone suggested that he didn't want her to get too comfortable or stay for too long. She kept her boots on, but wiped them carefully on the mat before stepping off it.

The main floor plan was open, with a dining area on one side and a living room on the other. The furniture was distressed leather with nail-head trim, oversize and masculine in design but perfect for the open space. Flames were crackling inside the river-rock fireplace, providing the room with both warmth and ambience. Jesse had moved to the kitchen, separated from the dining room by a long, granite-topped counter.

"Do you want a cup of tea?" he asked, already filling the kettle.

"That would be nice, thank you."

Even she winced at the cool politeness of their conversation. It was as if they were strangers meeting for the first time rather than lovers who had spent hours naked together. Yes, it had only been one night, but it had been the most incredible night of her life. The way he'd touched her, with his hands and his lips and his body, had introduced her to heights of pleasure she'd never imagined.

Even now, the memories of that night made her cheeks flush and her heart pound. Though it took a determined effort, she pushed them aside and forced herself to focus on the here and now.

"You've lost weight," he noted, his gaze skimming over her.

"A few pounds," she admitted. Actually, she'd been down nine pounds a couple of months earlier, but she'd managed to gain six of them back.

Jesse studied her carefully, noting the bony outline of her shoulders in the oversize sweater she wore over slim-fitting jeans, and guessed that she'd lost more than a few pounds. She was pale, too, and those beautiful brown eyes that had haunted his dreams looked even bigger and darker than he remembered.

The last time they'd spoken on the phone, she'd told him that she'd been feeling unwell, fighting some kind of virus. He'd thought it was just the latest in a long line of excuses for why she'd chosen not to return to Rust Creek Falls. It seemed apparent now that there had been at least some truth in her explanation.

He poured the boiling water into a mug, over a bag of peppermint tea. The day that she'd made him dinner, she'd told him it was her favorite flavor. And, sap that he was, he'd not only remembered but had bought a box so that he'd have it on hand when she came to visit.

The box had sat, unopened, in his cupboard for almost four months. Now, finally, she was going to have a cup—and the other eleven bags would probably sit in the box in his cupboard for another four months before he finally tossed them in the trash.

"Are you feeling okay?" he asked.

She looked up, as if startled by the question.

"You said that you'd been fighting some kind of virus," he reminded her. "I just wondered if you've fully recovered from whatever it was you had."

She wrapped her hands around the warm mug. "I'm feeling much better, thanks."

"It must have been quite a bug, to have laid you up for so long," he commented.

"It wasn't a bug." She lifted her gaze to his. "It was—is—a baby."

Jesse stared at her for a long minute, certain he couldn't have heard her correctly.

"A baby?" he finally echoed.

She nodded. "I'm pregnant."

He hated to ask, but he hadn't seen her since July and he knew he'd be a fool if he didn't. "Is it…mine?"

He held his breath, waiting for her response, not sure if he wanted it to be yes or no. Not sure how he would feel either way.

She winced at the question. "Yes, it's yours."

"I'm sorry," he said automatically.

"That it's yours?"

"That I had to ask," he clarified.

But she shook her head. "I knew you would. If you were one of my clients, I'd insist that you get proof," she admitted. "And if you want a DNA test, I'll give it to you, but there isn't any other possibility. I haven't been with anyone else in more than two years."

"You're pregnant with my child," he said, as if repeating the words might somehow help them to make sense.

His thoughts were as jumbled as his emotions. Joy warred with panic inside of him as he realized that he was going to be a father—a prospect that was as terrifying as it was exciting.

"I'm not here because I want or expect anything from you," she explained. "I just thought you should know about the baby."

Irritation bubbled to the surface. "I don't know which part of that outrageous statement to deal with first."

"Excuse me?"

"We made that baby together," he reminded her. "So you should want and expect plenty.

"As for letting me know—should I thank you for finally, in the fourth month of pregnancy, telling me that you're going to have my child?"

She winced at the harsh accusation in his tone. "It's not as if I was deliberately keeping my pregnancy a secret."

"You were accidentally keeping it a secret?"

"I didn't know."

He stared at her in disbelief. "You didn't know?"

"I didn't," she insisted.

"I'm sure you didn't figure it out yesterday."

"No," she admitted. "But for the first few weeks after I returned to LA, I was so busy with work that I thought the

fatigue and nausea were symptoms of my erratic schedule and not sleeping well or eating properly. Even when
I missed my first period—" her cheeks flushed, as if she
was uncomfortable talking about her monthly cycle despite
the intimacies they'd shared "—I didn't think anything of
it. I've skipped periods before, usually when I'm stressed."

He scowled but couldn't dispute her claim. Instead he
asked, "So when did you first suspect you might be pregnant?"

"Mid-September. And even then, it was my mother who
brought up the possibility. Which I didn't think was a possibility, because we were careful both times."

Both times. He didn't carry condoms in his wallet anymore, and she'd only had two in her makeup case. So they'd
done all kinds of things to pleasure one another but they'd
only made love twice.

And both times had felt like heaven on earth—the
merging of their bodies had been so perfect, so right—

He severed the unwelcome memory.

"So I took a home pregnancy test." She continued her
explanation. "And even when it showed a positive result,
I wasn't sure I believed it. The next day, my doctor confirmed the result."

"This was mid-September?" he prompted.

She nodded again.

"So you've known for six weeks, and you only decided
to tell me now?"

"I didn't know how to tell you," she admitted. "It wasn't
the kind of news I wanted to share over the phone, and my
doctor advised me not to travel until the morning sickness
was under control."

"Did you ever think to invite me to come out to LA to
see you?"

She blinked, confirming his suspicion that she had not.

That the possibility of reaching out to him had not once entered her mind. "You never showed any interest in making a trip to California."

"If you'd asked, if you'd said that you needed to see me, I would have come." And he would have been glad to do so, overjoyed by the prospect of seeing her again.

"I'm sorry," she said. "I never thought... And when I called to tell you that my planned visit to Rust Creek Falls was further delayed, you sounded as if you'd already written me off. And that's okay," she hastened to assure him. "I know neither of us expected that one night together would have such long-lasting repercussions."

"I didn't think it was going to be only one night," he told her.

"I bet you didn't think you'd end up having this conversation four months later, either," she said.

"No," he agreed.

"I know you've only had a few minutes to think about this, but I wanted you to know that I'm planning to keep the baby."

He scowled, because it hadn't occurred to him that she might want to do anything else. "You thought about giving away our baby?"

"There were a few moments—especially in the beginning—when I wasn't sure what I would do," she admitted. "I was stunned and scared—having a baby at this stage of my life wasn't anywhere in my plans."

"You don't just give away a baby because it wasn't in your plans," he told her.

"Some people do," she told him.

Only then did he remember that she was adopted, given up by her sixteen-year-old birth mother when she was only a few days old.

While he was busy trying to extract his foot from his

mouth, she continued, "And not necessarily because it's the easy choice. I don't know whether my birth mother wanted to keep me or not—Christa and Gavin always told me that she recognized that she couldn't give me the kind of life that I had with my parents, and I've always been grateful to her for that. So yes, I thought about giving up my baby, because I know that's sometimes the best option.

"But," she continued before he could protest, "I don't think it is for my baby. And maybe it's maternal instinct or maybe it's because I was adopted, but I felt an immediate bond with this baby who shares my DNA, and I can't even imagine letting him or her go."

"The baby shares half of your DNA," he pointed out. "The other half is mine."

She nodded. "And if you want to be part of our baby's life, I'd be happy to accommodate whatever kind of visitation you—"

"Visitation?" he interrupted, his voice dangerously soft.

She eyed him warily. "If that's what you want."

"It's not."

"Oh. Okay. In that case, I'll have papers drawn up—"

He interrupted her again. "The only paper we're going to need is a marriage license."

Chapter Three

Maggie stared at him, certain she couldn't have heard him correctly. "Excuse me?"

"We're having a baby together, which means we should get married to raise that child together." His tone was implacable.

"You can't be serious."

"Of course I'm serious. I'm not going to shirk my responsibilities."

"There's a lot of ground between shirking responsibility and marriage," she said, determined to remain calm and reasonable despite the outrageousness of his proposition.

"I want to be a father to my child."

"You are the baby's father."

"I want the baby to have my name."

She'd been so apprehensive about this meeting—worried about how he'd respond to the news of her pregnancy. Obviously she knew he'd be surprised, and she'd prepared herself for the possibility that he might deny paternity. But in all of the scenarios that she'd envisioned, she'd never once considered that he might propose marriage. And while she'd feared that he might reject both her and the baby, his grim determination to do "the right thing" was somehow worse.

This wasn't at all how she'd planned things to happen in her life. Yes, she wanted to get married someday. Her parents had given all of their children the wonderful example of a true partnership, and Maggie wanted to find the same forever kind of love someday. And when she did, she would get married and *then* have a baby. So while she hadn't planned to get pregnant just yet, she didn't intend to change anything aside from the order of things. She would be the best mother she could be to her child, but she wasn't going to settle for a loveless marriage with a stubborn cowboy—even if his kisses had the power to make her lose all sense and reason.

If Jesse had been offering her something more… If he'd given any indication that he'd been genuinely happy to see her, if he'd wrapped his arms around her and kissed her with even half of the passion and enthusiasm she knew he was capable of, she might have ignored all of her questions and doubts and followed him to the nearest wedding chapel. But the coolness of his initial response to her return to Rust Creek Falls proved that he didn't want her—he only wanted to ensure the legitimacy of his child.

"We don't have to get married for your name to go on the baby's birth certificate," she told him. "I would never deny my child's paternity."

"*Our* child," he reminded her. "And it's about more than just a name. It's about giving our baby the family he or she deserves."

"What about what *we* deserve?" she challenged. "Don't you want to fall in love and exchange vows with someone you really want to be with instead of someone you inadvertently got pregnant?"

"What I want—what you want—isn't as important as what our baby needs," he insisted stubbornly.

She blew out a breath. "I don't think our baby needs to be raised by two parents trapped in a loveless marriage."

"You don't have to make it sound so dire. If we want to, we can make this work."

"What if I don't want to?"

He ignored her question as if she hadn't even spoken. "We should be able to make all of the necessary arrangements for a wedding within a couple of weeks."

"Did you get kicked in the head by a horse? I am *not* marrying you."

The lift of his brows was the only indication that he'd heard her this time, as he steamrollered over her protest. "We can have a quick courthouse ceremony here or a more traditional wedding in LA, if you prefer."

"So I *do* have some say in this?"

"The details," he agreed. "I don't care about the where and when so long as it's legal."

There was something about his determination to make her his wife that thrilled her even as it infuriated her. And she suspected that, deep in her heart, she wanted what he was offering: to get married and raise their baby together.

But she didn't want a marriage on the terms he was offering. She didn't want a legal union for the sake of their baby but a commitment based on mutual respect and affection. Unfortunately, that offer wasn't on the table. And even if it was, there were other obstacles to consider.

"What about the detail also known as my job?" she challenged.

"What about it?"

"How am I going to represent my clients in Los Angeles if I'm living in Rust Creek Falls? Or am I supposed to happily sacrifice all of my career ambitions for the pleasure of becoming Mrs. Jesse Crawford?"

His only response was a scowl that proved he hadn't given much thought to the distance that separated them geographically.

"I'm sure you can find a job in Rust Creek Falls, if you want to keep working."

"Or maybe you could find work in Los Angeles," she countered.

"Now you're just being ridiculous."

"And you're being completely unreasonable."

"It's not unreasonable to want our child to be raised by two parents."

"Look at us, Jesse. We can't even have a simple conversation without fighting and you want us to get married?"

"Yes, I do," he said again.

She shook her head. "Obviously we have a fundamental difference of opinion."

"I don't recall there being any differences of opinion when we were in bed together."

And with those words, the air was suddenly charged with electricity.

The heat in his gaze spread warmth through her veins, from her belly to her breasts, throbbing between her thighs. He wasn't even touching her—and she was fairly quivering with desire.

No one had ever affected her the way this man did. No one had ever made her feel the way she felt when she was with him. But even more unnerving than the wanting of her body was the yearning of her heart.

She pushed away from the breakfast bar and carried her empty mug to the sink. She had to leave, to give them both some time and space to think about how they should proceed.

"Maggie."

She looked up, and he was there. Close enough that she couldn't breathe without inhaling his clean, masculine scent. Close enough that he had to hear her heart pounding. And although his eyes never left hers, she felt the heat of his gaze everywhere.

He lifted a hand to touch her hair, his fingers skimming over the silky tresses to cradle the back of her head. Then his mouth was on hers, his lips warm and firm and sure, and she melted against him.

She'd forgotten how strong he was, how solid every inch of his body was. Hard and unyielding. And yet, for all of his strength, he was incredibly gentle. It was that unadulterated masculine strength combined with his inherently gentle nature that had appealed to her from the first.

His hands slid down her back, inched up beneath the hem of her sweater. Then those wide, callused palms were on her skin, sliding up her torso to cup her breasts. Her blood pulsed in her veins, hot and demanding. His thumbs brushed over her nipples through the delicate lace, and she actually whimpered.

He nibbled on her lips. Teasing, tasting, tempting.

"I want you, Maggie."

She wanted him, too. And though she knew it might be a mistake to let herself succumb to that desire while there was still so much unresolved between them, that knowledge didn't dampen her need.

"Tell me you feel the same," he urged.

"I do," she admitted. "But—"

She forgot the rest of what she'd intended to say when he lifted her off her feet and into his arms.

He carried her up the stairs and down a short hallway to his bedroom with effortless ease. When he set her on her feet beside the bed, she knew that if she was going to protest, now was the time to do so. Then he kissed her again, and any thought of protest flew out of her mind.

Her mouth parted beneath the pressure of his, and his tongue swept inside, teasing the soft inside of her lips. His hands slid down her back, over the curve of her buttocks, pulling her close. The evidence of his arousal fueled her own. Blood pulsed in her veins, pooled low in her belly, making her want so much that she actually ached.

She lifted her hands to the buttons of his shirt and began

to unfasten them. She wanted to touch him, to feel the warmth of his bare skin beneath her palms. But the cotton T-shirt under the flannel impeded her efforts. With a frustrated sigh, she tugged the T-shirt out of his jeans and shoved her hands beneath it.

Jesse chuckled softly. "I didn't realize this was a race."

"I want to feel your body against mine," she confessed.

He released her long enough to get rid of his clothes. She sat on the edge of the bed, intending to do the same, but she was still struggling with her boots when his jeans hit the floor. As he kicked them away, she couldn't help but admire the knit boxer briefs that molded to the firm muscles of his buttocks and thighs at the back and did absolutely nothing to hide the obvious evidence of his arousal at the front.

Her mouth went dry and her fingers froze on the knotted laces. He knelt beside her and efficiently untied the boots and pulled them from her feet. Then he unfastened her jeans and pushed them over her hips, down her legs, finally stripping them away along with her socks.

"Your feet are cold," he realized, warming them between his palms. "You need thicker socks."

Not in California, she thought, but didn't say it aloud. She didn't want to speak of the distance that separated their lives; she didn't want anything to take away from the here and now.

"Or I could get under the covers," she suggested.

"That's a better plan," he agreed.

But first, he lifted her sweater over her head and tossed it aside, leaving her clad in only a lace demi-cup bra and matching bikini panties. He sat back on his haunches, the heat in his gaze roaming over her as tangible as a caress, making her nipples tighten and her thighs quiver.

"You absolutely take my breath away," he told her.

She tugged the covers down and rolled over the bed to

snuggle beneath them. Jesse immediately slid in beside her, his hands skimming over her, tracing her curves. He lowered his head to nuzzle the tender skin at the base of her throat, making her shiver.

He glanced up. "Are you still cold?"

She shook her head; he smiled slightly before he lowered his head again, his lips skimming across her collarbone, then tracing the lacy edge of her bra. She could feel his breath, warm on her skin, as his mouth hovered above her breast. Her hand lifted to his head, silently urging him closer. He willingly acquiesced to her direction, laving her nipple with his tongue. The sensation of hot, wet heat through the silky fabric made her gasp, then his lips closed over the lace-covered peak, sending fiery spears of pleasure arrowing to her core.

He found the center clasp of her bra and released it, peeling the fabric aside so he could suckle her bare flesh, making her groan. He tugged the straps down her arms, dropped the garment to the floor. His hands stroked down her torso, his fingers hooking in her panties and dragging them down her legs and away, so that she was completely naked. All the while, his hands and his lips moved over her, teasing and tempting, until her body was fairly quivering with wanting.

Genetics had blessed her with a naturally slim build and the loss of those few pounds had pushed her from slender toward skinny, but she knew that was only a temporary state. Because although her hip bones and ribs were visible now, there was also a subtle roundness to her belly— evidence of the baby she carried.

He splayed his hand over the curve, his wide palm covering her almost from hip bone to hip bone, as if cradling their child, and the sweetness of the gesture made tears fill her eyes.

"Everyone says that a baby is a miracle," he said. "But

the idea of you growing our baby inside of you is every bit as miraculous."

"You call it *miraculous* now. In a few more months, you'll be calling it *fat*."

She'd been teasing, attempting to lighten the mood, but as soon as she spoke the words, she wished she could take them back. Talking about the future as if they would be together was a mistake, even if it was—deep in her heart—what she wanted.

But he shook his head. "You'll always be beautiful to me—the most beautiful woman I've ever known."

Which might have sounded like a well-rehearsed line from another man, but the sincerity in his tone made her heart swell inside her chest.

"I want to be with you through every step of your pregnancy," he continued. "I want to see the changes in your body as our baby grows. I want to be the one who runs to the grocery store in the middle of the night when you have a sudden craving for ice cream."

"I didn't think the store in Rust Creek Falls was open in the middle of the night."

"Lucky for you, I have a key."

"That is lucky," she agreed. "But I don't want to worry about the future right now."

"What do you want?"

She lifted her arms to link them behind his neck. "You. I only want you."

"Well, that's convenient," he said. "Because I want you, too."

Then he captured her mouth in a long, slow kiss that went on and on until her head was actually spinning. The hand that was on her belly inched lower. His fingers sifted through the soft curls at the apex of her thighs and her hips automatically lifted off the bed, wordlessly encouraging his exploration. He parted the slick folds and dipped inside. She didn't know if it was the pregnancy hormones or Jesse, but all it took was that one stroke, deep inside, and she flew apart.

He continued to stroke her while the convulsions rippled through her body. Her hands fisted in the sheet, as she tried to anchor herself against the onslaught of sensations. "Jesse, please."

He leaned forward to reach into the drawer beside his bed and pulled out a small square packet.

Though she was reassured by this evidence of what was obviously a long-ingrained habit, she had to smile. "Isn't that a little like closing the barn door after the horse is out?"

"I guess it is," he agreed. "Although there are more reasons than pregnancy for using protection."

"Oh." She blushed. "Of course."

"But there's been no one since you," he said sincerely. "And no one for more than six months before that."

She took the square packet out of his hand. "Then we don't need this," she said, and set it on the bedside table.

He parted her legs and settled between them, burying himself deep in one thrust as she arched up to meet him.

He groaned in appreciation as she wrapped her legs around his hips. "You feel...so...good."

"You make me feel good," she told him.

He smiled at that and lowered his head to kiss her, long and slow and deep, as he moved inside her.

Maggie had never thought of herself as a particularly sensual woman. She certainly wasn't the type to get carried away by passion. She'd always thought sex was enjoyable, if unremarkable, but that was before she'd had sex with Jesse.

Over the past few months, she'd decided that her memories of the one night they'd spent together had been exaggerated by her imagination. It wasn't really possible that just standing close to him had made her knees weak, that breathing in his unique scent could make her insides quiver, that the touch of his mouth against her was enough to make her bones melt. Of course it wasn't. For some reason, she'd romanticized the memory, turned their one-night affair into something it never was and was never meant to be.

And then she'd seen him again, and her knees had gone weak. He'd stepped closer to her, and her insides had quivered. It didn't matter that his gaze had been guarded and his tone had been cool. All that mattered was he was there, and every nerve ending in her body was suddenly and acutely aware of him, aching for him.

Then, finally, he'd touched her. Just a brush of his hand over her hair, but that was enough to have her heart hammering inside of her chest. And then he kissed her, and not just her bones but everything inside of her had melted into a puddle of need. There was no thought or reason, there was only want. Hot and sharp and desperate.

As he moved inside of her now, she felt the connection between them. Not just the physical mating of their bodies but the joining of their souls. Maybe it was fantastical, but it was how she felt. She couldn't think of anything but Jesse, didn't want anyone but him.

The delicious friction between their bodies was every bit as incredible as she'd remembered—maybe even more. Every stroke, every thrust, sent little shock waves zinging through her blood. She could feel the anticipation building inside of her. Her body arched and strained, meeting him willingly, eagerly, aching for the ecstasy and fulfillment she'd only ever found in his arms.

Her hands gripped his shoulders, her fingers digging into his muscles, her nails scoring his skin. Her breath came in quick, shallow gasps as he drove her higher and higher to the pinnacle of their mutual pleasure.

Yes.

Please.

More.

And he gave her more. With his hands and his lips and his body, he gave and he gave until it was more than she could take. Pleasure poured through her, over her, a tidal wave of sensation that was so intense it stole her breath, her thoughts, her vision. There was nothing but bliss... and Jesse.

He was everything.

With a last thrust and a shudder, he collapsed on top of her, his face buried in the pillow beside her head.

She lifted a hand to his shoulder, let it trail down his back. His deliciously sculpted and tightly muscled body was truly a woman's fantasy—and he'd proven more than capable of satisfying every one of her fantasies, even the ones she hadn't realized that she had.

He lifted his weight off her, shifted so that he was beside her. But he kept his arm around her, holding her close. "Are you okay?" he asked.

Her lips curved. "I'm very okay."

He pulled her closer, so that her back was snug against his front and her head was tucked beneath his chin. "I almost forgot how good it was between us."

"I tried to convince myself it couldn't have been as good as I remembered." It was somehow easier to make the admission without looking at him. "But I was wrong."

"I missed you, Maggie."

"I missed you, too. But this...chemistry," she decided, for lack of a better term, "between us doesn't really change anything."

"You don't think so?"

"Wanting you—and wanting to be with you—doesn't alter the fact that our lives are twelve hundred miles apart."

"We'll figure it out," he told her.

He made it sound so easy, but Maggie knew there wasn't a simple answer. His suggestion that they should get married and raise their baby together wasn't a viable one. She couldn't—wouldn't—give up her career and her life in LA simply because he wanted to be a hands-on parent to their child. She admired his willingness to step up and respected his commitment to his ideals of fatherhood, but she was determined to focus on reality. And the reality was that her life, her family and her career were in California.

It wasn't likely that they were going to figure anything out—certainly not easily. She suspected it was more likely that there would be a lot of disagreement before any decisions were made, but it wasn't a battle she wanted to wage right now. Not while she was cradled in the warm strength of his arms, her body still sated from their lovemaking.

Within a few minutes, his breathing had evened out, and she knew he'd fallen asleep. As her own eyes started to drift shut, she found herself thinking about his impromptu offer of marriage. Not that she intended to accept—there were too many reasons to refuse, too many barriers to a relationship between them. But she couldn't deny that the prospect of sharing a bed with him for more than a few hours was undeniably tempting.

Chapter Four

When Jesse woke up, he was alone.

He could still smell Maggie's scent on his sheets, and there was an indent on the pillow where she'd slept, so he knew she couldn't have been gone long. He rose from his bed and moved to the window.

He didn't realize that his chest felt tight until he saw that her rental car was behind his truck in the driveway and the tension lessened. He'd been left with nothing more than a note on his kitchen table once before, and he didn't want to go through that again. He hadn't chased after Shaelyn—he'd had no interest in forcing her to stay in Rust Creek Falls when it was obvious she didn't want to be there.

But the situation with Maggie was different—she was carrying his baby, and that meant they had to figure out a way to work things out. If she had gone, he would have chased after her. He was glad he didn't have to.

He retrieved his jeans from the floor and tugged them on, then shoved his arms into the sleeves of his shirt and headed down the stairs. He found her standing at the stove, a spatula in her hand. The pressure in his chest eased a little more.

A glance at the numeric display on the stove revealed that it was after eight o'clock. "I guess we skipped dinner."

She looked up and offered a shy smile. "I hope you don't mind—I woke up hungry, and I thought you might be, too."

"I don't and I am," he told her. "French toast?"

"Is that okay?"

"Perfect."

She flipped the last piece of bread out of the frying pan and onto the plate, then carried the plate to the table, already set for two.

As she sat down across from him, he put a couple of slices on his plate, then liberally doused them with maple syrup. She took one slice, slowly ate it, cutting neat little squares that she dipped in a tiny puddle of syrup on her plate.

"I thought you said you were hungry."

"I was." She popped the last piece of toast into her mouth, then folded her napkin and set it on top of her plate. "And now I've eaten."

"You had one piece of French toast."

"I had two." One corner of her mouth tilted up in a half smile. "I ate the first one as soon as I flipped it out of the frying pan."

"Two whole slices?" He transferred another two to his own plate. "You must be stuffed."

"Don't make fun of me—I'm just happy to be able to keep down what I'm eating these days."

"I'm sorry," he said, sincerely contrite. "That must have been awful."

"It wasn't fun," she agreed.

"You should have called me."

She nodded. "I'm sorry I didn't."

He wanted to stay angry with her, but what was the point? Nothing could change what had happened since she left Rust Creek Falls in July, nothing could give them back the first four months of her pregnancy. But he couldn't help but think that, if she'd told him sooner, they might be in a different place right now.

Instead, he'd spent weeks dealing with the tangled emotions inside of him. He'd been hurt and angry and frustrated that he couldn't stop thinking about her. He'd tried to get over her—he'd even let his younger brother, Justin, set him up with a friend of the girl he was going out with. The date had been a complete bust, primarily because he couldn't stop thinking about Maggie. But recently he'd managed to convince himself that he was starting to forget about her—right up until the minute he saw her standing outside the paddock at Traub Stables.

"So," he began, thinking that a change of topic was in order, "things have been busy for you at work over the past couple of months?"

She nodded. "Busier than usual. Maybe too busy."

"Can you cut back on your hours?"

"Not if I want to keep my job."

"Do you?"

"Of course," she answered immediately, automatically. Then her brow furrowed as she picked up her glass of water and sipped.

"Tell me about your new job," she finally suggested. "When I was here in the summer, you were working here, at your family's ranch, and now you're training horses."

"I still help out here, but it's the horses that have always been my focus."

"I heard they call you the horse whisperer in town—what exactly does that mean?"

"It's not as mystical as it sounds," he told her. "It just means that I don't use restraints or force when I'm training."

"How did you end up working at Traub Stables? I thought there was some long-standing feud between the Crawfords and the Traubs."

"There is," he acknowledged. "Although no one really

seems sure about its origins, whether it was a business deal gone bad or a romantic rivalry. Whatever the cause, I think my sister's marriage to Dallas Traub in February has helped build some bridges between the two families."

"So your family doesn't mind that you're working for Sutter Traub?"

His lips curved in a wry smile. "I wouldn't go that far," he acknowledged. "My father saw it as a betrayal. My mother warned that I was being set up—for what, she had no idea, but she was certain it was some kind of disaster in the making."

"Did you take the job despite their objections—or because of them?"

"Despite," he said. "I've wanted some space from my family for a long time, but that doesn't mean I don't love and respect them."

"And you don't mind that your boss is a Traub?"

"Sutter's a good guy who values the animals in his care and appreciates what I bring to his stables."

"I read a series of books when I was a kid, about a girl who lived on a ranch and raised an orphaned foal," she told him. "She fed it and trained it and entered riding competitions with it. After reading those books, I was desperate to experience the feeling of racing across open fields on horseback. I begged my parents to put me in a riding camp for the summer.

"They were always encouraging us to try new experiences, so they found a local camp and signed me up. I was so excited...until the first day. I'd never seen a horse up close until then," she confided. "And when we got to the Northbrook Riding Academy and I saw real, live horses galloping in the distance, I was terrified."

"What happened?" he asked, both curious about and grateful for this voluntary glimpse into her childhood.

"I begged to go home as passionately as I'd begged for the camp, but they made me stay. My parents are very big on commitment and follow-through. I was the one who wanted the experience, and they weren't going to let me quit."

"Did you ride?"

She shook her head. "The instructors tried to help me overcome my fear of the horses, but whenever I got too close, I would actually start to hyperventilate. Of course, the other kids made fun of me, which made the whole experience that much worse.

"Then I met Dolly. She was a white Shetland pony who was too old and lame to do much of anything, but she had the softest, kindest eyes.

"I spent most of the week with her. I brushed her and fed her and led her around her paddock. At the end of the week, I still hadn't been on the back of a horse, but I'd fallen in love with Dolly. For the next six months, I went back to Northbrook once a week just to visit her."

He didn't need to ask what had happened after six months. Considering that the pony had been old and lame, he was certain he knew. Instead he said, "Did you ever get over your fear of horses?"

"I haven't been around them much since that summer."

He pushed away from the table. "Get your coat and boots on."

"What? Why?"

"I want to introduce you to someone."

She shook her head. "I got over my childhood fascination with horses—I'm good now."

"Not if you're still afraid," he told her.

"I wouldn't say *afraid*," she denied. "More…cautious."

He took her coat from the hook, brought it over to her.

"I need to clean up the kitchen."

"The dishes will wait."

"Has anyone ever told you that you're pushy?"

He took her hand and guided it into the sleeve of her coat. "Not pushy—persuasive."

"I'm not feeling persuaded," she told him, but she put her other arm in her other sleeve. "My boots are still, um, upstairs."

In his bedroom, where he'd taken them off her along with the rest of her clothing before he'd made love with her.

"I'll get them," he said.

When he came back down, she had her coat zipped up to her chin, a hat on her head and a scarf wrapped around her throat.

He held back a smile as he knelt at her feet and helped her on with the boots. To someone who had lived her whole life in Southern California, Montana in November—even the first of November—was undoubtedly cold, but he knew it would be a lot colder in December, January and February.

He hoped she would be there to experience it.

Maggie could tell that Jesse was amused by her efforts to bundle up against the climate. As she carefully tucked her hands into woolen mittens, he stuffed his feet into his boots and tugged on a jacket, not even bothering to button it.

She stepped outside and gasped as the cold slapped her in the face and stole the breath from her lungs.

"It was seventy-two degrees when I left Los Angeles," she told him.

He slid an arm across her shoulders, holding her close to share body heat—of which he seemed to have an abundance. "The weather takes some getting used to for a lot of people."

She couldn't imagine ever getting used to the cold—or wanting to. Thankfully, the barn was only a short distance from his house, and she was grateful to duck into its warm shelter.

The facility was brightly lit and immaculate. The alleyway was interlocking brick and the wooden walls fairly gleamed. Jesse pulled the door closed and stood beside her, giving her a minute.

"Are you okay?" he asked gently.

She nodded, because she wanted it to be true, but she wasn't entirely certain. She'd heard that the olfactory sense was one of the strongest for evoking memories, but she'd never experienced it herself until she stepped inside the barn and breathed in the scent of hay and horses. Suddenly her brain was flooded with memories of that long-ago summer camp, and with the memories came apprehension and anxiety.

"Just breathe," he said.

It was only then that she realized she'd been holding her breath. She let it out now, and drew fresh air into her lungs. But that fresh air carried the same scent, and made her heart pound hard and fast inside her chest. "I feel stupid."

"Why?"

"Because I'm scared," she admitted.

"I won't let anything bad happen to you," he promised.

"It's late," she said. "I should get back before Lissa starts worrying."

He took her hands, holding her in place. "Do you trust me?"

She nodded without hesitation.

"So let's just stand right here for a minute until you relax."

"I'm not going to relax in here."

"You just need to focus on something other than the horses," he said.

And then, before she could assure him there was absolutely nothing that would take her focus off the enormous beasts behind the flimsy wooden doors, his lips were on hers. And within half a second, her mind went completely, blissfully blank.

He released the hands he'd been holding to wrap his arms around her, pulling her closer. Then his hands slid up her back, and even through the thick layers of clothing, she could feel the warmth of his touch. Or maybe the heat was all in her veins, stoked by his caress. His tongue traced the curve of her bottom lip, teasing, coaxing. Her mouth parted on a sigh, not just allowing him to deepen the kiss, but demanding it, as her tongue danced in a slow and seductive rhythm with his.

Her blood was pumping and her head was spinning as she gave herself over to the pleasure of his kiss. She could still smell hay and horses, but mixed in with those scents was the essence of Jesse. His heat, his strength, his heart.

He eased his mouth from hers, but continued to hold her close as they each took a moment to catch their breath.

"What are you thinking about now?" he asked.

"That I won't ever be able to walk into a barn without thinking about you and remembering this moment."

He smiled. "Good."

"My heart's still racing."

"But not because you're afraid," he guessed.

"No." She blew out a breath and tipped back her head to meet his gaze. "Is that your usual method for helping people overcome their apprehensions?"

"It's not one I've ever used before," he told her.

Her brows lifted. "So I was a guinea pig?"

"No, you're the woman who makes me forget all thought and reason."

The words, and the sincerity in his tone, mollified her.

"But I haven't forgotten why we came out here," he said, looping his arm around her waist and gently guiding her along the alleyway.

They'd moved only about six feet when a huge head appeared over the top of the door of the closest stall. She let out a squeak and immediately jumped back.

Jesse's arms came around her, holding her steady. He didn't force her to move any closer, but he didn't let her back any farther away, either.

"This is Honey," he told her. "And she is as sweet as her name."

"She's…beautiful," Maggie realized. The animal had a sleek chestnut coat that gleamed in the light, a white blaze, glossy mane and tail and eyes the color of melted chocolate. "And…big."

The horse tossed her head, almost as if she was nodding, and Maggie couldn't help but smile.

Jesse chuckled softly, and she felt the warmth of his breath on the back of her neck.

"Do you see how her ears are turned forward?"

She nodded.

"That shows that she's relaxed and paying attention to you."

"Is she hungry?"

He chuckled again. "No, she's had her dinner," he promised, reaching around Maggie to tug her mittens off. Then he took her hand and guided it toward the horse's long muzzle.

She felt herself start to tremble and had to fight against the urge to snatch her hand away.

"Steady," he murmured.

The mare watched her, its huge, liquid eyes patient and trusting. With Jesse's guidance, she stroked the smooth hair of its blaze. Honey blew out a breath—an equine sigh of contentment—and Maggie fell in love.

"Now I really wish I'd learned to ride," she admitted.

"I could teach you," Jesse said. "Not now, obviously. But after."

After.

The word seemed to hang in the air for a long minute, teasing her with possibilities. Neither of them knew what would happen *after*—they didn't even know what the next five months would hold, but she couldn't deny that she liked the idea of *after*.

"I think I'd enjoy that," she finally said.

"What are the rest of your plans for the weekend?" Jesse asked Maggie, as they made their way back to the house.

"I didn't really have any other plans," she told him. "I came to Rust Creek Falls to tell you about the baby, and I've done that."

"Maybe we could spend some more time together," he suggested. "Get to know one another a little better before we bring a baby into the world."

"That baby's coming in another five months whether we know one another or not," she pointed out.

"Then we shouldn't waste any time."

"What did you have in mind?"

"Nothing too crazy," he assured her, opening the back door to lead her into the house. "Maybe a drive up to Owl Rock to see the falls or a walk through town. Dinner at my parents' house."

"I'm sorry—what was that last part?"

"Dinner at my parents' house," he said again.

"You want me to meet your parents?"

"And I want them to meet the mother of their grand-child."

She blew out a breath. "I didn't think about the fact that our baby will have a lot more family in Rust Creek Falls than a daddy."

"We don't have to tell the grandparents-to-be right away. I just thought it might be nice if they had a chance to meet you before I told them that I got you pregnant."

"I guess that's reasonable," she allowed.

"We don't even have to spend a lot of time with them," he promised. "In fact, I'd prefer if we didn't."

She smiled at that. "Are you trying to talk me into—or out of—this?"

"I'm not sure."

"Okay, we'll have dinner with your parents."

"What about *your* parents?"

"It's a long way for them to come for dinner."

He managed a wry smile. "Don't you think I should meet them?"

"Maybe not," she teased. "Because they already know I'm pregnant."

"Then they should also know that I want to marry you."

"I thought we'd agreed that wasn't a good idea."

"You said it wasn't a good idea, then we spent some time together in bed, proving that it is, in fact, a very good idea."

"That is definitely my cue to be going."

"Or you could stay."

She shook her head. "If I stay, we're both going to start thinking that this is something it's not."

"What do you think it isn't?" he challenged.

"A relationship."

He hung his coat on a hook. "We've had sex, we're having a baby, but we don't have a relationship?"

"We've spent the past four months in different states,"

she reminded him. "Does that sound like a relationship to you?"

"Obviously it's a relationship that needs some work."

Her lips curved, but the smile didn't reach her eyes. "I don't want to give anyone—including you—the wrong idea about us."

"I appreciate that," he said. "But this isn't LA, and I think people around here will have an easier time accepting the fact that you're having my baby if they believe we were involved in a real relationship—even if it didn't work out."

"Is that the story you want to go with?"

"I'd rather give the real relationship part a chance—to see if we can make it work."

"Jesse—"

"Don't say no, Maggie. Not yet."

She sighed. "I'll see you tomorrow."

"I'll pick you up around ten."

"Actually, I have an appointment with Lissa in the morning," she told him. "Can I meet you here again?"

"Sure." He brushed a quick kiss over her lips. "Drive safe."

"I was about to send out the sheriff," Lissa said, when Maggie walked into the house twenty minutes later.

The sheriff was currently lounging on the sofa in front of the television, so Maggie waved to him. "Hi, Gage."

He lifted his hand to return the greeting. "I told you she wasn't eaten by bears," he admonished his wife.

"As if that was all I was worried about," Lissa muttered.

"Well, you can see that I'm safe and all in one piece," Maggie said.

"Hmm." Her cousin's gaze narrowed, as if she wasn't entirely convinced. "How did it go?"

"Better and worse than I expected."

"What's the 'better'?"

"He's not disputing that the baby's his."

"I should think not," Lissa said indignantly.

Maggie shook her head. "I haven't seen him since July—he wouldn't be human if he didn't ask questions."

"And the 'worse'?" her cousin prompted.

"He thinks we should get married."

"Oh. My. God." Lissa jumped up and hugged her. "This is sooo great."

"Obviously you got kicked in the head by the same horse that he did."

Gage chuckled; Lissa scowled at him.

"You don't think it would be great if Maggie married Jesse and moved to Rust Creek Falls?" she said to her husband.

"I think your cousin has a life—and a job—in LA that need to be taken into consideration," he countered reasonably.

"Thank you," Maggie said to him.

"But you could get a job here," Lissa implored. "Unlike LA, Rust Creek Falls isn't plagued by an abundance of lawyers."

"Now you sound like Jesse," Maggie grumbled.

"Just think about it," her cousin suggested.

"I will." The problem was, she really couldn't think straight when she was around Jesse. When she was with him, she wanted to believe that they could defy both the odds and geography and somehow make a relationship work.

But that had been the plan when she'd gone back to SoCal after the night they spent together in July. They were going to keep in touch and see one another whenever possible. Except that complications—in the form of her job and then her pregnancy—hadn't allowed it to be possible, and Jesse had grown tired of her excuses and the distance and stopped communicating with her.

Of course, there was more incentive now to make it work. But their baby wasn't a magical glue that could bond them together, nor should they expect him or her to be.

And if she was ever going to say yes to a marriage proposal, she wanted to be in love with the man who was asking. She just wasn't ready to admit to anyone—even her cousin and best friend—that she already was.

Chapter Five

"There's been a little snag to our plans," Jesse said, when Maggie showed up at his house just after 10:00 a.m. Saturday morning.

"What kind of snag?" she asked curiously.

He stepped away from the door so she could enter. When she did, she saw a baby girl standing at the coffee table.

The child had wispy blond hair, big blue eyes and was dressed in a pair of pink overalls. And there was something about her—the shape of her eyes, the tilt of her chin—that launched her stomach into her throat.

She swallowed, and managed to find her voice. "You already have a baby?"

"What? No." The shock in his voice was real. "This is Noelle—my niece."

"Oh." She exhaled an audible sigh of relief.

Jesse scrubbed a hand over his face as he let out a nervous laugh. "Don't you think I would have told you something like that?"

She would have thought so, but she really didn't know him that well. If she had, she might have known that he had a niece. "I just saw the baby and my mind started spinning," she admitted.

"I would have warned you—if I'd had any warning myself," he told her. "Dallas took the boys to Kalispell to see a movie and Nina had to fill in at the store at the last minute. Usually she would take the baby with her, but No-elle's teething and cranky and Nina was afraid she'd scare off the customers."

"She doesn't look cranky to me."

"Give her a few minutes," Jesse said drily, hanging Maggie's coat on a hook.

"Do you babysit very often?"

"No. Nina can usually handle everything on her own, and when she does need help, there's a lineup of volunteers, including her husband, stepsons, grandparents on both sides and numerous aunts and uncles. But no one else was available today, so Noelle was dumped in my lap."

Maggie sat on the storage bench by the door and untied her boots. "So this wasn't part of your plan? Because I have to admit—this kind of feels like a test."

"A test?"

"To see how badly I'm going to screw up as a mother."

"It's not a test," he assured her. "And you're not going to screw up."

On the table in front of the sofa was a small plastic bowl containing a few cereal O's, with more scattered on the table and the carpet. When Maggie sat down, the little girl shuffled sideways toward her, holding on to the table as she went. Then she looked up at Maggie with a wide, droolly smile that revealed four tiny white teeth.

"She's adorable."

"She is pretty cute," he agreed. "But don't tell my sister I said so."

"Why not?"

"Because Noelle looks just like Nina when she was a baby." He sat on the floor and began to stack up the wooden blocks that were scattered around.

Noelle put her hand on Maggie's thigh and uncurled

her fist to reveal a crumbly cereal O. She left it on Maggie's pants, like a present, before she plopped down on the floor and crawled over to see what her uncle was doing.

Jesse was on the fourth level of blocks when his niece reached out with both hands and pushed them over.

"Oopsie," he said, and the little girl clapped her hands and laughed gleefully.

Maggie watched them play the same game for several minutes, amused by the easy interaction between them. "You're so natural with her."

"She makes it easy," Jesse told her. "She's a good baby."

"I don't have a lot of experience with kids," she admitted.

"That will change fast," he told her.

Noelle moved from the blocks to a ball that lit up and played music when it was rolled. When she gave up on the toys and went back to her cereal, Jesse decided it was time to make lunch, and he left Maggie supervising the baby.

She decided that she could stack blocks, too, and she sat down on the floor to do so. But Noelle wasn't overly interested in the structure Maggie was building. Instead, she was scouring the carpet for lost pieces of cereal. Only when she'd found them all did she crawl over to investigate Maggie's construction efforts. Of course, the house tumbled down and Noelle laughed and clapped. Then she picked up one of the blocks and shoved one corner of it into her droolly mouth.

"I don't know if you're supposed to be eating that," Maggie said dubiously.

The little girl continued to gnaw on the corner of the wood.

"I know you're probably hungry, but Uncle Jesse's getting your lunch ready so you might want to save your appetite."

Noelle kept her gaze fixed on Maggie, as if fascinated by what she was saying. Her lips curved in recognition of *Uncle Jesse*, but she continued to chew on the block.

"Why don't you give me that?" Maggie suggested, reaching for the square of wood. "Then we can use it to build a castle for—"

That was as far as she got, because when she managed to gently pry the block from the little girl's hand, Noelle started to scream like a banshee.

Panicked, Maggie immediately gave the piece of wood back to her. The little girl snatched the cube from her hand and threw it—bouncing it off Maggie's cheekbone and bringing tears to *her* eyes.

"What the heck—?" Jesse asked, appearing from the other side of the couch.

"I took her block away," Maggie admitted.

"Why?"

"I've read stuff…about lead paint and chemicals in children's toys, and I didn't think she should be chewing on the blocks."

"There's no paint on those blocks," Jesse pointed out. "They were handmade by my grandfather for Nina when she was a baby." Then he seemed to notice the red welt on Maggie's cheek and winced. "She's got a good arm, doesn't she?"

Maggie just nodded.

"I'll be right back," he said.

Noelle, having recovered her favorite wooden cube, was gnawing happily again, her explosive outburst apparently forgotten.

Jesse returned a minute later with a baggie filled with frozen peas and laid it gently against Maggie's cheekbone. "How's that feel?"

"Cold."

He smiled. "How do you feel?"

"Ridiculous," she admitted.

"Hungry?" he prompted.

"Sure."

Lunch was remarkably uneventful. Jesse had made grilled cheese sandwiches and French fries for everyone. He cut the little girl's sandwich into bite-size pieces, gave her a few fries and added a spoonful of corn niblets to her plate.

"Because her mother doesn't consider potatoes in fried form to be a real vegetable," he explained to Maggie.

Before the meal was done, Noelle was yawning and rubbing her eyes with a fist.

"Someone looks ready for her bottle," Jesse noted.

"Ba-ba," his niece confirmed.

"Why don't you give Noelle her bottle and I'll clean up the kitchen?" Maggie suggested.

"KP being the lesser of two evils?" Jesse teased.

She felt her cheeks flush. "It just seems fair, since you cooked, that I do the cleanup."

"In that case, I'll take you up on your offer," he said, scooping up the baby with his free arm. "But I think diaper change before bottle, because this little princess looks ready for a nap."

While Jesse tackled the diaper change—no way was Maggie ready for *that* challenge—she filled the sink with soapy water.

As she washed up and then dried the dishes, she could hear Jesse talking to the baby while she drank her bottle, his tone quiet and soothing. But as she put the dishes away, she realized he'd been silent for a while now, and she suspected that the little girl had probably fallen asleep.

She folded the towel over the handle of the oven and wandered into the living room.

She was right—the baby was asleep. So was Jesse.

And something about the image of the big strong man with the beautiful baby girl in his arms made her heart completely melt. There was absolutely no doubt that he loved his sister's child—or that he was going to be a fabulous father to their baby. She only wished she could be half as confident about her own parenting abilities.

Maggie touched a hand to her belly and thought of the tiny life growing inside her womb, suddenly assailed with doubts about her ability to meet all of her baby's needs, to be the mother her child deserved.

Noelle's mother worked full-time, but she was able to take her baby to work with her and she had family who were willing and able to help out with the baby as needed. Those same options weren't available to Maggie. Even if there was room in her shared office for a playpen—and there wasn't—she couldn't imagine the partners would ever approve that arrangement.

As for her family, she knew her parents would help in any way that they could, but they both had demanding careers of their own. And because she was at the start of hers, Maggie worked an average of ten hours a day, six days a week. Who would take care of her baby for all of that time?

Despite the size of the firm, there was no on-site day care at Alliston & Blake. Of course, most of the female lawyers on staff were primarily focused on their careers. She knew a few of them had children: Deirdre McNichol had three kids, but she also had a husband who was a playwright and able to work at home with their children; Lynda Simmons had invited her mother to move in so that she could look after her grandchild while Lynda was working; and Candace Hartman had a nanny—of course, she was a partner, so she could afford to pay someone to come into her house to take care of her child. Obviously none of those options was viable for Maggie, so she'd have to figure out something that was.

But first, she had to face dinner with Jesse's parents.

Dinner at the Crawfords' was always an experience—and probably not one that Jesse should have subjected Maggie to just yet. And definitely not while he was still hoping to convince her to marry him.

No one had ever accused his parents of being subtle, and as soon as Maggie sat down across from Jesse at the dinner table, the interrogation began. From "Where do you live in California?" and "What brings you to Rust Creek Falls this weekend?" to "How did you meet Jesse?" and everything in between.

No subject was off-limits, as his father proved when he asked, "What do you think about a woman planning to have a baby out of wedlock?"

Not surprisingly, the question made Maggie choke on her water.

"Really, Todd," his wife chided. "That's hardly appropriate dinner conversation." Which suggested that she at least had some boundaries, although Jesse didn't really believe it.

In an effort to divert the focus away from Maggie, he chimed in. "There are a lot of women who pursue nontraditional options to satisfy their desire for a family," he said, in a direct quote of the explanation his sister had once given to him.

"Nontraditional options," his father sputtered. "Nina got knocked up by some stranger through a turkey baster."

"Now she has a beautiful baby girl," his wife said soothingly. "*And* a husband."

"And three more kids she didn't plan on having," Todd noted.

"Three wonderful boys, who are now our grandchildren, too," Laura agreed. "And if we're lucky, Nate and Callie won't wait too much longer to give us even more."

"Give them time," her husband urged. "They're not even married yet."

"But they're so perfectly suited," Laura said. Then she turned to Maggie and said, in a confidential tone, "I had some concerns at first. There was a whole group of women who came here after the big flood last year, each one of them looking to hook up with a cowboy, and when Callie set her sights on Nate—as she did from the get-go—I was afraid she was just like them. Some of those women don't understand the life of a rancher—it isn't nearly as romantic as it looks in books and movies."

"Nothing ever is," Maggie agreed.

"But the important thing is that Callie and Nate are happy together." Laura paused to glance at her son. "We just hope Jesse will find someone who suits him so perfectly someday."

The implication being, of course, that Maggie couldn't be that someone. And though she kept a polite smile on her face, Jesse knew that his mother's remark had not been lost on her.

But still his mother had to hammer the point home, as she did when she asked, "So when are you going back to California?"

"Tomorrow," Maggie admitted.

"Well, I hope you'll stop by again the next time you're in town. Whenever that might be."

It was a dismissal—and not even a polite one. But he should have realized that Maggie wasn't the type of woman to let herself be dismissed, and while he was trying to figure out what he could say to clarify the situation, she responded.

"I'm sure it will be soon," Maggie said, matching his mother's cool tone. "We've got a lot to figure out before the baby comes."

Laura's fake smile froze on her face.

Todd turned to Maggie, his thick brows drawn together in a thunderous scowl. "You're pregnant?"

She nodded. "But don't worry—there were no turkey basters involved. I got knocked up the old-fashioned way."

Jesse hadn't intended to share the news of his impending parenthood with his own parents just yet, because he knew what they would expect him to do—it was the same thing he expected of himself: to marry the mother-to-be and give their child a family. And while he knew he wouldn't be able to keep Maggie's pregnancy a secret for much longer, he hadn't been anxious to go another round with his parents.

Their relationship had hit a serious snag when he'd told his mom and dad that he'd been offered a job at Traub Stables and they'd forbidden him to accept it. Forbidden him—as if he was a teenager rather than a twenty-nine-year-old man.

So while he hadn't planned to tell them about the baby, he couldn't regret that Maggie had done so—especially when her announcement had actually struck his mother mute for a whole three minutes.

"I can't believe I said that. To your parents." She dropped her face into her hands as they drove away from The Shooting Star. "I'm a horrible person."

"You were magnificent," he told her.

She shook her head. "Your mother pushed all of my buttons."

"She has a knack for that."

"I shouldn't have let her push my buttons. I should have just smiled and kept my mouth shut."

"I'm glad you didn't."

"Now they hate me."

"They don't hate you."

"They hate me," she said again. "And yet, they still expect you to marry me. How screwed up is that?"

He shrugged. "My family's big on taking responsibility."

"I thought they were big on finding someone who would suit you 'so perfectly.'"

"Apparently a baby trumps everything else."

"At least I understand a little better now why you felt compelled to propose."

He turned into the Christensens' driveway. "I do agree that a baby should have two parents."

"We've been through this once already tonight," she reminded him.

"But you still haven't agreed to marry me."

"Because I'm a big-city liberal who isn't morally opposed to nontraditional families."

"I'm not, either," he said. "Except when it comes to my child."

"Our lives aren't just in different cities but different states," she reminded him.

A fact of which he was painfully aware. And he didn't know what he could say or do to convince her to give them a chance to build a life together; he didn't have any new arguments to make. So he reiterated the most important one: "Our baby needs both of us."

He parked the truck in front of the sheriff's house, and although she was reaching for the handle before he'd turned off the engine, he scooted out of the vehicle and around the passenger side to help her out.

"There's no doubt your parents raised you to be a gentleman."

He lifted a finger to tip back the brim of his hat. "Yes, ma'am," he said, and made her smile.

But her smile quickly faded. "I wish I could say yes."

His heart bumped against his ribs. "It's a simple word—just three little letters."

"Those three little letters can't miraculously span twelve hundred miles." She started toward the house, and he fell into step beside her.

"We can figure it out," he said, desperately hoping it was true.

"I'm going back tomorrow," she reminded him. "I've got an early flight."

He sighed. "Will you let me drive you to the airport?"

She shook her head. "I've got to return my rental car, anyway."

"Can I call you?"

"Of course."

He caught her hand as she reached the door. "I know you have a lot to think about, but let me add just one more thing to the list," he said.

And then he kissed her.

Maggie didn't like to leave her car in the airport parking lot if she didn't have to, and she usually managed to cajole her brother Ryan into playing taxi driver. But when she got off the plane Sunday afternoon, she discovered that he'd somehow talked their mother into doing the pickup.

And when she saw Christa, Maggie felt her throat tighten and her eyes fill with tears. It both baffled and frustrated her that she could keep her chin up in the face of almost any kind of adversity, but as soon as she saw her mother, all of her defenses toppled and she felt like a little girl in need of her comforting embrace.

Christa, sensing that need, instinctively opened her arms and drew Maggie into them.

"What story did Ryan concoct to get out of airport duty this time?"

"There was no story," Christa said. "I volunteered."

"You hate driving around the airport."

Her mother shrugged. "I thought you might want to talk."

"I do," she agreed. "I just don't have the first clue where to begin."

Christa didn't press her. In fact, she didn't say anything else until they were in the car and driving away from the airport—except to ask for directions.

Once they were on the highway, Maggie finally vocalized the question that had been hovering at the back of her mind. "How did you manage to juggle a legal career and three kids?"

"I'd be lying if I said it was easy," Christa told her. "And I'm not sure I could have done it when you were babies."

"You weren't working then?"

Her mother shook her head. "I took a leave of absence when we adopted Shane and didn't go back to work full-time until you were in kindergarten."

"You took twelve years off?" She guessed at the number, since it was the age difference between herself and her oldest brother.

"It was actually closer to sixteen, although I did work a few hours a week at Legal Aid, to keep my hand in," her mother explained. "But your dad and I both agreed that if we were going to have children, our children needed to be a priority. I didn't want to work to pay someone else to raise you.

"That's not a choice every woman can make," she acknowledged, "but I was lucky to have your dad's support in that decision."

"I don't want to give up my career," Maggie said. "But I don't want to be so wrapped up in my career that I miss out on being a mother to my child."

"You don't have to choose one or the other," her mother pointed out.

"I'm not sure Brian Nash would say the same thing."

"Then maybe you need a new boss."

"I've dedicated almost half a decade to Alliston & Blake."

"Yes, you have," Christa agreed.

And Maggie heard what she didn't say—that maybe the time she'd already given them was enough. But leaving Alliston & Blake, trying something new and different, was a scary prospect. A little bit exciting but mostly scary, especially now that she had more than her career to think about—she had a baby on the way.

"I don't know what's the right thing to do," she admitted. "I know how to research precedent and draft motions and argue cases—I don't know how to be a mother."

"Being a parent is the toughest job you'll ever have, and the most important."

"What if I screw up?"

"You will," her mother said easily. "Every mother does once in a while. Every father, too."

"That was subtle, Mom."

Christa smiled. "I wasn't trying to be subtle."

"If you have questions about the baby's father, why don't you just ask them?"

"I don't have any specific questions—I just want you to tell me something about him. There was a time when you used to tell me everything about the boys you liked, but you've been awfully closemouthed since your trip to Montana in the summer."

Maggie wondered if it was possible to sum up Jesse in a handful of words, if there was any way to describe the way she felt when she was with him, any way to explain the conflicting emotions that she didn't understand.

"His name is Jesse Crawford," she said, deciding to start with the simple facts. "His family owns the general store in Rust Creek Falls and The Shooting Star ranch, but Jesse trains horses."

"So he's a cowboy," Christa mused.

Maggie nodded. "He's strong and smart, a little bit shy but incredibly sexy. There's an intensity about him, a single-minded focus. And he has a real gift for working with animals. They respond to him—his hands and his voice."

"I'm thinking he has the same gift with women," her mother noted drily.

Maggie felt her cheeks flush. "Maybe. But Lissa assured me he doesn't have that kind of reputation. In fact, since she's been living in Rust Creek Falls, she hasn't heard of him dating anyone at all."

"So what brought the two of you together?"

"Happenstance? Luck? Fate?"

Her mother's immaculately arched brows lifted. "Fate?"

"Something just clicked between us when we met," she said. "It was almost like…magic. I know that sounds corny, but I can't explain it any better than that."

"You're in love with him," Christa realized.

"I think…maybe…I am," she agreed hesitantly. "But is that even possible? I only met him a few months ago, I haven't spent that much time with him and I don't know him that well. But there's this almost magnetic draw that I can't seem to resist—that I don't want to resist when I'm with him."

"Have you told him how you feel?"

She shook her head.

"Why not?"

"Because I don't know how he feels."

"Love shouldn't be given with strings—it's a gift from the heart."

"Even if I told him, even if he—by some miracle—felt the same way, it doesn't really change anything."

"Honey, love changes everything."

"Maybe that's what makes me uneasy," Maggie finally admitted. "I like my life the way it is—and I get that having a baby will require some changes. But since I told Jesse, he's suddenly gone all Neanderthal, insisting that we should get married."

"You don't sound very happy about that."

"I'd be happy if I thought he wanted to spend the rest of his life with me," she admitted, startled to realize it was true.

"Isn't that usually the motivating factor behind a proposal?"

"The motivating factor for Jesse is our baby."

"Are you sure about that?" her mother asked gently.

"I told him I was pregnant and he said 'we should get married.'"

"And what did you say?"

"I said no."

"Did he accept that?"

"No," she admitted.

Christa smiled. "When do we get to meet him?"

Chapter Six

Since Jesse couldn't leave his animals unattended for a weekend, he called his brother Brad and asked him to take care of them. Of course, his brother showed up Friday just as Jesse was getting ready to head out.

"So where are you going this weekend?" he asked curiously.

"Los Angeles."

"California?"

"No, Los Angeles, Montana."

"Okay, it was a stupid question," Brad allowed. "But why are you going to California?"

"To see Maggie."

His brother narrowed his gaze. "That lawyer you were all ga-ga over in the summer?"

"No one over the age of twelve uses the expression *ga-ga*," Jesse chided. "But yes, Maggie is an attorney."

"I didn't even know you were dating her."

No one knew they were dating—because they weren't. But they were having a baby together and although his parents were now aware of that fact, they'd been surprisingly closemouthed about the situation. Probably because they were waiting for him to announce a wedding date, which he didn't think was going to happen anytime soon.

While he knew that Maggie's pregnancy couldn't remain a secret forever—and probably not very much longer—he wasn't ready to share the news with Brad. So he decided to go with the same explanation that Maggie had given to Jared Winfree. "We wanted to keep our relationship under the radar, to avoid small-town gossip."

"You definitely did that," Brad allowed. "I guess it's pretty serious, though, if you're going to LA to see her."

"I want to marry her," Jesse admitted.

His brother shook his head. "Why would you want to tie yourself to one woman when there are so many of them out there? And if you insist on settling down, why wouldn't you choose a local girl? Why would you hook up with another big-city gal who's only going to break your heart?"

"Thanks for the vote of confidence," Jesse said drily.

"You were devastated when Shaelyn left," Brad reminded him. "I don't want you to go through something like that again."

Actually, he'd been more relieved than devastated, having realized even before Shaelyn did that their engagement had been a mistake. But he didn't argue the point with his brother because Brad was right about one thing—Maggie was a big-city gal and it was entirely possible that he was making a big mistake.

Again.

Busy. Crowded. Frantic.

Those were Jesse's first impressions of Los Angeles, and that was before he left the airport terminal.

Thankfully everything he'd needed had fit into a carry-on, so he didn't have to battle the mass of people at baggage claim. He weaved through the crowd, feeling like a salmon swimming upstream. Or maybe the more appropriate analogy would be like a fish out of water.

Except that when he finally spotted Maggie, everything and everyone else seemed to fade away.

She offered him a quick smile and a kiss on the cheek. "Is that everything?" she asked, indicating the duffel bag slung over his shoulder.

"That's everything," he confirmed.

She nodded and led him toward the exit. "I got caught up in a meeting and didn't have a chance to pick up a file that I need this weekend. Do you mind if I make a quick stop at the office now?"

"Of course not," he said. In fact, he was curious to see where she worked—the big-city lawyer in her natural milieu.

But that was before she pulled out of the airport parking lot and onto the highway and he realized that Los Angeles traffic was insane. He'd never experienced anything like it and was beyond grateful that he didn't have to drive in it. And when Maggie began to zip from lane to lane, he just closed his eyes and held on.

They arrived at the offices of Alliston & Blake twenty minutes later. Maggie pulled into an underground parking garage and led him from there to a bank of elevators. She punched the call button for the one designated Floors 10–21, and once inside, they began the ascent toward the eighteenth floor.

"Are you okay?" she asked. "You look a little pale."

"I think so," he said. "I'd heard about California traffic, but I didn't anticipate anything quite like that."

"That was nothing compared to rush hour," she told him.

"I'll happily skip that experience, if it's an option."

She smiled. "I'll try to get in and out as quickly as possible."

He followed her into a small office with two desks and the same number of filing cabinets and bookcases. She went to the closer desk, the one with a neatly engraved nameplate that said Maggie Roarke. A similar nameplate on the other desk said Samantha Radke.

Maggie must have noted the direction of his gaze, because she said, "Sammi's working out of the San Francisco office this week."

While she sifted through a neat stack of folders, he moved farther into the room, checking out the diplomas on the wall and noting the summa cum laude designation on Maggie's certificate from Stanford Law.

"Got it," she said, just as a brisk knock sounded on the open door, immediately followed by a man's voice, "Good—you're back."

Maggie's smile froze on her face. "And on my way out again, Brian."

The man—Brian—didn't seem pleased by her response. And that was before he spotted Jesse standing beside her desk.

"Who's the cowboy?" he asked, speaking to Maggie as if Jesse wasn't even in the room.

"Jesse is…a friend of mine," she said. "Jesse Crawford. Brian Nash."

His hands were soft, his grip weak. The suit was obviously a pencil pusher who wouldn't be able to wrestle a fifty-pound sack of grain never mind a two-thousand-pound bull. Which didn't surprise Jesse or concern him—but he didn't like the way the other man put his hand on Maggie's shoulder, then let it linger there.

"I'm glad I caught you," Brian was saying to her now. "I have a meeting with Perry Edler tonight that I thought you might want to attend."

Perry Edler—the Chief Operating Officer of Edler Industries, one of Alliston & Blake's biggest clients. The invitation—and the possibilities that it implied—made Maggie's pulse quicken. Then she glanced from Brian to

Jesse, and her pulse quickened again, but for an entirely different reason.

"Tonight?" She shook her head with sincere regret. "I can't."

Brian frowned. "What do you mean—you can't?"

She couldn't blame him for sounding confused. In the almost five years that she'd worked at Alliston & Blake, she had probably never before uttered those same words. Her job had always been her number one priority and she'd happily juggled every other part of her life to accommodate it.

"I'm sorry," she apologized automatically. "But I already have plans for tonight."

"Plans?" Her boss's frown deepened as his gaze skipped to Jesse again. "Plans can't compare to opportunities, and this is an incredible opportunity for you, Maggie. Mr. Edler specifically asked that you be assigned to his team for this new project."

She looked at Jesse, her conviction wavering. His expression was guarded, giving her no hint of what he was thinking or feeling. He was leaving the choice entirely up to her, and she knew that if she told him this meeting was more important than their dinner plans because it had the potential to make her career, he'd probably wish her luck.

But was it?

Was one meeting with Perry Edler more important than the conversation she needed to have with her baby's father—a conversation for which he'd traveled more than twelve hundred miles?

Maybe the answer to that question should have been immediately obvious to her, but it wasn't. Because her job wasn't just important—it was vital. If she didn't have her job at Alliston & Blake, she'd have no income to provide the essentials of life—food, clothing, shelter—for her baby.

And okay, working as an attorney she'd have to add day care to that list, and day care was expensive, which meant that she'd have to increase her billable hours, which meant working more hours. The cycle was endless, and it made her head ache just to think about it.

If she let this one client meeting take precedence, where would it end? When would her job stop being more important than her life? When would the needs of her child finally matter more than the demands of her boss?

Brian took her silence as acquiescence. "We have an eight o'clock reservation at Patina—I'll see you there."

She looked at Jesse. "Can you give us a minute, please?"

"Sure," he agreed easily, already moving toward the door with the long, loose stride that was somehow both easy and sexy.

She waited until he'd closed the door before she turned back to her boss. "I'm sorry," she said again, but more firmly this time. "I can't make it."

His brows lifted. "This is a major career opportunity, Maggie."

She knew that it was—but she didn't much care for the strings that were obviously attached. "For the past five years, I've done everything you've asked of me— and more. I've come in early and stayed late. I've worked weekends and holidays that no one else wanted to work."

"And that's why you've earned this opportunity," he confirmed. "But if you're unavailable tonight, I'm sure Patricia will be pleased to join Mr. Edler's group."

Patricia was another junior associate who had made no secret of her ambitions—or her willingness to step on other people as she climbed her way to the top at Alliston & Blake.

"I thought Mr. Edler specifically asked for me."

"He asked for a young up-and-comer with lots of energy and enthusiasm." Brian amended his earlier claim. "I thought that was you."

"And now it's Patricia," she realized dully.

"You're good, but you're not indispensable," her boss said.

"I see."

"Do you?"

She was afraid that she did. And she was angry and frustrated because she knew there was nothing she could do—notwithstanding everything that she'd already done—to sway his opinion. If she couldn't be available to the firm every minute of every day, he would find someone who could.

She glanced from her boss to the door through which Jesse had exited. She could see him through the glass, leaning on a horizontal filing cabinet and chatting to one of the secretaries. Brian was a company man, from his neatly styled salon-trimmed hair to his immaculately polished Italian leather shoes. Jesse was every inch a cowboy—with a capital *C*. He was rugged and rough, charming and sweet, and he'd crossed state lines to be with her this weekend.

She'd never known anyone like him and it was immediately evident to her why—because he didn't, and wouldn't ever, fit in her corporate world.

Brian, obviously having followed the direction of her gaze, lifted his brows. "Do you really want to throw away this opportunity for some cowboy that you're having a fling with?"

"We're not having a fling," she told him. "We're having a baby."

He frowned. "You're joking."

"Actually, I'm not."

"You're really pregnant?"

She nodded. "Due in April."

"Well, that puts a different spin on the situation."

"Why is that?"

"As you already noted, I need someone who is available to come in early and stay late, someone who can work weekends and holidays. Are you still going to be able to do that when you have a baby at home?"

"I don't know," she admitted.

"That's not an answer that's going to get you very far in this firm," he warned.

"Are you firing me?"

"No," he said quickly. "Of course not. You're a valued associate and an important member of the Alliston & Blake team."

Which only meant that he knew he couldn't fire her without risk of being sued for unlawful termination.

"And I won't ever be anything more than an associate here, will I?"

"You know that's not my decision to make."

"You're a partner, Brian—one of the most senior, aside from Mr. Alliston and Mr. Blake. When you make a recommendation, the rest of the partners listen."

"If you're asking if I would recommend you for the partner track, I would have to say that, right now, I would not."

Though it was the answer she'd anticipated, it was still a shock to hear him say the words aloud. "That's not fair."

He shrugged. "It's a fact of life, Maggie. A partner is expected to put the needs of the firm first. Always."

"I can, and I would," she said, although without much conviction.

"Tell me," Brian said, "what you would do if you were on your way to court for closing arguments in a trial and the day care called because your child was feverish and vomiting?"

She didn't say anything, because she knew the answer

she would give him wasn't the answer he wanted to hear. And he knew it, too.

"Being a mother is a noble undertaking, but not one that's compatible with a partnership at Alliston & Blake."

Maggie dropped the file she'd come into the office to retrieve back on top of her desk.

"I'll see you on Monday."

Maggie didn't say anything to Jesse about her conversation with Brian. She didn't want him to feel sorry for her; she didn't want to give him any ammunition to manipulate her emotions to his own purposes; but mostly she didn't want his empathy, because she was afraid that would be her undoing.

"Do you like sushi?" she asked, when they exited the building.

He made a face. "No, and you shouldn't eat it, either, while you're pregnant."

"Suddenly you're an expert on pregnancy?"

"I've been reading up, learning a few things."

"Can I have steak?"

He nodded, either oblivious to or ignoring the sarcasm in her tone. "Red meat has lots of protein and iron, but it should be thoroughly cooked to ensure there is no residual bacteria."

"You really have been reading up," she noted, feeling duly chastised.

"I'm interested," he said simply.

She was, too, and she'd gone out to buy all of the best-reviewed books when her doctor had confirmed that she was going to have a baby. But they were still in a neat pile on her bedside table because she was usually too tired when she got home at the end of the day to want to crack the cover of a pregnancy guide or child-care manual.

"I'm hungry," she said, and led him through a set of frosted glass doors and into Lou's Chophouse.

The atmosphere was upscale casual, the decor consisting of glossy wood tables and leather-padded benches, with frosted glass dividers separating the booths and pendant-style lights hanging over the tables. When they were seated, the hostess handed them menus in leather folders, ran through the daily specials and promised that their server would be over momentarily to take their drink order.

Maggie ordered the peppercorn sirloin with basmati rice and steamed broccoli. He opted for the twelve-ounce strip loin with a fully loaded baked potato and seasonal vegetables.

But when her meal was delivered, she found she had no appetite. Mindful of the tiny life in her belly, though, she forced herself to cut into the steak and eat a few bites.

She didn't fool Jesse. He was halfway through his own steak when he said, "You're picking at your food."

"I guess I'm not as hungry as I thought I was."

"Is that all it is?"

She stabbed at her broccoli. "No," she admitted. "But I don't want to talk about it."

"Have you changed your mind?"

"About what?"

"Keeping the baby."

"No," she answered without hesitation. "I'm not sure about a lot of things, but I'm sure about that."

He exhaled an audible sigh of relief. "You probably know there aren't a lot of lawyers in Rust Creek Falls. In fact, Ben Dalton is it, but word around town is that he's interested in bringing in an associate."

"I have a job," she reminded him.

"I'm just presenting you with another option."

"Except that it's not an option, because I'm not licensed to practice in Montana."

"You'd have to pass the State Bar," he acknowledged.

"Have you been reading up on that, too?"

"A little."

"Then you should know that writing a Bar exam is a little more complicated than going to the store to pick up a quart of milk."

"Do you think the Montana exam is more difficult than the one you wrote here?"

"No," she admitted. "But I wrote the California Bar five years ago."

"And you've forgotten how to study since then?"

One side of her mouth tipped up in response to his teasing. "I don't think so."

"Then it's something you could at least consider?"

"Yes, it's something I could consider," she agreed. "But if I did get a job in Rust Creek Falls, what would I do about day care?"

"We have day care in Montana. In fact, the Country Kids Day Care is just a few blocks from Ben Dalton's office."

"Why are you okay with me putting our baby in day care in Rust Creek Falls but not in LA?"

"Because you wouldn't need day care for twelve hours a day," he pointed out logically. "Because even if you had to work late, I'd be there to help out, so our child would have more time with both parents."

"You make it sound so logical."

"It *is* logical."

She sighed. "I used to have a plan for my life and confidence that I knew exactly what I was doing. Now...I don't have a clue."

"So we'll figure it out together," he said.

"And what if we don't?"

"When you walk into a courtroom, do you worry that you can't handle the case?"

"I never walk into a courtroom unprepared."

"Exactly."

"I'm not sure the same rules apply to pregnancy and parenthood."

"I'm not sure there are any rules for parenthood—more like guidelines."

"Thanks, Captain Barbossa."

He grinned, pleased that she'd recognized the movie reference.

Maggie just sighed. "I used to be able to think things through—now my emotions seem to be all over the map, and I don't know if that's just the pregnancy hormones or…"

"Or?" he prompted.

"Or maybe this baby is giving me the excuse I need to make the changes to my life that I've wanted to make for a while."

"I have an idea for a change," he said. "You could marry me."

She shook her head.

"Why not?"

"Because I'm trying to be rational," she reminded him.

"You're pregnant with my baby, we have good chemistry—which might explain the baby," he acknowledged, earning a small smile from her. "You like to cook, I like to eat."

"Wow, your argument is…underwhelming."

"I'll be faithful, Maggie. I can promise you that." He knew it wasn't a declaration likely to make a woman swoon, but it was honest.

"I'm not sure that should be enough for either of us," she said softly.

"I'm not looking to fall in love."

"Why not?"

"Can we focus on what's relevant here?"

"What do you consider relevant?" she asked.

"The fact that I want to be a husband to you and a father to our baby." He reached across the table and covered her hand with his. "And maybe give that baby a brother or a sister someday."

"How do you know you want to be a husband to me?" she challenged. "You don't even know me."

"I know that you're beautiful and smart and warm and compassionate. I know that your family is important to you. You're close to your parents and your brothers and our baby is a real, biological connection to me and will bind us together forever.

"I know you enjoy your work, and I don't think you'd be happy to give up your career. But I also don't think you'll be happy, long-term, in a career that takes everything from you and gives nothing back—as it seems your job at Alliston & Blake is doing.

"The fact that you want to have and keep this baby proves you want to be a mother, and since you don't do anything in half measures, you want to be a good mother. Which means that you need to find a way to balance work outside the home with responsibilities to the child that we're bringing into the world."

She didn't know if anyone had seen into her heart so clearly, and the realization that he'd done so was a little worrisome. If he could read her thoughts and feelings that easily, it wouldn't take him long to figure out that she had strong feelings for him, and she was afraid he would manipulate those feelings to get what he wanted.

"You missed one thing," she told him.

"What's that?"

"I was raised by two parents who love one another as much as they love their children, and I always promised myself that if and when I did get married, it would be because I'd found someone that I loved the same way."

"I'd say the baby you're carrying trumps that idealistic dream."

Idealistic dream.

The dismissal in those two words cut to the quick. Just when she'd almost been ready to let him persuade her that they could make a marriage work, those two words told her so much more than he'd likely intended.

"She must have really done a number on you," Maggie mused.

"Who?"

"The woman who made you afraid to risk your heart."

Chapter Seven

Jesse didn't want to talk about the past but the future—his future with Maggie and their baby.

Except that her insight, as uncomfortable as it made him, was valid. And it forced him to ask himself some hard questions: Why *was* he pushing for marriage? Why was he trying to convince Maggie to move to Rust Creek Falls? How long did he really think an LA transplant would last in a small Montana town? Didn't he learn anything from his painful experience with his ex?

He'd met Shaelyn Everton when he was a student at Montana State University. She didn't really have a major—she was just taking some courses that interested her while she tried to figure out what she wanted to do with her life. Their paths had crossed at a pub on campus—his friend had been hitting on her friend, leaving the two of them to make conversation with one another.

She'd been pretty and sweet and he'd fallen fast and hard. Some of his friends had warned that she didn't want an education just an "MRS" degree, but he didn't care. All that mattered was that they were going to be together.

He'd proposed to her the day of his graduation, and she'd happily accepted. She'd promised that she was excited to go to Rust Creek Falls with him, to spend time with his family and start to plan their wedding.

She'd visited his hometown with him at Christmastime,

a few months earlier, but they'd been so busy with family and holiday events, she didn't have much time to experience the town. She admitted to him, after only a few days, that she was feeling a little bit of culture shock.

He didn't understand what she meant—having been born and raised in Rust Creek Falls, he was certain the town had all the amenities anyone could need. And anything that wasn't readily available in town—specialty shops and fancy restaurants—was close enough in Kalispell.

Her frustration had come to a head one night when she decided to make Salisbury steak for dinner. Unfortunately, she'd forgotten to buy mushrooms when she'd gone into Kalispell to get groceries. She went to Crawford's, but they only had canned, and she had a complete meltdown. Jesse tried to reassure her, suggesting that she could make the recipe without the mushrooms—he wasn't a huge fan, anyway. But she'd refused, insisting that it wouldn't be the same.

It hadn't seemed like a big deal to him, but it had been the beginning of the end for Shaelyn. She didn't know what to do with herself in Rust Creek Falls. She hated that his work at the ranch kept him busy for so many hours of each day. She wanted to spend time with him, to linger in bed late in the morning and enjoy long, leisurely lunches. Then she expected him to come in early and spend the evening hours entertaining her. After a few weeks, he talked his sister into giving Shaelyn a job at the store, but his fiancée had studied art history at university and was appalled by the idea of working in retail—especially in a small-town general store that sold cookies, canned goods and fishing gear, all under one roof.

He'd tried to make her happy. Though it got to the point where he almost dreaded coming home at the end of the day, he reminded himself that there had been a reason he'd fallen in love and planned to spend his life with her. So he would come in after working all day, shower off the dirt and sweat and take her into Kalispell to dinner or to see a movie. He wanted her to be happy, but trying to keep her happy was exhausting him. In retrospect, he was relieved it had only taken her three weeks to realize she couldn't stay in Rust Creek Falls.

She'd claimed to love him but, in the end, she hadn't loved him enough to really try to make their relationship work. He'd come in from checking fences one day to find her engagement ring on the table with a note.

Jesse,
I can't do this anymore. I really thought we would be together forever, but I can't stay in this town one more day. If you ever decide you want more than what you've got here, you know where to find me.
Love,
Shaelyn

Three weeks was all she'd lasted before deciding that Rust Creek Falls was too small-town for her. And she'd been from Billings. Billings had a population of 165,000 people—a booming metropolis in comparison to Rust Creek Falls, but an insignificant speck on the map in contrast to the more than three million that lived in Los Angeles.

If Shaelyn had been unhappy in Rust Creek Falls, what made him think that Maggie would feel any differently? Why was he pushing for marriage to another woman who would be completely out of her element in the small Montana town?

Maggie was a successful attorney comfortable with

the fast pace and bright lights of the city. She'd spent a few days in Rust Creek Falls—a few days that were an interlude from her ordinary life. In California she could have any kind of cuisine delivered to her door; food options in Rust Creek Falls were limited to the Ace in the Hole, Wings To Go and Daisy's Donuts. LA had concerts, comedy clubs, live theater and multiplexes; the only place to see a movie in Rust Creek Falls was the high school gymnasium, and only there on Friday or Saturday nights.

Of course, people were already talking about how the opening of Maverick Manor—his brother Nate's new resort—could change the atmosphere in Rust Creek Falls. Not everyone was in favor of those changes, but in Thunder Canyon, the opening of their resort a few years ago had brought about big changes and seriously boosted the local economy. It was hoped that Maverick Manor might do the same thing. There would be new shops and eateries, obviously targeting visitors but also benefitting local residents with the expanded availability of goods and services and the creation of new jobs. But those changes wouldn't happen overnight, and even when they did, would they be enough for Maggie? Could a big-city attorney ever be happy in a small town?

Because no matter how many more shops and restaurants moved into the area, Rust Creek Falls was always going to be a small town, and Jesse suspected that asking Maggie to stay would only be setting himself up for another heartache.

Unless he was careful to ensure that his heart didn't get involved.

Maggie had hoped to postpone the inevitable meeting between her parents and the father of her baby, but as soon as Gavin and Christa learned Jesse was coming to town, they were eager for the introductions. So after dinner, she drove to her parents' Hollywood Hills home, where Christa met them at the door.

After kissing her daughter on the cheek, she offered her hand to their guest. "You must be Jesse."

"Yes, ma'am," he confirmed.

And her mother, who rubbed elbows with judges and politicians and movie stars, almost swooned in response to his boyish country charm.

"Please," she said, "call me Christa."

"It's a pleasure to meet you," he said.

"We're eager to get to know you," she told him.

"Too eager to wait until tomorrow," Maggie noted.

Her mother just smiled. "It's a lovely night, so we're having drinks out on the patio, by the pool."

Jesse followed Maggie through the wide-open French doors that led to the enormous stone deck that spread out to encircle the hot tub and kidney-shaped swimming pool. Flames crackled in the outdoor fireplace, adding warmth and light to the seating area.

Her father had been relaxing on one of the dark wicker sofas with a glass of his favorite scotch in his hand, but he set the glass down and rose to his feet when they stepped out onto the patio.

"Maggie's brought her young man to meet us," Christa said to her husband.

Maggie winced at the *her* more than the *young man*, as the possessive pronoun suggested a relationship that didn't really exist.

"Jesse Crawford," he said, offering his hand to her father.

Gavin accepted, probably squeezing Jesse's hand with more force than was necessary—or even polite. She was confident that Jesse could handle anything her father dished out—she was more worried that her baby's father and her own father might find common ground in their belief that an expectant mother should have a husband.

"Can I get you something to drink?" Gavin asked Jesse. "Whiskey? Wine? Beer?"

"I'll have whatever you're having," Jesse said.

"Maggie?"

"I'll just have a glass of water."

Her father dispensed the drinks, then resumed his seat beside his wife. He asked Jesse about his education and his employment, his family and friends, and life in Rust Creek Falls. The questioning wasn't dissimilar to what she'd been put through by Jesse's parents, although she liked to think hers were a little more subtle.

Jesse answered the questions with more patience than Maggie had. When her father paused to sip his drink, she finally asked, "Is the interrogation part of the evening finished yet?"

"I'm just making conversation," Gavin told her.

"Really? Because you've served me steaks that haven't been so thoroughly grilled."

"Maggie," Christa chastised.

But her husband chuckled.

"She's always been quick to defend," he told Jesse. "But if the baby she's carrying turns out to be a girl, she'll undoubtedly be asking the same questions someday."

"Or I will," Jesse said.

Gavin nodded. "Or you will."

"Don't forget you've got a seven-fifteen tee time with the governor's son-in-law in the morning," Christa said to her husband when he got up to refill his drink.

"*If* it doesn't rain," he clarified.

"There's no rain in the forecast," his wife assured him.

"But every time I think there's no rain in the forecast, we get rained out."

"What are you two up to tomorrow?" Christa asked, turning back to her daughter.

"I'm going to show Jesse some of the local sights," Maggie responded. "And since we plan to get an early start, we should head out."

"I know you don't have a spare bedroom in your condo, but you've got a pullout sofa," her father said pointedly.

"Gavin," his wife chided.

He ignored her gentle admonishment. "She might be twenty-eight years old and on her way to becoming a mother herself, but she's still my baby girl," he said.

"Maybe I should move to Montana," Maggie muttered under her breath.

"If only you really meant that," Jesse said, not under his breath at all.

There was a lot to see and do in Los Angeles, and Maggie was happy to play tour guide for Jesse. She took him to Venice Beach, where they skated along the bike path, browsed the shops along the boardwalk, admired the public art walls, detoured around a filming crew and had lunch at a vegetarian café—but only after he made her promise she would never tell any of his friends or family in Montana. He seemed to enjoy spending the time with her, just talking and laughing and getting to know one another. And when they finally got back to her condo at the end of the day, she was sorry to realize the weekend was more than half over.

Less than twenty-four hours after that, she took him back to the airport again. She was glad that he'd come to Los Angeles, that he'd made the effort to see her. Except that she knew it had been an effort, that maintaining a relationship—or trying to establish one—over such a long distance wasn't easy.

And despite the time they'd spent together during the days—and their lovemaking in the nights—they hadn't resolved anything with respect to the baby or their future, and she was afraid they wouldn't anytime soon.

"We're not going to be able to do this every weekend, are we?" he asked when she walked him through the airport to the security checkpoint.

His question confirmed that his thoughts had been following the same path as her own. "Probably not," she admitted.

"When do you think you'll be able to get back to Rust Creek Falls?"

"I don't know. I've got a lot of stuff going on at work this week—" and she hadn't told him the half of it "—but I'll figure something out."

"I wish I had more to offer you."

"What do you mean?"

"My life in Montana is a lot more modest than everything you've got here."

She lifted a shoulder. "Believe me, the shine of Tinseltown wears off after a while."

And as much as she'd enjoyed this weekend in the city with Jesse, she couldn't deny there was a part of her that wished she was going back to Montana with him.

She was still feeling restless and unsettled when she went into work Monday morning. She'd always loved being part of the well-oiled machine that was Alliston & Blake and had thrived in the busy environment. But after her conversation with Brian Nash on Friday, she realized that it really was a machine—and she was just one of hundreds of gears—interchangeable and replaceable.

By early afternoon, she'd reviewed a restructuring proposal, drafted a motion for an injunction and written her letter of resignation—although she hadn't yet decided what, if anything, she was going to do with it.

Needing to stretch her legs, she went into the staff room to get a drink of water.

On her way, she crossed paths with Perry Edler as he was leaving Brian Nash's office.

"Mr. Edler," she said, offering her hand to the man she'd worked with on numerous occasions in the past.

He shook it automatically.

"I'm sorry I wasn't available to meet with you Friday night."

His expression was polite but blank, as if he wasn't entirely sure who she was or why he might have been meeting with her.

"I trust that Amanda was able to respond to any concerns you might have had about your new venture." She was well aware that it was Patricia and not Amanda who had attended the meeting, but she wondered if the COO of Edler Industries was aware.

"Yes," the older man assured her. "Amanda was most helpful."

Which confirmed Maggie's suspicion that he had never asked for her by name, that the associates at Alliston & Blake were all one and the same to the clients. So long as the work was done, they didn't care who did it. And that was okay—the head of an international company was obviously more concerned with the answers to his questions than the identity of the person answering them.

"But maybe you'll be at the next meeting," he said solicitously, because the head of an international company understood that it was easier to stay on top when you had people below to keep you there.

"Maybe I will," she said, but she didn't think it was likely.

She knew that her work mattered, but she was only beginning to realize that she wanted more than that—she wanted to matter. And she would never be anything more than one of those interchangeable gears if she stayed at Alliston & Blake.

She went back to her office and printed her resignation letter.

Chapter Eight

Maggie wasn't usually an impulsive person, but less than twenty-four hours after her brief conversation with Perry Edler, she was back in Rust Creek Falls to meet with Ben Dalton.

"We do a little bit of everything here," the attorney said, in response to her question about his areas of practice. "Although most of it is wills, real estate transactions, the occasional divorce, traffic offenses, minor criminal stuff. What did you do in LA?"

"Mostly corporate law for the past few years, with a focus on mergers and acquisitions," she admitted. "I've already looked into taking the Montana Bar, and I know it's only offered twice a year—in Helena in February or Missoula in July. I was hoping to write in February, but I missed the registration deadline."

"If you think you can be ready to write in February, I might be able to get your name on the list."

"I think I'd do better writing it in February," she admitted. "Because I'm expecting a baby in April."

"Are you planning to get married before then?"

The unexpected question made her pause, because she couldn't imagine any interviewer in LA ever daring to ask any such thing.

"It's a possibility," she told him.

"Because folks around here are pretty conservative,"

Ben warned. "And likely to be suspicious enough of a big-city attorney setting up practice in their backyard. But if you were married to a local boy—assuming the baby's father is a local boy—that would go a long way with the people in this town."

And she knew that if he did offer her a position, she'd have to remember that things were done a little bit differently here. With that thought in mind, she nodded. "One of the reasons I wanted to move to Rust Creek Falls was to be closer to the baby's father, so that we can share the parenting."

"A smart decision," Ben told her. "My wife chose to be a stay-at-home mother, and I'm grateful our six kids had the benefit of having her around full-time, but she'll be the first to admit that every aspect of parenting is made easier by sharing it with someone."

He talked about his wife with an easy affection that spoke of their thirty-seven years and the experience of raising half a dozen kids together. He had a copy of their wedding picture in a gold frame on his desk and told Maggie it was a lucky man who could, after almost four decades, honestly say he loved his wife even more now than the day he married her.

Rust Creek Falls might have been a small town, but there were still a lot of people that Maggie had yet to meet and a lot of familial connections she hadn't begun to make. For example, it wasn't until Ben pulled out his cell phone to show off the latest snapshots of his brand-new grandson that she learned his daughter Paige was married to Sutter Traub, the owner of Traub Stables—Jesse's boss. They'd recently had a baby boy—Carter Benjamin Traub—and the proud grandpa had more than a hundred photos of the little guy on his cell phone.

The baby was adorable, and just looking at the pictures

made Maggie long for the day when her baby would finally be in her arms. Except when she remembered her first interaction with Jesse's ten-month-old-niece—then her anticipation was tempered by a healthy dose of apprehension.

"He offered me a job," Maggie told Lissa, when she got back to her cousin's house after the interview.

"Of course he did," Lissa said smugly. "He's never going to find a more qualified candidate than you to add to his practice."

"I'm not qualified yet," she reminded her cousin. "I still have to pass the Montana Bar."

Lissa waved a hand dismissively. "I'm more interested in the details about your wedding, such as what your matron of honor will be wearing."

Maggie shook her head. "The only thing I accepted today a job, not a marriage proposal."

"But you *are* going to marry Jesse, aren't you?"

"I don't know," she admitted.

"So let me see if I'm following this," Lissa said. "You felt an instant connection to Jesse and fell into bed together. It was the best sex of your life and you hoped it was the start of a real relationship, then you found out you were having his baby and he proposed, but you don't know if you should marry him?"

Maggie nodded. "That about sums it up."

"I need a little help with the 'why' part," her cousin admitted.

"Why what?"

"Why you don't want to marry him."

"Because I love him."

Lissa took her hands. "Sweetie, you're not just my cousin but one of my best friends in the world, but I have to admit that right now, I have serious concerns about your sanity."

Maggie managed a smile even as her eyes filled with tears. "I want him to love me, too."

"You don't think he does?"

"I know he doesn't." And she told Lissa what Jesse had said about common goals being more important to the success of a marriage than love.

"Clearly Jesse Crawford is an idiot. But," Lissa continued, when Maggie opened her mouth to protest, "since he's the idiot you love, we're going to have to come up with a plan."

"A plan?"

"To make sure he falls in love with you, too."

"I don't think that's something you can plan," Maggie said.

Her cousin smiled. "A smart woman has a plan for everything."

Gage and Lissa decided to go into Kalispell for dinner. They invited Maggie to go with them, but she declined. She needed some time to think about her future—and she needed to call Jesse. Before she had a chance to do so, there was a knock on the door, and when she opened it, he was there.

"Jesse—hi." Her instinctive pleasure at seeing him was mixed with guilt as she realized that she hadn't told him about her plans to come to Rust Creek Falls this week. "I guess news travels fast in a small town."

He nodded. "Of course, I didn't believe it when Nina told me she overheard Lani Dalton tell Melba Strickland that her father was interviewing 'that city lawyer.' But then Will Baker told me that he saw you and Ben having lunch at the Ace in the Hole."

"Who needs Twitter when you've got the Rust Creek Falls grapevine?"

"Why are you here?" Jesse asked. "I thought you had some big project to work on with your boss at Alliston & Blake."

She stepped away from the door so that he could enter. "Why don't you come in so we can talk about it?"

He followed her into the kitchen, hanging his jacket over the back of a chair before settling into it.

"Do you want anything to drink?"

He shook his head. "No, I'm fine, thanks."

She turned on the kettle to make herself a cup of peppermint tea, more because she wanted something to do than because she wanted the tea.

"I handed in my resignation at Alliston & Blake yesterday."

He opened his mouth, closed it again, as if he wasn't quite sure what to say, how to respond to her news. "Okay—I'll admit I didn't see that one coming."

She shrugged. "It was time. Maybe past time. Technically, I'm supposed to give two weeks' notice, but since I haven't used all of my vacation this year—actually, I haven't used all of it in any of the past few years—I'm officially on vacation right now."

"And your lunch with Ben today?" he prompted.

"He offered me a job." She didn't tell him that she'd accepted, because she didn't want him to immediately rush to the same conclusion that Lissa had done.

"You're thinking about moving to Rust Creek Falls?"

She nodded. "I'm not sure of any of the other details yet, but I'm sure that I want you to be part of our baby's life." She poured the boiling water over the tea bag inside her cup, then carried it to the table and sat down across from him. "You went away to school, right?"

"Montana State University in Bozeman."

"When you graduated, did you ever think about exploring options anywhere else?"

He shook his head. "Nowhere else is home."

She couldn't help but smile at his conviction. "It must be nice, to know without a doubt that you are exactly where you belong."

"You don't feel like that in LA?"

"I wouldn't be making this move if I did," she told him.

"Are you going to marry me?"

She hesitated. "I still think marriage is a little extreme."

"And yet people have been doing it for thousands of years."

She smiled. "Yes, and since it's the twenty-first century, our child is unlikely to be ostracized by society if his or her parents aren't married."

"Archaic attitudes are still pervasive in society," he said, in an echo of Ben's comments earlier that day.

"And more so in Montana than California," she acknowledged.

"Undoubtedly," he agreed.

"Despite that, there are aspects of this town that really appeal to me, too."

"Such as?"

"The teacher-to-student ratio in the schools. It's widely theorized that students in smaller classes learn better. The public high school I went to had two thousand students. The secondary school here has a population that isn't even one-tenth of that."

"And only one teacher."

She laughed, because she was almost 100 percent certain he was joking. "And I like the sense of community," she said. "Everywhere you go, you cross paths with someone you know."

"I don't always consider that a plus," he admitted.

"It is," she insisted. "You might not always agree with your friends and neighbors, but you know you can count on them.

"Lissa told me what it was like, after the floods last year. How the residents rallied to help one another. Even the Crawfords and the Traubs worked together."

"That's true."

"You don't see a lot of that in LA. I'm not saying that neighbors don't ever help neighbors, but it's not the usual mindset. It's a town built on glitz and glamour and climbing over other people to get to the top."

"Why would you ever want to leave such a place?"

She smiled at his dry tone. "I also like the idea of a job with more regular hours, so that I'd have more time to spend with my baby."

"And your husband."

She shook her head. "You're like a wave crashing against a rock, determined to erode my resistance."

"Is it working?"

"It might be," she acknowledged. "And if I did decide to marry you, then what would you do?"

"Call the preacher to book a date for the wedding before you changed your mind," he replied without hesitation.

"The wedding is the easy part—it's the marriage I'm worried about."

"I'm not going to tell you that you shouldn't worry," he said. "Because I think you're right—if we want our marriage to succeed, we're both going to have to work at it. But the fact that you're having my baby means that we both have a vested interest in its success, and I'm willing to do whatever it takes to give our child the happy and stable family that he—or she—deserves."

"Then I guess, since it seems we both want the same thing, you should call the preacher."

"Really?"

She nodded.

He whooped and lifted her off her feet, spinning her around. And the sheer joy of being in his arms and sharing his joy convinced Maggie that she'd made the right decision.

She still had some concerns—aside from agreeing to marry a man who didn't love her, there was the uncertainty about whether or not she would be able to make the transition to life in the country. But if Lissa could do it—if her cousin could make the change from Manhattan to Montana—then Maggie was confident she could adjust, too.

But Lissa had worked her butt off to prove herself to the people of Rust Creek Falls after the flood the previous year. On behalf of Bootstraps, a New York–based charitable organization, she'd rallied volunteers, coordinated their schedules and duties, and essentially gone door-to-door assisting families in need and helping repair damage. Along the way she'd fallen in love with the highly respected sheriff, which had helped the townspeople fall in love with her. Even so, Gage's mother had expressed concern when her son had got involved with Lissa. Apparently the local residents had some pretty strong opinions about "city people" and not necessarily good ones.

And then Maggie had swept into town from Los Angeles, and what had she done? She'd helped get Arthur Swinton out of jail—and while his illegal activities had targeted the residents of Thunder Canyon, the people of Rust Creek Falls weren't unaware of what he'd done. As if representing the convict wasn't bad enough, she'd seduced Jesse Crawford and got pregnant in order to trap him into marriage.

Of course, that wasn't at all how things had really happened, but she didn't doubt that at least some of the locals would view the situation in exactly that way.

"At the risk of you changing your mind before I've even put a ring on your finger, I have to ask—do you think you'll miss the hustle and bustle of LA?"

"It's not as if I'm never going back there," she pointed out. "I do still have family in California."

"How are they going to feel about you moving so far away?"

"My parents have always encouraged me to follow my own path."

"Even if that path leads you to a small town in the middle of nowhere?"

"Are you trying to convince me to stay or go?"

"I just want to be sure you know what you're getting into," he told her. "I couldn't imagine living anywhere else, but I know the open space and isolation aren't for everyone. Winters, in particular, can be harsh, especially for someone who is accustomed to having all the amenities of the big city within walking distance."

"So who was she?"

"Who was who?"

"The girlfriend from the big city who did a number on you," she clarified.

He didn't say anything.

"Don't make me go into town searching for tidbits of gossip," she teased.

It wasn't a sincere threat, of course, but Jesse finally answered.

"Her name was Shaelyn," he said. "And for all of three weeks, she was my fiancée."

"Oh." And how silly was it that Maggie was disappointed to realize she wasn't the first woman he'd ever proposed to. "How many times have you been engaged?"

"Just two."

"Was she pregnant?"

He shook his head.

"So you proposed to her because you loved her," she realized.

"I thought I did," he admitted.

But Maggie knew it had been more than a thought to have scarred him so deeply.

He'd told her he didn't want to fall in love—but that was only because he'd already been there, done that. And while her heart was filled to overflowing with feelings for him, his heart was still in pieces, broken by another woman.

Not exactly the auspicious start she'd envisioned for their life together.

True to his word, Jesse called the preacher that same night, and their wedding was scheduled for Saturday afternoon—only four days away.

Christa, Gavin and Ryan all had to do some serious rearranging of their schedules, but they managed to fly into Montana on Friday. Shane and his wife, Gianna, drove up from Thunder Canyon on the same day, and the Roarkes had an impromptu family reunion at Strickland's Boarding House, where they were all staying.

On Wednesday, Lissa had taken Maggie into Kalispell to go shopping. Maggie didn't want to buy her wedding dress without her mother's approval, so every dress that she tried on, Lissa took a picture and emailed it to Christa, who would email back her thoughts and suggestions.

After the fourth picture, Lissa's cell phone rang. Christa was crying happy tears on the other end of the line because she knew that dress was "the one," and she gave her credit card information to the clerk over the phone to ensure that Maggie walked out of the store with it in hand.

And on the day of the wedding, as she helped her daughter into the gown, Christa's eyes misted over again. "Look at you," she said softly, almost reverently.

Maggie did so, smiling as she took in her reflection in the full-length mirror. "I look like a bride," she said, turning to show off the dress from all sides.

It was a strapless design with a sweetheart neckline, a bodice covered in sparkly beads that hugged her breasts, and a full skirt that skimmed the floor.

"The most beautiful bride I've ever seen," her mother said, brushing moisture from her cheeks.

"I'm sure Dad would have something to say about that," Maggie countered. Then she lifted up the hem of her skirt to show her the cowboy boots on her feet. "What do you think? Lissa says she's going to make a cowgirl out of me yet."

"I think, if Lissa says so, I wouldn't bet against it."

Maggie smiled again. "I can't believe it's my wedding day already."

"It seems like only yesterday that you called to tell us you'd accepted Jesse's proposal," her mother said.

"You mean instead of actually being four days ago?"

Christa fussed with the headpiece. "I've never heard of anyone putting together a wedding in four days."

"That's because no one else had Lissa taking care of all the details."

"Probably true," her mother agreed.

Maggie turned to take her hands. "Are you disappointed that we wanted to get married here?"

"It's *your* wedding," her mother said. "And I can understand why you'd want to take your vows where you're going to start your life with your new husband. If I'm disappointed about anything, it's only that we didn't have enough time to plan a proper wedding."

"So you think this is going to be an improper wedding?"

The gentle teasing made Christa smile, even through her tears. "You always did know how to twist words to make your point. It's one of the reasons you're such a good attorney."

"I learned from the best," she said.

"Hopefully I also taught you that there's more to life than the law."

"That's why I left my job at Alliston & Blake."

"I only wished you'd left there sooner," her mother admitted. "They demanded far too much of you and gave you very little in return. If you'd come to work at Roarke & Associates—"

"I would have always wondered if I earned my position or got it on the basis of my name."

Christa sighed. "As much as it frustrates me to know that you believed it, I can understand."

"You'll get to meet my new boss and his wife at the wedding."

"I'm looking forward to it," her mother said.

"Knock, knock," Lissa said, pushing open the door. "Mabel sent me up to let you know that the photographer's here."

"Then I'll go get the father of the bride and meet you both downstairs in ten minutes."

Since Jesse had to pick up his tux in Kalispell the day of the wedding, he decided to take it directly to the church and get ready there.

So much had happened since the day Maggie told him she was pregnant, it was hard to believe that only two weeks had passed. He'd known right away that he wanted to marry her and be a father to their child, and his conviction had not wavered. But as the clock ticked closer and closer to four o'clock and their scheduled wedding, he found himself worrying more and more that Maggie might be having second thoughts.

He suspected Shaelyn's most recent phone call was responsible for some of his concern. Although he hadn't spoken to his former fiancée, there had been a message on his machine when he got home the night that Maggie had finally agreed to marry him. Shaelyn had asked him to call her back, but of course he hadn't. She was his past and he was determined to focus on his future with Maggie.

He should feel jubilant—Maggie was going to make her life with him and their child in Rust Creek Falls. He was getting everything he wanted. But what was she getting? She was moving away from her family, her friends, giving up a career. Yes, she was planning to write the State Bar exam in the new year, and he had no doubt that she would soon be licensed to practice in Montana, but he also knew that she wouldn't have the same kind of career here that she could have if she stayed in LA.

Which was one of the reasons she'd agreed to do this— to give her life balance, so that she could be a mother *and* an attorney. But it seemed to him that she was giving up more than she was getting in return, and he couldn't help but wonder if she might come to resent him because of the changes she'd felt compelled to make to her life.

But if there was another—a better—way to work things out, he couldn't see it. He didn't want to live more than twelve hundred miles away from his child. And he didn't want his child raised by someone else while Maggie worked sixty hours a week to pay for that care.

A knock on the door jolted him out of his reverie. Assuming it was Nate, his best man, he invited him to come in.

But when the door opened, it wasn't his oldest brother who walked through it—it was his former fiancée.

Chapter Nine

"Shaelyn."

Jesse stared at her for a long moment, not knowing what else to say. He couldn't believe she was here, and he couldn't begin to fathom why.

"Hello, Jesse." She smiled at him—the same slow, seductive smile that used to be the prelude to all kinds of things.

She looked good—but then, Shaelyn always did. She had the fragile beauty of a china doll: silky hair, porcelain skin, delicate features. She was the type of woman that a man instinctively wanted to cherish and protect, as he'd once vowed to do.

But looking at her now, he felt nothing more than surprise—and maybe some apprehension. He hadn't seen her in seven years and couldn't understand why she'd shown up after so long—and on his wedding day, no less. "What are you doing here?"

"I saw your mother and your sisters in Missoula," his former fiancée explained. "Natalie told me that they were shopping for dresses for your wedding."

"Why were you in Missoula?"

"I've been working at the university for the past four years—at the Museum of Art & Culture."

"I thought you were in Helena. Isn't your husband some kind of advisor to the governor?"

"Ex-husband," she said with a small smile. "I moved to Missoula after the divorce, almost three years ago."

"Oh." He wasn't quite sure what else he was supposed to say. "I'm sorry it didn't work out?"

She offered a weak smile. "I should have realized our marriage was doomed from the start—because I never stopped loving you."

She waited a beat, but Jesse remained silent.

"I was hoping you would say that you feel the same way."

"I don't," he said bluntly.

"I know it's been a long time—"

"Speaking of time, I really don't have time for this right now."

"If we don't do this now, it's going to be too late."

"It's already too late."

She shook her head. "You told me that you loved me."

"Because I did," he confirmed. *"Seven years ago."*

"And now?"

"Now I'm marrying someone else."

She lifted her chin, her gaze challenging. "Do you love her?"

"Why else would I be marrying her?"

"That's what I'm trying to figure out," she said.

"We've been apart longer than we were together," he pointed out. "And I promise—I'm *not* still in love with you."

As he said those words, he realized—without a doubt—that they were true. He was completely over Shaelyn. Yes, he'd loved her once, but that was in the past. He'd been young and infatuated, wanting to be with the woman who claimed she wanted to be with him. When she'd gone, he'd realized that he hadn't missed Shaelyn so much as he'd missed being with someone.

"But you still haven't said that you're in love with her."

"I'm in love with Maggie," he said, because it seemed that speaking the words was the only way to get his former fiancée out of the way so he could marry the mother of his child.

"Okay, then—" she took a step back "—I guess I should offer my congratulations."

"Thank you, Shaelyn."

But, of course, she couldn't leave it at that. "I hope she loves you, too, Jesse. Enough to trade in the glitz and glamour of Hollywood for the tedium and simplicity of Big Sky Country."

And with those words, she tossed her hair over her shoulder and stalked out, passing the groom's best man on the way.

"What the hell was *she* doing here?" Nate wanted to know.

"I'm not entirely sure," Jesse admitted.

His family had never taken to Shaelyn, despite the fact that he'd planned to marry her. Nate, specifically, had expressed disapproval of her apparent lack of ambition to do anything other than get married.

"What did she say to put that look on your face?"

Jesse just shook his head.

"Don't let her mess with your mind," Nate warned.

"She didn't say anything that I haven't already heard a thousand times."

Except for the fact that she was still in love with him, and he wasn't going to get into that with his brother. Because, as he'd said to Maggie when he first proposed to her, he wasn't looking for love.

So why was he bothered by Shaelyn's suggestion that Maggie might not love him enough?

* * *

As his wife fussed with his tie, determined to get it just right before he walked their daughter down the aisle, Gavin stared stonily ahead, trying *not* to think about the reason he was in this tux.

"You're the father of the bride—try to look happy."

"Even if I'm not?"

Christa sighed. "You should be happy for your daughter— this is what she wants."

"She's only twenty-eight years old and she's been so busy building a career, she's barely dated. How can she know what she wants?" he demanded.

"No one knows her mind like our Maggie," his wife assured him. "A fact that you've been lamenting since she was a toddler."

He smiled, because it was true, but the smile quickly faded. "You don't think he coerced her into this marriage because she's pregnant?"

"I think she wouldn't let herself be coerced if she didn't want to be."

He continued to scowl. "She's our baby girl."

"Our baby girl's going to have a baby of her own in a few months," Christa reminded him gently.

"And she's going to have that baby more than a thousand miles away from us."

"I know you think Montana is the middle of nowhere, but we managed to get here today, didn't we?"

"You think I'm being ridiculous," he realized.

"I think you're being a father." She tugged on his tie, bringing his mouth down to hers for a quick kiss. "And a very handsome father of the bride you are."

"The mother of the bride looks pretty good, too."

She arched a brow. "Pretty good?"

He grinned and slipped his arm around her waist. "I love you, Christa."

"I love you, too."

"I just hope that, forty years from now, Maggie and Jesse will be as happy as we are."

"No one can know what the future holds," she told her husband, "but I have no doubt that when you walk our daughter down the aisle today, she will be marrying the man she loves."

The groom's parents, already seated in the church, weren't any more enthusiastic about the forthcoming nuptials than the bride's father.

"I hope he isn't making a mistake," Todd Crawford said, drumming his fingers on his knee.

His wife clasped her hands together in her lap. "What else could he do, under the circumstances?"

"Nothing," her husband admitted. "A man needs to take responsibility for his actions, and a child needs a father."

"Then why are you griping?"

"I just wish, if he had to knock up someone, he'd chosen a local girl who might actually stay put in this town."

"Except that one or more of his brothers has dated most of the single women in Rust Creek Falls," she pointed out drily.

"There are plenty of women in Kalispell or even other parts of Montana."

"Like Billings?"

He winced at the mention of the hometown of the groom's former fiancée. "Okay, so that didn't work out so well for him. But I'm not sure this is going to be any better. She's from Los Angeles for Christ's sake."

"Don't swear," his wife admonished.

"She's not going to be happy here."

"You don't know that—look at her cousin, Lissa. She came from New York and yet she settled in with the sheriff with no difficulty."

As was usual when Todd couldn't refute an argument, he said nothing. But his jaw remained stubbornly set.

"This all started when he went to work at Traub Stables," he said, after another minute had passed.

Laura frowned. "What?"

"It's those damn Traubs—they lured Jesse away from home, from his roots."

His wife sighed. "You know Jesse's heart has always been with the horses."

Todd shook his head. "As if it wasn't bad enough that everyone in town knows that our son is working for a Traub, now he's marrying a California girl."

"Could you try to focus on something else—at least for today?"

"Like what?"

"Like the fact that we're going to be grandparents again."

"That's if she sticks around long enough for us to meet the baby," her husband grumbled.

Maggie had lived her whole life in Los Angeles, where there was no shortage of handsome men. She worked in a law firm where men lived in suits. But she was certain she'd never seen anyone as handsome as Jesse Crawford. And she knew none of those other men had ever affected her the way he did. Never had any one of those men made her breath catch in her throat or her heart pound so hard and fast against her ribs she was certain everyone must be able to hear it.

But when she took her first steps down the aisle and saw Jesse standing at the altar, that's exactly what happened.

She didn't even remember the exchange of vows; the words were somehow lost in the excitement of the realization that she was going to be Mrs. Jesse Crawford. She did remember the kiss. Although it was chaste in comparison to other kisses they'd shared, there was heat in the brief touch of his mouth to hers, enough to heighten her awareness and anticipation.

Now she was in his arms again, sharing their first dance as husband and wife.

As she turned around the floor, she caught a glimpse of her parents—Christa dabbing her eyes with Gavin's handkerchief—and Jesse's parents—Laura's smile obviously forced, Todd's attention on the drink in his hand.

"I think your mother disapproves of the fact that I'm wearing a white dress," Maggie said.

Jesse looked down at his bride—the most beautiful woman he'd ever known, looking even more beautiful than ever. "You don't need to worry about my mother's—or anyone else's—approval."

At nineteen weeks, Maggie wasn't obviously pregnant. It was only because he'd been intimate with her slender body that Jesse was aware of the subtle bump that was proof of their baby growing inside of her.

"I'm not really. But I know people are already speculating about the reasons for our getting married so quickly."

"People are always going to talk about something."

"I know," she admitted. "Although it's a little unnerving to realize that the Hollywood paparazzi has nothing on the Rust Creek Falls grapevine."

"You're a celebrity here," he told her.

"The city slicker who shamelessly seduced the quiet cowboy and trapped him into marriage?"

He tipped her chin up, forcing her to meet his gaze.

"I don't feel trapped," he promised her. "I feel incredibly lucky."

Then he brushed his lips against hers.

And the way she kissed him back gave him hope that, before the night was out, he'd get even luckier.

After the cake-cutting ceremony, Maggie slipped away to use the ladies' room. Lissa had been taking her duties as matron of honor seriously and had barely left the bride's side, but she was dancing with her husband now and Maggie didn't want to interrupt.

It was a bit tricky to maneuver her skirts in the narrow stall, but she managed and was just about to flush when she heard the *click-clack* of heels on tile. Several pairs, by the sound of it, accompanied by talking and laughter.

The words she heard made her pause with her fingers on the handle.

"Guess who stopped by to see the groom before the wedding," an unfamiliar female voice said.

"Who?" a second woman wanted to know.

"Shaelyn Everton."

"Who?" the second speaker asked again.

"Jesse's ex," yet another voice responded, sounding impatient. "The one he was engaged to for all of three weeks."

Inside her bathroom stall, Maggie sucked in a breath. Thankfully, the other women were too focused on their conversation to hear her.

"How do you know this?"

"Brad told me that Nate caught them together in the anteroom before the ceremony."

"Caught them doing what?" There was more glee than curiosity in the tone, suggesting that the second woman enjoyed a juicy scandal.

Maggie pressed a hand to her stomach, desperate to still its sudden churning.

Her friend laughed. "Nothing like that," she chided. "They were just talking."

"Oh." Woman Number Two didn't hide her disappointment while the bride exhaled a long, slow breath. "What was she doing here?"

"Trying to make a final play for Jesse would be my guess."

"Because breaking his heart once wasn't enough?"

"She messed him up, that's for sure," the first woman commented. "I remember hearing his mom tell my mom that she didn't think he'd ever get over her."

"That was a long time ago," someone else said. "And he seems happy with Maggie."

"For now," the first speaker allowed.

"Give her a chance," the third woman suggested.

"Kristin's just mad that Maggie got him into bed and she never did."

"I've always liked the strong, silent type," the first speaker, now identified as Kristin, admitted. "But Brad is every bit as cute as his brother—maybe even more."

"But why was Shaelyn here?" The second woman finally circled back to the original topic of conversation. "I thought she married some other guy."

"She did, but they're divorced now. And while she might have been the one to leave Jesse, the rumor is that she never got over him."

The women had apparently finished their primping and started toward the exit, as evidenced by the *click-clack* on the tiles and their fading voices. "I don't think he..."

Maggie stayed in the bathroom stall until she was sure they were gone, and then for a few minutes more to compose herself.

She didn't know what to make of that entire exchange. What she did know was that, even if Shaelyn still wanted Jesse, she wasn't going to get him.

Because the shy, sexy cowboy was Maggie's husband now.

Jesse warily eyed the beer that Maggie's oldest brother offered to him. "Is it poisoned?"

Shane Roarke grinned. "You haven't given me any reason to want to make my sister a widow…yet."

"Then I'll make sure I don't," he said, accepting the bottle.

"I wish I could be sure that Maggie will be happy here."

"You don't think she will be?"

"Let's just say I have my doubts." Shane sipped his own beer.

"Wasn't it just a couple of years ago that you decided to make your home in Montana?"

"Yeah, but I moved around a lot before then," his new brother-in-law pointed out. "Maggie, on the other hand, has been working her tail off for the past five years to establish herself at Alliston & Blake."

"From my perspective, she worked too long and too hard for too little."

"I don't disagree—but it was her choice."

"So was this," Jesse assured him.

"That's what I have to wonder about," Shane said. "Because this whole situation—quitting her job, moving twelve hundred miles away, having a whirlwind wedding—isn't Maggie. She doesn't rush into anything."

She hadn't dragged her feet at all the day they met, but that was hardly something that would gain him points with her brother.

"She walked down that aisle of her own free will."

"It looked that way," Shane agreed. "But one of the women I work with just had a baby, and I have to tell you—pregnant women have all those hormones to deal with that mess with their heads and their hearts.

"I'm not sure Maggie knows what she wants right now, but you managed to convince her that you should be together for the sake of your baby. She's smart, but she's probably scared, too. The prospect of having a baby on her own had to be a little daunting, especially when her pregnancy ended any hopes of ever getting a partnership at Alliston & Blake."

He must have noticed Jesse's scowl, because he swore softly. "I guess she didn't tell you about that."

"No, she didn't."

"I think she was planning to leave, anyway," Shane said now. "But when her boss found out she was pregnant, it expedited the process."

"So you think she married me because she was in danger of losing her job?"

"No. She wouldn't have had any trouble getting another job in LA—and not just at our parents' firm. But I think marrying you gave her the excuse she needed to make a big change.

"I'm just not sure, because everything happened so fast, that she's not going to regret it in a month or two and realize she isn't cut out for life in Small Town, Montana."

Jesse thought about what Shane had said for a long time after the other man had gone.

There was no doubt he'd pushed Maggie to the altar because it was what he wanted for their baby. She'd voiced some objections, and he'd disregarded each and every one. Even her concerns about her clients in LA had been discounted, because they hadn't been as important to him as giving their baby a family. But they'd been important to her…

Damn.

He didn't know if what Shane had said about pregnancy hormones was true—but in case it was, he was going to give her time and space to decide if this was truly what she wanted.

As was usual for a bride, Maggie spent a lot of time dancing with various guests. After the first dance with her new husband, she took a turn around the floor with her father, then Jesse's father, then Ben Dalton. She danced and chatted with each of her new brothers-in-law and several other residents whose names she wasn't even sure she would remember. When her brother Ryan snagged her for a spin, she was grateful that she didn't have to keep up any pretenses—at least for the next three minutes.

"When you decide to make some changes in your life, you do it in a big way," he mused.

"It was time," she said lightly.

"Maybe," he acknowledged. "But this is the twenty-first century—you don't have to get married to have a baby."

"I know," she said, and she loved her brother for his ability to support nontraditional choices.

"You should also know that I'm having a really hard time not kicking that cowboy's ass for doing the things he did with you that resulted in you getting pregnant."

She held back a smile. "You could *try* to kick his ass."

Her brother's eyes narrowed. "You don't think I could take him?"

"I'm a big girl, you know. It's not like I was an innocent virgin seduced by a big bad cowboy. I wanted him every bit as much as he wanted me."

Ryan winced. "I don't need to know things like that."

"Apparently you do."

"I just want you to be happy, and I'm not convinced you will be with him. He's not at all like any of the other guys you've dated."

"No, he's not," she agreed. "And I think it says something that I never fell in love with any of those other guys."

He looked at her carefully. "You really are in love with him?"

"This is the twenty-first century," she said, echoing his words back to him. "I wouldn't be marrying him for any other reason."

"So I can't kick his ass?"

"You can't even try."

"Okay," he relented. "But if he ever makes you unhappy, you let me know."

"I'll let you know," she promised.

"Maybe I should kick Shane's ass," Ryan suggested.

"Why?"

"Because if he hadn't enlisted our help to get Arthur Swinton out of jail, there wouldn't be any Grace Traub Community Center, and you would never have come to Rust Creek Falls and met Jesse Crawford."

"I would have come anyway for Lissa and Gage's wedding," she pointed out to him.

"I guess you would have," he allowed.

"Look on the bright side—now you have twice as many reasons to visit Montana. And maybe you'll find the woman of your dreams in Big Sky Country, too."

"There's only one woman for me—Lady Justice."

"Does she keep you warm at night?"

"No, but there are other women who satisfy those needs."

"I don't need details," Maggie said.

"You weren't going to get any," he assured her.

The song ended, and he stepped back but continued to hold her hands. "I'm going to miss you."

"You're going to miss stealing the Yorkshire pudding from my plate at Sunday-night dinner."

He grinned. "That, too."

Jesse caught up to his bride as she was kissing her younger brother's cheek. Since he'd already done the verbal sparring routine with her older brother, he merely nodded to Ryan and spoke to Maggie.

"Apparently the guests want the bride and groom to share one last dance."

"It's barely ten o'clock," she protested.

"Most of the people here are ranchers who will be up before the sun rises in the morning," he reminded her.

"Then I guess we should have that dance."

He took her hand and led her back to the middle of the floor. His youngest sister, acting as DJ, announced their final dance, and Maggie lifted a brow when she recognized the opening bars of the song.

"Did you request this?" she asked, as they moved in time to the Rolling Stones' "Wild Horses."

He shook his head. "It was Natalie's choice."

But Maggie just smiled, appreciating his sister's offbeat sense of humor. Or maybe she just appreciated that it wasn't a traditional sappy ballad.

"How are you holding up?" he asked her now.

"I'm doing okay."

"It's been a long day."

"It's been a crazy week," she clarified. "I can't believe we managed to put together a wedding in only three days."

"With a little help from our friends and families."

"A *lot* of help."

He nodded his agreement. Shane Roarke, head chef at

the Gallatin Room, the four-star restaurant at the Thunder Canyon Resort, was their connection to the resort's pastry chef, who had agreed to make the wedding cake; Nina had a friend who did the flowers; Lissa, Maggie's matron of honor and the undisputed queen of organization, had supervised the decorating, ensuring that the utilitarian community room was transformed into a winter wonderland, including potted Christmas trees with white lights and silver bows, silver and white streamers, bouquets of helium-filled balloons and white poinsettias in silver pots on the tables.

It was beautiful and festive, but what made the day perfect for Maggie was the identity of her groom.

And she was looking forward to their perfect night that would follow their perfect day.

Chapter Ten

Someone had brought Jesse's truck to the front door of the community hall to expedite the bride and groom's exit from the reception.

Maggie smiled when she saw that the vehicle had been decorated with paper flowers and an enormous heart proclaiming Just Married. Jesse offered his hand to help her into the cab, and when she took it, a definite frisson of electricity passed between them.

Neither of them said much on the drive back to his house. Maggie's mind and heart were so cluttered with emotion and anticipation, she could barely hold on to a thought. But when she looked down at the hands folded in her lap, and at the rings on her finger that confirmed that she was definitely and undeniably Jesse Crawford's wife, she knew—maybe for the first time in her life—that she was exactly where she wanted to be.

It wasn't until he shut off the engine that she realized they'd arrived at his house. Now her home, too. And it was their wedding night. Nerves and excitement tangled in her belly as she reached for the gift bag that Lissa had thrust into her hands as she was leaving the hall.

Jesse came around to her door again and helped her out of the truck. But she'd barely put her feet on the ground when he swept her off them and into his arms.

"What are you doing?"

"It's traditional for the groom to carry his bride over the threshold," he told her.

She knew that, of course. And the fact that he'd insisted they marry before the birth of their child proved he was a traditional guy. But both of those facts were lost in the giddy excitement and sheer pleasure of being carried in strong arms.

He turned the handle and pushed open the door. "Welcome home, Mrs. Crawford."

She smiled at him. "Thank you, Mr. Crawford."

He gently set her onto her feet, only then seeming to notice the silver bag in her hand with the pale pink tissue sticking out of the top. "What's that?"

"A gift. From Lissa."

"I thought Justin loaded all of the presents into his truck to bring over tomorrow."

"All except this one," she confirmed.

Thankfully, he didn't ask any more questions about it. Instead he said, "I'll go get your suitcases."

"Okay."

He disappeared outside again, returning a few minutes later with the two bags of what she'd deemed to be essential clothing items and toiletries. The rest of her belongings were still in LA, but packed up and ready to be shipped. He set them down inside the door to remove his coat and boots, then carried the suitcases up the stairs.

Maggie hovered inside the door, not quite certain what to do. Reminding herself that she wasn't a guest here—although she still felt like one—she sat down on the bench beside the door and removed her wrap and boots.

She'd loved the sleeveless-style dress when she'd tried it on in the bridal shop in Kalispell, but she wished now that someone had warned her that a November bride in Montana should have sleeves. Long sleeves. And a high collar. But then she remembered the way Jesse had looked at her when he first saw her in the dress, how the heat in his eyes had warmed every inch of her body from her head to her toes.

She moved toward the stone fireplace and imagined flames crackling and flickering as they'd been the first day she'd been here—was it really only two weeks earlier? So much had happened since the day that she'd told Jesse about their baby, it was hard to believe such a short span of time had passed.

She wondered if Jesse would build a fire tonight. She had a fantasy—perhaps born of reading too many romance novels—of making love by a fire, and the thick sheepskin in front of the hearth only fueled that fantasy.

She curled her toes into the fluffy rug as the scene played out in great detail in her mind. He would move slowly toward her, his eyes—filled with unbridled heat and wicked promises—locked on hers. Then he would take her hands in his, drawing her down to the carpet, so they were kneeling and facing one another. Then he would slowly peel away her clothes as he kissed her, his lips moving from her mouth to her throat to her breasts—

"Maggie?"

She gasped, as his voice jolted her out of her fantasy. "I didn't hear you come back down the stairs," she admitted.

"Are you okay?"

"Fine," she said quickly. "I was just thinking a fire might help take the chill out of the air."

"It's kind of late," he told her. "If I started one now, I wouldn't be able to go to bed until it was completely out."

"I didn't think about that," she admitted, trying not to feel disappointed that his response had been more practical than romantic. Besides, he'd carried her over the threshold, which was an undeniably romantic gesture. Not quite as romantic as carrying her directly upstairs and to his bed, but romantic nonetheless.

"Did you want anything?" Jesse asked. "A cup of tea or a glass of water?"

She shook her head. "I think I'll just go get ready for bed."

"Okay."

"Can I just get your help with something?" She turned around, showing him her back. "There's a little hook at the top of the zipper that I can't reach."

"Oh. Um. Sure."

She felt the brush of his knuckles against her bare skin as he wrestled with the tiny closure, and goose bumps danced up her spine. The catch released and he lifted his hands away.

"And the zipper," she prompted. "If you could just lower it a couple of inches."

The soft rasp of the pull tracking along the twin rows of tiny teeth—the only sound in the quiet room—was tantalizingly seductive. As the zipper inched downward, the fabric of her bodice parted, exposing a V of skin between her shoulder blades. The air was cool, but she felt hot all over. Hot and achy and needy.

"How's that?" His voice was low, husky, and she knew he was as aroused as she was.

Maybe he didn't love her, but he wanted her, and that would be enough for now.

"That's great—thanks."

She picked up the gift bag again and carried it upstairs to the bathroom.

She didn't know what was going on with Jesse—why, after campaigning relentlessly for her to marry him, he'd been keeping her at arm's length since she'd agreed to do so. Maybe it was another one of those traditions—abstaining from lovemaking until the night of the wedding. Again the horse-and-barn-door analogy came to mind, but she could pretend to be understanding. Because tonight, finally, was their wedding night.

She unzipped her dress the rest of the way and slid it down her body, then hung it on a hook on the back of the door. The snug bodice had eliminated the need for a bra, so she was left in only a pair of lacy bikini panties and thigh-high stockings. She debated for a minute and then removed them, too, before reaching into the bag for the peignoir set her cousin had bought for her.

The sleeveless gown had a soft, stretch lace bodice that dipped low between her breasts, and an empire waist from which fell a long flowing skirt of semi-sheer chiffon. It was feminine and romantic and sexy, and Maggie loved the feel of the soft fabric against her skin. The long-sleeved chiffon wrap had wide lace cuffs and delicate pearl buttons with satin loop closures at the bodice. She slipped her arms into the sleeves but decided to leave the wrap unfastened, then eyed herself critically in the mirror.

Would he see the truth of her feelings for him when he looked at her? Did it matter if he did? She knew he didn't feel the same way, but she couldn't help hoping that maybe, someday, he would.

She was under no illusions about why he wanted to marry her: *it's about giving our baby the family he or she deserves.* He wasn't looking for love, and now—thanks to the conversation she'd overhead in the ladies' room—she knew why. It was because Shaelyn had broken his heart so badly even his mother had worried that he'd never get over her.

She pushed the conversation between those unknown women to the back of her mind. Maybe Jesse's former fiancée had come back to Rust Creek Falls hoping to lasso her cowboy once again, but he'd sent her away and married Maggie. Even if he didn't love her, she knew he cared about her and he loved their baby. That was a pretty good starting point, and she wasn't going to let anything or anyone ruin her wedding night.

They'd shared a connection in the bedroom, and she was confident they would reconnect tonight. She craved not just the physical joining but the emotional intimacy they'd shared; she wanted to make love with him, to show him the true depth of her feelings with her lips and her hands and her body. But she would hold on to the words until he was ready not just to hear them but to believe them.

With her heart pounding against her ribs, she opened the door and stepped out of the bathroom.

"Jesse?"

She tapped her knuckles on the partially closed bedroom door. There was no response. She pushed it open and found the room was empty. His tuxedo was draped over the back of the chair in his bedroom, but her husband was nowhere to be found.

She made her way down the stairs, past his dark office, through the quiet kitchen to the empty living room.

"Jesse?" she said again.

It was then that she noticed his boots and coat were missing from the hook by the back door.

He was gone.

Her husband had left her alone on their wedding night.

Or maybe she was being melodramatic. He'd probably expected it would take her longer to get ready for bed, and he'd decided to go out to the barn to check on the horses while he was waiting. Her spirits buoyed by this thought, she went back upstairs. It was then that she noticed a light spilling out of the doorway of one of the spare bedrooms farther down the hall.

She pushed open the door and found her suitcases neatly aligned at the foot of the bed, undeniable evidence that her husband didn't plan on sharing a bed with her tonight—or anytime in the near future.

She felt the sting of tears behind her eyes as hurt and confusion battled inside of her.

Had she been so blinded by her own feelings that she'd misinterpreted what she'd believed was evidence of his desire for her? How were they supposed to make their marriage work if they were sleeping in separate rooms? And why had he insisted on marrying her if he didn't want to be with her?

Of course she didn't have the answers to any of these questions. All she had was an aching emptiness in her heart, and all she could do was slip between the cold sheets of a bed that wouldn't be shared with her husband and cry herself to sleep.

The next morning, Maggie's first as Jesse's wife, she woke up as she'd fallen asleep: alone.

She climbed out of bed and headed for the bathroom. After she'd washed her face and brushed her teeth, she stepped into the hallway. The scent of fresh coffee wafted up the stairs, luring her to the kitchen. Jesse wasn't there, but the empty cereal bowl and mug in the sink confirmed that he was up—and probably already out in the barn. Rumor around town was that Jesse Crawford liked animals more than he liked people, but Maggie hadn't believed it was true. At least not until he'd left her alone on their wedding night.

She opened three different cupboards before she found the mugs. Although she'd severely cut back on her caffeine consumption as soon as she knew she was pregnant, she still needed half a cup of coffee at the start of the day to feel human in the morning.

She looked out the window over the sink, slowly sipping her coffee and wondering if she might catch a glimpse of her husband. She didn't see him, but she heard the back door open and then close, indicating that he'd returned to the house.

As his footsteps came toward the kitchen, her heart started to pound a little bit faster. But she kept her eyes focused on the window, not wanting to appear overly eager to see him.

"Good mor—" The greeting halted as abruptly as the footsteps.

Her curiosity piqued, Maggie slowly turned to face him, and caught his gaze—hungry and heated—skimming over her.

"What—" He swallowed. "What are you wearing?"

She'd forgotten about the ensemble she'd donned in anticipation of her husband taking it off for her on their wedding night. Had she been thinking about anything but how much she wanted her daily half cup of coffee, she might have covered up. But the blatant masculine appreciation in his eyes warmed every inch of her—from the top of her head to the bare toes on the ceramic tile floor—and made her glad that she hadn't.

"It's called a peignoir set," she told him. "Lissa bought it for me."

He continued to stare at her, as if he couldn't tear his eyes away, but when he spoke, his tone was gruff. "Your cousin should know by now that the winter nights are cold in this part of the country. You'd be better off with something a little less see-through and a little more flannel."

Flannel—as if separate bedrooms wasn't a big enough hint that he didn't want her.

Except that he hadn't looked at her as if he didn't want her. Even now, even though he was staying on the far side of the kitchen, there was something in his gaze—and it wasn't disinterest.

But she only nodded in answer to his statement. "I guess I'm going to have to do some shopping."

He moved to the fridge and yanked on the door handle. "I can't ignore my responsibilities to take you around the shops today."

She blinked, sincerely baffled by his response. "I didn't ask you to take me anywhere."

He dropped a package of bacon on the counter. "No," he finally acknowledged. "I guess you didn't."

That did it. Maggie put her mug on the counter with a thud. "What's going on, Jesse?"

"What do you mean?" He set a frying pan on the stove, turned on the flame beneath it.

"We've barely been married—" she glanced at the clock "—fifteen hours, and you're acting like you're sorry you ever proposed."

"I'm not," he said quickly. "You know this is what I wanted."

"I *thought* it was what you wanted," she acknowledged. "But clearly I'm having trouble reading your signals, because when you asked me to marry you, I didn't think you intended for us to sleep in separate bedrooms."

He opened the bacon, peeled off several strips and placed them in the pan. "When you accepted my proposal, you didn't say you wanted to share a bed," he countered.

"I'm carrying your baby," she reminded him. "And there was nothing immaculate about the conception."

"We've done some things out of order in our relationship," he said, keeping his gaze focused on his task as he moved the slices of bacon around with a fork. "I just thought we should take some time now to get to know one another."

She tried to think about what he was saying objectively. The words sounded reasonable—considerate, even. But she couldn't help but wonder when exactly he'd decided they should take this time: Before or after he'd seen Shaelyn?

Maybe seeing the woman he'd once loved had made him realize he'd made a mistake in proposing to Maggie. But if that was true—why hadn't he called off the wedding?

"If it's so important to you that we take time to get to know one another, why didn't you want to take that time *before* we got married?"

He shrugged. "I wanted to make sure our baby would be born to parents who were legally married."

She nodded. From the moment he'd learned that she was pregnant, he'd been clear that the baby was his primary concern. Maybe his only concern.

What I want—what you want—isn't as important as what our baby needs.

She'd accepted his proposal because she'd been certain that there was more between them than their baby. She'd believed that their relationship was founded on mutual attraction and growing affection.

Now she knew the truth. Jesse didn't want her—he only wanted their baby.

If her silence wasn't evidence enough that he'd said something wrong, the white-knuckle grip in which Maggie held her cup further substantiated the fact.

He'd never been good with words—or relationships, but he'd never had so much at stake before. He decided a shift in topic toward something less personal was warranted.

"Did you have breakfast?" he asked.

She shook her head. "No. I'm not hungry."

"You have to eat," he admonished. "Skipping meals isn't good for the baby."

Apparently he'd said the wrong thing again, because when he glanced up, he saw that her eyes shone with tell-tale moisture.

Damn. His brain scrambled for something, *anything,* to divert the ensuing flood of tears and recriminations, but he came up empty.

To his surprise—and relief—Maggie lifted her chin. "You're right." She took a banana from the bowl of fruit on the counter. "I'm going to check my email."

And then she was gone, and he didn't know whether he was relieved or disappointed.

The only thing that was certain was that he'd lost his mind—most likely sometime between the minister proclaiming he and Maggie to be husband and wife and his return to the house to make breakfast this morning. It was the only possible reason that might explain why he'd suggested his wife should sleep in something less see-through and more flannel.

Not that what she'd been wearing was exactly see-through, but the morning light coming through the window had backlit her so that her silhouette was clearly visible. And those delicious curves had tempted him to touch, to trace her feminine contours and revel in the satiny softness of her skin. He'd had to curl his fingers into his palms to prevent himself from reaching out for her. And then she'd turned to face him, and the outline of her peaked nipples pressed against the gauzy fabric had actually made his mouth water.

The first time he saw her, he wanted her. In the five months that had passed since their initial meeting, he hadn't stopped wanting her. And being with Maggie had escalated rather than satiated his desire.

She was right—he hadn't planned on separate bedrooms when he'd asked her to marry him. He couldn't think of anything he wanted as much as he wanted Maggie in his bed again—just imagining her naked body wrapped around his was enough to make him ache. He'd been eager for their wedding day to conclude so that their wedding night could begin. And then he'd been cornered by her brother at the reception.

His conversation with Shane Roarke had made him realize that he'd pushed Maggie into this marriage because it was what *he* wanted. He hadn't asked what she wanted. In fact, he'd ignored her efforts to tell him.

On more than a few occasions, he'd been accused of being stubborn and single-minded, because he rarely gave up until he got what he wanted. And usually the end justified the means—except that, in this situation, he wasn't entirely sure what "end" he wanted. Why had he insisted on this marriage? To ensure he would have a place in his child's life? Or to hold on to Maggie?

Because he didn't know the answers to those questions, and because he wasn't comfortable acknowledging the possibility that he might have pushed her into a marriage she wasn't ready for, he'd forced himself to take a step back.

The fact that she'd slept in that—what had she called it?—peignoir set, suggested that she hadn't planned on sleeping alone.

But the weight of her brother's words continued to echo in the back of his mind.

He'd never even taken Maggie out on a date. They'd gone from introductions to intercourse in a matter of hours. They'd both been on the same page, had both wanted the same thing, but their compatibility in the bedroom aside, what did he really know about her?

After she'd gone back to LA, they'd had several long

telephone conversations, they'd exchanged emails, they'd planned to get together again. But it hadn't happened.

Weeks and then months had passed, and he'd been certain their relationship was over. If what they'd shared could even be categorized as a relationship. After a few more weeks, he'd even managed to convince himself that he didn't care. Yeah, and that conviction had lasted right up until he'd looked up and saw her standing outside the paddock where he was working with Rocky.

He'd been genuinely happy to see her—and mad at himself for being so happy. She'd unceremoniously dumped him, and then reappeared out of nowhere, and his heart had practically leaped out of his chest.

Now, only two weeks later, they were married.

He didn't doubt that they'd done the right thing for their child. Whether it was right for him and Maggie remained to be seen.

Chapter Eleven

Over the next few days, Maggie and Jesse started to become accustomed to living together—albeit as roommates rather than husband and wife. They shared conversation and ate their meals together, but it was all superficial.

They talked mostly about the weather, which Jesse described as alternately chilly/nippy/frosty/blustery or simply cold, and which Maggie interpreted as unbelievably mind-numbingly and bone-chillingly frigid, and the local news: old Mr. Effingham slipped outside of the post office and broke his hip; six-foot-five-inch local basketball star Wendell Holmes was caught with his girlfriend in a compromising position in the backseat of a Chevy Spark at the high school; three ranch hands spent a night in lockup after the most recent brawl at the Ace in the Hole; and Tom Riddell's yellow lab had given birth to a litter of puppies that confirmed the doggy daddy was Liza Weichelt's German shepherd, despite her repeated assertions that Rex never showed any interest in Taffy. The discussion of which might have been more interesting if Maggie knew any of the people involved.

Maggie did most of the cooking, because she enjoyed it, and Jesse did the cleanup. And as they went about their respective duties, he didn't touch her—either by accident or design. It was as if every movement he made was deliberately intended to ensure there was no contact between them. If she asked him to pass the salt, he put the shaker in front of her plate rather than in her hand. If she needed help reaching something on the top shelf of the pantry, he'd wait until she moved aside rather than reach over her.

On Wednesday morning, just four days after her wedding, Maggie was scheduled to start working for Ben Dalton. She woke up early—both nervous and excited about her first day.

Although she'd learned a lot in her tenure with Alliston & Blake, she'd also had almost limitless resources at her disposal. At Ben's office, there weren't a dozen other junior associates to ask for help, there was no senior associate assigned to review her work. There was only Ben, his secretary, Jessica Evanson, and his paralegal, Mallory Franklin. Which meant that if she didn't know how to do something, she would have to ask her boss.

She hoped she didn't have to ask her boss, because she really wanted to make a good impression.

She knew that the people of Rust Creek Falls were reserving judgment—that they were wary of outsiders and didn't trust her not to run out on Jesse the way his former fiancée had done. Only time would convince them of that. She was more concerned with proving that she was smart and capable and independent of the man she'd married.

Ben had confided that he was usually in the office before eight-thirty, but he told her that she could start at nine. Since she was accustomed to early hours and Jesse was up as well, she decided she might as well head into town. She pulled into the small parking lot beside the building at eight-twenty-two and found Ben's Suburban was already there.

She picked up her briefcase and drew in a deep breath, trying to calm the butterflies that were swooping around in her tummy. Apparently it was early for most of the townsfolk, as the streets were quiet. Quite a different scenario from the nearby ranches, where the men would have been up at the crack of dawn, feeding stock and mucking out stalls and whatever else ranch hands did at the start of the day.

Jesse always began his morning at The Shooting Star. After he'd taken care of the animals there, he'd drive over to Traub Stables, where he'd put in several hours training other people's horses. She didn't know what exactly it was that he did, but she knew that when people spoke his name, they did so with respect. Aside from the fact that he had an undeniable gift when it came to animals, he was also universally regarded as a good man.

Maggie didn't disagree, but she would add *enigmatic*, *confusing* and *frustrating* to his list of attributes. And apparently, since their marriage, *celibate*—which contributed in no small part to the *frustrating*.

As she made her way around the building, she was startled to find Homer Gilmore sitting on the bottom step that led to the front door of the law office. She'd seen him around town before, but she didn't know much about him. She didn't put much stock in gossip or rumor, although the consensus was that he was a crazy old coot. She thought *lost* was a more apt description, as if he wasn't quite sure where he was or how he got there, but he seemed harmless. Certainly she'd never had reason to fear him, so she greeted him pleasantly now.

"Good morning, Mr. Gilmore."

He scrambled up from the step and moved out of her way. "The past is the present."

She wasn't sure if the mumbled words were intended as some kind of cryptic response to her greeting or if he was talking to himself.

"It's a little chilly this morning," she said, making her

way up the steps. Actually, it was more than chilly by LA standards, but she knew that saying so would only highlight her status as an outsider.

"The past is the present."

"O-kay."

"The past is the present." He muttered the same statement again, so quickly now the words almost ran together.

"Well," she kept her tone cheerful, "I should get in to work."

"Thepastisthepresent."

She opened the door and stepped into the outer office, concerned that the rumors about his sanity might be true.

Maggie spent the first hour and a half in her new office reviewing the client files her boss had put on her desk for later discussion. Jessica arrived just before nine and settled at her desk; Mallory came in a few minutes later, after she'd taken her niece Lily to school.

Everyone seemed to have their own routines and enough work to keep occupied—except for Maggie.

Just before ten o'clock, Ben Dalton knocked on her open door. "I've got a settlement conference in Kalispell," he said. "If you want to come with me, I can introduce you to the court staff and some of the local Bar members."

"I'd like that," she agreed readily.

On the way, he gave her some background information about the issues to be discussed, his client—an employer trying to negotiate an agreement with a former employee— the opposing counsel and the judge who was scheduled to preside over the conference.

Afterward, they went for lunch and while they were waiting for their food to be delivered, they discussed the files Ben had asked her to review. One was an application for a variation of a custody agreement, another was a

landlord-tenant dispute and the third was a breach of con-
tract case. Maggie had not just familiarized herself with
the details of the cases but made notes of relevant statutes
and precedents for each.

Ben seemed pleased with her initiative and insights,
and confided that he'd been thinking about expanding his
practice for a few years. Hiring Mallory Franklin as a
paralegal had been the first step, and because she now did
a lot of the paperwork that he used to do, he was able to
keep more regular hours than he had in years. He hadn't
given up on his plan to bring in a second lawyer, but there
hadn't been any qualified candidates in Rust Creek Falls—
until Maggie.

"With your background and experience, we can expand
the services offered to our clients," he told her.

"I'm looking forward to being able to help," she said.

Ben nodded. "And maybe we can even work out some
kind of partnership agreement after you pass the Montana Bar, so that you can work with me instead of for me."

Maggie stared across the table at him, too stunned to
reply.

"What do you think—should it be Dalton & Roarke or
Dalton & Crawford?"

She hadn't thought about whether she would take Jesse's
name professionally. As for a partnership, she hadn't thought
about that at all.

"Or maybe that's more responsibility than you're looking for?" he asked, when she didn't respond.

"No," she said quickly. "That's *exactly* the kind of responsibility I'm looking for.

"I guess I'm just…surprised," she admitted. "I worked
more than sixty hours a week for years at Alliston & Blake
before there was any mention of a promotion, and I haven't

even worked here for six hours and you're offering me the possibility of a partnership."

"You think a small-town Montana lawyer doesn't have sense to know what he's doing?"

"On the contrary, I think you're a lot smarter than any of my bosses in Los Angeles."

He chuckled. "And I like to think you'd be right. I did my research," he assured her. "Beyond the work experience that was outlined on your résumé, I know that you graduated in the top five percent of your class from Stanford Law and passed the California Bar on your first try. In addition to the sixty-plus hours a week that you worked at your firm, you somehow found time to be an active member of the Women Lawyer's Association of Los Angeles and volunteer at a local women's shelter."

"That's pretty thorough research," she noted.

"I assure you, Maggie, I didn't hire you on a whim because your husband works for my son-in-law or because your cousin is married to the sheriff. I hired you because I want to expand the range of legal services available to the people of Rust Creek Falls and because I want to know this firm will be in capable hands when I decide to retire."

"Then I guess we should talk about the specific areas of expansion," she said, already looking forward to it.

Jesse spent the majority of his time at Traub Stables with the horses, but he always ended his day in front of the computer. He made detailed notes of his interactions with every animal and meticulously documented those notes in individual folders on Sutter's computer so they could be easily referenced by the owner.

He was at the computer on Thursday when Sutter strolled into the office with a baby carrier in hand.

Jesse looked over and couldn't help but smile at the wide-eyed infant.

"Good-looking kid," he said. "Must take after his mama."

Sutter chuckled, unoffended. "That he does. But his mama had a meeting at the school today, so the men are hanging out together."

"Drinking beer and smoking cigars?"

"Maybe in a few more years."

"Good call," Jesse told him.

"I hear you're going to have a baby of your own in a few months."

"News travels," he said, not at all surprised by the fact.

"Are you excited or terrified?"

"Both," Jesse admitted.

"I was, too," Sutter said. "Truthfully, I still am. But I wouldn't give him back for anything in the world."

As he spoke, he set the baby carrier on the desk to pull his cell phone out of his pocket and glance at the display.

"Brooks is here," Sutter said, naming the local vet. "Do you mind if I leave Carter with you while I go talk to him?"

"No problem," Jesse assured him.

"I won't be more than ten minutes," his boss promised.

It was the longest ten minutes of his life.

While Carter had seemed perfectly happy to gurgle and coo while his daddy was in his line of sight, as soon as Sutter walked out of the room, the baby began to squirm and fuss. Jesse tried rocking the carrier, to no avail. The fussing escalated to crying. He unbuckled the straps and lifted Carter out.

The little guy looked at him, his big blue eyes filled with tears, his lower lip trembling.

"Daddy's going to be right back," Jesse promised.

Carter drew in a long, shuddery breath, as if considering whether or not to believe him. But when "right back" was not immediate, the crying started anew.

Jesse tucked him close to his body, the baby squirmed; he cradled him in the crook of his arm—a favorite position of his niece Noelle's when she was younger—the wails grew louder; he propped him up on his shoulder and patted his back. The baby let out a belch surprisingly disproportionate to his size—and the crying began to quiet and, finally, stopped.

"That feels better now, doesn't it, buddy?"

Of course, the baby didn't respond. He let out a long, shuddery sigh, rubbed his cheek against Jesse's shoulder, and his eyes drifted shut.

Jesse couldn't help but smile.

His sister's little girl was the epitome of sugar and spice. She was soft and feminine and heartbreakingly beautiful. Sutter's son, although only four months old, was already snakes and snails. He was solid and sturdy and 100 percent boy.

Jesse hadn't given much thought to the gender of his own baby. When he'd learned that Maggie was pregnant, his primary concern had been marrying her to ensure his place in their baby's life. Now, however—

That thought was severed by the sudden realization that the back of his shirt was wet.

Carter hadn't just released an air bubble—he'd spewed the contents of his stomach all over Jesse.

"Why is there a sticky note on the fridge that says 'burp cloths'?" Maggie asked when Jesse came in for dinner later that night.

"I thought we should start making a list of things we'll need to get before the baby comes," he said.

She eyed him skeptically. "And the first thing that came

to mind wasn't a car seat or crib or even diapers—it was burp cloths?"

"I spent some time with Sutter and Paige's little guy today."

"His proud grandpa has shown me about a hundred pictures," she said.

"He puked all down my back."

She laughed. Then pressed a hand to her lips in a belated attempt to hide the fact that she was laughing.

His gaze narrowed.

"I'm sorry," she apologized, not sounding sorry at all. "I'm sure it was disgusting."

"I know that babies puke and poop and cry," he acknowledged. "But it's one thing to read about it in a book and another to experience firsthand."

"Noelle never puked on you?"

He shook his head. "She's spit up a little, but nothing more than that."

Maggie put a plate of chicken parm on the table in front of him.

"How was your day?" he asked her.

"Well, I didn't have to deal with any puking babies." She sat down across from him with her own plate. "In fact, I didn't have to do much of anything.

"Ben took me to Kalispell for an arbitration today. We chatted on the drive, lingered over coffee when we got there, he presented his case to the arbitrator, then we had lunch and returned to Rust Creek Falls around three o'clock, at which point he decided we'd done enough for the day."

"Most people would be happy to finish their day at three o'clock," he pointed out to her.

"I know. I just felt kind of…useless," she admitted. "Ben

promised he'd make me earn my salary, but I'm not sure that will happen until I pass the Bar."

"Maybe you need to remind yourself that you're not in LA anymore and relax a little bit," he suggested.

"That's what Ben said," she admitted.

"Imagine… I gave the same advice as an attorney without charging two hundred dollars an hour for it."

"Which is less than half the rate of most lawyers in California. Of course, the cost of office space is a lot higher there, too."

"Do you miss it?"

She shook her head. "Having time on my hands is a new experience but I think, once I get used to it, I'll enjoy the slower pace and lessened pressure. And I really like Ben and Mallory and Jessica—I'm not sure I could say that about any of the people I worked with at Alliston & Blake. I'm sure they were all great people, but I was so busy focusing on my clients and cases that I never really got to know any of them very well."

"I didn't have the chance to get to know your boss very well, but I'm sure I didn't like him," Jesse told her.

"Brian was always fond of saying he was in the business of business, not making friends."

"That's probably one of the reasons I prefer to work with animals than people." He pushed away from the table and carried his empty plate to the sink.

She appreciated that Jesse always insisted on doing the dishes if she did the cooking, but she wished he didn't shoo her out of the kitchen so that he could do the cleaning up. She just wanted to be with him, to do the things that most married couples did together. And since—for reasons she still didn't understand—that didn't include sex at the present, she was so pathetically eager to spend time with him she would settle for sharing chores.

She began to clear away the rest of the table. When she picked up a towel to dry the dishes he'd already washed, Jesse said, "I'll do that."

But this time, she didn't let him ban her from the room. "I don't mind," she told him.

Short of wrestling the towel from her, there was nothing he could do, so he shrugged and focused his attention on the washing again. He didn't say anything while he completed the chore, but she didn't mind the silence.

She put the last pot back in the cupboard then turned to hang the towel on the oven handle. She hadn't realized he was right behind her, and when she turned, her breasts brushed against his chest. The shock of the contact might have jolted her backward, except that the counter was at her back and Jesse was at her front, so she had nowhere to go.

She lifted her gaze to his and saw both heat and hunger reflected in his eyes. Her heart pounded harder and faster and her mouth went dry. The atmosphere crackled with heat and tension. She instinctively moistened her lips, and his eyes darkened as they followed the movement of her tongue. His gaze shifted from her mouth to her breasts, zeroing in on nipples that were already peaked, begging for his attention.

Jesse drew in a slow, deep breath. Then he took a deliberate step back, away from her.

"I have to go out...to check on Lancelot."

She swallowed, torn between frustration and disappointment. "Now?"

"Nate asked me to take a look at him—said he was favoring his right foreleg."

She nodded, because she could hardly dispute the importance of checking on an injured animal.

But as she watched him grab his coat and walk out the

back door, she wondered if she'd have to grow a tail and a mane to make him take a look at her.

And so it went for the next several days—except that Maggie banned herself from the kitchen after dinner. She didn't mind playing with fire, but she hated being the only one who felt the burn.

She tried to talk to her cousin, in the hope that Lissa might have some insights into Jesse's behavior. But although Lissa was puzzled by the distance he was deliberately keeping from his bride, she had no words of wisdom except to say that no man could resist a woman intent on seduction—especially if that woman was his wife.

The problem was that Maggie didn't know the first thing about seduction. She could count the number of lovers she'd had on one hand, with two fingers left over.

The first had been the editor of the law review. She'd fallen in love with his mind and decided that she liked the rest of him well enough to take their relationship to the next level. But the actual event, when it finally happened, was less than spectacular. Still, they'd stayed together for another four months before the relationship eventually fizzled away.

The second had been a former client at Alliston & Blake. She'd never actually worked with him, but she'd been in the elevator when he'd left a meeting with David Connors, one of the senior IP attorneys. He'd asked her to have dinner with him; she'd declined, telling him that it was against company policy for attorneys to fraternize with clients. He'd responded by calling David Connors on his cell phone, right then and there, and firing him. They'd dated for almost a year, and while the physical aspect of their relationship had been pleasant enough, he hadn't exactly rocked her world.

No one had—until Jesse.

She didn't know if the sex had been so great because she felt a deep, emotional connection that she'd never experienced with anyone else, or if she felt a deep, emotional connection to him because the sex had been so great.

Or maybe it hadn't been as great as she remembered... Or maybe it had been great for her but not for him... Or maybe she should stop driving herself crazy speculating about things and figure out what was keeping her husband so busy he was out of the house more than in it.

Because it seemed that every night he had one excuse or another to escape from the house right after dinner. If she'd still been working at Alliston & Blake, she wouldn't have minded being married to a man who was absent for frequent and extended periods—she probably wouldn't even have noticed.

A glance at her watch revealed that it was just past eight o'clock. Jesse's truck was parked out front, so she knew that he hadn't gone far.

She put on her boots and bundled into her coat, wrapping her scarf around her throat, tugging a hat onto her head and slipping thick mittens over her hands. She didn't know if she'd ever get used to Montana temperatures, but she was learning to cope with them.

It helped if she didn't check the daily forecast for LA, as she'd done that morning, only to discover that it was sixty-four degrees in SoCal—forty degrees warmer than in Rust Creek Falls. No wonder she hadn't owned a winter coat until she'd gone shopping in Kalispell with Lissa before the wedding. Unlike the peignoir set her cousin had purchased for her, she actually used the coat.

Her breath puffed out in little clouds, and the snow crunched under her feet as she made her way toward the stables. It wasn't a long trek from the house, but her cheeks and nose were numb by the time she reached the door. The light inside gave her hope that she would find her husband there.

The scent of hay and horses no longer filled her with panic. Instead, it reminded her of Jesse's kiss—the comfort of his arms around her, the warmth of his mouth against hers—and renewed her determination to track down her errant husband.

Honey poked her head over the gate when Maggie ventured near. She was tempted to go closer, to rub the animal's long nose the way Jesse had taught her, but she wasn't nearly as brave without him beside her. She just kept walking, toward what he'd explained was the birthing stall at the back of the barn and from which the light emanated.

She didn't know what she expected to find him doing—but whatever possibilities had crossed her mind, finding him rubbing sandpaper over a carved piece of wood was not one of them.

She didn't know if she made some kind of sound or if he sensed her standing in the open doorway, but his movements suddenly stilled and he looked up at her.

She stepped into the stall, her curious gaze taking in the assortment of pieces spread out over a large worktable—along with the plans for a baby's cradle.

"Oh." Her heart, already his, went splat at his feet. "Is this why you didn't put *crib* on one of your sticky notes?"

He smiled. "We'll need one eventually, but I wanted to do this."

"I thought horses were your thing."

"They are—but sometimes I like to putter."

She looked at the pieces of wood, meticulously carved and sanded. "You're a very talented putterer."

"Is that even a word?"

"I don't think so," she admitted, running her hand over

what she guessed—based on the picture—was the top of a side rail. But referring to him as a putterer was safer than saying that he was good with his hands. Because he undoubtedly was, but that kind of comment would bring to mind all kinds of things that he could do with his hands, things he had done with his hands, things she wished he would do with his hands again. Pushing those tantalizingly torturous thoughts aside, she asked, "Where did you learn to do this?"

"My grandfather was a carpenter as well as a rancher. He taught me a lot of tricks to working with wood."

"The one who made Noelle's blocks?" she guessed.

He nodded.

"Did he make the blanket chest at the foot of my bed?"

"No. I made that."

She'd thought it was a family heirloom, and knew that someday it would be. Just as this cradle would be enjoyed by their child, and maybe, eventually, their child's child.

"There's something else on your mind," he guessed. "You didn't come out here to talk about puttering."

She managed a smile. "No, because I didn't know about the puttering until I got out here."

"Something you want to talk about?"

"I'm not sure," she admitted.

He picked up a soft cloth and began to wipe down the sanded pieces in preparation for staining. "When you decide, you can let me know."

It would be easier, she decided, to ask the question when he wasn't looking at her. When he couldn't see the doubts and insecurities she feared might be reflected in her eyes.

So with his attention focused on his task, she blurted out, "Why didn't you tell me your ex-fiancée was in town?"

Chapter Twelve

Jesse looked up, sincerely startled by the question. "I didn't know that she was."

"I don't mean today," Maggie amended. "I meant the day we got married."

"Oh."

"Why didn't you tell me?" she asked again.

"Because I didn't think it was important."

"The woman you were once planning to marry shows up in town on the day of our wedding and you don't think it's important?"

He sighed. "I don't know how much you know about that engagement—"

"As much as you've told me, which is nothing."

"Because there isn't much to tell. We were engaged for a few weeks—not even long enough to plan a wedding."

"That's longer than we were engaged," she pointed out.

"What do you want me to say, Maggie?"

"I don't know," she admitted. "But I guess I've been wondering... Are you still in love with her?"

"No." His response was immediate and unequivocal.

She didn't look convinced.

"The truth is, I hadn't seen her in almost seven years," he told her. "And I never knew if seeing her again might stir up any old feelings. But it didn't. Any feelings I once had for her are long gone."

"Well, I guess that's good," she said. "Considering that you're now married to me."

"And I'm happy to be married to you."

She opened her mouth, then closed it again without saying a word.

"If there's something you want to say, just say it," Jesse suggested. "I'm not a mind reader."

"One of the first things a lawyer learns is to never ask a question that she doesn't already know the answer to."

"Was it a legal question you were wondering about?"

"No," she admitted. "But in this situation, I think the same rule applies."

He decided to ask a question of his own. "How did you find out about Shaelyn's visit?"

"I overheard some women talking about it at our reception."

"Why didn't you ask me about it then?"

"Because I was hoping you would tell me about it," she admitted.

"I didn't tell you because I forgot about her the minute she walked out the door."

She had no reason not to believe what he was telling her, but his casual dismissal of his former fiancée made her wonder if, during the four months that he and Maggie had been apart, he'd forgotten about her just as easily.

If she hadn't been pregnant, she might not have seen him again. She wouldn't have had any reason to seek him out, and he hadn't shown any inclination to track her down. They were only together now because of their baby—and while she was exactly where she wanted to be, she wasn't convinced the same was true for Jesse.

"I'm sorry I interrupted your work," she said.

"I didn't mind the interruption," he told her. "But you kind of ruined the surprise."

"I'll be surprised when it's all put together," she promised him, heading toward the door.

"Maggie—"

She paused with her fingers wrapped around the handle and turned back.

"I don't want to be with anyone but you," he told her.

She managed a smile. "Same goes."

As she headed back to the house, she told herself that she should be satisfied. He wanted to be with her, and that should be enough.

But it wasn't—she wanted him to love her as much as she loved him.

At Alliston & Blake, there was an office manager in charge of ensuring supplies were documented and maintained. At Ben's office, Jessica usually went into Kalispell once a month to replenish supplies as required. If anything was needed in the interim, it could usually be obtained from the General Store.

Which was why Maggie was at Crawford's to pick up a package of printer paper on Friday afternoon. Natalie directed her to the stationery section at the back of the store, where she found Nina pacing with Noelle in her arms.

"Someone doesn't look too happy today," she said, noting the runny nose and teary eyes of the little girl in her mother's arms.

"That's why my sister's working the register and I'm hiding out back here," Nina admitted.

"Is she sick?" Maggie asked.

"Teething," her sister-in-law clarified. "She's been teething for six months—but every new tooth seems to make her grumpier than the previous one."

Maggie stroked the back of a finger over the child's red cheek. Noelle looked at her and let out a shuddery sigh.

"I was just about to take her upstairs to see if she'll nap," Nina said. "Do you have time for a cup of tea?"

Maggie glanced at her watch, although, aside from printing the memorandum she'd drafted and which didn't need to be submitted until Monday, she had absolutely nothing pressing at the office. "I do if you do," she told her sister-in-law.

Nina led the way through the store to the staircase behind women's sleepwear.

"I lived up here before I moved in with Dallas. Because I manage the store, it was convenient. I decided to keep the apartment, at least for now, so that Noelle can be close by when I'm working. It makes it easy for me to slip away to nurse her—or take a nap with her."

"You're nursing even while she's teething?"

"For now," Nina agreed. "We've been supplementing with formula for a few months, because it gives me a little more freedom, but they say that breast milk is best for the first year, so even when I'm not nursing, I'm pumping."

The door opened into a big living room that was separated from the kitchen and dining area by an island counter. It was bright and spacious but as warm and inviting as the woman who had decorated it.

"This is nice," Maggie said sincerely.

"I like it," Nina said. "It was where I originally planned on living with Noelle—until I fell in love with Dallas. Now he's going to add on to his house—our house—so that we'll have a master suite on the main level and then the current master bedroom can be divided into two rooms and each of the kids will have their own."

"Are you planning to add to your family?" Maggie asked.

"I think four is a good number." Nina passed the baby to her sister-in-law so that she could make tea. "But I have to admit, I've been thinking that it would be nice to have a baby with Dallas."

"What does he say about that?"

"It took some getting used to for him with Noelle. Robbie is seven now, so dealing with midnight feedings and dirty diapers was a big adjustment for him, so I haven't even mentioned the idea yet. I was thinking I'd give him a little more time before I bring up the subject—and to make sure it isn't just a whim on my part."

Watching Nina's ease with and obvious love for her baby, Maggie didn't think it was a whim. Jesse's sister was clearly one of those women who was meant to be a mother, and she knew that her husband was lucky to have found a woman who loved the children from his first marriage as much as she loved her own.

"Speaking of homes," Nina said. "Did you know that Jesse built his? Well, not by himself," she clarified. "My dad and my brothers helped."

"He didn't tell me." But the information reminded her that she'd wondered about something else. "How long has he lived there?"

"Four years, I think." And then, demonstrating a startling insight into her sister-in-law's mind, she said, "It was definitely post-Shaelyn."

Maggie nodded, grateful for the information. "Did he design it, too?"

"Inside and out," Nina confirmed.

"He's got a good eye—and great hands."

"Please," Nina said. "There are some details a sister doesn't need to know."

Maggie felt as if her cheeks were as red as Noelle's. "I meant that he's good with tools."

Her sister-in-law raised a brow.

She blew out a breath. "I saw the cradle he's making for the baby."

"He's making a cradle?" Nina's eyes misted. "That's so sweet—and so Jesse."

"Is it?"

"He's over the moon about this baby."

Maggie looked down at the little girl now sleeping in her arms. "I'm pretty excited, too. I can't wait to hold my own baby just like this."

"He—or she—will be here before you know it, and then what you'll want more than anything in the world is a few hours of uninterrupted sleep."

"I'm sure that's true," Maggie agreed. "But I still can't wait. Of course, I'm as terrified as I am excited, but since there's no turning back now, I'm trying to focus on the positive."

Nina was silent for a minute, seemingly content to just watch Maggie cuddle with Noelle. But when she spoke again, the sincere concern in her tone even more than the question warned Maggie that the other woman suspected all was not wedded bliss for her brother and sister-in-law.

"Is everything okay?" she asked gently.

Maggie managed a smile, in an effort to convince Nina as well as herself. "Everything's great."

"The day that you and Jesse got married, you were absolutely glowing," Nina said. "You're not glowing anymore."

Since Maggie couldn't dispute that, she said nothing.

"Are you unhappy here?" her sister-in-law prompted.

"No. I'm really coming to love Rust Creek Falls."

"Are you missing your family?"

"Sure," she admitted. "But I'm building a new family here, with Jesse." When Nina's only response was patient silence, Maggie sighed. "I guess I just hoped that we'd have more time together. He's so busy, between his work at Traub Stables and chores at The Shooting Star, that I hardly ever see him."

Nina's brow furrowed. "I would expect a new husband to make more time for his bride."

"You know why we got married," Maggie reminded her.

"I know why you got married as quickly as you did," her sister-in-law allowed. "I also know that Jesse started to fall for you the first time he saw you—long before there was a baby in the picture."

Maggie was surprised by the statement. What Nina apparently "knew" was news to her.

Yes, Jesse had been attracted to her from the start—which was why there was a baby on the way—but she didn't know if she'd go so far as to say that he'd fallen for her. Even if she'd fallen head over heels for him a long time ago.

"Did he tell you about Shaelyn?" Nina asked.

"Only that he was engaged to her, briefly."

"That's true, but not even close to being the whole truth." She picked up her tea, sipped. "It's not really my place to tell you the story—or at least what I know of it—but I think you should know the basics, so that you won't lose all patience with my idiot brother."

"I'm not sure how to respond to that," Maggie admitted, making Nina laugh.

"You don't have to—as much as I love him, I'm not blind to his faults."

She sipped her tea again while she considered what—or maybe how much—to say. Maggie set aside her own cup, unable to drink her tea while her stomach was twisting itself into knots.

"He loved her," Nina finally said, and with those words, the knots tightened painfully. "In that innocent first love kind of way. You have to understand what it was like for

Jesse growing up in our family. He's always been the quiet one, the more introspective one. And he's sensitive, which is probably why he's so good with animals, and why he doesn't like to play with anyone's emotions.

"All of the local girls chased after Nate and Justin and Brad. Jesse was every bit as good-looking, smart and charming, but he was overlooked because he let himself be.

"When he went away to college, he was no longer competing with our brothers for attention, and the girls started to notice him for who he was. Shaelyn set her sights on him from day one. He didn't have a lot of experience deciphering subtle signals, but there was nothing subtle about Shaelyn."

"You didn't like her," Maggie realized.

"I wanted to—for Jesse's sake. But Shaelyn didn't have many redeeming qualities, aside from the fact that she loved my brother."

"And he loved her."

"He was infatuated," Nina allowed. "I'm not sure it was anything more than that, although he certainly thought it was, at least at the time.

"And his experience with Shaelyn did make him wary. So I'm going to ask you to try to be patient with him. To give him the time he needs to accept how he feels about you."

"What if you're wrong about his feelings?"

"I'm not," her sister-in-law promised.

Maggie wished she could be half as certain, but her conversation with Nina had at least given her hope.

Jesse's excited anticipation about the impending birth of his child was tempered by his fear that the baby's mother would wake up one day and realize she hated life in Rust Creek Falls. Because if that happened and Maggie decided to go back to Los Angeles, he'd lose everything that mattered most to him.

It was this fear that kept him from admitting—to her and himself—the true depth of his feelings. It was easy to keep busy around the ranch: mending broken fences, mucking out stalls and working with the horses. But that hadn't taken up all of his time, so he'd decided to build a cradle. It was something he wanted to do, and it gave him an excuse to stay out in the barn, away from Maggie. Because he couldn't be around Maggie without wanting Maggie, and giving in to that want would inevitably tangle up his heart, and he wasn't ready to go down that road again.

Except that he was almost finished the cradle, and he didn't know what project to tackle next. Maybe he would see if he could find a good plan for a crib.

He was assembling the stand when Honey nickered a happy greeting. Curious, he left the worktable and rounded the corner to discover Nina rubbing an affectionate hand down the horse's muzzle.

"What brings you out here?" he asked his sister.

"Maybe I just wanted to see my big brother."

"More likely you want something from your big brother," he guessed. "Like a babysitter?"

She smiled, unoffended by the assumption. "I really just wanted to see how you were doing—how you're settling into married life."

"Fine."

She lifted her brows in response to his single-word answer. "I don't know if I can express how incredibly reassured I am."

"I don't know why you'd need reassurance," he said. "But I'm glad I could help."

"Maggie told me you were making a cradle for the baby."

"When did you see Maggie?"

"She came to the store yesterday?"

"Yesterday?" he echoed incredulously. "And you waited a whole twenty-four hours to track me down to no doubt tell me that my marriage is doomed?"

"I don't think your marriage is doomed," she denied. "Although it's interesting that you would project that forecast onto me."

"I'm not projecting anything."

"Can I see the cradle?"

Happy to turn her attention to something other than his marriage, he led her to the workbench.

"Oh," she said, when he removed the protective cloth he'd draped over it. "Wow. Jesse, this is—" she ran a hand over the smoothly curved footboard "—gorgeous."

"I think it turned out pretty good," he agreed.

"This was obviously a labor of love."

"I wanted the baby to have—"

"This isn't for the baby," she interjected softly. "It's for Maggie."

"I'm pretty sure Maggie won't fit in it."

"You know what I mean," she chided. "This is your way of showing Maggie—because God forbid you should actually use words—how you feel about her."

His only response was to pull the blanket back over the cradle.

Nina sighed. "What are you afraid of?"

"I'm not afraid of anything."

"Good—because she married you, Jesse. She let you put a ring on her finger and she put one on yours and she promised to stay with you 'so long as you both shall live.'"

"Your point?" he prompted.

"You've got to stop waiting for her to leave," she said gently.

He scowled. "I'm not."

"Maybe not consciously, but I know you, and I see the way you look at her—and the way you don't let her see you look at her."

He frowned. "I'm not sure what you just said even makes any sense."

"Okay, I'll put it in simple terms that even you can understand—Maggie isn't Shaelyn. Don't make her pay for what Shaelyn did to you."

"I know she's not Shaelyn."

"Do you?" his sister challenged. "Do you realize that she looks at you as if you're everything she wants and needs? Or do you look at her and think—she's going to hate it here? That after having lived her whole life in Los Angeles, she's never going to adjust to life in Rust Creek Falls?"

"I can't deny that the possibility has crossed my mind, but I'm not waiting for it to happen."

"Here's another question—when you asked her to marry you, did you tell her how you feel about her or did you make it all about the baby?"

"I'm really glad that you're in love and happily married—even if you did choose to marry a Traub—but I don't want or need your marital advice."

She shook her head. "You haven't told her how you feel, have you?"

"Maggie and I both know why we got married."

"I don't think either of you has a clue about the other's reasons."

He scowled at that.

"She's not going to break your heart," Nina told him. "But if you're not careful—or maybe I should say if you don't stop being careful—you might break hers."

"I've got things to do, so if that's all…"

"There is one more thing."

"What is it?" he asked, not bothering to disguise his impatience.

"The holiday pageant at the elementary school is on Monday night. Ryder's part of the stage crew, and Jake and Robbie both have parts. I'd like you and Maggie to come."

"I don't think—"

"Most of Dallas's family has already said that they'll be there," she interjected to cut off what she no doubt knew was going to be a refusal.

He tried again. "I'm not sure a school play is Maggie's kind of thing."

"You might be surprised—by a lot of things."

He scowled. "What's that supposed to mean?"

"It means, ask her," his sister said, heading toward the door. "The show starts at seven."

So Jesse asked her.

When he got back to the house, Maggie was on her computer, looking on Pinterest for decorating ideas for the nursery. Her study manuals for the Bar exam were closed on the table beside her.

"My brain needed a break," she said.

He took a bottle of beer from the fridge, twisted off the cap. "I'm not surprised," he said. "You've been working nonstop since you got here."

"I used to take work home from the office all the time. Now I'm lucky if I have enough work to keep me in the office until five o'clock."

"Are you bored?"

"No, I enjoy what I'm doing. I'm just not accustomed to having so much time on my hands."

He felt another twinge of guilt as he realized it was true. Not only did her job demand fewer hours, but she didn't have the number of friends and acquaintances that she'd had in California. Yes, her cousin, Lissa, was here—but Lissa and Gage were head over heels in love and rarely more than ten feet away from one another.

"Do you have some time Monday night?"

"For what?" she asked, just a little warily.

"There's a Christmas pageant at the elementary school," he explained.

"Actually, it's a holiday pageant."

"Huh?"

"They're billing it as a holiday pageant this year because of the earlier date. There's going to be a short Thanksgiving play, holiday songs performed by the school choir and then the Christmas production."

"How do you know all of this?"

"Ben's daughter Paige teaches at the elementary school. Well, she's not teaching right now because she just had the baby, but she was talking about it when she came into the office last week. The earlier date—apparently a result of Winona Cobbs forecasting some big snowstorm—left the teachers scrambling to get everything ready on time."

He chuckled. "She's forecasting a big snowstorm?"

"You think she's wrong?" she asked hopefully.

"I think winter snowstorms in Montana are inevitable."

She sighed. "Obviously I'm going to need more than one pair of long johns."

She was making a joke—at least, he thought she was joking—but just the mention of her needing more long johns started him thinking about her nonthermal underwear. He'd had the pleasure of undressing her a few times now and he remembered—in scorching detail—that she liked to match her panties and her bras. But even more tempting were the feminine treasures he'd discovered hidden within the delicate scraps of lace.

"About the pageant," he prompted, in a desperate attempt to get his own thoughts back on track. "Do you want to go?"

"Sure," she agreed. "But why do you sound less than enthusiastic?"

"It's not exactly my idea of fun."

"Then why did you ask me to go?"

"Because misery loves company, and Nina guilted me into going."

"How did she do that?"

"She said that all of the Traubs were going to be there."

"So?"

"You know about the rivalry between the Crawfords and the Traubs," he reminded her.

"I thought Nina and Dallas getting married had put an end to all of that."

"Their wedding might have started to bridge the divide," Jesse allowed. "But the tension between the two families is still there, beneath the surface, with this ongoing one-upmanship. If Dallas's family is all going to be there, then Nina's family all needs to be there to show that we're just as supportive as they are."

"Sounds...exhausting," Maggie decided.

"Yeah," he agreed. "And mostly I don't care, but since Nina asked..."

"You feel obligated."

He nodded. "But if you don't want to—"

"I'm not going to be your excuse for begging off," she told him.

"I wasn't going to use you as an excuse, but only because I didn't think of it," he admitted. "I was just going to say that you aren't under the same obligation, so if you don't want to go, you don't have to."

"And give your parents another reason not to like me?" She shook her head. "I don't think so."

He frowned. "My parents don't dislike you."

"They think I trapped you into marrying me."

"No, they don't," he denied, uncomfortable to realize that she believed such a thing, and that he'd done nothing to reassure her. "They do have some concerns about the fact that we got married quickly and don't know each other very well, but they'll come around."

"Before or after our child graduates from college?"

He smiled at her wry tone. "Hopefully before."

"Well, in the meantime, I would like to go to the holiday pageant with you."

"You would?"

"Sure," she agreed. "What time does it start?"

"Seven o'clock. But we should probably be there by six-thirty if we want to get a seat in the auditorium."

"Are you expecting the show to sell out?"

"There's not a lot of entertainment in Rust Creek Falls," he reminded her.

Chapter Thirteen

It hadn't taken Maggie long to realize the trick to tolerating the frigid Montana weather was layers. Lots of layers. So she started with long johns under her dark jeans and a long-sleeved knit top beneath a bulky cable-knit sweater in pale pink. Then she added some dangly earrings, just for fun.

She didn't miss the cocktail parties and dinner meetings that were so much a part of her life in LA, but she did miss dressing up and feeling pretty. In need of a little extra boost, she added mascara to her lashes and a darker than usual shade of gloss to her lips.

Jesse was ready and waiting for her when she came downstairs. He'd showered and changed into a clean pair of jeans with a dark blue V-neck sweater over a lighter blue crewneck T-shirt. He hadn't bothered to shave, and the dark shadow on his cheeks and jaw made him look even more rugged and sexy—and made her heart slam against her ribs.

It was the closest thing they'd ever had to a date. She wondered if he would hold her hand, and chided herself for the flutters of anticipation that danced in her tummy.

She'd had sex with him—more than once even, but not at all since their wedding—and now she was desperate for any sign of interest or affection.

Sometimes when he looked at her, she thought she saw

a flicker of heat, a glimpse of desire, but then he'd look away, leaving her to wonder if she'd only imagined it. She didn't understand why he'd pushed so hard for her to marry him, and then completely withdrawn once his ring was on her finger.

He looked at her, his gaze skimming from the boots on her feet to the top of her head, lingering at certain spots in a way that made her breasts ache and her thighs tingle. But when he spoke, it was only to say, "You're going to want a hat. It's cold outside."

"It's November in Montana—of course it's cold outside," she noted drily. But she found the new pink hat and matching gloves she'd bought on a recent trip into Kalispell and put them on.

"How many hats do you own?"

"Hopefully enough."

"You do know that you can only wear one at a time?" he teased, flicking the pom-pom on top of her head.

"I like to accessorize."

"You look good in pink," he told her.

She was surprised—and pleased—by the compliment.

"And in skirts," he said. "Although I haven't seen you in one since we got married."

"And you probably won't until spring," she warned. "There's no way I'm baring my legs in this weather."

"That's too bad—because yours are spectacular. Especially when you wear those heels that make them look a mile long."

The comment seemed to surprise him as much as it surprised her. But she kept her tone light when she said, "So you're a leg man, are you?"

"I like *your* legs," he admitted, his gaze skimming down her body, then slowly up again. "Actually, I like every part of you."

"Really?"

"You're a beautiful woman, Maggie," he said.

She blew out an unsteady breath. "And you're a confusing man."

He held her gaze for a long minute, as if there was something more he wanted to say. But in the end, he only asked, "Are you ready to go?"

As soon as they got to the doors of the auditorium, Maggie realized that Jesse had not exaggerated the popularity of the event. Although there was still more than half an hour before the pageant was scheduled to start, almost all of the seats were taken.

"This is quite the gathering," Maggie noted.

Jesse shrugged. "Folks around here will take their entertainment any way they can get it."

"Or maybe they appreciate the time and effort that the teachers and students put into the productions."

"Maybe," he allowed, guiding her closer to the front, where his sister and the rest of the family were sitting.

Looking around as they made their way down the center aisle between the rows of seats, Maggie was surprised by how many familiar faces were in the crowd.

Caleb Dalton was there with his fiancée, Mallory Franklin, whose niece Lily was singing in the choir and one of the angels in the pageant. In addition, Maggie recognized several members of the Rust Creek Falls Newcomers Club, including Vanessa Brent—recently engaged to Jonah Traub—Jordyn Leigh Cates and Julie Smith. She knew some of their stories—Lily Franklin had played a big role in bringing her aunt and the boss's son together; Vanessa had met Jonah while they were both working onsite at the soon-to-be-completed Maverick Manor—and that some of the others were still looking to lasso the cowboy of their dreams.

She also knew that several of the single newcomers probably envied her the attention of the handsome cowboy she'd married. But while she might have Jesse's ring on her finger, she didn't have the one thing she really wanted: his heart.

Although she was undoubtedly a newcomer, too, she'd married Jesse so quickly after moving to Rust Creek Falls that a lot of people viewed her as his wife first, forgetting that she was also a transplant. Which was funny, because Jesse never did. In fact, she didn't think a single day had gone by since they'd married that he hadn't made at least one passing reference to the life she'd left behind in LA.

He wants you to stay, but he's afraid you won't.

Nina's words echoed in the back of her mind as Maggie took a seat beside her husband. In the row immediately in front of them was Jesse's sister with her husband. On the other side of Nina were her parents, and on the other side of Dallas were his. The Hatfields and the McCoys of Rust Creek Falls playing nice—or at least pretending to—for the sake of their children and grandchildren. Seeing them here together gave Maggie hope that the baby she was carrying might also succeed in bringing her and Jesse closer together.

As far as school plays went, Jesse decided it was entertaining. But not quite entertaining enough to keep his attention on the stage while he was seated beside his bride. He wasn't usually so easily distracted, but being close to Maggie made it impossible for him to focus on anything else.

With every breath he took, he breathed in the scent of her skin—something light and spicy. The scent was too subtle to be perfume, so he guessed it was probably some kind of lotion she rubbed on her body. A conclusion that tantalized his mind with the mental image of her delicate hands smoothing fragrant lotion over the bare, silky skin of her shoulders, her arms, her breasts...

The sound of applause jolted him back to the present. He automatically put his hands together as the kids on stage took a bow.

"There will now be a fifteen-minute intermission," the eighth-grade emcee announced. "Please help yourself to the cookies and hot drinks available outside."

The auditorium was suddenly filled with the sound of chair legs scraping against the floor as parents and grandparents and other guests hurried for the snacks.

"Do you want anything?" he asked Maggie.

She shook her head as she rose to her feet. "Just to stretch my legs."

He noticed that several older kids, not in costume, were on the stage now, pushing aside the long table that had been the setting of the Thanksgiving feast to set up a makeshift stable for the upcoming nativity scene.

"It's hard to believe that we're going to have a son or a daughter up on that stage someday," he said.

"Not for several years yet," Maggie pointed out to him.

"I know, but it started me thinking... Do you know if our baby is a boy or a girl?"

She shook her head. "Do you want to know?"

"I'm not sure," he admitted. "In some ways, I think it would make planning easier."

"We'd know whether to buy pink or blue burp cloths."

He smiled in response to her teasing. "There is that."

"I have an appointment for an ultrasound tomorrow. We should be able to find out the baby's gender, depending on his or her position." She hesitated a second, then said, "I know it's short notice, but you could come with me, if you want."

"I'd like that," he immediately replied.

"I should have asked you before, but you've been so busy…" Her explanation trailed off.

Yes, he'd been busy making himself busy, and he suspected that she knew it. But he still couldn't admit it to her now, because that would also require admitting that he didn't know how to be the husband she wanted—the husband he wanted to be to her.

Before he could manufacture an appropriate reply, Tara Jones—the third-grade teacher—stopped beside them.

"Mr. and Mrs. Crawford—how wonderful to see you here tonight."

Although her greeting encompassed both of them, she seemed to be speaking to Maggie, making Jesse suspect that she was a client. Her next words dispelled that theory.

"I know I said it before—but I have to thank you again for all of your help with the costumes and props."

"I really didn't do very much," Maggie said.

"We would never have had everything ready on time without you," Tara insisted. Then she turned to Jesse. "In case your wife didn't tell you, she made thirty pilgrim hats and an equal number of native headbands, painted the starry sky for the nativity scene and designed the wings and halos for the angels."

"You might want to save your thanks until after the pageant, in case the sky falls down."

Tara chuckled. "It's not going to fall down. And even if it did, it wouldn't matter. What matters is that you gave us the extra hands we desperately needed to get everything done in time for tonight."

Maggie smiled. "And that the kids all seem to be having a good time."

"They definitely are," the teacher agreed. "And now I'm going backstage to make sure their costumes are on before we continue the show."

Jesse waited until she was out of earshot before he turned to his wife. "I didn't know you'd helped out with this."

"I put in a few hours when I had nothing to do at the office," Maggie admitted, settling into her chair again as the other audience members began to return to their seats.

"It sounds like you put in more than a few hours."

She shrugged. "I had time on my hands."

He impulsively reached for one of those hands—it was small and soft in comparison to his, but for all of its delicacy, it was also strong. Not unlike Maggie herself.

She was a California girl experiencing a Montana winter, and he wondered if it was only her first or also her last. If she made it through the season, would she stay through the spring and the summer? How long would she last so far away from the bright lights of the big city? And how long did she need to stay before he stopped anticipating that she'd pack her bags and hightail it back to LA?

Right now, she seemed happy enough, and he hadn't been doing anything to make her happy. He'd been leaving her to her own devices, certain she would get bored and be gone. Maybe he was pushing her away, or at least testing her steadfastness. And yeah, it had only been a couple of weeks, but so far, she'd stuck. Which got him to thinking... What if he actually let her know that he wanted her to stay? What if he made an effort to make her want to stay?

There was a connection between them—he'd felt it from the first. It was real and strong. She made him want to open up to her in a way that he hadn't opened up to a woman in a long time, to share not just his home but his life and his heart, and that was more than a little scary.

Watching her watch the kids onstage, he let himself consider the possibilities. Maybe she could grow to love Montana—and him—enough to want to stay. Maybe they really could raise this child—and other children—together.

But there was still a part of him that was afraid to let himself believe, certain that as soon as he started to plan for their future together, she'd knock him down and stomp on his heart.

Don't make Maggie pay for what Shaelyn did to you.

Nina's words echoed in the back of his mind.

He knew that most of his family had had concerns when he'd told them that he and Maggie were getting married—and why. And although only ten days had passed since the wedding, Nina had become her new sister-in-law's biggest cheerleader.

But not her only supporter. Ben Dalton had nothing but praise for the young attorney he'd taken on. And even Sutter had mentioned how appreciative Paige was of Maggie's work at the law office, because it freed her father up to spend more time with his family.

Obviously their faith was well-placed. She was willing to tackle whatever legal issues were assigned to her, she was studying for her exams, and even outside her area of expertise she'd stepped in to help where help was needed. She was making an effort to fit in, to be accepted by the community, and the residents of Rust Creek Falls were starting to give her a chance—which, he realized, was more than he'd done.

Even while she'd been reciting her vows, he'd been holding his breath, waiting for her to announce that she'd changed her mind.

But despite his best efforts, he'd got used to having her around. He looked forward to seeing her at the breakfast table in the morning and having dinner with her every night. He enjoyed talking to her about his day and hers, and he enjoyed the silence when they didn't feel like talking. He felt comfortable around her—except when being in close proximity to her was decidedly *un*comfortable because she tempted him to want more, to believe they could have more.

They were connected by their baby and their marriage. But he'd meant it when he'd told her he wasn't looking for love, and he knew that he needed to maintain some kind of boundaries between them if he was going to protect his heart. He was already sharing his name, his house and almost every part of his life. If he shared his bed, there would be no more boundaries between them, nothing to prevent him from falling the rest of the way in love with her.

It was that certainty that prevented him from giving in to the ever-growing desire he felt for her.

At least for now.

Maggie had been referred to Dr. Gaynor in Kalispell by her ob-gyn in Los Angeles, and the first time she met her, she was impressed by the doctor's warmth, compassion and efficiency. Dr. Gaynor didn't believe in overbooking her patients, which meant that while emergencies did occasionally arise, it was unusual for there to be more than one or two women in the waiting room.

So it didn't surprise her that she was taken into an exam room at 10:59 a.m. for her eleven o'clock appointment, or that the doctor entered the room only three minutes later.

It did surprise her when the doctor said to Jesse, "You must be the husband."

He nodded and offered his hand. "Jesse Crawford."

"Susan Gaynor." She must have noticed Maggie's surprise, because she smiled. "The last time I saw you, you said that you might be getting married," the doctor reminded Maggie. "This time, you came with a man and a ring on your finger."

"We got married on the fifteenth," Maggie confirmed.

"Congratulations," Dr. Gaynor said to both of them. "And thank you—" her gaze shifted to Jesse "—for taking the time to come here today. It's always nice to see a husband supporting his wife through her pregnancy."

"I'm happy to be here," he said sincerely. "And to do anything I can to help Maggie over the next five months."

"The next five months are the easy part," the doctor teased. "The real challenges—and joys—come with the baby."

Jesse reached for her hand, linked their fingers together. "We're looking forward to both."

"Good answer," Dr. Gaynor said. "And I'm happy to report that everything looks great with both your wife and the baby. In fact—" she turned to Maggie now "—you've gained two pounds since I last saw you."

"I knew I shouldn't have eaten those Christmas cookies that Nina sent home with us last night," the mom-to-be grumbled.

The doctor chuckled. "A special treat every once in a while isn't going to hurt you or your baby so long as you're also eating lots of fruits, vegetables, whole grains and proteins."

"I'm eating lots of everything," Maggie confirmed.

"Good. That first trimester weight loss could have been problematic, but it's apparent that you've been taking good care of yourself and your baby.

"Have you felt any movement?"

"I don't think so," Maggie said, her grip on his hand instinctively tightening.

"It's nothing to be concerned about," the doctor assured her. "A lot of first-time moms don't recognize the little flutters as fetal movement. If you haven't noticed anything yet, you will soon enough."

Dr. Gaynor's glance shifted from Maggie to Jesse and back again. "Do either of you have any questions at this stage?"

He looked at Maggie, who shook her head.

The doctor followed the silent exchange, then directed her next comment to him. "A lot of first-time fathers worry about sex."

"Nope," he said quickly, vehemently. "No worries there."

"Good." The doctor nodded, but she didn't leave it at that. "But just in case you were wondering, there are absolutely no restrictions on intercourse right up to the day of delivery, so long as Maggie's comfortable and there aren't any complications in her pregnancy."

"Okay...um...yep. That's great."

Maggie didn't know if Jesse was looking at her, because she didn't dare look at him. Obviously they'd had sex—she wouldn't be here otherwise. But the doctor couldn't know, thankfully, that they hadn't been intimate for some time. In fact, for reasons she didn't understand and that her husband hadn't bothered to share with her, they hadn't even consummated their marriage.

Not that she was going to discuss that with him in the doctor's office—or anywhere else, apparently. Because although it was a question that continued to keep her awake at night, she wasn't entirely sure she wanted to know his answer. She didn't want to hear him confirm that he didn't want her—he only wanted their baby.

But she couldn't help wondering when and why he'd stopped wanting her. When they'd made love the first time after she'd told him that she was pregnant, he'd seemed captivated by the subtle changes in her body, awed by the realization that there was a tiny life growing inside of her.

Of course, with each day that passed, that tiny life was getting a little bit bigger. And although she'd only gained two pounds since that day, she was barely able to fasten the button on her pants now, which meant that she was going to have to start wearing maternity clothes soon. And if Jesse found her barely noticeable baby bump unappealing, how was he going to feel in a few more months?

"Are you ready to have a look at that baby of yours now?" Dr. Gaynor's question interrupted her musing.

It was only when Jesse squeezed her hand that Maggie realized he was still holding it—had been holding it almost from the minute they walked into the doctor's office.

She nodded in response to the doctor's inquiry.

"I'll send the technician in."

The technician, who introduced herself as Carla, wheeled in a cart with the ultrasound machine on it. It only took her a minute to set up, then she asked the mom-to-be to lift her shirt.

Maggie's pregnancy wasn't yet obvious—at least not to Jesse and not in the clothes she usually wore. In fact, she did such a good job of hiding any evidence of her pregnancy that he sometimes almost forgot she was pregnant— except he knew that she would never have chosen to move to Rust Creek Falls and marry him if not for their baby. He suspected the loose-fitting tops were a deliberate choice, to postpone the inevitable gossip and speculation that would run rampant when her condition became public knowledge. While he understood her reasons, he wanted to shout the news of her pregnancy from the rooftops for all of the world to hear. But because she'd done such a good job disguising her baby bump, he was surprised when she lifted the hem of her tunic-style top and he saw that there was an undeniable roundness to her belly.

The technician squirted gel onto the exposed skin and pressed a probe to her belly. A rhythmic whooshing sound filled the silence and the fuzzy display on the monitor screen began to take shape.

"Oh. Wow."

Jesse felt stunned—and humbled—as he registered the shape of their baby: the outline of the head and the body, even the skinny little legs and arms, and—most awesome and overwhelming—the rapid beating of the heart inside the chest.

He had some experience with ultrasounds—mostly with respect to equine fetuses. But this was completely outside his realm of experience. This was an actual human baby—his and Maggie's baby. He knew that he'd done very little to help grow this miracle inside of her. Yes, he'd contributed half of the baby's DNA, but since then, he'd done nothing. She was the one who was giving their baby everything he or she needed, the only one who could.

He wanted to say something to express the awe and gratitude that filled his heart, but his throat was suddenly tight, so he settled for squeezing Maggie's hand.

"Your baby is almost eight inches long and weighs about fourteen ounces," Carla told them. "Completely within normal range for twenty-one weeks."

"I've gained eight pounds and less than one of that is the baby?"

"Which is completely normal," the technician said patiently. "Now that I'm finished with all the measurements, do you want to know your baby's gender?"

Maggie looked at Jesse. They'd talked about the possibility but hadn't made a final decision, and he was grateful that she was asking for his input now. He considered, wavered, then nodded.

"Can you tell?" Maggie asked.

"I can tell," Carla said. "But I never do unless the parents want to know."

"We want to know," she decided.

The technician smiled. "It's a girl."

A girl.

Maggie honestly hadn't thought she had any preference, but she would have guessed that Jesse wanted a boy. But when she looked at him now, trying to gauge his reaction to the news, he didn't look disappointed. In fact, he was smiling like the proud father he would be in another few months.

"Were you hoping for a boy?" she asked softly.

He immediately shook his head. "My only hope is that both you and the baby are healthy."

The sincerity in his tone assured Maggie that he meant it. And the way he was looking at her—with warmth and affection—gave her hope that sharing the experience of "seeing" their baby for the first time together might bring them closer.

The technician gave her a paper towel to wipe the gel off her belly, and the moment was broken.

"Do you feel up to making another stop before we head back home?" Jesse asked when they left the doctor's office.

"Does that stop include lunch?"

He chuckled. "That stop can definitely include lunch," he promised. "What do you want to eat?"

"A burger," she answered without hesitation.

"Then we'll get you a burger."

Chapter Fourteen

They found a diner around the corner from the medical center. It was an old-fashioned-style eatery with Formica tabletops and red vinyl benches and stools lined up at the counter. The menu was quite extensive, offering more than a dozen different types of burgers with countless toppings, French fries, sweet potato fries, onion rings, coleslaw or green salad, and milk shakes and ice-cream floats.

Maggie ordered a bacon cheeseburger and a side salad, then picked at the fries on Jesse's plate. Not that he minded—it was all he could do to finish the spicy barbecue chicken sandwich on sourdough bread that he'd ordered—but he was curious.

"If you wanted fries, why didn't you just order fries?" he finally asked.

"Because the salad is healthier."

"But you're eating fries, anyway."

"Only a few," she said defensively. "And only after I ate my veggies."

He nudged his plate closer to her. "I don't mind sharing," he assured her. "I was just wondering about your rationale."

"I never even used to like French fries all that much," she said. "But lately, I can't seem to get enough."

"Any other unusual food cravings?"

"Red meat," she said.

"I noticed we've been eating a lot of beef."

Her gaze tracked the slice of apple pie that a waitress carried past their table to deliver to another customer.

"And apple pie?" he prompted.

She turned her attention back to him. "Sorry?"

He smiled. "Do you want dessert?"

"I probably shouldn't."

"Which doesn't actually answer the question," he said.

"I'm not sure if I want dessert or if that pie just looked really good."

"Should I get a slice of pie and ask for two forks?"

"Only if you want pie," she said. "With ice cream."

So he ordered the apple pie with ice cream and two forks.

After it was delivered, he watched her fork slide through the flaky crust and layers of sweet, sticky apple slices. Her lips closed around the tines of the fork, her eyes drifted shut and she let out a sigh of pure pleasure that stirred an appetite inside him that had nothing to do with dessert.

She chewed slowly, savoring the flavor, and finally swallowed.

"You have to try this," she told him.

"I ordered it for you."

She shook her head. "I'd feel way too guilty if I ate the whole thing myself."

So he picked up the second fork and took a bite.

There was something intimate about sharing a dessert. Maybe it went back to the communal consumption of ancient times, when a hunter shared his catch with his mate and their children, proof of their relationship to one another. Or maybe it was that watching Maggie eat was an incredibly erotic experience.

The pie was good, but he much preferred letting Maggie savor it.

Her tongue swept over her bottom lip, licking away the smear of ice cream. He knew that her lips were even sweeter than ice cream, and he had an almost insatiable desire to lean across the table and sample her flavor. It seemed as if it had been years since he'd kissed her, rather than the ten days that had passed since their wedding. But it wasn't easy holding his want of her in check, and he knew that if he gave in to the urge to kiss her, he wouldn't be able to stop with one kiss.

"I'm glad you're enjoying your dessert," he said.

"It's always a treat to eat something that someone else has prepared."

"And I haven't taken you out to eat anywhere since we got married," he realized. Equally startling was the realization that he hadn't taken her out at all *before* they were married. They had gone out for dinner in LA, and although he'd insisted on paying the bill, she'd chosen the restaurant, so he didn't figure he should get credit for that.

"We're going to your parents' house for Thanksgiving."

"That hardly counts."

She shrugged. "I don't need to be taken out or entertained."

And maybe it was because she didn't that he found himself wanting to make the effort. "I haven't been a very attentive husband," he acknowledged. "My only excuse is that I don't have a lot of experience with this kind of thing."

"It's my first marriage, too," she said lightly.

"I meant...dating and other courtship rituals."

"I'm your wife, Jesse. You don't have to court me."

"I should have courted you properly before we were married."

"I guess we did things a little out of order," she agreed. "But I'm not sorry, because they got us to where we are now."

"You don't miss LA?"

"Only my family," she told him. Then she gave him a half smile. "And the weather."

"The weather can be a challenge, even for those who were born and bred in Montana," he admitted.

"I asked Lissa how she survived her first winter in Rust Creek Falls—she said she wouldn't have survived at all if she hadn't had Gage to snuggle up to every night."

"I don't think I like the idea of you snuggling up to your cousin's husband," he teased.

"I don't think Lissa would, either," she admitted.

And although she smiled, her gaze shifted away, as if she was disappointed by his response. Which made him wonder—had she been suggesting that she wanted to snuggle up to him?

Before he could decide whether or not to pursue the possibility, the waitress brought the bill to their table.

When Jesse asked if they could make a stop before heading back to Rust Creek Falls, she'd assumed it was to pick up something that he needed for the horses. So she was more than a little surprised when he pulled into the parking lot of a strip mall—and parked in front of a toy store.

He strode purposefully through the front doors, as if he'd been there before and knew exactly where he was going. Considering the way he doted on his eleven-month-old niece, she would bet he'd been there several times before. He guided her down the main aisle to a section titled Cuddly Critters that was lined with big cubes stacked floor to ceiling and filled with stuffed animals of various breeds, sizes and colors.

Jesse zeroed in on the pink teddy bears, rifled through the selection, then pulled one out and handed it to Maggie.

Her fingers sank into fur that was unbelievably soft and plush. The bear was the color of cotton candy, with skinny arms and legs ending in oversized paws. The head was big, too, with a slightly paler muzzle, a brown nose, and eyes and a half smile stitched onto the fabric. It was, without a doubt, the cutest baby teddy bear she'd ever seen, and when he put it in her arms, her heart just melted.

She looked up at him. "For our baby?"

He shook his head. "For you. To remember the day that we found out about our baby girl."

"I have a very old pink teddy bear that sits on my bedside table at home," she said wistfully.

"I saw it when I was there," he admitted.

"My parents gave it to me the day I was adopted."

"I guess teddy bears are a pretty common theme."

But there was nothing commonplace about his gesture, and tears filled her eyes as she impulsively hugged him, squishing the bear between them. "Thank you."

"I should be thanking you," he said gruffly. "You're giving me the greatest gift of all in our baby, and I don't know how to tell you how grateful I am. Looking at our daughter on the ultrasound monitor, I realized how different things might have been...if you'd chosen not to tell me...or if you'd decided to give her away."

"I wouldn't have," she promised him. "It might have taken me a while to share the news, but I would never have kept it from you."

He brushed a strand of hair off her cheek, tucked it behind her ear. His deep blue eyes reflected so much of what he was feeling: affection, warmth—want?

Her breath caught in her throat as she thought, for one brief moment, that he was actually going to kiss her. She didn't care if they were standing in the middle of a toy store, she wanted to feel his lips on hers. It had been so long since he'd kissed her, too long.

But instead of lowering his head toward her, he took a step back, away from temptation. Or maybe she was the only one who was tempted.

She'd seen the surprise on his face when she lifted her shirt and he realized the tiny curve of her belly was bigger and rounder since the last time he'd seen her naked. And although she was still on the small side for twenty-one weeks, there was no longer any denying that she was pregnant. The body that he'd so thoroughly explored with his hands and his lips back in the summer was growing and changing—her subtle curves weren't nearly as subtle anymore, and his desire for her wasn't nearly as palpable.

She sat with the teddy bear in her lap throughout the drive home and consoled herself with the knowledge that at least now she'd have something to cuddle up with at night.

It wasn't what—or rather who—she wanted to be with, but the company of a plush bear was better than nothing…

Maggie went into the office for a couple of hours after she and Jesse returned from Kalispell. He, predictably, went to Traub Stables and warned her that he wouldn't be home until late. When the phone rang around nine o'clock that night, she thought it might be him calling to tell her that he was on his way home. She was only a little disappointed when she heard her mother's voice on the other end of the line.

"I just called to see how you're doing," Christa said when her daughter answered. "You had a doctor's appointment today, didn't you?"

Maggie had to smile. "You're twelve hundred miles away, in the middle of discoveries for a multimillion-dollar class action lawsuit, and you remembered the date of my doctor's appointment?"

"Of course," her mother said simply.

"Everything's fine," Maggie told her. "The baby is healthy and growing."

"And the baby's mom?"

"She's fine, too. In fact, I've gained back almost all of the weight I lost in the first trimester."

"That's good."

"I think I'm going to wear that Isabella Oliver wrap maternity dress that you sent to me for Thanksgiving." She didn't tell her mother that she'd also be wearing faux fur–lined knee-high boots and a down coat, because she did not want to hear about the balmy weather in SoCal.

"Maybe you could make a quick weekend trip this way sometime soon for us to do some more shopping," Christa suggested. "For you and for the baby."

"I'd like that," Maggie agreed.

"I wish you could be here for Thanksgiving," Christa said. "Both you and Jesse, I mean."

She was glad for the distance that separated them, so her mother couldn't see the tears that stung her eyes. "We'll make the trip for Christmas," she promised.

"Christmas still seems so far away."

"It will be here before we know it."

"So what are your plans for this holiday?"

"We're having a big meal with Jesse's family—all fifteen of them."

Christa laughed. "That should be an experience."

"No doubt."

"How's the new job?"

"Good," Maggie said. "Different, but good. I'm doing a little bit of everything, but not a lot of anything."

"I'm sure you don't miss working sixty hours a week for Brian Nash."

"No," she agreed. "I feel a little bit like I'm at loose ends right now, but I know I'll be glad for the slower pace when the baby comes."

They chatted a little more, about the class action suit, a new movie star client—unnamed to protect the solicitor-client privilege—who had hired Gavin to fight a paternity claim, and the new woman—a Laker girl—that Ryan was dating.

"Are you sure everything is okay?" Christa asked when their conversation had finally wound down. "Because LA might seem like a long way from Rust Creek Falls, but if you need anything at all, you just say the word and I'll be there."

Maggie was glad that her mother couldn't see the tears that filled her eyes. "Thanks, Mom. But everything's fine."

"You don't sound fine."

"I guess I'm just missing you and Dad. I've never not been home for Thanksgiving."

"You don't feel like Rust Creek Falls is your home now?" her mother asked gently.

"No, I do," Maggie hastened to assure her, again grateful that her mother couldn't see her face because Christa always could tell when any of her kids was being less than honest. "Like I said—I'm just missing you and Dad. Even Ryan."

That made her mother chuckle. "Happy Thanksgiving, Maggie."

"You, too, Mom."

Maggie was putting her boots on when Jesse came in from his final check on the animals Wednesday night.

"Going somewhere?" he asked.

"To the grocery store."

Because she'd specified *grocery*, he knew she didn't mean Crawford's. "We were just in Kalispell yesterday for your doctor's appointment," he reminded her.

"I know," she admitted. "But I wasn't thinking about Thanksgiving then."

"And you're thinking about Thanksgiving now?"

"Because it's tomorrow," she reminded him. "And I can't show up at your parents' house empty-handed."

"My mom's been doing Thanksgiving dinner for more years than I've been alive," Jesse pointed out. "I assure you, everything is covered."

"I want to make something," she insisted.

He sighed. "It's late and it's already been a long day."

"I don't expect you to go with me—I just thought you might want to know where I was going."

"Is Lissa going with you?"

"No."

He frowned. "You're going by yourself?"

"I know the way," she assured him.

"But it's late," he said again.

"It's not quite seven-thirty and the store's open until nine."

She made the statement matter-of-factly, as if she was perfectly capable of driving twenty minutes to an out-of-town grocery store to pick up a few items. And, of course, she was—he was just taken aback by her independence.

He'd lost count of the number of times he'd suggested to Shaelyn that she should go into Kalispell to go shopping or to a movie or even just to get one of those fancy over-priced iced coffee drinks that she liked and that couldn't be found in Rust Creek Falls.

But she never wanted to go anywhere without him. And she had a knack for making him feel guilty for even suggesting she should be on her own for half an hour when he'd been away from her for most of the day. And what if something happened when she was driving *all the way* to and from Kalispell?

As if he needed any further proof that Maggie was nothing like Shaelyn, she already had her boots and coat on and her keys in hand.

"Wait."

She paused at the door. "Did you want something from the store?"

"I want to go with you," he decided.

"That's really not necessary."

And he knew it was true. She didn't need him to go to the grocery store with her. In fact, she didn't seem to need him for much of anything. There wasn't anything she couldn't do on her own—including having and raising a child.

Which supported what Nina had said—that Maggie wasn't with him because she needed him but because she wanted to be with him.

And he realized that he didn't like the idea of her driving to Kalispell on her own. Not because he was worried about anything that might happen, just because he wanted to be with her.

"I know," he finally said. "But I'd like to come, anyway."

She looked at him for a moment, then turned back to the door. "Then let's go."

Maggie was undeniably apprehensive about spending Thanksgiving with Jesse's family. Partly because the last time she'd been invited to Todd and Laura's house, she'd abruptly—and rudely—dropped the bombshell about her pregnancy on them, and partly because this was the first time since the wedding that she'd be in the same room with all of Jesse's siblings—and the first time she'd see most of them since her husband had shared the news about their baby.

"What have you got there?" Laura asked, gesturing to the covered bowls in each of Jesse's and Maggie's hands.

"This one's coleslaw," she said, holding it up. "And Jesse's got the mac and cheese carbonara."

"Mac and cheese *what*?" Todd asked.

"It's got bacon in it," Jesse said, knowing that was his father's weakness.

"Well, I'll have to try that," he decided.

"You didn't have to bring anything," her mother-in-law protested.

"It's a lot of work to make a meal for so many people," Maggie acknowledged. "I wanted to at least make a small contribution."

"Well, that was real thoughtful," Laura said, basking a little in her new daughter-in-law's compliment. Then she gestured for them to join the rest of the family in the living room. "Come in, come in. We'll be putting dinner on the table shortly."

"Can I give you a hand with anything?" Maggie offered.

Her mother-in-law shook her head. "We've got everything covered. Oh—except that we do need one more place set at the table."

"I'm doing it now," Callie said from the dining room.

"One more?" Jesse queried.

Laura nodded to her husband. "Ask your father."

His father shrugged. "When I stopped by the store to pick up a pint of ice cream, I saw Homer Gilmore wandering the street. Since I knew we'd have more than enough food to feed the army reserves, I asked him to join us for the meal."

"That was…generous," Jesse noted.

And, Maggie could tell by his tone, unexpected.

"Everybody sit," Laura directed, as Nina and Natalie began to set bowls and platters of food around the table. "Justin—you can pour the wine. Brad—get Noelle's high chair from the kitchen. Jesse—you make sure everyone finds a seat. Nate—you come get the turkey."

Justin made his way around the table, pouring the wine. "Oops—forgot about the bun in the oven," he said, lifting the bottle away from Maggie's glass.

"Gramma took the buns out of the oven," seven-year-old Robbie said, pointing to the basket on the table.

"Yes, I did," Laura confirmed, sending a narrow-eyed look in her son's direction.

"What would you like to drink?" Natalie asked Maggie.

"Water's fine," she replied, because glasses of that were already set around the table along with a pitcher for refills.

When everyone was settled, Todd said grace, expressing thanks for the bountiful feast on the table and the gathering of family and friends. Then the bowls and platters were passed around, and people chatted easily as they filled their plates.

Laura Crawford had indeed prepared enough food to feed an army—or at least the army reserves—confirming Jesse's assertion that Maggie's contribution was unnecessary. But she was pleased to note that Dallas's three sons all wanted to try her mac and cheese.

"What's that?" Brad asked, warily eyeing the bowl that Jesse offered to him.

"It's coleslaw."

Brad scowled as he looked more closely at the salad. "But it's got raisins…and nuts."

"And it's delicious," Natalie said.

"Did you make this?" Brad asked his youngest sister.

"Maggie did."

"Oh." He glanced apologetically at his new sister-in-law. "I usually eat my fruit after dinner, inside a pie crust."

"He says as he spoons cranberry sauce onto his plate," Nina noted drily.

He scowled at that. "Cranberry sauce isn't fruit—it's a condiment."

"It's fruit," his mother informed him.

"Well, my plate's kind of full right now," Brad said, passing the bowl of coleslaw to Nate's fiancée, Callie, on his other side. "I'll try some on the next go-round."

"Can I have some more mac 'n' cheese?" Robbie asked, lifting his plate up.

"Eat some of your veggies and meat first," his father admonished.

"But I like the mac 'n' cheese best," the little boy said.

Which reassured Maggie that she'd at least made one good choice.

"What kind of cheese is in that sauce?" Laura asked.

"There are four different kinds," Maggie said. "Cheddar, Asiago, Fontina and Parmigiano Reggiano."

"Do we carry those in the store?" Laura asked her oldest daughter.

"Cheddar and Parmigiano," Nina said. "But even I go shopping in Kalispell to pick up items that we don't stock on a regular basis."

And all three of Dallas's boys were devouring the mac and cheese carbonara as if they'd never tasted anything so good.

Jesse slid an arm across her shoulders. "Better than the stuff that comes out of a box, that's for sure."

"You haven't tried the coleslaw."

"Fruit and nuts are for dessert," he echoed his brother.

"And I can say that because I don't eat cranberry sauce, either."

Across the table, Justin was drowning his mashed potatoes in gravy as he spoke to Nate. "How is construction of the resort coming along?"

Other conversations quieted as everyone wanted to hear the details. Maggie had been surprised to learn that, only a few months earlier, Nate had been thinking about leaving Rust Creek Falls. Instead, he'd decided to buy a piece of local property to open a resort, similar to what was in Thunder Canyon. Work had progressed steadily, and Maverick Manor was scheduled for a Christmas Eve grand opening.

"Is there going to be a honeymoon suite?" Nina asked.

"You've already had a honeymoon," her oldest brother reminded her.

"But Jesse and Maggie haven't," she pointed out.

"There is a honeymoon suite," Callie confirmed. "On the top floor, of course, with a gas fireplace in the lounge area and a jetted tub big enough for two in the bath."

"It sounds impressive," Maggie said, because Callie seemed to expect her to say something.

"Let us know when you've got a couple of days free and I'll reserve it for you," Nate promised.

Jesse looked at his wife. "What do you think?"

She was tempted to ask Nate if the room had two beds, because she didn't think Jesse would be willing to go if they actually had to sleep under the same covers.

"That's a generous offer," she said instead. "But we're going to be in Los Angeles for Christmas this year."

Which would present them with the same dilemma under a different roof. As close as Maggie was to her parents, she didn't want to explain to them that she wasn't sharing a bed with her husband. So they were going to have to share a bed—or one of them would have to sleep on the floor, and it wasn't going to be her.

But they had several weeks before they had to worry about that. Right now, she was focused on getting through this holiday with Jesse's family.

She was grateful that his siblings seemed to have accepted her. His parents were still lukewarm, and she didn't really blame them. They didn't know her well enough to know that she hadn't set out to trap their son.

On the other hand, her parents didn't know Jesse very well, either, but they didn't blame him for the situation. Maybe because they at least knew her well enough to know that she wouldn't be here now if she didn't want to be. Baby or no baby, she wouldn't have married him if she didn't love him. She wondered if Jesse was ever going to figure out the same thing.

"How about New Year's Eve?" Nate suggested now. "We've taken a few reservations for December 31 already, but the honeymoon suite is still available."

"I promise you'll love it," Callie said to Maggie. "The painting's done and the window coverings are going to be installed this week. Then it's just the finishing touches—bedding, towels, decorations, et cetera. If you get a chance, you should stop by for an informal tour."

Maggie appreciated the overture. "I'd like that—thanks."

"I'll pencil you in for New Year's Eve, then," Nate decided.

To which Homer responded, "We must rescue the child."

Maggie looked at Jesse, not sure if the old man was referring to their unborn child or Noelle or one of Dallas's sons. The old man didn't appear to be looking at anyone in particular but was staring at his plate and shaking his head. "We must save the child."

"Why's he saying that?" Robbie asked Nina.

"I have no idea," she admitted to her youngest stepson.

"He's creepy," Ryder muttered.

Thankfully the boy was far enough away from Homer that the old man couldn't hear him. And, truthfully, Maggie couldn't help but agree, at least with respect to his behavior today.

"Who wants pie?" Laura asked brightly.

"I think we're going to skip dessert and get the kids home," Nina told her mother.

The family matriarch looked as if she wanted to protest, then she glanced at Homer again and finally nodded. "I'll get you some pie to take with you."

Nina and Dallas ushered the kids away from the table, and Homer turned his attention to Maggie.

"We must rescue the child," he told her, his tone imploring.

While his eyes were on her, his gaze was unfocused, and she realized he wasn't looking at her so much as past her.

Were his strange prognostications merely the ramblings of a crazy old man—or were his words intended as some kind of warning to her? Was it possible that the child he was referring to was her own? And if so, why did he think her child needed to be saved?

Chapter Fifteen

"I think we should invite Homer Gilmore to the table every time we have dinner with your parents," Maggie said to Jesse when they got home that evening.

"Why is that?" her husband asked, sounding amused.

"Because his sporadic outbursts meant that people were staring at him instead of me every once in a while."

"Was it that bad?"

She shrugged.

"Well, you survived your first Crawford family Thanksgiving relatively unscathed."

"Pun intended?"

He just grinned.

"Since it's a day to count our blessings, I'll say that your mother is a fabulous cook."

"And she always makes sure there's enough so that everyone has some leftovers to take home."

"She even packed a turkey sandwich for Homer Gilmore before your dad took him back to town."

"Did he freak you out?"

"Homer or your dad?"

Her husband chuckled. "Homer."

She shrugged again. "Not really. Although sometimes, the way he looked at me when he talked about saving the baby, I wondered if he was talking about our baby."

"I don't think even he knew what he was talking about," Jesse said. "He's just a crazy old man."

"Maybe," she allowed. "But he seemed sincerely worried. Does he have any children?"

"I have no idea. He's not originally from around here. And while it's hard to imagine him in a relationship with anyone, I suppose it's possible."

"I just wish there was something I could do to help him."

"Maybe you should keep your distance from him."

"He's not dangerous."

"Probably not," Jesse agreed. "But I'd rather you didn't take any chances."

"I wouldn't do anything to risk our baby," she assured him.

"I'm not just worried about the baby."

She looked up at him, obviously surprised by his statement.

"Don't you realize how much I care about you, too?"

Care. There it was—a four-letter word that described his feelings for her. Unfortunately, it wasn't the four-letter word she'd been hoping to hear.

"Well, I'm not going to let anything happen to me or our baby," she said lightly.

He nodded. "Good. Now, how about a turkey sandwich?"

She shook her head. "I can't believe you're hungry again already."

"Turkey sandwiches are a Thanksgiving evening tradition."

"Not for me," she told him. "I couldn't eat another bite."

"How about pie?"

She started to shake her head again, paused. "Pumpkin?"

He chuckled. "We've got apple and pumpkin."

"Maybe just a sliver," she allowed, and followed him to the kitchen.

"Sit," he said, pointing to the breakfast bar. "I'll get it for you."

She sat. He cut a slice of the pie his mother had sent home, slid it onto a plate, added a fork and set it on the counter in front of her.

"I said a sliver," she reminded him.

"You're eating for two."

Actually, her doctor had warned her that was a fallacy, but considering the fact that her weight wasn't an issue— not yet, anyway—she picked up the fork and dug into the pie without further comment.

"I wish we had some of that mac and cheese left over," he said. "I barely got to sample it."

"It was a hit with the kids," she agreed.

"Not just the kids—even Brad had two helpings."

"But he wouldn't try the coleslaw."

Jesse just shrugged and washed down his sandwich with a tall glass of milk.

She expected him to push away from the table and escape to the barn with the excuse of one chore or another. Sure enough, he slid back his chair and stood up to clear away both of their plates, but then he surprised her by asking, "Do you want to watch some of the football game with me?"

She shook her head. "It's been a long day and I'm ready for bed."

"Are you feeling okay? You didn't overdo it, did you?"

"I'm fine," she assured him. "Just…tired."

And she was—not just physically, but emotionally. She was tired of wanting what she knew she couldn't have, tired of pretending that their marriage was something it wasn't, tired of hoping that he might one day love her the same way that she loved him.

It was her own fault. He'd told her from the beginning that he didn't want to fall in love—he just wanted their baby to have two parents.

It had seemed like a reasonable request at the time, but after almost two weeks of living together, so close and yet with so much distance between them, she realized this was going to be more difficult than she'd anticipated. Not just difficult, but painful, and she wasn't sure that she could continue like this for much longer.

They'd been married for twelve days and living like roommates. She thought they'd made some progress today. They'd spent several hours together, shared some quiet moments and comfortable silences. And he'd admitted that he cared about her. True, it was a long way from caring to loving, but she had to believe it was a step in the right direction.

Maybe she should stay up with him, at least for a little while. But being near Jesse wreaked havoc on her mind and her heart. What she really needed was distance—some time away from him to figure out what she really wanted and needed.

"I talked to my mom yesterday," she told him. "She invited me to LA for a shopping trip. Well, the invitation was to both of us, but I don't imagine that would be your idea of fun."

"It's not," he agreed. "And it seems a long way to go to do some shopping."

"Aside from the fact that I'd also get to spend some time with my parents, there are some fabulous baby stores in SoCal."

"Rust Creek Falls might not be a shopping mecca," he acknowledged, "but it has other advantages."

"I wasn't making a comparison."

But obviously he thought that she was, because he said, "I just wanted to remind you that this is a great place to raise a child.

"That's why I'm here," she reminded him. "So that we can raise our child in Rust Creek Falls, together."

"You're sure this is where you want to be?"

"This is exactly where I want to be," she said, wanting to reassure him. But then she realized that while it was true, it wasn't the whole truth. "Or *almost* where I want to be."

He frowned at the clarification. "Almost?"

She hesitated, doubts creeping in. Did she really want to go down this path without knowing where it might lead? But she decided that she did, because it beat the alternative of continuing to live the way they'd been living for almost two weeks. She hadn't married Jesse so they could live separate lives under the same roof.

She'd married him because she loved him and she wanted to be his wife in every sense of the word. But she didn't think he was quite ready for that heartfelt declaration just yet, so she only said, "I'd rather be in the bed across the hall from where I've been sleeping."

Across the hall was…his bed.

Jesse's gaze locked with hers, silently seeking—begging for—confirmation.

She didn't falter, didn't blink, and in the depths of her eyes he saw a reflection of the same desire that hummed in his veins. She wanted him—and he wanted her. He would be a fool to turn down what she was offering, and he never liked to be a fool.

But he realized now that he had been. Living in close proximity to Maggie since the wedding had been a delicious torture. She'd been close enough to touch, but he hadn't been certain she wanted his touch. He'd let himself be swayed by her brother's concern that she didn't know what she wanted instead of asking her what she wanted.

"I put your stuff in the other room because I didn't want to assume we'd share a bed just because we were married."

"I kind of hoped we'd share a bed because we wanted to," she told him. "If that is what you wanted."

"It's what I wanted—what I want," he confirmed. "I haven't stopped wanting you since the first day I saw you, and believe me, I've tried."

"Why?"

"Because I pushed you into marriage, and then it bothered me to think that you only married me because I pushed."

"If you knew me better, you'd know that nobody pushes me to do something I don't want to do."

"You wanted to marry me?"

She nodded. "I've never felt about anyone else the way I feel about you. And I've never experienced anything like the pleasure I've known in your arms."

In response to that, he lifted her into his arms and carried her to his bedroom.

He set her back on her feet beside the bed and lowered his mouth to hers. Her eyes drifted shut as her lips parted, welcoming a deeper kiss. Her tongue danced with his, a sensual rhythm that had his blood pounding in his veins, hot and demanding.

It took him a minute to figure out the wrap-style dress she was wearing. He thoroughly enjoyed running his hands over her torso, tracing her feminine curves in an effort to find the hidden zipper, but he really wanted to feel her bare skin beneath his palms. When he finally discovered the tie at her side—when she finally guided his searching hands to it—he nearly chuckled with giddy relief. With one quick tug, the knot loosened and the fabric parted. Then he was touching *her*, and the silky softness of her skin was even more tantalizing than he remembered.

He pushed the dress off her shoulders and let it fall to the floor, then he took a step back to look at her. She was wearing a pale pink bra, matching bikini panties and those thigh-high stockings that he'd always suspected were designed to drive a man to his knees. Literally.

He dropped to the floor in front of her, splayed his palms on her belly then slid them around to her back, pulling her closer to kiss her belly. Then his mouth moved lower to nuzzle the sweet heat between her thighs. Maggie sucked in a breath. He stroked her with his tongue, through the thin barrier of lace, and felt her thigh muscles quiver. He wanted her to tremble for him, but he didn't want her to sink to the floor.

He rose to his feet again and peeled away her bra, her panties, one stocking and the other. Then he eased her back onto the mattress and started to lower himself over her.

She lifted her hands, holding him away. "I want you naked, too," she told him.

He quickly stripped away his own clothes, then glanced at her with his brows raised. She answered his silent question with a smile and lifted her arms to embrace him.

He kissed her again, softly, sweetly. "You are so beautiful," he told her.

When Jesse looked at her the way he was looking at her right now, with warmth and affection in his gaze, Maggie felt beautiful. When he touched her the way he was touching her now, gently and reverently, she knew he saw her that way.

But if she was beautiful, he was breathtaking.

Maybe the life of a rancher wasn't as romantic as it was

depicted in the movies, but there wasn't any big-screen star who could hold a candle to Jesse Crawford. She let her hands roam over him, absorbing the smooth texture of bronzed skin stretched taut over all those glorious muscles, sculpted not in some Hollywood gym to look like a cowboy but through years of hard work actually *being* a cowboy.

She'd never known anyone like him, had never felt the way she felt with him, and the memory of what he had done—could do—to her body left her breathless and aching for him.

"Jesse…please."

"I will please you," he promised.

And he did. He made his way down her body, kissing and caressing every inch of her. Loving her with his mouth and his hands until everything inside of her twisted and tightened—and released.

He held her close—he was her anchor in the storm as endless waves of sensation washed over her. When those waves gradually subsided to ripples, he finally parted her thighs and buried himself in the wet heat between them, and the storm started all over again.

As they moved together in the thrillingly familiar rhythm of lovemaking, she felt connected to him in a way that was so much more than physical. And the way he looked at her, their gazes linked as tangibly as their bodies, she was sure that he must feel it, too.

Afterward, he held her tight against him, as if he couldn't bear to let her go. And she fell asleep listening to his heart beating, steady and strong, beneath her cheek and knew she was exactly where she wanted to be.

Maggie wasn't sure why she'd awakened—a quick glance at the clock on the bedside table confirmed that it was still early. Not surprisingly, Jesse was already up—and getting ready to walk out the door.

"Where are you going?"

"You're awake."

"After last night, I didn't expect to wake up alone." She sat up, tugging the sheet to cover her breasts.

"I got a message from Sutter."

"It's the day after Thanksgiving—a holiday for almost everyone in this country who doesn't work in retail."

"One of his friends has a yearling with some behavioral issues and he asked me to take a look at him," he said, as if that explained everything.

"And you have to go right now?"

"I told him I would."

And because Jesse was nothing if not a man of his word, she nodded. "When do you think you'll be back?"

"I don't really know."

It wasn't just the noncommittal response, it was the way his gaze kept shifting away, as if he couldn't bear to look at her, as if he was already out the door.

No—she wasn't going to jump to conclusions. They'd had a fabulous night together. She wasn't going to assume anything was wrong and sabotage the closeness they'd shared.

"Will you be home for lunch?"

"Probably."

But he didn't say that he'd keep her posted, and he didn't kiss her goodbye. He just said, "I'll see you later," and then he walked out the door.

She sat there for another minute, naked in his bed, staring at the empty doorway through which he'd disappeared and trying to make sense of what had just happened. But she couldn't, and tears welled up along with her frustration.

She didn't understand what was going on with him.

The night before, she'd felt so connected to him, not just physically but emotionally. She'd been certain that they'd turned a corner, that they were finally going to start living as husband and wife, building a life and preparing for the birth of their child together.

She'd expected to wake up in his arms; she'd even hoped they might make love again. She knew he had things to do around the ranch, that even on the day after Thanksgiving, stalls needed to be mucked out and animals fed, so she didn't expect he'd stay in bed with her all day. But she'd hoped he'd at least show *some* reluctance to leave her side.

Instead, he'd already been up and dressed and on his way out the door when she'd awakened. She wasn't just hurt by his disappearing act, she was baffled. Why was he so anxious to put distance between them? Did he really not have any feelings for her?

No, she didn't believe that. There was no way he could have kissed her and touched her and loved her the way he had unless he felt something. But she was tired of guessing the breadth and depth of those feelings. She couldn't keep doing this—she couldn't keep putting herself out there only to have him pull back every time they started to get close. She couldn't continue to live under the same roof with the man she loved if he didn't feel the same way.

She dried her tears and picked up the phone.

When the call connected at the other end, she took a deep breath and said, "Nina—I need to ask you a huge favor."

Jesse was more than halfway to Traub Stables before he finally acknowledged the question that had been hammering at his mind since he'd responded to Sutter's text: *What was he doing?*

Why had he walked away from the beautiful—and

naked—woman who was still in his bed? What was he afraid of?

Maggie wasn't Shaelyn. The woman he'd married wasn't anything like the girl he'd been engaged to for a short time so many years before. Maggie was smart and beautiful, warm and compassionate, sexy and fun. She was also making a real effort to meet people and make friends, to fit in—and she was succeeding. He'd heard nothing but positive comments from everyone who had got to know her, his brothers and sisters all liked her, and even his parents were starting to come around.

And most significant to Jesse, she'd left her job and her family in LA and moved to Rust Creek Falls so that they could raise their baby together. He'd been so grateful for that decision he hadn't really asked why. He hadn't dared let himself hope that she'd made the choices she had because she loved him—as he loved her.

And with sudden clarity, he realized that was exactly what he'd been afraid of.

They'd both agreed to this legal union in order to give their baby a family. He'd made it clear that he didn't want to fall in love. But apparently his heart hadn't got that memo, because that was exactly what had happened.

He should have known, from day one, that he was fighting a losing battle. Because he'd started falling the first day he met her—no, even before then. The first time he saw her.

Had he really thought he could share a life with her—his home, his bed—and keep his emotions out of it? If so, he was obviously a bigger fool than he thought.

He might not have wanted to fall in love, but that's what had happened. And now he wanted more. He wanted everything.

So why was he pulled over on the side of the road near

Traub Stables instead of with Maggie, telling her how he felt?

His tires kicked up gravel as he made a quick U-turn and headed toward home.

As he took the stairs two at a time, he could hear Maggie moving around in the spare bedroom. He paused in the doorway to catch his breath and saw she was removing her clothes from the dresser. At first, he actually thought she might be moving her things across the hall to his room.

Then he saw the suitcases open on the bed.

For just a moment, his heart actually stopped beating.

"What are you doing?"

She looked up, and he saw the wet streaks on her cheeks, evidence of the tears she'd recently shed. His heart, beating once again but in a slow, painful rhythm now, twisted inside his chest, because he knew that he was responsible. He'd hurt her and made her cry, and he'd never wanted to do that.

"This is your house," she said to him. "Instead of you always making excuses to run off, I figured it made more sense for me to go."

"Go," he echoed numbly, not wanting to believe it. He'd rushed home to tell her that he loved her—and she was leaving him? He felt as if she'd reached inside his chest and ripped his heart out.

And yet, there was a part of him that wasn't really surprised, that understood he'd been on tenterhooks since their wedding in anticipation of this exact moment. But expecting it didn't mean that he was prepared for it—especially not now. Not when he'd finally accepted how much she meant to him.

"Don't do this," he said. "Please, don't go."

She folded a sweater and placed it in the suitcase. "I can't live like this."

"I know we have some things to figure out, but we can't do that if you're not here."

"I'm not the one who rushed out of here this morning," she pointed out to him.

"I told you where I was going."

"I know," she admitted. "And the fact that you'd rather spend time with a horse than me says everything that needs to be said."

"That's not true," he denied.

"Isn't it?"

"No," he insisted.

But she continued to pack.

"If you won't stay for me, please stay for our baby."

"I'm not going to keep you from our baby," she assured him.

"You don't have to—the twelve hundred miles between here and Los Angeles will do it for you."

"I'm not going back to LA."

"You're not?"

"My job and my life are here now. I have no intention of leaving town. I'm just going to Nina's apartment over the store until I can find something else."

He was torn between relief and confusion. "Why would you stay in Rust Creek Falls if you're not staying with me?"

"I'm staying in Rust Creek Falls because I made a promise to Ben Dalton when he hired me, and I don't renege on my promises."

"Really?" he challenged. "What about the promise you made to me when we exchanged wedding vows?"

She zipped up the first suitcase, and when she looked up at him, the tears that shone in her eyes were like another dagger to his heart. "I would have been happy to love, honor and cherish you for the rest of my life," she said softly, "if I thought there was any chance you might someday feel the same way."

"Wait a minute." He pried her fingers off the handle of her suitcase, linked them with his. "Are you saying that you love me?"

"I would never have married you if I didn't." She kept her gaze riveted on the suitcase as she responded. "But I can't live with someone who doesn't feel the same way."

"But I do," he told her. "I was just too stubborn and stupid to admit—even to myself—how I felt." He nudged her down onto the edge of the mattress, then sat beside her. "I fell for you, hard and fast, even before we were officially introduced. I know it sounds crazy, but it's true. And when you shook my hand—it was like something inside of me just clicked."

She eyed him warily, as if she didn't trust what he was saying. "I thought it was just me."

"And I thought it was just me—until you kissed me."

That first kiss was tame compared to the intimacies they'd shared since then, but her cheeks colored at the memory.

"I think I fell in love with you that night," he told her. "The next morning, I was so happy, certain it was only the first night of many. Then I found out that you were going back to LA that same day.

"And yes, I wondered if our relationship would end the same way my relationship with Shaelyn did. But when you promised to come back, I believed you. I *wanted* to believe you."

"And then I kept making excuses as to why I couldn't," she realized.

He nodded. "And I thought you were brushing me off. I figured you'd gone back to LA and realized you couldn't consider giving up your glamorous life in the city to settle down with a quiet cowboy."

"You barely got a glimpse of my life in LA," she said. "Or you would have known that it wasn't very glamorous."

"But you had palm trees and temperatures that rarely ever dip below freezing."

She managed a small smile. "There is that."

"My point is that I was so worried that you wouldn't want to stay here, with me, that I acted like an idiot in an unsuccessful attempt to protect my heart."

"Are you done acting like an idiot?"

"Probably not completely," he warned. "But I'm done pretending that I don't love you with my whole heart, because I do. And if you can forgive me for being such an idiot, I promise that I will never give you reason to doubt my feelings for you ever again."

"I can forgive you."

He leaned forward and brushed his lips against hers. "I love you, Maggie."

"Show me," she said.

He shoved the suitcases aside, onto the floor, and complied with her request.

Afterward, while their bodies were still joined together and sated from lovemaking, he held her as if he would never let her go. Maggie, her head cushioned on his shoulder, exhaled a soft, contented sigh.

Jesse stroked a hand over her hair, down her back. "I'm sorry."

"For what?"

"Missing out on almost two weeks of mornings just like this because I was an idiot."

"I thought we moved past that part."

"I guess it's easier for you than for me."

She pulled back, just far enough to prop herself up on an elbow so she could see his face. "Well, stop beating up on the man I love."

He lifted a hand to cradle her cheek. "What did I ever do to deserve you?"

"You loved me," she said simply.

"I do," he told her. "You are everything to me—my wife, the mother of my children, my partner in life and the woman I love, for now and forever."

"And you are everything to me," she replied. "My husband, the father of—" Her breath caught as she felt a little flutter low in her belly. "Oh."

His brows lifted. "Oh?"

The flutter happened again, and she took his hand and placed it over the curve of her belly. "Can you feel that?"

"What?" And then he felt it, too. His eyes went wide, his lips curved. "Is that...our baby?"

She nodded. "I think she's happy that her mommy and daddy are finally, truly together."

"And always will be," Jesse promised.

Epilogue

"Thanks for helping me out with this," Nina said to Maggie and Jesse. "The Tree of Hope was a big success last year and I wanted to do it again, but decorating with a baby underfoot turned out to be more difficult than I imagined."

The newlyweds, who had stopped in at Crawford's just to pick up a few staples before Nina conscripted them into service, were happy to help.

"This time next year, we'll have a little one of our own to interfere with our decorating," Maggie said to her husband, already anticipating that day.

Jesse grinned. "An eight-month-old baby whose mother graduated summa cum laude from Stanford Law will probably be directing our every move."

"Unless she takes after her father," his sister teased.

Maggie hooked another ornament over a branch and turned to her sister-in-law. "She?"

"You've slipped up and used the feminine pronoun a few times," Nina told her. "But if the baby's gender is supposed to be a secret, I won't tell."

"I don't know that we'd planned to keep it a secret," Maggie admitted. "But I didn't realize I'd given it away so quickly."

"We only found out at Maggie's ultrasound appointment last week," Jesse told his sister.

Since then—and since his wife's move across the hall

had happily turned "his" bedroom into "their" bedroom—they'd started to set up the nursery in anticipation of their daughter's arrival. Maggie had picked out new paint for the walls and ordered curtains from an online home decor warehouse, and the cradle Jesse had made was already set up in the middle of the room with a big pink bow tied around it.

"Well, I'm thrilled," Nina said. "Because I know Noelle will love having a female cousin to hang out with."

"Does that mean you've given up on the idea of giving her a little sister?"

"No, I still want another baby," Nina confided. "And I think my husband is on board with the plan, but all of the evidence would suggest that Dallas begets boys."

"At least you know Noelle will always have three big brothers to look out for her."

"And I'm sure they'll look out for their little cousin, too," Nina said.

The bell at the front of the store jingled as the door opened and Winona Cobbs entered.

The renowned psychic was a regular customer, usually stopping into the store a couple of times a week to pick up a few things. But this time she chose a cart instead of a basket and moved purposefully through the aisles, filling it with items. Toilet paper, bottled water, canned goods.

"Anticipating a long winter?" Nina asked her.

"There's a storm coming," Winona said.

"Considering it's nearly December in Montana, I'd say you're probably right," Jesse noted drily.

The older woman sent him a dark look as she pushed her cart toward the checkout. "A storm isn't always connected to the weather."

"That was...odd," Maggie said.

"Winona's odd," Nina said, as if that explained everything. "But she wouldn't have the reputation she does if her predictions weren't accurate at least once in a while."

"Even a broken clock can tell time twice a day," Jesse noted.

"You don't believe she has a gift?" Maggie asked him.

"I'm more concerned about finishing this tree so the deserving kids in the community will have gifts," he said, resuming his task.

After the tree was done, Jesse and Maggie headed toward home—just as big fluffy flakes started to fall from the sky, adding to the white blanket that already covered everything in sight.

"It looks like our first Christmas together is definitely going to be a white one," Maggie commented.

"I feel like we've already had Christmas, because I got the greatest gift ever when you became my wife." He gave her a slow, sexy smile that made her knees weak. "And the best part is that you're a gift that can be unwrapped again and again."

She lifted a brow. "Is that a promise?"

"Absolutely," he assured her.

And when they got home, he proved it.

Again and again.

* * * * *

THE RELUCTANT HEIRESS

SARA ORWIG

Many thanks to Stacy Boyd and Maureen Walters.

Prologue

"I don't have a clue why I'm here," Garrett Cantrell, company CFO, said at the family gathering in the Dallas office of Delaney Enterprises.

"Because Sophia Rivers is our father's child. She's as stubborn as Dad ever was," Will Delaney stated, combing his fingers through his black hair.

"We won't give up. There's too much at stake," Ryan Delaney added, resting one booted foot on his knee. "We can be as stubborn as she is. There has to be a way to reach her."

"We need to outsmart her instead of the other way around," Zach Delaney grumbled.

"Right," said Will. "That's why I asked Garrett to join us."

"I'm sure finding out you have a half sister at the reading of your dad's will was a shock," Garrett said, "but you should face the fact that she doesn't want to meet any of you. I'd say give it up."

"If we don't get her on the board of the Delaney Foundation, we can kiss our inheritances goodbye," Zach snapped. "Also, she's family. We have a sister—all these years."

"I agree," Will added. "She's part of our family and we'd all like to know her."

"Even if she doesn't want to know you?" Garrett asked.

"I think that's because of Dad and not anything we've done. We just want to unite this family and we don't stand a chance if she won't speak to us," Will said. "Each of us has tried and failed to make contact with her. I think the next thing is to send someone neutral."

Garrett straightened in his chair, his good humor vanishing. "Go through your dad's lawyer. She communicates with Grady."

"Her attorney communicates with Grady," Will replied drily. "Grady has never met the lady."

"The bottom line is, we want our inheritances," Ryan stated. "She's costing each of us four billion dollars. Too much to blow off."

As Garrett looked at the Delaneys, he reflected on how his life had been tied to theirs from the day he was born. His father's life had been closely linked with the family patriarch, Argus Delaney. Besides ties of work and family, Will Delaney, the Delaney CEO, was Garrett's best friend. Garrett had been raised to feel indebted to the Delaneys, just as his dad had felt obligated. As he thought about what they were about to ask of him, his dread grew exponentially. "I suggest the three of you try again to meet her," Garrett said.

"C'mon, Garrett. You can contact her because your

name isn't Delaney. Spend time with her, get to know her, find out why she's resisting, and we'll take it from there," Will said. "Just open the door for us. Go to Houston. You have a family business and a house there. It's a perfect plan."

"I own the property management business in Houston—I don't work there. Give it up, guys. Don't ask me to do what you can't do."

"We think you *can* do this," Will argued. "You've been our spokesperson many times. We'll make it worthwhile for you. Help us get her on the board and it's another five hundred million for you."

Garrett was already wealthy— He didn't care about the money. But he couldn't turn down the brothers because his obligation to the Delaneys ran deep. He sighed as Will handed him a manila folder.

Garrett looked at a picture of a raven-haired, brown-eyed beauty. *Maybe their request isn't so bad after all,* he thought.

"If she cooperates, she will inherit three billion dollars. It's not like you're trying to cause her trouble," Ryan pointed out.

"How can she turn down that kind of money?" Zach asked, shaking his head.

"She must be angry as hell," Garrett remarked. "That kind of anger isn't going to change easily."

"We have to try," Will stated. "Will you do it?"

Garrett glanced at the picture again. He had just inherited three billion from their father. Will was his closest friend. How could he refuse to help them now?

"Garrett, we're desperate. And we have a time limit," Ryan said.

"All right," Garrett replied reluctantly. "I can't say no to any of you."

There were thanks from all and a high five from Will, who grinned. "Everything's going for you. You're not a Delaney."

"I might as well be one," Garrett grumbled. "I don't think your half sister will be one degree happier with me than she was with any of you." Garrett shook his head. "Meeting Sophia Rivers is doomed from the start."

One

Sophia Rivers sipped champagne and gazed beyond the circle of friends surrounding her. Her small Houston gallery was filled with guests viewing her art and helping her celebrate the second anniversary of her gallery's opening. The crowd was the perfect size, and she was completely satisfied with the turnout.

"Sophia, I have a question."

She turned to see Edgar Hollingworth, a father to her and a mentor, as well as a man whom she and her mother had been friends with before she ever moved into the art world. "Excuse me," she said to the group around her, and stepped away.

"Edgar, what can I do for you?" she said to the tall, thin man.

"You looked as if you needed rescuing," he said quietly. "You also look ravishing. The black and white is striking on you, Sophia."

"Thank you," she replied, shaking her long black hair away from her face.

"Shall we at least act as if I've asked you about a painting?" Edgar motioned toward the opposite side of the room and she smiled as she strolled with him. "You have a sizable crowd tonight. I'm glad you were able to make it. I haven't seen you in a long time."

"I hadn't planned to come until about three hours ago. I've been in New Mexico, painting. Who's the couple ahead to our right?" she asked.

"The Winstons. They're probably on your guest list because they bought a painting recently."

"Now how do you know that?"

"I sold it to them," he said, smiling at her, causing creases to fan from the corners of his blue eyes. "I still think you should move your gallery nearer mine. Our galleries would complement each other."

Sophia smiled at the familiar conversation that always ended with her saying no. "I do appreciate your gallery carrying my art. You were the first and I'll always be indebted to you for that."

"You would have been in a gallery anyway whether it was my place or another's. You have a fine talent."

"Thank you, Edgar," she said.

Sophia glanced around the room again and was slightly surprised when she saw another unfamiliar face. Except this one took her breath away.

Perhaps the tallest man in the room, he stood in profile. His brown hair had an unruly wave to it and his hawk nose and rugged looks made her think instantly that he would be an interesting subject to paint. He held a champagne flute in his hand as he looked at a painting.

"There's someone else I don't know," she said.

"His name is Garrett Cantrell. We talked awhile. He

has a property management business here and he's a financial adviser. He, too, bought one of your paintings last week. Another satisfied customer."

A woman approached Edgar, who excused himself, leaving Sophia to contemplate the tall, brown-haired stranger, strolling slowly around the gallery. She suddenly found herself crossing the room to stand near him.

"I hope you like it," she said.

"I do," he replied, turning to look at her with thickly lashed eyes the color of smoke. Her breath caught. Up close he was even more fascinating—handsome in a craggy way—and his gray eyes were unforgettable.

"That's good," she replied, smiling and extending her hand while still held in his compelling gaze. "Because I'm the artist. I'm Sophia Rivers."

"Garrett Cantrell," he said, shaking her hand. His warm fingers wrapped around hers and an uncustomary tingle ran to her toes. She gazed into his smoke-colored eyes and couldn't get her breath. Her gaze slipped lower to his mouth. She wondered what it would be like to kiss him. The temperature in the room rose. She knew she should look away, yet she didn't want to stop studying him.

"The artist herself. And even more beautiful than your paintings," he said as he released her hand. "You've caught the atmosphere of the West."

"It's New Mexico, around Taos. And thank you," she added. Her pulse jumped at his compliment and she was keenly aware of him as they moved to view another painting.

"You're very good at what you do. I look at these and feel as if I'm there instead of standing in a steamy metropolitan city."

"That's what I hope to achieve. So this is the first time you've been to my gallery."

"Yes, but I own one of your pictures," he said, moving to the next painting. "You must spend a lot of time in New Mexico. I assume you have a gallery there?"

"Actually, I don't. I intend to open one early next year, but I haven't launched into that yet. It will take time away from painting."

"I understand." He sipped champagne and moved to another painting. "Ah, I really like this one," he said and she looked at a familiar work. It was an aged cart in front of a brown adobe house with bright hollyhocks growing around it. A small mesquite tree stood at one corner of the house.

He looked at the next series of paintings. "These are my favorites. The Native American ones," he said, indicating a man with a long black braid standing beside a horse in an open stretch of ground dotted with mesquite. Overhead, white clouds billowed against a blue sky and a large hawk sailed with widespread wings.

"That's a great painting," he said. "The light and shadows are an interesting contrast." Happy with his compliment, she smiled. "I'll take this one. Any chance the artist will help me decide where to hang it? A dinner is in the offering."

Again, she had a flutter in her heartbeat. "We're strangers, Mr. Cantrell."

"It's Garrett. We can fix the 'strangers' part. When you can get away tonight, why don't we go around the corner to the hotel bar and have a drink? Tomorrow evening we'll hang my painting and then I'll take you to dinner."

"You don't waste time. I'd be delighted to have a drink tonight. I should be through here in another hour."

"Excellent," he said, glancing at his watch.

"I'll get one of my staff to wrap your painting and we can deliver it tomorrow if you'd like."

"That will be fine. The delivery person can leave it with my gatekeeper."

She smiled and left to find one of her employees. "Barry, would you help Mr. Cantrell? He wants number 32. Please take care of the sale and get the delivery information."

She had to resist the temptation to glance over her shoulder at Garrett.

Instead, she strolled around, speaking to customers and friends, meeting Edgar again.

"I see Cantrell bought a painting."

"Yes. I'm having a drink with him after this."

"That was quick," he said, glancing across the room. "Seemed nice enough. Wealthy enough, too. Last week he bought your painting from me without hesitation. Now, a week later, he's buying another one. The man knows what he likes."

"I see the Santerros. I have to speak to them."

"Have fun this evening," Edgar said as she left him.

"I intend to," she stated softly. "Garrett Cantrell," she repeated, glancing back to see him at the desk, handing a business card to Barry. Her gaze drifted over his long legs while her heartbeat quickened. Dressed in a navy suit with a snowy dress shirt and gold cuff links, the handsome man was a standout even in the well-dressed crowd.

She spent the next hour all too aware of where Garrett stood.

When she saw him talking to a couple she recognized, she waited until he moved away, then worked her way around to them.

"How are the Trents tonight?" she asked.

"Fine," Jason Trent answered.

"We love your new paintings," Meg Trent said. "Thanks for the invitation."

"Thank you for attending. I saw you talking to Garrett Cantrell. I just met him, but it looked as if you two already know him."

"We do," Jason replied. "I lease a building from his company. He keeps up with whether everything is going smoothly, which it is. Good bunch to work with."

"We're getting one of your watercolors for the family room," Meg said. "It's the one with the little boy and the burro."

"I'm glad you like that one. I hope you enjoy having it in your home."

"You're a prolific painter," Jason remarked.

"I enjoy it."

"More than the financial world," he said, smiling.

"I have no regrets about changing careers."

"That's what I keep trying to talk Meg into doing— She'd love to have a dress shop."

"Accounting seems to hold fewer risks. You're established now, but weren't you nervous when you started?" Meg asked.

"I suppose, but it was absolutely worth it," Sophia said. "It was nice to see you both," she added, moving on, aware of Garrett across the gallery talking to two people. She wondered whether he knew them, too.

She stopped at the desk to look at his card. "Cantrell Properties Inc." It was a plain card with a downtown address, logo and phone number, but little else. She returned it to the drawer.

Garrett appeared at her side. "Can you leave? You still have quite a few people here."

"I can leave. My staff can manage quite well. They weren't expecting me to be here tonight anyway."

"I'm glad you are," he said.

"We can go out the back way and it'll be less noticeable." She led him through a door, down a hallway that opened onto offices, a mailroom and a studio and out the back into a parking lot where five cars were parked. Four tall lampposts illuminated the area as brightly as if it were day. A security guard sat in a cubicle watching a small television. He stepped to the door.

"Good night, Miss Rivers."

"I'll be back after a while to get my car, Teddy."

"Sure thing. Evening, sir," he said, nodding at Garrett who greeted him in return.

"My car is in front," Garrett said, taking her arm.

"It's a nice night. We can walk if you want," she said, pleasantly aware of his height because she was taller than some men she knew and as tall as many.

"I saw you talking to Meg and Jason Trent. Jason said he leased property from you."

"Yes, he's a good tenant," he said. "They like your art."

"I've had a gratifying response from people," she said.

They entered the bright hotel lobby, then the darkened bar where a pianist played a ballad for couples who were dancing.

Garrett got a booth with a small lamp at the end of the table. It spilled a golden glow over his fascinating features, highlighting his prominent cheekbones and leaving the planes of his cheeks in dark shadows. She felt breathless again, a steady hum of excitement that she couldn't explain.

They ordered drinks—a cold beer for him and an

iced soda for her. When they came, he raised his glass in a toast. "Here's to a new friendship. May it grow."

"A toast to friendship," she repeated, touching his cold bottle lightly. She sipped her soda and set the glass down.

He reached across the table to take her hand, his warm fingers enveloping hers. Again, a current streaked through her like lightning. "Shall we dance?"

As she stood, he shed his coat and tie, folding them once on the seat of the booth.

Sophia followed him to the small dance floor and stepped into his embrace. Her hand was in his, her other hand on his shoulder, feeling the warmth of him through the fine cotton shirt. She enjoyed dancing around the floor, aware of how well they moved together. He was agile, light on his feet.

"I've been waiting all evening for this moment," he said, setting her heart fluttering again. She had never had such an instant and intense reaction to a man. "I'm glad I decided to come tonight. I didn't expect to see the artist, but I knew I would enjoy looking at your art. Now, the whole world has changed."

She smiled. "I don't think it's been a world-changing night," she said, though she actually agreed with him. She wasn't sure things would ever be the same after having met Garrett Cantrell.

"The night isn't over yet," he reminded her, obviously flirting.

She slanted him a look. "Perhaps you'll change my mind."

"That's a challenge I'll gladly take."

The ballad ended and a faster number began. Garrett released her and she put a little distance between them. The man had sexy moves that set her pulse at a faster pace. She was unable to tear her gaze from his until she forced herself to turn and the spell was broken.

By the time the music finished, she needed to catch her breath.

Garrett took her hand. "Shall we go back to our drinks?"

They returned to the booth. He loosened the top buttons of his shirt. The temperature climbed a notch and her desire revved with it.

Her cell phone chimed. She looked down, reading a brief text from Edgar.

How is your evening with G.C.? Call me when you get home. I promised Mom.

She had to laugh. "I have a text from my friend Edgar. You bought a painting of mine from him."

"Yes. I remember."

"He once promised my mom that he would look out for me and he's been like the proverbial mother hen ever since. He's checking on when I'll get home."

Garrett flashed a breathtakingly handsome smile. "Is he jealous?"

Shaking her head, she laughed. "Definitely not. Edgar always loved my mother. They dated some, but for Mom it was a good friend sort of thing. Then as my interest in art developed, Mom told Edgar. He became a friend and mentor, helping me in so many ways."

She sent a text back.

Go to bed, Edgar. I'm fine and he's fun.

"I let him know that I'm okay and we're having a pleasant time."

"A pleasant time. I'll have to try harder if I want to move that into the 'world-changing' arena."

She smiled as she put away her cell phone. "So tell me about yourself," she said.

"I grew up with the proverbial silver spoon. Well, my dad began to make big bucks when I was about seven years old. Life was easy in some ways."

"What wasn't easy?"

"My mom died when I was fifteen. My dad and I were close. I lost him this past summer."

"Sorry. It hurts. My mom died a couple of years ago."

"Your dad?"

"I never knew him," she said, her eyes becoming frosty as she answered him.

"I'm glad you and your mom were close. So how did you get into art?"

"It's my first love. I went to college, got a degree in accounting, got a good job, moved up. I began to invest my own money and did so well, I finally took over managing my mother's finances, which was far more than I had. Finance became my field, but art was—and is—my love. We have something else in common—our financial backgrounds."

"So we do."

"The difference is, you love it and pursue it. I wanted something else."

"Sometimes I think about something else, but I'm locked into where I am."

"What else do you think about doing?" she asked.

"Nothing serious. I'm where I should be, doing what I've been trained to do and have a knack for doing."

"There's something else you like," she persisted, tilting her head to study him. "I don't think it's art. I'll bet it's far removed from the world of property management."

"Yes, it is. It's not that big a deal for you to even try to guess. Someday when I retire, I'll make furniture. I like working with my hands."

"It's getting a little scary how alike we are," she said, noticing how his thick lashes heightened the striking effect of his gray eyes.

"Perhaps it's an omen indicating we will get along well."

"Usually, it's the other way around. Opposites attract."

"Well, I'll see where we're opposite—one thing, you're living your dream. I won't leave the business world."

"Why not?"

He shrugged a broad shoulder. "I was raised to do this. When Dad was alive, I wouldn't have changed for anything because it would have hurt him terribly. He hasn't been gone long and I just can't think about changing when I know how badly he wanted me to do what I'm doing. There are other reasons, too, but that's the biggest."

She nodded. "We're different there, all right. My mom was okay with the change I made. I'm sorry she didn't live to see the success I've been lucky enough to have, especially since she's the one who told me to chase my dream."

"Be thankful. I've been told the opposite all my life."

"I am thankful," she said, wondering about his life as the topic of conversation shifted. As she looked at him, desire smoldered, a steady flame. She knew he would kiss her tonight and she wanted him to.

"So there are no other men in your life?" he asked, tilting his head.

"No, no other men and you're not exactly in it either since I've known you all of a few hours."

"I'm in it now," he said in a tone of voice that stirred sparks. "So Mr. Right has not come along. And there's no one vying for that title."

"I'm definitely not looking for Mr. Right. The past few years I've been incredibly busy and my social life has suffered."

"I can understand about incredibly busy. And I'll see what I can do to remedy that a little for both of us."

"And what about the women in your life? You can't convince me there are none."

"There isn't anyone special, or even anyone really 'in' my life at this point. I'm free as a bird, as they say."

"Workaholic?"

"I'm not arguing that one."

When her phone chimed again with a text that the gallery was cleaned and closed, she noticed the late hour. "I didn't know the time. I should go home."

As they walked back to the gallery, Garrett stopped her. "Why don't I take you home? I'll pick you up for breakfast and bring you back to the gallery to get your car."

"That seems a lot of trouble for you."

"No trouble at all," he said, unlocking the door of a black sports car.

After a moment, she climbed in, gave Garrett her address and watched him drive, studying his hands with neatly trimmed nails. A gold cuff link glinted in the reflection of the dash lights.

They drove through a gated area and up the front drive of her sprawling house. He parked and came around to open the door for her. They crossed the porch and she unlocked the door before turning to face him.

"You have a nice home."

"Thanks. As you said, it's comfortable. It's too late to invite you in but I had a great time tonight."

"It's too early to exchange goodbyes," he said, slipping his arm around her waist to draw her close.

Sophia's heart raced as she looked up at him. His lower lip was full, sensual. She leaned slightly closer, pressing against him and closing her eyes as his mouth covered hers lightly, then firmly, his tongue thrusting into her mouth. A wave of longing rippled, tearing at her while she felt as if she were in free fall. Her breathing altered, heat pooled low in her. His kiss was demanding, enticing and she returned it. She moaned softly, the sound taken by his mouth on hers.

Her heart pounded so violently she was certain he could feel it. When she pressed against his lean, hard length, his arm tightened around her. Leaning over her, holding her tightly, he didn't let up. She was lost, consumed in kisses that were magical, that set her on fire.

One hand slipped down her back, a light caress, and the other was warm on the nape of her neck. His kisses were earth-shattering, rocking her world. She had never been kissed this way. She wanted to stay in his arms for hours.

Finally she leaned away to look at him. "Garrett, slow down," she whispered, caution and wisdom fighting to gain control over desire. All she wanted was to kiss him endlessly.

As he gazed at her intently, she realized that his ragged breathing matched her own.

"Sophia," he said, her name a hoarse whisper. "I

want you." The words—stark, honest and direct—set her pulse galloping.

"We have to say good-night," she declared. She had just met him and barely knew him. She should not fall into his arms instantly and lose all control.

Locks of his dark, unruly hair had tumbled on his forehead, escaping the neatly combed style he'd worn when she first saw him. She ached to run her hands through them.

Instead, she took a deep breath and stepped back. "We have to say good-night," she repeated. "I had a wonderful time."

"It was world-changing for me," he whispered, his voice still only a rasp. He framed her face with his hands. "I mean it. Tonight was a special night that I never, ever expected. I'd hoped to meet you but I never once thought I'd have an evening like this." As he spoke, his fingers combed lightly through her hair. His words carried a sincerity that made her heartbeat quicken again, his smoky, intense gaze consuming her.

"I didn't expect anything like this either," she whispered, wanting him with an urgency that shook her.

"When I walked into your gallery, I wanted to meet you for one reason. After meeting you, I want to be with you for an entirely different reason," he said.

He leaned down to kiss her again, passionately. When he released her, he stepped away, but his hand stayed on her shoulder as if he didn't want to break the physical contact with her.

"I'll see you in the morning. How's seven?"

She nodded, and he turned and strode away. She stared at him—broad shoulders, narrow waist, long legs, thick brown hair, handsome. The man took her breath and set her heart pounding.

"Good night, Garrett," she said softly. She closed the door and switched on lights while her lips tingled. Desire was a scorching flame. Garrett Cantrell. She would be with him again in just hours and yet she couldn't wait.

Her cell phone's tune signaled a call. She looked at the number with curiosity as she answered. Her heart missed a beat when she heard Garrett's deep voice.

She laughed. "You do know that we just parted?"

"We did. It now seems like a serious mistake. Tell me more about growing up, your dreams, your day tomorrow."

Smiling, she sat in a rocker in her bedroom, gazing at her shelves of familiar books and pictures. "I grew up in Houston. I've always dreamed of painting and having my own gallery. Tomorrow—"

"Wait a minute. Back up. You grew up in Houston. House? Apartment? Best friends through your school years or did you move a lot? Tell me about your life, Sophia."

When he said her name in his deep drawl, her pulse beat faster. "It can't possibly be that fascinating. I grew up in one house, went to neighborhood elementary schools and then private schools later. I had the same close friends through elementary and then new friends in the private school. See? All very routine and ordinary."

"There is absolutely nothing ordinary about you," he said, stirring another thrilling physical reaction in her that threw her completely off base. She wasn't used to feeling like this because of a man.

"What about you? You said you had it easy growing up?" she asked.

"I always went to private schools. I've had the same

best friend all my life since I was too young to remember. Our fathers were best friends. I've had the same family home my whole life. I'm an only child."

"We're so much alike, I'm surprised we can stand each other, Garrett." When he laughed, she felt her stomach drop, like she was in free fall. He was turning her inside out with just the sound of his voice.

"You're already living your dream. Do you feel fulfilled, complete?" he asked.

"I think people always want more and keep striving. I am very happy with my life, though, and what I do."

"Surely there's something else you want."

"Another successful gallery in Taos. I'd like to live in Santa Fe. But I already have a home and studio, and I have a cabin in the mountains near Questa, where I go for solitude to paint."

"The Questa cabin sounds isolated."

"No cell phone reception whatsoever, which is a plus. I have a caretaker. He and his family have a cabin close to mine, so there are people nearby. He has four dogs. Two take up with me when I'm there, so that's a bit of company. It's a good place to work with no interference—a good place to improve my skills as a painter."

"I'd say you can settle for how well you paint right now."

"No, I can definitely improve. So tell me about you, Garrett. Do you really dream of building furniture someday?"

"It's pushed to a burner so far back, it will take years to get to it."

As they talked, she moved to the window, switching off a lamp and gazing outside at the full moon. By the time she glanced at the clock, she was shocked to see it was half past three.

"Garrett, we have to get off the phone. It's after three a.m., and you're picking me up at seven."

"All right. Sophia, you're a remarkable woman," he said in a solemn tone. She suddenly had a funny feeling that he had expected something different from her.

"And you are a remarkable man," she replied softly. "Good night, Garrett. I will see you soon—very soon."

"Night, Sophia," he said, and was gone.

She turned off her phone and crawled into bed, Garrett dominating her thoughts completely. "Garrett," she whispered, enjoying saying his name while she thought about his magical kisses. She had never expected to meet someone like him tonight. This wasn't a time in her career to be distracted, yet he made her feel things she had never felt before. Morning couldn't come quickly enough. She was already anxious to be with him again.

Two

Setting aside his phone to strip to his briefs, Garrett replayed the night, thinking of the first moment he had seen Sophia at the gallery. In high heels, she had to be six feet tall. Her midnight hair was straight and fell freely over her shoulders in a black cascade.

A dramatic black-and-white dress left one tan shoulder bare. The slit in the straight skirt revealed long, shapely legs with each step. Her mother's Native American blood had given her smooth, olive skin, beautiful raven hair and her prominent cheekbones, yet she bore a striking resemblance to Will and reminded Garrett of Zach in her forthright, practical manner.

From the first moment she had captivated him. Dancing with her had fanned his desire until he ached to kiss her.

He shook his head to clear his thoughts.

While he hadn't lied to her, he had still deceived

her by not mentioning his ties to the Delaneys and his mission in Houston. At the moment she could be at her computer, looking him up and discovering he was an executive with Delaney Enterprises. A chill slithered through Garrett, turning him to ice. By breakfast time, she might already know the truth.

He didn't want her to find out that way. He wanted to tell her about his relationship with the Delaneys himself. But if he did, he wouldn't see her again, and neither the Delaneys nor she would get their inheritances.

His thoughts drifted to her soft, lush curves, her silky, midnight hair and her large, dark brown eyes...

After twenty more minutes of tossing and turning, he went to his indoor pool and swam laps, trying to stop thinking about Sophia yet wanting morning to come so he could see her again.

What if he did tell her about the Delaneys at breakfast? Maybe they already had enough of a connection that she'd agree to meet them.

Who was he kidding? Anyone who felt strongly enough to turn down billions wouldn't change her mind because of a few kisses and one exciting night.

Glumly, he executed a flip-turn and mulled it over as he swam another lap. Three billion dollars—no one could turn down money like that, yet she had. Why? Was her anger at Argus Delaney that deep?

From what the P.I. had unearthed, Argus had continued seeing her mother until she died. At the end of her life, he had done everything to keep her comfortable, taking care of her medical bills and seeing that she had the best care possible. Why was Sophia so bitter? She didn't seem a bitter, grudge-holding type. Sophisticated, intelligent, an inner core of steel, obviously hardworking, optimistic—all were qualities that he would use to describe her. It seemed difficult to imagine that she would have enough anger and hate to give up a three-billion-dollar inheritance.

He had to confess or risk Sophia discovering on her own the deception that grew larger with every passing hour.

Yet if he told her now, it was the end of what they'd only just started. And the termination of hope for the Delaneys.

Trying to shut off his nagging thoughts, he swore and swam harder.

It was another half hour before he was dry, sitting in his bedroom and staring out the window. Sleep eluded him. Worse, he was no closer to a decision about what he would do in a few hours when he saw her. Either way—tell her or wait—their relationship was doomed.

In spite of his disturbed sleep, the next morning he was eager to see Sophia again. His uncustomary inability to reach a decision about her added to his restlessness. Before he left to pick her up, Garrett phoned Will and gave him an update.

"Fantastic. So she can be civil and you like her," Will said. "That's promising."

"Will, for her to cut all of you off and lose her inheritance, her anger must run really deep. I can't imagine being able to persuade her to change her mind."

"We're counting on you to work a miracle. You're already getting close to her."

"Not that close," Garrett snapped and then curbed his impatience. "I wanted you to know that I'll be with her tonight so don't call."

"I'll wait until you call me. You're doing great—I knew you would."

"Will, stop being the ultimate optimist. She doesn't have a clue yet about my connections. Everything will change when she learns the truth."

"Maybe. Maybe not. Thank heavens women can't resist you."

Garrett had to laugh. "Oh, hell. Goodbye, Will. I'll call when I can."

Garrett ended the call and tried to get Will out of his thoughts and stop worrying about him. As he headed to his car, he focused on Sophia, his thoughts heating him to a torrid level.

When Sophia opened the door, her heart missed beats. Dressed in a charcoal suit and matching tie, Garrett looked as handsome as he had the night before.

His warm gaze roamed over her and he smiled. "You look gorgeous," he said.

"Thank you," she replied, thinking about all the different outfits she had tried on before settling on a plain red linen suit. Her hair was tied behind her head with a matching red scarf and he gave it a faint tug.

"Very pretty, but if we were going out for the evening, I would untie that scarf and let your hair free, which is the way I like it."

"But I won't," she replied lightly, locking up and walking to his car with him. "I have to go to the gallery and it needs to be tied and out of my way."

As he held the car door, she noticed he watched her legs when she climbed in. He closed the door and went around to slide behind the wheel. "So how did you sleep?" he asked.

"Great."

"I must be slipping if my kisses didn't keep you awake a little."

"You think I would tell you if I had stayed awake all night?"

As they both smiled, she felt the sparks between them, that electrifying current that had sizzled the whole time they were together last night. She hoped he never realized what a strong impact he had on her. She had a busy life and a time-consuming career. Garrett had come into her life at a time when she was trying to make a name in the art world. She didn't want him to realize how he affected her. She didn't want to lose control of her emotions.

At the restaurant, they were seated on an outdoor patio—the breezes were cool, the sun bright. As soon as they had ordered and were alone, Garrett smiled. "So when will my painting be delivered?"

"This afternoon."

"Excellent. Let me pick you up, we'll go to my house to hang the painting and then I'll take you out."

Her heartbeat quickened yet again. "You really don't waste time, do you," she replied.

"I'll pick you up around seven. So how much time do you spend in New Mexico?" he asked.

"Most of the summer. It's cool at night and I enjoy being there part of the year. Do you have a home anywhere else?"

"My home is in Dallas and I have a condo in Colorado because I like to ski. I also have a place in Switzerland."

"Nice."

"Painting is a reclusive occupation. Do you get out much in Santa Fe?"

"Sure, when I want to. But I enjoy the quiet and solitude. Chalk that up to being an only child." As Sophia talked, she couldn't help but study Garrett. His brown hair had been neatly combed, but the breeze soon shifted the locks and they tumbled over his forehead. His rough handsomeness—his hawk nose and firm jaw—and his spellbinding gray eyes fascinated her. When he began to speak, her gaze lowered to his mouth and she recalled his kisses, not hearing what he was saying as heat suffused her and the temperature of the cool morning changed.

He touched her chin with his fingers. "I don't believe you're hearing a word I'm saying. What could you possibly be thinking about?" he asked in a husky voice as if he guessed exactly why she hadn't heard a word he had said.

"My mind drifted, sorry," she said, embarrassed, looking into his knowing gaze. She felt the heat flush her cheeks and couldn't do anything to stop it.

"So, Sophia, where did it drift? What were you thinking?"

She gave up because he knew full well what she had been thinking about.

"I don't think you need me to tell you that, do you, Garrett?" He gave her a slight smile as she changed the subject. "Do you travel much with your job?"

To her relief he moved on with the conversation and the moment passed. But she suspected it had not been forgotten.

After breakfast Garrett took her to the gallery and parked beside her car. As he walked her to the door, he said, "We're early. May I come inside with you in case your building is empty?"

"Actually, people should start arriving in about ten minutes, and there is a guard outside."

"I'd rather stay until someone does arrive."

"Garrett, it's safe, and I'll lock the door once I'm inside." She turned to unlock the door and reached inside to switch off the alarm. When it became clear that he had no intention of leaving, she headed down the hall and said over her shoulder, "I'll show you my office."

She stepped into her office and he followed, taking in the beige room with bright splashes of color from her paintings. He studied the paintings for a moment, and then turned to her, making her pulse skip. "I expect people any minute now."

"I'll wait and be certain. Why don't you give me the key and I'll unlock the front and switch on lights."

She handed him the key and he caught her wrist, drawing her to him. Her "no" died on her lips before she ever uttered a sound. His arm banded her waist and he looked down at her. "I didn't sleep well and I suspect you didn't either. This is what I've wanted since I woke up this morning." His mouth covered hers, his lips warm and firm as he kissed her.

Her heart thudded while heat made the room a furnace. Wrapping her arm around his neck, she combed her fingers through his thick hair while their kiss turned to fire. Forgetting her surroundings, she held him tightly.

She never heard the car but Garrett raised his head and stepped away. "I hear one of your employees."

Garrett's erratic breathing matched hers. She felt disoriented, trying to ignore her desire and get her focus off Garrett and back to the real world.

He left to unlock the front for her just as she heard a car door slam. One of her male employees came in the back door, and Sophia introduced him to Garrett when he returned to the office.

"I'll pick you up at home tonight. How's six? Too early?" he asked.

"It's fine," she said, still slightly dazed, thinking six o'clock sounded eons away. "Thanks again for breakfast." He gave her an incredible smile, said goodbye and closed the door behind him. Sophia felt like she was in a daze until her phone rang.

"You were out late last night," Edgar said.

"Hello to you, too, Edgar," she said, amused. "I can't recall having a curfew. I don't think this is what Mom had in mind when she asked you to look out for me."

"I think it's exactly what she had in mind. You didn't answer the text I sent you this morning."

"Sorry, Edgar. I went out for breakfast."

"Uh-huh. With the Cantrell fellow?"

She laughed. "Yes, with the Cantrell fellow—Garrett, to be exact."

"Oh, dear," Edgar said, sighing audibly. "I suppose I will have to remember his name. So you're seeing him again?"

"Correct. Am I going to have to check in, Mom 2?"

He chuckled. "No. I'll keep tabs. Just answer your text messages."

"Yes, Edgar."

"Last night seemed a huge success."

"I'll hear shortly when everyone arrives at work."

"I'm certain I'm right. Have lunch with me and we'll celebrate your success."

"Thanks. That'll be nice." She made arrangements with him and a minute later, her assistant appeared to show her the receipts from the gallery.

Last night had indeed been a success—in more ways than one.

Sophia pulled on a blue wool-and-crepe sweater with a deep V-neck, a straight, short skirt and matching pumps. She put her hair up in a French twist. She was nervous, anxious, excited.

Get a grip, she silently lectured herself.

It wasn't easy. Garrett captivated her more than any other man she had known. He was exciting, handsome, interested in her life. If she let herself think of kissing him, she could get lost in memories of the previous night. But she didn't want that to happen. She needed to stay in control.

When she was ready, she studied herself thoroughly to make certain she was at her best for the evening.

When she opened the door to face him, her heart raced, despite all her commands to the contrary. In a navy suit, he looked breathtakingly handsome and commanding. His smile warmed her as his gaze drifted slowly over her.

"You're gorgeous," he said in a husky voice that was like a caress. She smiled, glad for the effort she had taken to get ready. "You have a nice home," he said.

"Sometime you'll get a tour, but right now, we're headed for your house."

"I'll hold you to that. Shall we go?"

Nodding, she closed the door behind her, hearing the lock click in place. Garrett took her arm to escort her to a waiting limo where the driver held the door while she climbed inside. She was surprised Garrett wasn't driving. Did he always travel in limos? Was she seeing another facet of his life? Garrett sat facing her.

"How were the gallery showings?"

"Very good. I'm gratified. I'll paint whether people buy my work or not, but when my paintings sell, I feel good about it. I keep the ones I don't want to sell. Some are just for me and they're not going to a gallery." As she talked, she was intensely aware of Garrett's smoky gaze on her. His fascinating gray eyes and knowledge of what his kisses could do kept her tingling with anticipation.

"If it suits you, we'll go out to my house to hang the painting. When we're through, we'll have dinner."

"Sounds like a great evening."

In a short time they drove through an exclusive residential area with acres of tall pines and estates set back out of sight. Black wrought-iron gates swung open to allow them entrance.

She was curious about his home, interested in finding out more about him. When the trees cleared, she saw the sprawling, three-story stone mansion.

"Garrett, your home is beautiful." A long narrow pool was centered in the formal gardens in the front yard. Various fountains held splashing water and sunlight spilled an orange glow over the house. Tall, symmetrical Italian pines stood at opposite ends of the wide porch that led to massive double doors.

The limo halted and the driver held the door as they exited. The door opened before they reached it and Garrett introduced her. "Sophia, meet Terrence, who is my right-hand man. He's butler and house manager and keeps things running smoothly here. Terrence, this is Ms. Rivers."

"Welcome, Ms. Rivers," Terrence said, stepping back and holding the door wide.

Garrett took her arm as they entered.

"Somehow this surprises me. I imagined you in a different type of home," she said, realizing Garrett had far more wealth than she had thought.

"Maybe I better not ask what kind."

"Something less formal, maybe more Western. Although this mansion has enough rooms to have all types of decor."

"I'll show you my shop and then we'll find the perfect spot for your painting."

He led her down the wide, elegant hall with potted palms and oils in ornate frames hanging on the walls. They entered another wing of the mansion and finally turned into a large paneled room that smelled of sawdust. The terrazzo floor was rust-colored with dark brown stones. Beautiful pieces of furniture in various stages were scattered throughout the room. The framework for an ornate credenza stood on a worktable, above which tools hung. One wall held handcrafted cabinets containing more tools.

She walked around the room, inhaling the sawdust smell, taking in the furniture in progress, lumber, power saws, a stack of sawhorses. "This is what you love, isn't it?"

He stood watching her and nodded. "You're the first woman who has ever been down here."

"I'm honored," she said.

"Sophia," he said and stopped. He stared at her intently.

"Yes?"

"I just wondered what you think about all this. Although I suppose I need to show you a finished product before I ask you that," he replied.

She had the feeling that he had been about to say something else, and she wondered what it was. The slight frown on his face made her curiosity deepen but she was certain if she asked, she would not get the answer.

She walked to a table to run her finger along the smooth finish. "This is beautiful, Garrett."

"That still needs a lot of work. It's intended to be a

reproduction of a French walnut refectory table. I also enjoy history."

"So do you do this when you can't sleep?" she asked.

"Do you paint when you can't sleep?" he said, by way of answering.

She smiled at him.

"C'mon. I'll show you some finished pieces."

As they made their way out into the hall, she still felt as if he towered over her—a unique sensation and one she enjoyed.

They paused by an elegant reproduction of a 19th-century French sofa with embroidered rosebuds in beige damask upholstery. "Here's a finished piece," he said.

She had expected his work to be nice, but this was beyond nice. "Garrett, this looks like a well-preserved antique. It looks like the real thing." She ran her fingers over the smooth wood. "This is truly beautiful," she said, impressed. "You could make another fortune from your craft."

He smiled. "That's the best compliment I've ever received," he said. He placed his hands on her shoulders. "You do look stunning, Sophia. Do you mind?" he said while he reached up and pulled a pin out of her hair. Locks spilled on her shoulders as she gazed up at him.

He stood close, removing pins, causing a gentle tingling sensation on her scalp. She looked at his mouth and her heart drummed. She wanted him to kiss her right now and was tempted to pull him to her.

Instead, she kept quiet while Garrett finished and her hair cascaded across her shoulders. She moved her head slightly, shaking out her hair and letting it swirl across her shoulders. She still watched him while he gazed into her eyes. His attention shifted to her mouth.

"Garrett, show me more of your work," she said, her

voice breathless. She wanted his kisses, yet she felt she should resist and have some control. Garrett had come into her life like a whirlwind and she needed to show some resistance before he totally uprooted her career and schedules. Deep down, she had an instinctive feeling that Garrett was more than just an appealing man who excited her.

"Better yet, come with me and I'll show you where I want to hang your painting. There are two possible rooms—one is the billiard room, the other is a large living area. I entertain there and it's not as formal as some of the other rooms."

She followed him down the wide hall. "You really need a map for this mansion."

He smiled. "Your place wasn't small either."

"I'm so accustomed to it, I don't give a thought to the size."

"Nor do I." He motioned toward open double doors. She entered a large room that had two glass walls. One end of the room bowed out in a sweeping glass curve, giving the room light and a sensation of being outdoors. The other end featured a massive brick fireplace. Leather furniture and dark fruitwood lent a masculine touch.

"This is a livable room. Very comfortable," he said. "I'm in here a lot." He led her across the room and she saw a familiar painting she had done a year earlier.

"I like it there," she said, looking at her painting on his wall with others in a grouping. "A prominent spot in a room you like and live in. Now you can think of me when you see it," she added lightly, teasing him.

"I'll always think of you when I see it," he said, his solemn tone giving a deeper meaning to his words.

"Sure you will," she said, laughing. "Is this the room where you'd like to hang the other painting?"

"Yes, possibly. Where do you think it should go?"

Aware of his attention on her, she strolled around the room, selecting and then rejecting spots until she stopped. "I think this is a good place."

"It is. One other possibility you should consider is over the hearth. It's a sizable painting. I think it fits this room."

"That would be the most prominent spot in the room," she said, surprised and pleased.

"I think it would look good there." He shed his coat. "Let me hold it up and see what you think."

She watched as he picked up the painting and held it in place.

She smiled at him. "It looks great there. Are you sure?"

He grinned. "I'll get tools and hang it."

"What can I do?" she asked.

"Let's have a drink and you can supervise the hanging."

"I can get the drinks," she said, moving to the bar in the corner of the room. "What would you like?"

"I think I'll have beer."

"And I'll have red wine," she stated. While she got a wineglass and opened a bottle, he disappeared. By the time he returned, she was on a leather couch in front of the fireplace with the drinks on a table. He placed an armload of tools on a chair and pulled off his tie. He twisted free the top buttons of his shirt—something so ordinary and simple yet it filled her with heat and she longed to get up and unbutton the rest for him. He picked up his beer, raising the bottle high.

"Here's to improving the looks of my house by adding a Sophia Rivers painting."

"I'll drink to that," she said, standing and picking up her drink to touch his cold bottle. Again, when she looked into his eyes, her heart skipped a beat. Each time they almost kissed, her longing intensified. How soon would they be in each other's arms?

Sipping her red wine, she stepped back. His gaze remained locked on hers. Watching her, he sipped his beer and then turned away, breaking the spell.

He picked up the painting. "I'll hold this and you tell me when I have it in exactly the right spot." He held the painting high, and then set it down. "Just a minute. I can put myself back together later," he said as he took off his gold cuff links and folded back his immaculate cuffs. "Now, let's try this again."

Slightly disheveled, he looked sexy, appealing. She tried to focus on the painting, but was having a difficult time keeping her attention off the man.

"To the right and slightly higher," she said. After several adjustments, she nodded. "That's perfect."

He leaned back to look while he held the picture. Setting it down, he picked up chalk to mark a place on the bricks before pulling the tape measure out.

She sipped her wine while he worked. In an amazingly short time he had her painting hanging in place and he stepped away.

"Let's look at it."

He took her arm and they walked across the large room to study the result of his work. She was aware of the warmth of him beside her. He looked at his watch. "Shall we go eat now, or should I just throw some steaks on the grill?"

"If we eat here, it's fine with me."

He leaned down to look directly into her eyes. "Are you certain you don't mind my cooking?"

"Now I'm curious," she said. "I'll view it as an adventure."

"Steaks at home it is." He draped his arm across her shoulders. "It's a nice evening. We'll eat on the terrace."

They carried their drinks outside, and Sophia was again surprised by the house.

"This isn't a terrace, Garrett—it's another kitchen, plus a terrace, plus a living area, plus a pool."

"With Houston's weather, it works well through the fall and winter," he replied, crossing to a stainless-steel gas grill built into a stone wall. In minutes he had the grill fired up and he sat with her on comfortable chairs in the outdoor living room.

"So where are you going, Sophia? What do you want out of life?"

"To pursue painting. To do charity work. I'd like to help with literacy. Also, try to do something to aid in getting more opportunities in school for children to take art and learn art appreciation. I want to open a gallery in New Mexico."

"Marriage and family?"

She shrugged. "I don't think about that. I'm accustomed to being on my own. I don't ever want to be in the situation my mother was in—in love with my dad who never returned that love fully."

"Your dad—you knew him?"

"What I told you last night wasn't completely accurate. He was around off and on all my life," she said, feeling a stab of pain and anger that had never left her. "My dad wouldn't marry my mother. He practically ignored me except for financial support."

"You said he was married?" Garrett said.

"Not by the time I was a teenager, but he didn't want to get tied down again. Whenever he came to visit, it tore her up each time he left. She would cry for several days. He was the only man she ever loved," Sophia stated bitterly. "He had a family—boys. He would go home to them. I couldn't do anything to help her or stop her tears. When I was little, we both cried. I cried for her and she cried over him."

"That's tough," Garrett said. "He ignored you?"

"In his way he provided for me. But looking back, I don't think he knew how to deal with a little girl. He brought me all kinds of presents. I can remember reaching an age where I smashed some of them to bits. Mom just started giving them to charities. I didn't want anything from him."

"How old were you then?"

"Probably about eight or nine. He was polite to me and Mom saw to it that I was polite to him, but we weren't together a whole lot. He never talked to me other than hello and goodbye. I rarely heard him say my name. When I was little I wondered whether he knew it. Often, I would be sent to my grandmother's, which I loved, or out with my nanny when he was coming. Worked fine for me. I didn't want to see him."

"Yet your mother always loved him."

"She did. And I don't ever want to fall into that trap. The best way to avoid it is to keep relationships from becoming too deep."

"Maybe you shouldn't base everything on the actions of your father."

"That's the legacy he left me—a deep fear of any relationship that isn't totally committed."

"Sorry, Sophia," Garrett said with a somber note.

"How'd we get on this?" she asked, wanting to avoid

thinking and talking about her blood father. She wanted him out of her life and thoughts as much as humanly possible.

"I'm interested in your life and finding out about you. Did he ever try to make it up to you?"

She thought of the inheritance Argus Delaney had left her. "He always showered Mom with money. Money was his solution for everything. He paid her medical bills, but by the time the end of her life came, we had enough money to manage on our own. No matter what happened, she always loved him. And I've always hated him," she said.

"At least he was good to her," Garrett said gently. "And generous."

"I suppose I should be grateful, but I can't be. He left money when he died—money I don't want one penny of," she said.

"He's gone. He'll never know whether you take his money or refuse it. Why not take it and enjoy it? It should be yours."

She shook her head, feeling the familiar current of fury that she had lived with as long as she could remember.

"I don't want anything to do with him."

"You could do a lot with your inheritance."

"I'll never touch it," she said, trying to shift her focus off the past and onto Garrett, thinking he would be fascinating to paint. His rugged features gave him a distinctive individualism and his unique gray eyes were unforgettable. Desire stirred and once again, she struggled to pay attention to their conversation.

He was studying her intently. "Sophia—" He paused, his eyes holding secrets. She couldn't tell what he was thinking.

"What? What were you going to say?"

He looked away. "I'll check on the steaks." She watched him stride to the cooker and she wondered for the second time this evening what it was he'd been about to say to her. Probably more advice about taking her inheritance, which she'd already heard enough of from Edgar.

"The steaks are ready."

She stood, going with him to help get tossed salads, potatoes and water on the table. Soon they sat on the terrace to eat thick, juicy steaks.

"It's a wonder you ever travel for pleasure. It's gorgeous here and you have every convenience."

"I like it here, but I like my other places, too."

"I guess I can understand since I enjoy Santa Fe and Taos and even the cabin in the mountains as much as living in Houston." She took a bite of her steak. "You're a very good cook. The steak is delicious," she said, surprised because he'd seemed to pay little attention to his cooking.

"I'm glad you think so."

"I should have watched you more closely. I invariably burn them."

"You can watch me as closely as you want," he replied with a twinkle.

"I opened the door for that one," she said, smiling at him. "So how did you get into property management?" she asked, picking up her water glass to take a sip. A faint breeze caught his hair, blowing it gently. His hair was thick, and she thought about how it felt to run her fingers through it.

"My dad had the business," he was saying. "He was into property management and finance. I was raised to follow in his footsteps and groomed to take over his businesses."

"Businesses? There are others?"

"Yes, but I'm not directly involved in most of them. Hardly involved at all. They're investments."

"And that leaves you free to play around," she said. "So what do you actually do?" she asked, flirting with him while trying to satisfy her curiosity about him and his life.

He smiled at her. "More than play around, although I hope to do that tonight. Dinner—get to know you—kiss you. That's what I want to do in the next few hours," he said, his voice deepening and making her tingle.

"I don't really know you. Do you work, Garrett, or does the playboy lifestyle fit you?"

"I work, but not tonight, so we can get away from that subject. You aren't eating, and I've lost my appetite for this steak. Let's sit where it's more comfortable to talk. We can take our drinks with us."

She was leaving a half-eaten steak, yet she couldn't resist his suggestion. Her interest in food had disappeared with Garrett's flirting. He took her hand and she stood, going with him, her insides tingling the moment he touched her.

Garrett sat close on the couch. Her perfume was an exotic fragrance and he liked the faint scent. Her long hair was silky in his fingers as he twisted and toyed with the strands. She was stunning and he couldn't get enough of her. And yet, he was racked with guilt.

When she had talked about Argus Delaney, Garrett felt awful that he wasn't telling her the truth about who he was. Twice he had been on the verge, almost confessing and then pausing, waiting because it seemed the wisest course to follow. If he confessed the truth now, he was certain he would be finished. It was too soon, but knowing that didn't ease his conscience.

"What about you and marriage?" she asked.

"I'm a workaholic, I suppose," he said, stretching out his long legs. "I haven't ever been deeply in love," he admitted. "I don't feel ready for marriage or getting tied down. Right now, my life is devoted to my work."

"Pretty ordinary attitude when someone is tied up in work," she stated.

As he gazed into her eyes, he wondered what it would be like to come home to her every night—to make love to her night and day. His thoughts surprised him. Sophia stirred him in a way no woman before her ever had. He had never had long-term thoughts or speculation about a woman before. Not even when he had been in a relationship. "I owe you an elegant dinner and dancing instead of sitting at my house and eating my cooking and helping me hang your painting," he said, trying to get focused again on the present and stop imagining a future with her. That kind of thinking disturbed him. Because it was totally uncustomary.

"I'm enjoying the evening. You don't owe me an elegant dinner," she said. "This has been nice and you're an interesting man, Garrett Cantrell."

Garrett smiled at her. "You barely know me. And I lead an ordinary life."

"Why do I doubt that statement? You've bought two of my paintings. That alone makes you interesting."

"Next time we go to your house and I get to see where you paint," he said.

"It's a typical studio with brushes and paint smears. I don't think it's quite as interesting as your workshop."

"If it's yours, it's interesting. Have you painted all your life?"

"Actually, yes. I loved drawing and painting. Of course, what little girl doesn't?"

As she talked about painting when she was a child, his mind returned to the problem. He hated not telling her about the Delaneys, yet he had heard the bitterness, felt her anger smoldering. He wanted to be up front with her—his guilt was deepening by the minute.

He realized she was staring at him with a quizzical smile. "What?" he asked.

"You haven't heard one word I've been saying, Garrett. Is there something you want to tell me? What are you thinking about?"

He focused on her lips before looking into her eyes again while desire consumed him. He didn't want to admit the truth yet and the burden of guilt was becoming unbearable, but one way to avoid both was to stop her questions with kisses.

Three

Sophia gazed at Garrett, waiting for an answer to her question, wondering what he had on his mind. Was it his business that had him so lost in his own thoughts?

Was it her?

"Garrett, what is it?" she asked, looking into his eyes.

Lust was blatant, causing her pulse to race. Perhaps it *was* her.

He leaned close, slipping his arm around her waist to pull her to him, ending her questions as his mouth covered hers. Her heart slammed against her ribs.

She inhaled, winding her arms around his neck while she kissed him in return. When he pulled her onto his lap, she was barely aware of moving.

He wound his fingers in her hair and she clung to him. Her body tingled, an aching need beginning. She moaned softly as he ran his hand down her back, over the curve of her hip to her thighs. He pushed the hem of her skirt higher to touch her bare skin. Hot, urgent longing consumed her. Her fingers worked free the remaining buttons of his shirt and she pushed it away to touch his sculpted chest. She ran her fingers lower over his muscled stomach. The touch caused the fires within her to blaze. She gasped over caressing him, realizing she had to stop or she would be lost in lovemaking, complicating her life in a manner she had always intended to avoid. She had never slept with a man and she didn't intend to take that step now.

She caught his wrist and raised her head. "This is crazy, Garrett. I barely know you. We're going too fast."

"We're getting to know each other, and I'd say the chemistry is pretty hot." As he talked, he ran both hands through her hair on either side of her face. "You're beautiful. You take my breath away. Sophia, I want to make love to you," he whispered hoarsely.

Her heart thudded but she forced herself to slide off his lap. "Let's take a breather and slow things down," she said, standing to face him.

He stood, his desire obvious. His shirt was unbuttoned to the waist and pushed open to reveal his broad, muscled, masculine chest. Her mouth was dry and she had to fight the urge to fling her arms around his neck and kiss him again.

"I haven't felt this way about anyone before," he said, sounding surprised, frowning slightly as if he weren't happy about it.

"Please sit, Sophia. We'll just talk," he said.

She sat, turning so she could face him. The moment he was seated, he wrapped his fingers in her hair. "We can sit and talk, but I can't keep from touching you."

"Garrett, I meant it when I said I'm not into affairs.

I watched my mother shed a million tears over my father. I won't put myself in that position."

"I can understand that completely. But we're not having an affair. We're kissing."

"I know. But things are escalating quickly," she said.

"Well, now I'm duly warned about your feelings,"
he said with a smile.

"I figure it's better to be forthright and upfront with
you. Why are you smiling?"

"I didn't mean to. You just remind me of a friend who
is forthright," he replied, combing his fingers slowly
through her hair, caressing her nape and then picking
up long strands to wind them in his fingers again. "Sophia, I already feel as if I've known you a long time."

"I like that," she said, trying to focus on their conversation, yet more aware of his hand lightly toying
with her hair.

"So. Let's talk. Do you have other relatives?" he
asked. "Did your mother have any brothers or sisters?"

"I have two aunts, one uncle and eight cousins, all
scattered around this part of Texas. I see them at family
events, but otherwise, we haven't been that close since
she's been gone. I never knew my father's family, nor
did I want to," she said coldly.

"You might be making a mistake there," Garrett said.

Sophia felt her blood turn to ice, and she glared at
Garrett. "No, I'm not. His family was the reason he
wouldn't marry my mother. I don't want to know them
or have anything to do with any part of him."

"Sophia, *you're* part of him. And they couldn't help
being part of him any more than you could."

She hadn't ever thought about how innocent they
were of what their father did, and the thought startled
her, but she pushed it away. His sons were still his blood.

"Even so, they grew up with him. They have his name and he's honored them." Why did Garrett keep taking Argus's side? She disliked talking about her father or even thinking about him. "Garrett, let's find something else to discuss. Do you have any other hobbies besides the furniture?"

"Sure. I work out. I ski. I play tennis, play polo and I swim. You?"

"More things we have in common. I love rodeos, country dances. I also like to ski, swim and I play the piano," she answered.

"With the storms that have gone through recently, they've already had enough freezing weather in the upper levels of Colorado mountains to ski. Fly up there with me for the weekend. We can leave early in the morning and come back Sunday evening."

"You're serious," she said, surprised by his invitation.

"Why not? We'll have fun, ski, nothing big. Just a fun getaway. My condo is large. You can take your pick of bedrooms."

"You are serious." A weekend with Garrett. Excitement bubbled and she wanted to accept, yet common sense reminded her again to slow down with him. He had come into her life like a whirlwind.

He leaned closer and held her chin. "Come with me. No strings. I'll bring you home anytime you want. We'll ski, relax, talk. Do whatever we want."

Her heartbeat quickened. She was surprised at herself because his offer held some appeal. On the other hand, years of being wary of getting too close to someone were ingrained in her.

"I don't think flying to Colorado with you is a good idea."

"Sophia, you're not going to risk getting hurt by spending the weekend skiing with me. We're not getting into anything remotely serious."

"But this is exactly how you get into something serious. Moment after moment together and then it's too late."

"Take a risk and live a little. This is simply two days. We're not going to fall in love over the weekend."

She blushed. She hadn't been worried about falling in love.

Had she?

"If you're worried, we can ask Edgar to join us."

She couldn't keep from laughing. "You're willing to invite Edgar, too?"

"If that's what it takes to spend the weekend with you, yes, I'll invite Edgar, too."

"Now you're making me feel foolish."

"That's not my intention. Listen, I understand why you don't want to follow in your mother's footsteps, but I don't think you run any risk of that happening with me."

Her eyes widened. "I guess I've lumped all males into the same group as my father."

"I can't blame you for being hurt, Sophia," he said solemnly and her heart warmed. He gazed intently at her while she debated, waiting quietly.

"I'll go with you," she said, smiling at him.

"Excellent. It'll be fun. No big deal."

It was a big deal because she didn't even spend weekends with men she knew. All she had to go on with Garrett was the information she had received about him from others and her own feelings.

"I'll tell Edgar I'm going, but we're not inviting him along. He hates cold weather and he can't imagine fastening his feet to 'long boards,' as he calls them. Thank you, though, for the offer to invite him," she said.

"Good. I'll check the weather right now. I don't fly into storms if I can possibly avoid it."

She watched as he pulled out his phone. He smiled broadly, sexy creases bracketing his mouth. "Good weather—cold nights, sunny days. I'll call my pilot. How early can we go?"

"Name your time."

"I'll pick you up at seven."

"Fine with me," she said. She'd surprised herself, she thought as eagerness bubbled in a steady current. The weekend with Garrett. Foolhardy, risky for her heart.

Exciting.

Walking away, Garrett talked with the pilot and made arrangements. When he was done, he sat beside her again. "We're set to fly at eight."

"So one of your traits is impulsiveness," she said. "I'm learning more about you."

"I don't think I'd describe myself as impulsive. Usually I'm predictable and methodical."

"If we get to know each other, I'll weigh in on that."

"We'll get to know each other, Sophia," he said softly in a husky tone that sent a tingle spiraling in her. "I definitely intend that we do."

Desire was constant with Garrett, keeping her intensely aware of him in a physical manner. Despite her concerns, she couldn't deny that she loved being with him, hearing about him, learning about him. In some ways, she, too, felt as if she had known him a long time. They talked until one and she promised herself by half past she would end the evening. Finally, when it was almost two, she stood.

"Garrett, I must get home."

"You don't have to go if you don't want." He waved his hand toward his house. "Needless to say, there is plenty of room here. Take any bedroom you want. Close to mine, far from mine or in mine with me," he teased. "I'll even promise to not wake you in the morning. Particularly if you make the last choice."

Shaking her head, she laughed. "It does seem silly for you to drive me home, but that's what I want. If I'm going to Colorado to ski, I want to go home and get some things."

"All right. Home it is. I told my chauffeur we'd take you home tonight."

"See, I should have driven."

"I would insist on taking you home even if you had driven. It's way too late for you to be out driving around by yourself."

"That's an old-fashioned notion."

"It's not the first time someone has accused me of having old-fashioned notions."

"I think old-fashioned is rather nice if it isn't over-done. Edgar gets a little carried away— I'll probably have a text waiting from him when I get in. He's probably running background checks on you as we speak."

She expected a laugh but Garrett merely gave her a smile and stood. "Shall we go?"

When they arrived at her house, the limo waited while Garrett walked with her to her door. He stepped inside, waiting while she switched off the alarm and then pulling her into his embrace to kiss her.

With her heart racing, she wrapped her arms around him and kissed him in return, pouring her feelings into her kiss, wanting to spend the rest of the night with him, wanting to touch and caress and make love, yet knowing she should do little more than what they were doing unless she wanted to risk losing her heart.

How much time passed, she didn't know or care. They were breathless, wanting more. Need became a raging fire. When Garrett's hands began to roam over her, she stopped him and stepped back.

"We'll say good-night," she stated. Her voice was breathless as she gulped for air. "Garrett, tonight has been so much fun," she said softly. His gray eyes had darkened to slate, desire burning in their depths. "Thanks for a grand evening."

"I'll see you in the morning, Sophia," he said, giving her a smile that nearly stopped her heart. He turned and left, the lock clicking in place behind him.

For a moment, she could barely move, resting against the door, trying desperately to catch her breath, wondering if she was about to make the biggest mistake of her life.

Garrett swore under his breath. He liked Sophia more than any woman he had known. He wanted to call Will immediately and tell him that he hated deceiving her and it had to end. But he knew that as soon as he told Sophia the Delaneys had sent him, she would break it off.

He was torn between admitting the truth to her and running the risk of losing her, or continuing the deception until he felt she liked him enough that they could weather the storm that would break when he told her the truth.

More than once he had mulled over resigning from Delaney Enterprises and devoting himself to building furniture. Sometimes he thought of working with his hands, living in a place near the ocean, creating instead of acquiring. He often wondered if the notion of changing careers was merely a pipe dream, yet Sophia had successfully done just that.

Only her situation had been different. He had been raised to do this kind of work and he felt he owed the Delaney family his services. Argus Delaney had taken his father out of poverty, given him a job and paid for his education because he said he saw potential in his dad. His father had worked hard and risen fast and Argus had helped him all along the way, opening doors and paying him well. In turn, his father had absolute loyalty to the Delaneys and had raised Garrett to feel the same. If he left Delaney Enterprises, Garrett felt he would be turning his back on all his father had wanted for him, and on Will's friendship. And he was inheriting a fortune from Will's dad.

Even so, the thought was tempting. Especially after being with Sophia.

For the first time he considered actually going through with telling Will he was resigning. If he resigned, he might have hope of some kind of future with Sophia.

How tempting. He could tell Sophia everything with a clear conscience.

Could he do it?

At his estate he glanced at his watch and picked up his phone to call Will. "Sorry for the early hour."

"I hope it's because you have good news."

"I don't, and I don't know whether I ever will. She told me more about your dad. She's incredibly bitter."

"Are you making any progress?"

"We're flying to Colorado to ski for the weekend."

"I call that progress. Just hang in there—sounds as

if you two get along fine," Will said, his voice rising with enthusiasm.

"We do," Garrett said in clipped tones. "I don't know what will happen when I tell her the truth. Will, I hate not being up front with her on this."

"You're doing her a favor, too—don't forget that."

"Dammit, Will, she's been hurt. She isn't going to change easily and I can't keep up this deception," Garrett said, startled by how deeply concerned he had become over Sophia's feelings. He cared more for her than he would have dreamed possible when he first took this assignment.

"You don't need to feel guilty. You're doing your job. Do your best is all we all ask—your best is mighty damn fine. We're counting on you."

"I know. I'll see how it goes today."

"Don't rush. Get her so close she'll do what you want."

Garrett hated the sound of that. "I'll talk to you tomorrow or Monday," he said.

"Have a real good time."

He hung up, wondering why he'd even bothered to call Will. He stared at the phone with Will's words echoing in his thoughts. *We're counting on you.* All his adult life they had counted on him. He couldn't toss that aside.

Doubting if he would sleep at all, he skipped bed and headed to the shower, thinking of being with her again, of her dark eyes and midnight hair, her laughter, her kiss. A whole weekend. By the time they flew back to Texas, he hoped to be closer to her.

The big question was: What would happen if he told her the truth? Would he lose her forever?

* * *

Sophia rummaged in her closet for ski clothes and other things she would need. Still marveling at the thought that she had accepted Garrett's offer, she decided to wait to text Edgar until the morning.

Anticipation kept a running current of excitement humming through her body. She kept glancing at the clock, anxious to see Garrett again. Was she falling into the same trap her mother had fallen into? Was she doing what she had tried all her adult life to avoid— falling in love?

A text message broke into her thoughts.

Are you home? I've been worried about you. All OK?

She fired back an answer.

I'm home, Edgar. Flying to Colorado tomorrow to ski with Garrett. Back Sunday. Don't worry about me. Go to bed.

Minutes after she sent the text, her phone rang. "Edgar, do you know what time it is?"

"I know you're still awake," he answered. "I hope you keep in touch. Sophia, this isn't like you. How important is Garrett Cantrell to you?"

"I like the guy and we're becoming friends. I can do that," she said, hoping she could hold true to her words. "We'll be back home early Sunday evening."

"I just want to keep my promise to your mother."

"Stop worrying. Mom had no idea you would take her request to this extent. I'm grown, Edgar. I can take care of myself."

"All right, I'll buzz off. Let me know when you're back in town. You can tell me all about your weekend."

Smiling, she put away her phone and climbed into bed.

Just a few short hours later, Garrett was at her door. As he stepped inside, his gaze roamed over her.

She smiled while her heart jumped. Each time they were together, she thought he was more handsome than the time before. Dressed in a cable-knit navy sweater and jeans, he took her breath away.

"You look gorgeous," he said, wrapping one arm around her waist and leaning down to kiss her. She wound her arms around his neck to kiss him in return.

With an effort she moved away. "This is not a weekend for seduction," she said with a smile.

"That's simply a good morning kiss," he said. "And I know what I promised you. We'll keep things light. Unless you change your mind," he added with a grin. "The weather report is good so we're on our way." He picked up her skis, shouldering her bag as she gathered her purse and jacket.

"Sorry, the tour of my house will have to wait," she said.

"Something to look forward to in the coming week. Perhaps Monday night."

She laughed at his attempt to make plans with her for Monday even though they hadn't even gone away for the weekend yet.

At the airport, they boarded a waiting jet that was far larger than she had expected. Its luxurious interior made her forget she was on board a plane for a few moments.

As they flew, Garrett sat facing her, their knees almost touching. It was difficult to keep her mind on the conversation because she was lost in looking at him. She still marveled at her reaction to him, alternating between enjoying it and being concerned by it. *Remember, it's just a fun weekend,* she told herself.

Far sooner than she expected they were driving through the small Colorado resort town to Garrett's condo.

His condo was built of stone with panoramic mountain views. Polished plank floors gleamed beneath high, open-beamed ceilings. Garrett built a roaring fire in the massive stone fireplace.

"What a change this is. It's a picture book," she said, looking out the window that covered almost the entire front wall.

Garrett stood behind her with his arms lightly around her. "We can hit the slopes or wait, if you prefer."

"We came to ski. I vote to ski."

"All right. I'll meet you back here in twenty minutes."

She went to the bedroom she had selected on the opposite end of the hall from Garrett's, which had made him smile. She changed into her gear, finally gathering her parka, sunglasses and gloves. They spent the rest of the day on the slopes, discovering they were well-matched skiers. They returned as the sun was setting.

"When we're changed, I'll take you to my favorite restaurant," Garrett said, stomping snow off his feet inside the entryway.

"Sounds good to me—I'm starving."

"Meet you here in, what?"

"Give me thirty minutes," she replied.

Certain he would be ready in far less time, she hurried. Thirty minutes later she made one last check. Her red wool pants and sweater were warm, as were her fur-lined boots. She let her hair go unpinned. With a toss of her head to get her long hair away from her face, she went to meet him.

As she entered the room, only one small lamp burned

and she could see the view of the sparkling lights through the picture window. The view was spectacular with twinkling lights below spreading out toward the snow-covered mountains that glistened beneath a rising full moon. But when Garrett entered the room, she only had eyes for him. He wore a bulky sweater that emphasized his broad shoulders, tight jeans and Western boots. He stepped closer and his direct gaze held her. Desire shone in the smoky depths of his eyes.

"Now this is best of all," he said. "You look beautiful. I love your hair down." He wrapped his fingers in her hair and his arm circled her waist as he pulled her close. "This is perfect," he whispered before he covered her mouth with his.

Ending their kiss, she tried to catch her breath, noticing that his breathing was as ragged as hers. Taking his cue from her, he stepped back.

"Shall we go?" he said in a husky voice while he caressed her nape.

He held her parka and she pulled on her gloves as they went downstairs to the car. During the ride she looked at the charming snow-covered town, but her thoughts tumbled over the excitement of being here with Garrett and the worry of how important he was becoming in her life.

At the restaurant they sat close to a blazing fire while piano music played softly. They ordered cups of steaming cider and hors d'oeuvres. Garrett had been famished when he finished dressing, but now his appetite had dwindled. He longed to hold Sophia, to kiss her. He ached to just touch her, to physically keep contact. Her hair fell loosely over her shoulders and around her face. Her luminous brown eyes were thickly lashed and captivating. And she looked happy.

Which made what he had to do even harder.

This withholding of information had gone on long enough. The closer they got, the more important it was to be honest with her. He had never been devious in his dealings before and he didn't want to start now.

It was a miracle she hadn't already discovered his connection with the Delaneys. But he was certain he would know when she had.

How he wished he didn't have this big secret. If only he were free to pursue her honestly the way he wanted, in a manner he had never dreamed of before.

Candlelight on the table reflected in her dark eyes. Each day he had been amazed by how much he wanted to be with her. She was becoming more important to him by the minute. Which meant he needed to tell her.

"You're an excellent skier," she said.

"I was going to tell you the same."

She smiled. "I think you held back to stay with me. It was invigorating, a real change from my regular life. You've turned my world topsy-turvy."

And there it was—the perfect opening to tell her about the Delaneys.

But he couldn't. He realized he didn't want to tell her in public. He wanted to be alone with her. And he also realized that no matter how guilty he was feeling, he should wait until they returned to Houston. It would give him the weekend to get closer to her and hopefully create a stronger bond between them that would be harder for her to break.

A voice inside him told him that that was a cruel thing to do, but he ignored it.

He didn't want to lose her. From the first moment he

had seen her, he'd been drawn to her and the thought of losing her made his insides churn. He had never expected to find her fascinating, to want a relationship with her.

"Maybe you've turned mine topsy-turvy, too."

"I seriously doubt that," she said. "All of this is scrumptious," she added, taking a bite of a mini-beef Wellington. I can see why this is your favorite restaurant."

"Good—I'm so glad you like it. So tell me, do you go to your gallery every day?"

"Not at all. I have a competent manager and excellent staff. They run the business so I can stay at the studio and paint."

"I don't blame you. If I ever build furniture full-time, I'll do the same."

"Why do you stay in property management? With your talent for woodwork, you could build a following very quickly."

"Blame my father for that one. I was raised to be in a productive, lucrative business. It was instilled in me as far back as I can remember."

"But your father is gone now, and you've already proved yourself in that area. Your furniture would be productive and lucrative."

"I'm wound up in obligations. Imagined or real, they are as much a part of me as my breathing. To Dad, who hasn't been gone that long, my fascination with building was entertainment and silly."

"Too bad," she said, shaking her head. "What did your dad want for you in your personal life?"

"The usual. Marriage and kids. But I've watched too many people have miserable marriages, and I'm not ready to get tied down."

"Tied down," she repeated, smiling. "So no long relationships in your past?"

"None. And evidently, none in yours."

"Absolutely not."

When he had first met her, her answer would have pleased him—a woman who did not want any deep commitment. Why now did he feel jolted slightly by her answer? Was Sophia weaving a web around his heart—something no woman had ever done?

It was nine before they left the restaurant. When they stepped outside a light snow fell, big flakes drifting, glistening in the light.

"Look, Garrett, this is enchanting," she said, spinning around with her arms spread wide. Her long hair flew out behind her, swirling around her face. He couldn't resist wrapping his arms around her to kiss her, tasting a wet snowflake on her lips.

When he released her, she stepped away. "We're in public."

"I couldn't resist," he admitted, thinking he would always remember her spinning around in the snow, a beautiful woman whose exuberance and zest for life were contagious. He looked up at the falling flakes and took out his phone. "We weren't supposed to have this kind of weather."

"It's gorgeous. I can't keep from being glad we have it."

"Even if you're snowbound with me?" he asked.

"Even if. I'll manage."

"Chance of a trace of snow," he read off his phone. "Clear Sunday." On impulse he glanced up. "Do it again. Let me get your picture."

Laughing but humoring him, she did and he took a picture that he expected to be a blur, a disappointment.

Instead, the picture was clear with her dark hair swinging out behind her head. He had caught her big smile and the essence of the moment. It would have been a perfect moment if it weren't for this big secret between them. He put away his phone, shaking off the thought. "A trace of snow tonight won't make any difference except to please you."

"It definitely does," she said. "Hey, wait. You're not the only one who wants a picture of this." She yanked out her phone. "Smile, Garrett."

He grinned while she took his picture and then flashed it briefly so he had a glimpse of himself. Linking his arm in hers, he waited for the valet to bring his car.

They stomped snow off their boots at his condo and he built another fire, which gave a low light. When he turned away from the hearth, he faced her.

Sophia stood at the window with the flickering orange flames playing over her. As his gaze drifted down over her lush curves and long legs, his heartbeat quickened. His longing was intense. He crossed the short distance to take her in his arms.

Four

Sophia's heart thudded as she wrapped her arms around Garrett. The day had been magical and she had grown closer to him, learning more about him and enjoying herself. All through dinner she had wanted to be alone with him so they could be together like this again.

Snowflakes had been the perfect touch, landing in his dark hair, sprinkling across his broad shoulders. His kiss had tantalized her. She wanted more of him, so much more.

She didn't believe in love at first sight, or second or third for that matter. She thought if she ever fell in love it would be with someone she had been friends with for years, yet Garrett shook her theories because he was already more important to her than anyone else she had ever dated. He was pure temptation.

He made her want to risk her heart.

She stood on tiptoe, her heart pounding while he

held her tightly against his long frame. His hand slid down her back and up beneath her sweater. She moaned softly, the sound muffled by his mouth on hers. His fingers trailed up her back in a feathery touch that was electrifying.

He picked her up and carried her closer to the fire, setting her on her feet while he still kissed her as flames crackled. Garrett stepped back and pulled her sweater over her head, tossing it aside. He unfastened her lacy bra and removed it, dropping it to the floor.

With a deep sigh he stepped back, cupping her breasts in his hands. "So beautiful," he said, his gaze as sensual as his caresses. His thumb traced circles on her nipples that sent currents streaming from his touch.

She tugged his sweater over his head to toss it aside. She moaned in pleasure again while her hands roamed over his broad, muscled chest, her fingers tangling in a thick mat of chest hair that tapered to a narrow line disappearing beneath his belt.

Firelight spilled over him, highlighting bulging muscles, leaving dark shadows on flat planes. His handsome features captivated her, and in some ways she felt as if she had known him for years instead of days, just as he had said to her.

Desire wracked her. She wanted to make love. She ran her hands over his flat stomach until he leaned down to kiss each breast, his tongue tracing circles. She gasped again with pleasure, closing her eyes and clinging to him while fire raged within her.

She wanted him with an urgency she had never felt before. Garrett was special, unique in her life and she didn't think Garrett would ever hurt her. It was a night, not a relationship. Was she succumbing in the same foolish way to temptation, just as her mother had done in allowing a man to become irresistible?

All her logic fled, driven away by passion when his arm banded her waist again, pulling her tightly against him. He picked her up again to carry her to a sofa, settling her on his lap. Her bare breasts were pressed against his warm chest, the thick mat of chest hair sensual against her naked skin. As they kissed his hands roamed over her, light caresses that scalded.

Kisses became hotter, deeper and more passionate and she didn't notice his hands at the buttons on her pants. He pushed them down, standing and setting her on her feet to let them fall around her ankles.

He paused, stepping back to lift one of her feet to remove her boot and sock and then he moved to the other foot, standing to hold her hips while his gaze drifted slowly over her. "You're lovely, so beautiful," he whispered. He yanked off his boots and socks, tossing them aside. When he stood, she unfastened his belt and pulled it free, dropping it and unbuttoning his jeans to push them off. As he kicked them away, he pulled her into his arms.

This was the time to stop if she was going to, but she had already made a decision that went against everything she had practiced. Take a chance with Garrett tonight. Tomorrow she could say no. She had never had a weekend like this one and might not ever again. She gazed into his gray eyes that were heavy-lidded, filled with sensual promises. She wanted him to an extent she had never wanted any man. She wanted to be loved by Garrett. She could take what she wanted, and then go back to her resolutions and her safe life.

Garrett drove all thoughts away with his kisses and caresses.

Her insides knotted, fires building low in her. He sat and pulled her onto his lap against his thick rod, caressing her while one hand dallied lightly along her legs, moving to the inside of her thighs, heightening desire.

Continuing to kiss her, he leaned over her while his fingers went beneath the flimsy bikini panties. She spread her legs slightly, giving him more access, moaning with pleasure and need.

He touched her intimately, kissing her, his other hand caressing her breast while his fingers were between her legs. Pleasurable torment built as he stood again to peel away her panties.

Freeing him, she removed his briefs, caressing his hard manhood, stroking and then kissing him. He closed his eyes, his hands winding in her hair while he groaned. In seconds, he raised her up, looking into her eyes.

He picked her up once again, carrying her to the bedroom, placing her on the bed and then shifting to her ankle to kiss her, trailing kisses along her leg to the back of her knee. Gradually, his tongue moved up the inside of her thigh. Writhing, she closed her eyes while he moved between her legs, driving her wild with his tongue and fingers.

She sat up swiftly, wrapping her arms around him and pulling him down. He held her tightly, kissing her fervently.

"Garrett, I don't have any protection," she whispered.

"I do," he answered. He left, and in seconds returned with a small packet, which he opened. He spread her legs and knelt between them to put on the condom and then he lowered himself.

He started to enter her and she wrapped her legs around him. As he lowered himself and thrust slowly, he stopped. "Sophia," he said, frowning and sounding shocked.

She held him tightly. "I know what I want," she whispered.

"You're a virgin," he said, starting to pull away.

"Garrett," she whispered, holding on to keep him from leaving. "Love me," she whispered. "I want you to," she said before kissing him passionately. He hesitated a moment and then slowly pushed into her, sending a sharp pain that was gone when he filled her and slowly moved in her.

In seconds she rocked with him, lost in desire. The tension increased. Garrett was covered in sweat, moving with her, trying to pleasure her while urgency grew. And then all control was gone. He pumped fast and she met him, clinging to him as relief burst and rapture poured over her.

"Garrett," she cried out, holding him tightly, spinning away in ecstasy, oblivious of all else.

He shuddered with his release and then showered kisses on her, slowing as his ragged breathing calmed.

They were finally still, wrapped together, her heartbeat returning to normal. She held him tightly while her fingers played over one muscled shoulder.

"You should have told me," he said.

"It didn't matter."

"Yes, it did. I tried to avoid hurting you."

She framed his face with her hands and kissed him lightly. "You couldn't hurt me," she said and saw something flicker in the depths of his eyes that was like a warning bell to her, yet had it been her imagination? The warmth in his eyes now enveloped her and she pushed away her worry.

He rolled over, keeping her with him, their legs entangled. He combed long strands of hair away from her face and smiled at her. "You're beautiful," he whispered, kissing her lightly.

"Garrett, when I flew up here, I was certain this would never happen," she said, running her fingers over his bare shoulder.

He showered light kisses on her temple down to her ear. "I actually hadn't planned on it either. I didn't think you'd want to make love." He propped himself up on an elbow to look down at her, gazing intently. "I'll never hurt you, Sophia. I'll never be like your father."

"Shh, Garrett. Let me enjoy the moment now," she said lightly, touched by his statement. She noticed his voice had deepened, his words sounding heartfelt. She combed his brown hair back from his forehead. "This was a one-time thing. I'll go right back to my former resolutions because that's the safe way to live and pro-tect my heart," she said.

He kissed the corner of her mouth lightly. "We'll see what the future brings," he whispered, placing more kisses on her throat.

She ran her fingers along his jaw. "This was perfect. I'll always remember it."

"I agree with that. Monday night I want to see your house, particularly your studio."

"That's a deal. But I think you'll be disappointed. My studio is just an art studio with all the mess that goes with painting."

"It'll be fascinating."

"If it is, you do lead a boring life." She smiled at him and shook her head in wonder. "I'm amazed there isn't one particular woman in your life right now."

"There is definitely one particular woman in my

life right now." He kissed her again on her throat and shoulders.

Through the night they made love and at dawn she fell asleep in his arms. Sometime later, she stirred and looked down at Garrett. The sheet was across his waist, leaving his chest bare. Even in sleep, his looks fascinated her.

She had no regrets. Garrett excited her more than any man she had ever known. He was intelligent, interesting, fun to be with, exceedingly sexy. She thought she could still keep her heart intact as long as she ended the intimacy when they returned to their regular lives in Texas.

But could she do that? She was realistic enough to know that she was not wildly in love. She was certain she could say no to intimacy.

She leaned down to kiss his shoulder so lightly her lips barely brushed him. His arm circled her waist, pulling her down against him as he slowly opened his eyes. He rolled over while she opened her mouth to tell him good morning. Before she could say a word he kissed her and all conversation was lost.

It was almost two hours later when he held her in his arms while sunshine spilled into the room.

"I have a suggestion for the day," he said. "I'll cook breakfast and then we can ski. Or I'll cook breakfast and then we'll stay right here in the cabin."

She laughed. "I say we cook breakfast and ski because that's what we came here to do. And we've been loving it up for hours."

"And I'm ready to love it up some more," he said, rolling over on top of her to end their discussion.

He finally cooked breakfast at one. They ate beside a

window with a view of the mountains that surrounded the small town.

"Do we have time to ski for an hour?"

"Of course," he replied, looking amused. "It's my plane. We can ski for three hours if you want, or longer."

"One hour will be sufficient and then I'll be ready to go back to Texas."

"One hour it is. But there's no need to rush back to Texas."

"Garrett, it's over."

He paused, gazing into her eyes. He cocked his head to one side. "Don't make up your mind hastily. You might change how you feel."

She shook her head. "No. Last night was special and I wanted it to be with you, but we won't pursue it because that could to lead to heartbreak. I'm not taking that chance."

"You're scared to live, Sophia." His gray eyes darkened slightly. He looked away and a muscle worked in his jaw, a more intense reaction than she would have expected. For an instant, anger flashed like a streak of lightning and then was gone.

"Maybe I'm just exercising caution and waiting for a deep, true love. This weekend was a brief idyll in my steady life."

"You're an artist and I doubt if there is any way you can describe your life as 'steady.'"

"Let's clean up and go ski."

"I have someone who will come in and clean after we're gone. We'll spend our time on the slopes."

She hurried to dress, thinking about their conversation and wondering if she could stick by her declarations. She had never expected to have this night of love and yet she had made the decision clearly and rationally and she had no regrets.

But she began to wonder: Was one of the consequences of her actions last night falling in love with Garrett?

She mulled over the question, unable to answer it. She didn't feel the same toward him as she had before they'd made love for hours. And to her surprise, the night simply made her want to be with him more, not less. Could she stand by her resolutions, do what she knew she should do?

Could she avoid a heartbreak with Garrett? Or was she blindly ignoring the truth that she might be falling in love with him already?

Or, more likely, that she had fallen in love with him that first night she met him?

They skied and returned to his condo by five after eating burgers on the way back. Garrett made a call to his pilot. "He'll be ready. I told him we can be there by six."

"I can be ready in just a few minutes. After all, I didn't bring much."

"I'll call him back and make it thirty minutes from now. Or maybe I won't," he said, his voice dropping. He tossed his phone on a table and crossed to take her into his arms, holding her tightly as he kissed her.

Their passionate kiss lengthened until clothes flew and they made love again with a desperate haste.

By seven, they were airborne. She looked below as twinkling lights disappeared and the night swallowed the plane.

"Garrett, it was a wonderful weekend," she said.

He leaned close to kiss her briefly. When he straightened up, he met her gaze. "It *was* a wonderful weekend," he repeated. "An unforgettable one, Sophia. I hope we have more unforgettable moments together. A lot more," he said.

"I don't think that will happen," she said. "We've both avoided any lasting relationship so I don't expect one to happen now."

"The heart is unpredictable."

"You sound like a romantic," she said, amused.

"That's the first time in my life I've ever been accused of being a romantic."

"Maybe I see a different side to you."

He smiled at her.

"When will you let me paint your portrait?"

"I'd love to have anything you paint, except a painting with myself as the subject. I can't exactly see hanging it in my house."

"Everyone should have a portrait painted. It's for posterity. You'll change your mind, and when you do, remember that I'd like to paint it. You have an interesting face."

"Another first. I've never heard that before either. I think you're seeing different things in me from what everyone else sees."

"I see good things."

"Sophia, listen. I want to be in your life for a long time."

"I'm all for continuing to get to know each other, Garrett," she said carefully.

He leaned close, placing his hands on both arms of her chair. "I hope you never change your mind," he said, startling her with his sincerity, a look of deep sorrow on his face.

"What is it, Garrett?"

He sat back and smiled at her, looking himself again. "I just hope we can keep spending time together."

While they talked, she thought about the past twenty-four hours and was still amazed at how her life had taken an unexpected turn since meeting Garrett.

It was after ten by the time they reached her house. "If you have a moment, come in and I'll show you the studio."

"Sure. Why put off until tomorrow what you can do today?" he teased.

They walked through a wide entry hall that had a twelve-foot-high ceiling. A circular staircase curved to the second floor. Double doors opened to a dining area on one side of the front hall while columns separated the hall from a formal living area.

He paused to look at Louis XVI furniture on the polished oak floor and an elegant marble fireplace. "I'm surprised. I expected you to have something rustic to match your paintings." One of her landscapes hung above the mantel. "That's a superb painting. No wonder you kept it."

"Thank you. I enjoy it. Mountains and a stream—I've been there and I like to look at the painting and remember."

She took his arm. "Come on. I'll show you the kitchen and my studio."

They entered a blue-and-white kitchen with ash woodwork and a casual dining area. "Now I can picture you in your house when I talk to you on the phone," he said.

Switching on lights, she led him into another spacious room. "Here's where I spend most of my time."

He stood looking at her studio with easels, drawing boards, a wide paint-spattered table. Paintings hung on the walls and stood on the floor. Empty frames of various sizes leaned against a wall. Garrett prowled the room and then paused at the large windows overlooking her patio and pool area. Crystal-blue water filled a free-form-shaped pool that had two splashing fountains.

He turned to her. "I like to see where you work. Now do I get to see the bedrooms upstairs?"

She smiled at him. "No, you don't. It's getting late and we've had a long weekend."

"So I'm not allowed to see your bedroom."

"You don't need to," she said, smiling at him as she linked her arm in his.

"I'm having the grand tour tonight but I still want to take you to dinner tomorrow."

"I look forward to it," she said as they walked to her front door.

Before they reached it, he stopped to face her, placing his hands on her waist. "This weekend was incredibly special," he said in a husky voice.

"It was for me," she said, looking up into his gray eyes that mesmerized her as always. Desire filled them and her heart drummed loudly.

"You're special, Sophia. I mean what I say. I never expected to feel the way I do toward you. From the first moment, knowing you hasn't been at all what I expected. So quickly, you've become important to me," he added with a solemn expression.

"So you had expectations about meeting me? That's interesting." In some ways, she wanted to cover her ears and stop hearing his words because she was falling in love with him and it scared her. But Garrett's words wrapped around her heart. He, too, looked as if he were wrestling with something, so their attraction was taking an emotional toll on him, too. "You've become important to me, too, Garrett," she whispered. She stepped close, going on tiptoe to kiss him.

Instantly his arms banded her waist and he leaned over her, kissing her hard.

As if unable to control her own actions, she twisted free his buttons swiftly, her fingers shaking, while she still kissed him.

He tossed off clothes and peeled away hers and in seconds, he lifted her while he kissed her.

"Protection, Garrett?"

"I have it," he said. When he picked her up again, she locked her long legs around him as he lowered her on his thick rod to make love to her.

Crying out, she climaxed, going over an edge while colors exploded behind her closed eyelids.

He shuddered with his release. "Sophia, love," he said in a gruff, husky voice. The endearment made her heart miss a beat.

She moved with him until they both began to catch their breath. He gave her light kisses and finally set her on her feet.

"Now I do need to be directed to a bathroom somewhere in this house."

"There's one in the guest bedroom at the back of the hall, across from my studio. Clean towels will be out."

He leaned down to kiss her again, then gathered his clothes. She picked up hers, pausing to watch him walk away. He was muscled and fit. He looked strong, masculine, sexy. Her gaze ran down his smooth back, over hard buttocks and then down his muscled legs. He was hard, solid and breathtaking.

She gathered her things and headed to her own bathroom off her studio.

In a short time she returned to the front hall to find

him waiting by the door. When she reached him, he pulled her close to kiss her tenderly.

"I don't suppose I'm going to be invited to stay the rest of the night."

"As adorable as you are, no invitation is forthcoming."

"Let me take you to breakfast again. I'll want to see you in the morning."

She laughed. "Garrett, that's crazy. And I can't go. I have appointments."

"I want to be with you."

"Again, Garrett, this has been a special weekend I'll never forget."

He kissed her again. When they moved apart, he opened the door and stepped outside. "Thanks for going with me."

After he left, she locked up and went upstairs to her bedroom.

Had she just done the most foolish thing of her life by making love with him? She hoped not. There was no denying he was becoming more significant to her all the time. In her room she spun around just as she had outside the restaurant in the falling snow in Colorado. Exuberance, excitement, memories dazzled her. Shoving aside worries, she thought about their loving, remembering Garrett in moments of passion, his magnificent body, his tenderness, his heat and sexiness. His kisses held promises and temptation. It had been one of the most wonderful weekends in her life.

She sang as she hurried to shower, moving as if by rote while she replayed the weekend in her mind.

Was this love? Was she already wildly in love with him?

Five

A car was parked at the gate of Garrett's estate. As his lights shone on it, the door opened and Edgar stepped out, patiently waiting.

Garrett's heart dropped. He knew why Edgar was waiting for him.

He put the car in Park and stepped out to walk to Edgar. His mind raced. Had Edgar already told Sophia? Was he here at Sophia's request or because of his own anger over Garrett's duplicity?

The gatekeeper stood in the doorway of the gate-house. "I tried to reach you on your cell," he said.

"It's all right," Garrett said. "I know Mr. Hollingworth." He turned to shake hands with Edgar, relieved slightly to see Edgar offer his hand.

"Sorry, Garrett," Edgar said. "I know this is a late hour, but I want to talk to you in person. This isn't something to deal with over the phone."

"That's fine. Come up to the house and we'll talk. You can follow me in."

"Thanks."

Garrett returned to his car to drive through the gates. Edgar turned in behind him. At least he had been civil, which was a hopeful sign. More than he expected from Sophia when she discovered the truth about his connections.

At the house, he led Edgar into the library where a decanter of brandy and small crystal glasses sat on a mahogany table.

"Would you care for brandy?"

"Yes, thank you."

Shedding his jacket, Garrett poured two brandies although he had no interest in drinking. He handed a glass to Edgar.

"You're more than CEO of a Houston property management firm," Edgar said. "You're CFO of Delaney Enterprises in Dallas. I assume the property management business here is a sideline of yours."

"It actually was started by my dad," Garrett said. He looked at Edgar, waiting for the rest. When Edgar didn't continue, Garrett asked, "Have you told Sophia yet?"

"No."

"I'll tell you what I'm doing here and why I haven't told her about my connection," Garrett said, proceeding to run through his history with the Delaneys and his purpose in meeting Sophia.

"I intended to get to know her so she would at least let someone talk to her about meeting with Will Delaney. So far, she won't even talk to their lawyer, much less to any of them. Edgar, I don't know what details she's told you, but she stands to lose an enormous inheritance and cost the Delaney brothers theirs. They are as innocent in this as she is."

"I know," Edgar said, swirling his brandy in the snifter and then looking up to meet Garrett's gaze. "She's told me. That's why I'm here. First, I don't want her hurt."

"I don't want to hurt her either. I hate keeping this secret from her. I've come to care very much about Sophia. To be honest, I've thought about resigning, but I have deep obligations to the Delaney family."

"Don't resign. I want you to succeed. I want Sophia to get her inheritance. It's absurd for her to toss aside that kind of money. I came to see you to learn what you intend and to make certain you're not going to hurt her. I feel like a father to her."

"I will try in every way I can to avoid hurting her."

"Sophia is very cautious with men. Therefore, she's rather naive. As far as the Delaneys go—I hope to heaven you succeed in making her listen."

"They want to know her and want her in their family. But they didn't even know she existed until the reading of Argus's will."

"Why am I not surprised. That man was arrogant."

"There's one grandchild, Caroline Delaney, who is five years old. This will hurt her, too," he said, pulling out his phone and touching it. He crossed the room to show a photo to Edgar.

"Great heavens!" Edgar exclaimed, taking the phone to stare at the picture. "Except for the curly hair, she looks like Sophia. Actually, Sophia and this half brother bear a strong resemblance."

"Yes, they do."

"Does Sophia know about the child?"

"She has to because Caroline is in the will. There's a

trust for her. Caroline's mother walked out when Caroline was a baby and the oldest brother, Adam, was her father. When he was killed in a plane crash, Will became Caroline's guardian. Caroline has lost enough in this life." Garrett put away the phone, retrieved his brandy and sat again.

Edgar sipped his brandy. "I'll do what I can, but I can't keep her from looking you up. I'm amazed she hasn't already. She must like you and take you at your word."

"I think she's been reassured because Jason Trent knows me. She knows I have a business here and you had already met me. I've had her to my house and now we've spent a weekend together."

"Believe me, that's unlike her. She's very cautious and I'm sure she's already told you why."

"Argus again and his treatment of her mother. I'm not Argus or even close, and not one drop of his blood runs in my veins."

"True. I hope you can talk some sense into her for her own sake. It's absurd for her to toss aside that fabulous inheritance. She doesn't have the kind of money to be so blasé about it."

"Thanks for letting me try to work this out. I just want her to talk to Will and to think about what she's doing to them and herself."

"If I can help in any manner, let me know." Edgar took another long sip of brandy and set down his glass. "I'll go now. I'm relieved to hear your purpose and I hope you succeed. I'll stay out of this until I'm asked to do otherwise."

He offered his hand and they shook again. "Thanks, Edgar. I appreciate it. I intend to tell her soon and I hope that doesn't end her speaking to me."

"I can't help you much if it does. Sophia has a mind of her own and is quite independent. She grew up that way."

At the front door, Garrett walked out on the porch. "Take care, Edgar. The gates will be open."

"Good luck. I will try to get her to listen to reason. Sooner or later she will tell me when she learns the truth about you."

As Garrett watched him drive away, his cell phone rang. It was Will Delaney.

"How did the weekend go?" he asked.

"It was fine. But suppose you had called in the middle of a moment when I would not have wanted to talk to you?"

"You wouldn't have answered your phone," Will said with a laugh.

"I'm actually glad you called. I've been thinking about it, Will. I don't want to accept any pay for this."

"What the hell? Is there something in the water in Houston that makes people not want money? She won't take her inheritance. Now you don't want your pay."

"Just accept that I am off the payroll on this. I'm doing the Delaneys a favor. It's free, gratis," he said, feeling a faint degree better that he wasn't taking money for keeping his purpose from Sophia. But he still hated being secretive.

"I'm not going to argue with you. You're a big boy now and if you don't want money, okay. We can renegotiate your salary."

"Don't push me, Will," Garrett said. He knew Will was teasing and being flip, but he didn't feel like horsing around.

"Sorry, Garrett, if this has turned sour for you. Okay,

no pay. We're all grateful as hell, as usual. So it went well?"

"Yes, it went well. I'll call you when I have something solid to report. Night, Will."

He clicked off. His thoughts shifted to Edgar and then to Sophia. Tomorrow night he had to tell her the truth. Would the intimacy they had shared this weekend be a strong enough bond to keep her from despising him? He couldn't answer his own question.

Sleep eluded him again. He mulled over the fact that she had been a virgin. He was the first man in her life, which shook him. She had strong feelings about intimacy and had avoided it all these years. He hadn't expected that and now, not telling her his connection to the Delaneys seemed even worse.

Why had she changed her mind this weekend? How deep did feelings run between them? Were they deep enough to withstand the shock she was going to receive?

Could she forgive him? If she did agree to meet the Delaneys and give them a chance, would it mean that she was willing to give her relationship with him a chance? Garrett clenched his fists. He was anxious to tell her while at the same time, he dreaded the moment. The fact that she had let him make love to her made him feel a bond with her that he hadn't experienced before. Thinking about making love last night, his thoughts shifted and memories flooded him until he had to get out of bed and do something physical because he couldn't sleep. The prospect of flying home and resigning still tempted him, yet he couldn't do that either. Obligations to the Delaneys, to Will, to memories of his father's wishes were all too strong. Now the Delaney legacy made him sink even deeper into his obligations to them.

He had to stay and confess his ties to the Delaneys to Sophia.

Not one thing about meeting Sophia had turned out the way he had expected. The most certain thing he knew, though, was that he wanted her with him. He missed her and wanted her in his arms and in his bed right now. He conjured up the memory of her spinning around in the snow, big flakes on her silky black hair and lashes and coat, her smile, her bubbling enthusiasm and zest for life. He ached to hold her again and he would remember the weekend all his life.

Would the truth destroy his budding relationship with Sophia? Or could he make her see how much he wanted to be with her even though he had kept this secret from her?

He had basically lied to her about who he was. How could he make it up to her? Would she even let him try?

Sophia tossed restlessly in bed. She missed Garrett, but she was annoyed with herself for reacting in such a manner. The weekend still dazzled her, memories bubbling up constantly that enveloped her and carried her away. Garrett had changed her feelings about intimacy. Had her feelings for Garrett become so strong, she was changing her basic views of life?

They would be together again in less than twenty-four hours. He would have stayed tonight if she had let him. Those two things made her wonder: Was she rushing headlong into a life like her mother's? Had Garrett so easily demolished all the barriers she kept around her heart?

Realizing that she needed a distraction from thinking about Garrett, she switched on a light and got up to paint, losing herself in her task and driving all thought of him away until morning came.

Monday night she dressed eagerly, trying various outfits and finally selecting a red crepe blouse with a low-cut rounded neckline and straight skirt that had a slit on one side. She pinned the sides of her hair up, letting it fall in the back.

Her pulse raced with anticipation and she was impatient to see him.

When she greeted him, he stepped inside and swept her into his arms. Words were lost as he kissed her. She locked her arms around him and kissed him in return.

Finally she stepped back. "Another minute and I won't look presentable to go out to dinner."

"That's impossible." He held her waist and stepped back to look at her. "You're beautiful, just perfect."

"I think you're the perfect one," she said, thinking his charcoal suit made his gray eyes appear darker. "I'm ready."

"So am I," he said in a husky voice, referring to more than just dinner.

"We're going to dinner. You promised," she reminded him.

"Yes, I did. We'll go eat and then we're coming back here and I'm going to kiss you the way I want to."

His words made her tingle and she smiled at him.

He took her arm to escort her to a sleek black sports car. She was surprised it wasn't his chauffeur and his limousine, wondering why he preferred driving. Was it because he expected to stay at her house a long time tonight when he took her home?

She wasn't exactly sure how she felt about that, despite the desire for him that had been burning through her since they'd last made love.

They drove through posts and a wrought-iron fence, winding up a drive past splashing fountains and tall pines with lights high in the branches. As they stopped in front of a canopied walk and he gave the keys to a valet, he took her arm. Lights twinkled in all the bushes and over the restaurant, creating a festive atmosphere.

Inside, a large bouquet of four dozen red and yellow roses in a sparkling crystal vase on a marble table stood in the center of the entryway. A maître d' met them, talked briefly to Garrett and led them to a table in a secluded corner that overlooked the dance floor on one side and a terrace on the other. Beyond the terrace were sloping grounds to a well-lit pond with more lights in the trees. Soft piano music played and a few couples were already on the small dance floor.

"I've never eaten here before, Garrett. I've heard of this place, but just haven't been here. It's lovely."

"The food is great. I think you'll like it." A candle flickered in the center of the linen-covered table. Garrett reached across to take her hand. Candlelight was reflected in his gray eyes and her gaze dropped to his mouth. "The weekend was special," he said in a husky voice.

"It was for me, you know that," she replied breathlessly, studying him as he watched her. He had one of the most interesting faces and she wished he would let her paint his portrait. The only problem was that she would want to keep it, and that was the last thing she needed in her house right now, especially if she was trying to slow things down.

"I brought you something to remind you of the weekend and to let you know that it was special for me," he said, handing her a small package.

Surprised, she looked up and smiled. "How sweet you are. You know you didn't need to do this."

She untied a silver ribbon and then unwrapped blue paper on a small box. When she opened it, another velvet box was inside. She removed it and took out a thin gold filigree bracelet.

"Garrett, it's beautiful," she said, touched and surprised. She looked up at him and then took it out to slip it on, turning her wrist as the candlelight highlighted the gold. "Thank you. It's lovely and I'll treasure it."

"Enjoy it, Sophia, and remember the fun we had."

"Of course I will," she said, picking up his hand and leaning forward to brush a light kiss across his knuckles. He inhaled, his chest expanding while desire burned in the depths of his eyes.

All through dinner and later as they danced, desire kept her tingly. Dancing with him was as much fun as everything else. She enjoyed the fast dances; the slow dancing was sexy, tantalizing, making her want to love again. When they stopped and she looked up to meet his gaze, he appeared to be thinking about the same thing she'd been thinking about.

Garrett had a thick steak while she had lobster tail with white wine. Her appetite fled as she watched him in the flickering candlelight. Garrett had ensnared her heart. There was no way she could keep things light with him or hold to her resolution to avoid a relationship. He was important to her and he turned her insides out just looking at him.

By ten, when Garrett asked her if she was ready to leave, she nodded.

At her house, she invited Garrett inside.

"You've had the tour, so would you like a drink—a cup of hot chocolate, soda?"

"If you have iced tea, I'll take that."

"Two iced teas it is," she said, heading for the kitchen. She crossed the room to get out glasses.

"Have a seat and I'll get our drinks. We can go where it's more comfortable."

Garrett moved closer and turned her to face him. "Sophia," he said in a husky voice, and her heart skipped. He leaned down to kiss her while his arm held her waist tightly.

The moment he touched her, her insides clenched and her pulse jumped. She hugged him tightly in return while her intentions to say no to making love vanished.

Nothing seemed as important as kissing and loving him.

"Now you'll have to show me a bedroom," he said, kissing her throat.

"There's one down the hall on this floor," she said, taking his hand to lead him to the bedroom where he stood her on her feet as he continued kissing her. His hands moved deftly over zippers and buttons, and her skirt floated to her ankles where she stepped out of it.

"This time we're taking it nice and slow," he said, taking time to shower kisses on her. He loved her with deliberation, trying to pleasure her and heighten desire every way he could until she was writhing beneath his touch, aching for him.

"Garrett, come here," she whispered, reaching for him.

He slipped on a condom and lowered himself, slowly filling her, withdrawing and entering again while she arched beneath him.

His loving was slow, a sweet torment that fanned the fires he had already ignited.

He was beaded with sweat, trying to maintain control until finally he let go and loved furiously.

She cried out as she climaxed and in seconds he shuddered with his release.

Gradually her heartbeat returned to normal and her breathing grew quiet. They helped each other up and went to shower together, drying each other off only to return to bed. He pulled her into his embrace, holding her while he combed her hair with his fingers.

"Garrett, I didn't know it could be this way," she confessed. "I couldn't say no to you."

"I hope you never can," he whispered, kissing her temple while he held her against his heart with his arms wrapped around her. "This is perfect, Sophia."

"You might as well stay tonight. There's no reason not to."

"I'm glad to hear you say that. I'm surprised you asked me."

"I surprised myself, but it seems logical. And my bracelet is beautiful. Thank you again."

"Just remember our weekend together."

"I will always. There's no way I can forget it."

He gazed into her eyes. "I hope you don't. It was special to me." He kissed her lightly. Though he'd told her many times before, his words thrilled her. She ran her hands over his shoulders, relishing being with him.

At two in the morning, he partially sat up. "I'm ready now for that cup of hot chocolate you offered. Is it still in the offering?"

"Of course. You have to wait a minute because I'm putting on a robe."

"That takes away the fun."

"Otherwise, we'll never get to the hot chocolate."

"True enough."

She stood, wrapping herself in a comforter and going to get a robe. "I'll meet you in the kitchen."

He grinned and waved, his gaze roaming over her as if mentally peeling away the comforter.

"You look gorgeous."

"It's my beautiful gold bracelet," she replied, holding out her arm and letting the bracelet catch glints of light. Smiling, she left to go upstairs and get her best robe, a black velvet robe with a silk lining. She brushed her hair and went down.

When she entered the kitchen, Garrett already had mugs with steaming cocoa on the table. Dressed in his white shirt and slacks again, he gazed at her, then walked to meet her and place his hands on her waist. His white shirt was unbuttoned halfway and she wanted to run her fingers through the hair on his chest. He had turned the fancy French cuffs back and he looked sexy.

"You look far too gorgeous for that to be called a bathrobe. And far too sexy for that to not be for the benefit of some man."

"You know absolutely there hasn't been a man—until now. It's my best warm and comfy bathrobe."

"I'm glad you said 'until now' and I hope it stays that way."

"Garrett, I've warned you about that from the beginning."

He leaned down to kiss her long and hard. Her heart raced as if it were the first time. She couldn't get enough of him. Fighting an inner battle between what she wanted and what she thought she should do, she shifted away.

"We're going to drink hot chocolate, remember?" she said breathlessly, placing her hand against his chest.

He still held her. "Sophia, you're important to me.

I know we haven't known each other long, but that really doesn't matter. You're essential and I want you in my life."

While her heart drummed, his words held her enthralled. "Saturday night wouldn't have happened if you hadn't been very important to me."

"I'm glad. Don't forget what I've said."

"Garrett, you've said that to me before. What am I missing?"

"Before we sit to drink our hot chocolate, I want to talk to you and I hope you'll listen to everything I have to say."

She looked at him and realized that whatever it was he was about to tell her, it wasn't good. "What is it, Garrett? Go ahead and tell me what's troubling you," she said, puzzled, wondering what he wanted to talk about.

"We've become friends, haven't we?"

"Yes, of course. But more than friends, Garrett. Lovers."

"Good. I want to keep it that way."

"What are you getting at?" she asked, growing chilled. What had he been keeping from her that might change her feelings for him? "What do you want to talk about?"

"I want you to promise me you'll listen and keep an open mind."

"I'll listen and I'll try to keep an open mind unless you're going to tell me you're married with a family," she said stiffly. Suddenly, all her fears about rushing into intimacy with him came back to her. All her life she had been cautious, but she threw caution to the wind when Garrett came into her life. And she had a feeling she was about to find out that she'd made a terrible mistake.

He shook his head. "Nothing like that."

Relief was slight because whatever he intended to tell her, it was serious. "I'll try to keep an open mind," she said, though she could already feel the walls closing down around her heart. "But I can't make any promises."

Six

Garrett framed her face with his hands and she watched as he took a deep breath. "I was asked to meet you and get to know you. I was hired to do so, actually, but I've told them I won't take the money. I swear I never expected it to turn out this way at all. I didn't dream I would get any closer to you than I had to in order to talk to you."

"You were hired? To meet me? I don't understand," she said, confusion flooding her. Garrett was struggling with his words, and he wasn't giving her information fast enough. "Answer me, Garrett! Who hired—" She stopped speaking and stared at him, her confusion changing to burning fury. There was only one group of people in the world who would have to hire someone to try to get her to meet with them. "No! It's the Delaneys, isn't it?"

"Yes, it's the Delaneys. Please, Sophia, you have to believe me. I never thought I, we would—"

"Damn you, Garrett," she said, astounded at his pretense and the advantage he had taken of her. She was furious with herself for letting down her guard. "I promised to listen and keep an open mind, but I'm not going to now. Everything you've done has been a sham. You've been conniving and false from the start," she accused. "All that asking about my family, listening while I told you about my father—you're as bad as he was," she said, shaking with rage. "You knew! You knew all the time who Argus was and what he had done! You knew how I grew up. You knew everything when you met me and passed yourself off as a Houston businessman."

"I am a Houston businessman. I own that business."

"How are you connected with the Delaneys?" she blurted, startled to hear he actually had the Houston business.

"I'm the CFO of Delaney Enterprises."

She felt as if he had delivered a blow to her. "So the best friend you talked about, the family obligations—that's all the Delaneys, isn't it?" She clenched her fists. "I'm not going to listen to you. Everything you've done has been underhanded and low. How could you?" she cried.

"Sophia, by denying your heritage and your inheritance, you're hurting innocent people and you're hurting yourself."

"You can't possibly justify your actions." She thought of what had happened between them in Colorado, devastation washing over her like a crushing wave. "How you must have laughed after this weekend. You seduced me for the Delaneys," she said, grinding out the words, tears of anger and hurt threatening, adding to her fury.

"No, I did not. I meant what I've said to you, Sophia. I swear. I meant what I said about how special this weekend was for me—about how special you are to me."

"Oh, please," she snapped, hating him for what he'd done and angry with herself for tossing aside all caution where Garrett had been concerned. She was shaking and hurting all over, and she wanted nothing more than to get rid of him and make sure she never had to lay eyes on him again. "You can get out, Garrett. Out of my house and out of my life."

"I'm not going until you listen to me and hear my side of the story."

"Get out of here," she cried. "I don't want to see you or talk to you. I want you out of my life." She tried to slip the bracelet off her wrist, her hands shaking as she fumbled. She finally succeeded, throwing it at him. He caught it and slowly put it into his pocket, never taking his eyes off her.

"I just want you to listen for a moment," he said, speaking quietly. "You're harming yourself as much as you're hurting them and they haven't done any more than you have. All they did was end up with Argus Delaney as their father. You can't select your parents, and neither could they. So why are you doing this to them, Sophia?"

"I already told you. I don't want anything from Argus Delaney. He never gave me love or attention or even acknowledgment that I was his daughter. Never," she declared bitterly, tears over Garrett's betrayal blinding her eyes as they spilled faster than she could wipe them away. "My father gave us money as a man gives cash to a prostitute. I'm not turning down the money to hurt my half brothers. I'm refusing it because it's the only way I can reject Argus Delaney. He gave it out of guilt at the end of his life, and I will do nothing to exonerate the way he treated me or my mother."

Garrett reached out to touch her and she jerked away from him as if he had scalded her with his touch.

"This isn't about them," she said. "It's about him. All those years from the time I was born until I was in my twenties, he treated me as if I was nothing. I'm not trying to hurt them."

"But you are hurting them. Can't you see? And not just your half brothers. Sophia, there's a grandchild. An adorable little girl, Caroline, who someday will inherit Delaney money. You're hurting that child."

Momentarily startled, she stared at Garrett. "There's a grandchild mentioned in the will. A trust was left for her, which has nothing to do with these inheritances. So how could this affect her?"

"Eventually, she'll inherit money left by her uncles. It's not as big a thing with Caroline, but she's in the family and will inherit family money," he said, pulling out his phone and holding it out for Sophia to see. "Here's Caroline with Will, who is her guardian since her father was killed. Look at it, Sophia. Here are two of the people you're hurting."

She snapped her mouth closed and looked at a picture of a beautiful child with long, black, curly hair and huge brown eyes. Shocked, Sophia stared. The little girl looked like her at a young age. She could see the family resemblance between herself and both the child and the smiling, handsome man in the picture.

"I hadn't thought about the future for her." She continued to stare at the picture, suddenly struck by the fact that she had a family, a family that she had never met, a family that looked very much like her. There was no doubt they were all related. Shaken, she couldn't stop staring at the picture—until she looked at the man who was holding it. Her hurt deepened and she walked away from Garrett to put space between them.

"They have money. The Delaneys are worth billions. This isn't going to hurt any of them." She spun around to glare at him, her anger returning. "If they don't get this inheritance, they'll still be enormously wealthy. They are young and into enough enterprises. They will make more money than they even know what to do with. I want no part of my father or anything that belonged to him. Not a dollar—not a fortune. I will have no part of him."

"He'll never know," Garrett answered, putting away his phone. "Your father is dead now, Sophia. You're not hurting him. The people whose lives you are affecting are Will, Zach, Ryan and Caroline," Garrett said quietly. "Sophia, they didn't even know about your existence— Don't punish them when they haven't snubbed you. When they found out they had a sister, they wanted to meet you. They feel you're part of the family and all of you should be united. Aside from the money, they would have tried to meet you and bring you into the family. They are great guys in spite of their father. They don't want to hurt you. They want you to have your money as much as they would like to have theirs. And they want to meet their sister."

"So they sent you to trick me into meeting them."

"There was no tricking you. They tried to meet you openly. Will called. Zach flew here. You've rejected every contact, including their attorney."

Sophia was losing her patience with Garrett, and

she couldn't stand here and have this conversation with him any longer. "I don't see why you are still standing here when you know you're unwanted," she said coldly, her eyes still blurry from tears that streamed down her cheeks. "Once again, I don't care about the Delaney brothers' inheritances or about meeting them. I don't want to see you again, and I never want to see the Delaneys. I want you to go. You deceived me, Garrett."

"You're not going to listen or give me any kind of chance, are you?"

"How could you do this?" she lashed out, her voice a hiss. She wanted him to get out of her house and her life. Why couldn't he understand?

"I did it because those guys are important to me. And all they want is for you to give them a chance. But I don't want to lose you," he said. Her burning anger had turned to a chill. She shook and couldn't stop tears from falling.

"Get out, Garrett. Just go. You can't change my mind, and you and I are through."

"Sophia, don't do this. You're being stubborn and foolish. If you don't want the money for yourself, give it to charity and do some good with it. You don't have to keep it or live on it."

"There is nothing you can say that will make me change my mind. I don't ever want to meet my half brothers. The only thing we have in common is Argus Delaney and nothing else. Garrett, get it through your head—I don't want to have anything to do with any part of my father, and those half brothers are all part of him."

"You're part of him, Sophia."

"Don't remind me. If I could do anything to erase that, I would." She walked toward the door, opening it to make it very clear that she needed him to leave. "You have to go now."

"Why the hell are you being so selfish about this?" he said. Momentarily, she was taken aback by his harsh accusation and then her anger surged again.

"Selfish? Haven't you been listening when I've talked about my father? His world revolved around him. He thought only of himself. His ego was enormous. Don't accuse me of being selfish. He took the prize."

"But what would it hurt to meet them? There's no way you can be harmed by a meeting. You're being stubborn and unreasonable about this—spiteful and hurtful for no reason. Argus will never know, Sophia. You are not getting back at your father," Garrett said, his voice rising.

"How dare you. How dare you call me spiteful and hurtful after what you've just done to me. In case I haven't made it abundantly clear, Garrett, I don't want to see you again ever."

"Sophia, I don't want to lose you. You're important to me and I thought I was to you. I thought we had something special between us. Other than my connections with the Delaneys, I've been open and truthful with you."

"Other than your connections with the Delaneys? How can you discount that? That is actually the first thing you should have told me about yourself. Because the problem now, Garrett, is that I don't believe you or trust you, and I never will. Get out of my life."

"I'm sorry, Sophia. I'm sorry about everything. About the way this worked out, about how long I kept the truth from you. Just please promise me that you'll think about this and stop having such a closed mind."

Sophia wasn't even going to grace his request with a

response. Instead, she walked out of the room. He followed and caught up with her at the door.

"Just think about what I've said to you. Give some thought to your half brothers who have done nothing to you." When she refused to look at him, he paused for a moment. "Maybe, Sophia, you're more like Argus than you care to admit."

"How dare you, Garrett!" she cried. His words cut like a knife. How could she possibly have given this man her body? Her heart? What on earth was she thinking? "Get out of my life!"

"That isn't what I want to do. I don't want things to end this way between us."

"There is no 'us,' Garrett."

"There was, and there can be, if you'll just give me a chance to explain. I put off telling you about the Delaneys because I was scared of losing you. What I feel for you is real."

"I can't believe you care."

He clenched his fists. "What I want is you in my arms, and in my life. What I feel for you, I've never felt for any woman. I can't tell you how many times I thought about calling Will and resigning. But I didn't, because I believed I was doing the right thing—both for you, and for them."

"Goodbye, Garrett," she said, unwilling to listen to another second of his plea.

"I wish you viewed this differently. You're stirring up a storm when you could have so much joy and give so much joy. And you're doing it for the wrong reasons. Actually, reason doesn't even enter into it. You're blindly striking out and trying to hurt whoever you can. Listen, if I had thought I could be up front with you from the first moment, I would have been. But I can see now that I was right. You wouldn't have talked to me, and so I did the only thing I could to get near you. You have a closed mind. You want me out of your life? I'm out," he stated coldly. He turned and left in long strides.

Sophia slammed her heavy door and sagged against it, sobbing and shaking. She hurt badly in every way.

Garrett had betrayed her—she couldn't perceive anything else. Their lovemaking had simply been a means to an end, nothing more. When they had made love, he hadn't been emotionally involved—he had been working. But as swiftly as that thought came, she replayed the pain in his voice as he confessed to her, and she believed his emotions were real.

Yet how could she trust him now?

She heard his car and then it was gone. And with that, Garrett vanished out of her life.

She sat on the nearest chair and cried. Hurt was overwhelming. Heartbroken, she hated herself for being duped just as much as she hated Garrett for deceiving her. How blind she had been to Garrett's purpose.

His accusations echoed in her thoughts—*you're selfish*; *you're blindly striking out and trying to hurt whoever you can.*

Was he right? Was she being selfish?

He had not succeeded or even come close to getting her to consider meeting the Delaneys. So would Garrett continue trying, or was he giving up?

Would she ever see him again? And could she admit to herself that after everything he had done to her, after everything that had happened, the possibility of never seeing him was the worst part of all of this?

Garrett slid behind the wheel and took deep breaths. Desperate at the thought of losing Sophia, he had been tempted to just grasp her shoulders and force her to talk to him. But where the Delaneys were concerned, Sophia had shut off reason.

Her actions shocked him even though he had known about her feeling rejected beforehand, and had heard her bitterness when she talked about the Delaneys, particularly her father.

Anger churned his insides. Along with fury was an uncustomary hurt. He had enjoyed being with her more than any other woman he had known. He wasn't ready for the hurt of losing her. He wasn't ready for the fallout from telling the truth, yet he had been compelled to do so. How could she be so stubborn?

Clenching his teeth until his jaw hurt, he drove home, charging into the empty house and tossing down his keys. Yanking off his jacket as he headed to his room, he tried to compose his thoughts and get a grip on his stormy emotions.

He'd always thought Will was the most stubborn Delaney—until now. Sophia was more stubborn than Will because Will would at least listen to reason and if you got through to him, he would cooperate. Sophia, on the other hand, turned deaf ears to his arguments.

He thought about the night and her passion. It was as if he had been with a different woman when they had made love. A warm, loving, passionate woman. He hurt and hurt for her.

He swore quietly, pacing his room, glaring at the phone. He needed to break the news to Will, but he wasn't ready yet.

Would she ever give him another chance to talk to her about the Delaneys—or to make it up to her? He doubted it and he didn't care to hang around with unreasonable expectations.

He went to the kitchen to get a cold beer. Reeling with anger and frustration, Garrett popped the top and took a drink, feeling the cold liquid wash down his throat.

Procrastinating, Garrett stared at the window. He did not want to call Will or any other Delaney. Yet he had to. What would he do if he were in Will's place? What could he suggest Will and his brothers do now? In future years, after the inheritances were dispersed to other places and no longer an issue, then would she meet with the Delaneys? The brothers truly wanted to know their sister, and Garrett knew they wouldn't stop trying. Surely then she would think more rationally about them and give them a chance.

But would she ever give *him* another chance?

Garrett paced the floor and sipped his beer while he thought. All the time he had argued with her, he had wanted to just wrap his arms around her and ask her to forgive him, believe him and go back to the way things had been. He knew that was unrealistic, but he wanted her badly and he hurt now in a manner he had never hurt before in his life.

Reluctantly, he picked up the phone. Will answered on the second ring.

"Will, it's Garrett."

"You're running true to schedule, waking me in the wee hours of the morning. What's the deal?"

"Here's the latest," he said, pausing. This was the second-hardest thing he had ever had to tell someone. "I did what I could for you with Sophia."

"Whoa, Garrett. You told her who you are?"

"Yes, I did. I had to. I think waiting longer would have made it worse and it's bad enough anyway."

"Go ahead," Will said, his voice becoming gruff, the

disappointment showing. "I'm not sure I want to hear, but I know I have to. This doesn't sound good."

"It's not," Garrett declared. "She's adamant about her decision. She still won't meet with any of you," he said, pain rippling through him as he remembered her cold remarks to him.

"Dammit, I thought you were getting close to her— I thought this would work."

"I did get damn close to her, but the instant she learned the truth… You can't imagine her fury. She doesn't want anything to do with me or any Delaney. Will, I did my damnedest with her."

"I'm sure you did. I'm disappointed, but not with you. You always give a job your best."

"We were getting along great and I thought I could safely tell her. I was wrong, but I don't think she would have been any different if I had waited a year. She won't listen to reason. She's stubborn, determined and filled with hate for Argus. Because of that, Sophia will pass up the inheritance and hurt herself along with all of you. I've been shocked by the depth of her anger toward your dad. It's monumental."

"Garrett, I gotta ask," he said. "I've been thinking about you giving up your pay for this. Do you care about her?"

Silence stretched between them. Garrett didn't want to answer Will, but he knew his silence was telling.

"Dammit," Will said. "We didn't want you getting hurt in the cross fire."

"Forget it, Will. None of us—not any of you, Sophia or even I—expected us to get involved. That's beside the point here."

"Sorry. That's bad news. When the time is up on the

inheritances, and we still want to meet her, do you think she'll at least meet us and let us try to be a family?"

"I can't answer that."

"We all want to know her. You liked her, so in the right circumstances, I suppose we would, too."

"Yes, you would. She's like you in some ways, like Zach in others. She's stubborn as hell—definitely a Delaney."

Another heavy silence ensued. "What do you suggest as a next step?" Will finally asked.

"I've been thinking about it and the only thing I can come up with is to go back to your lawyer. Or get a different lawyer and see if he can reason with her."

"Like I said, she won't even talk to our attorney. She has her attorney talk to our attorney."

"All right, but get him to tell her attorney everything you want her to know. Try to get him to convince her attorney this is in her best interests, which it is. Also, try to get across that you want to know her and include her in the family."

"We'll do that."

"How can her attorney not want to argue in your favor when the size of the inheritance is so huge?" Garrett asked.

"I don't know. Maybe a female attorney might get farther."

"I don't think it'll matter. Man or woman, just get someone who is very clever and competent."

"We'll try. Don't come home yet. Stay a few days longer and see if Sophia relents and has a change of heart."

"Will, I'm coming home. Sophia doesn't want to talk to me or see me again."

"How could she be this bitter when he provided for them and her mother was in love with him?"

"She hated seeing her mother hurt by him, especially when he wouldn't marry her. As a child she felt shut out and ignored by him."

"That wasn't so different from how he dealt with us. We had nannies, boarding schools. It wasn't until we were adults that he began to show real interest in us."

"She doesn't know that and won't care. Since she's never met any of you, you're not real to her and she is lashing out at him. She's financially independent and she's content with what she has."

"The one person on earth who doesn't want more money and she has to turn out to be our sister."

"Sorry, Will. I failed all of you, but I tried," Garrett said. "Will, other than this facet to her personality, she's great. She truly is. You would like her."

"Too bad she's not one of those people who wants to be reunited with her long-lost relatives."

"Work with your lawyer. Beyond that, I can't think of any way to reach her."

"Thanks, Garrett. I know you tried. I still say you might hang around in case she has a change of heart. Miracles happen and you had a chance to say some good things about us."

"Will, I couldn't say anything about you, much less sing your praises."

"You surely did a little tonight."

"I didn't have much of an opportunity. I'll wait a few days but it's hopeless as far as I can tell."

"Okay, I'll let the others know," he said, and paused. "Damn, thanks seems inadequate if the two of you had something going and then this killed the relationship."

"Don't worry about me."

"Hang in there, Garrett. And keep in touch."

"Sure. Sorry, Will. I'm damned sorry," Garrett repeated.

He told Will goodbye, then raking his fingers through his hair, he swore. As bitter as Sophia had been and as stubborn, he couldn't imagine her changing.

He looked at his phone and pulled up the picture he had taken of her. His anger transformed to pain as he stood mesmerized by the picture of the moment that remained magical in his memory. She looked breathtaking, happy, sexy. He remembered reaching out to pull her into his arms and kiss her, and he longed to feel her against him now. Even though he was angry with her stubborn refusal to open her mind a little, he was torn with guilt about making love to her when he had been deceiving her. There were reasons he deserved her anger. He wanted to hold her right now.

He hurt for the loss. While he hadn't known her long, it had seemed as if she had become a permanent part of his life.

He shook his head and swore again. The familiarity and closeness had been pure delusion. For her to become so furious with him, he must have meant nothing to her.

He couldn't stop glancing at the picture even though he knew the futility of longing to see her. Wasn't going to happen. He ran his thumb over her smiling image. Tonight would she think over what he had said? Or was she almost as angry with him as she was with Argus? Garrett missed her far more than he would have dreamed possible.

There was no going back, no setting aside the Delaneys and having something with Sophia. He might as well start trying to move on with his life.

* * *

Sophia painted until six, knowing she was merely going through the motions until she had to get dressed for some appointments. Her anger was overshadowed by pain over the break with Garrett and the deceit he had practiced. She couldn't believe it— Argus Delaney was still causing her pain even after his death. Garrett's arguments nagged at her, but she didn't want to think about them or consider them in the least. He had completely betrayed her trust—in more ways than one.

She didn't believe for a second that the Delaneys wanted to meet her and would still want to after the deadline had passed. They had to be just like their father and after more money. She was certain greed ruled their lives.

When she went to her closet, she barely glanced at her red suit that she had worn with Garrett. Pulling out a black suit that matched her mood, she stepped out of her robe and began to dress. She tried to put last night out of her mind as she got ready to go to the gallery.

She called Edgar and they agreed to meet for lunch. Friday was the anniversary of the opening of his first gallery and he was celebrating with an open house. He had planned to send invitations to clients with a listing of the artists who would be present, including her. Now she wished she could cancel so she could go to Santa Fe and try to forget Garrett, the Delaneys and everything that had happened since Garrett had come into her life. She wouldn't do that to Edgar, but it was a tempting thought.

At her gallery, she tried to get things done as quickly as possible so she'd be ready to leave Houston as soon as she could. Also, she found that the gallery held memories of being with Garrett.

She had to rush to meet Edgar on time. Standing beside their table, he smiled as she approached.

"Oh, my," he said as soon as she was close. He held her chair for her. "Something is wrong. I take it this is not just a fun lunch."

"You're too astute, Edgar," she said lightly. She sat and picked up a menu although she ate there often with Edgar and knew what she liked. She just needed a moment behind her menu before she told Edgar the whole story. It wasn't going to be easy. Their waiter came and they both ordered. As soon as they were alone, she met Edgar's curious gaze.

"I'll give you a clue. When you're upset, you always fasten your hair up in a tight knot," he said.

Startled, she glanced at him. "I don't," she replied and he shrugged. She could tell he didn't want to argue, but he was probably right. "I didn't even realize."

"We don't notice ourselves sometimes. So tell me—what's the problem?"

"I would really like to go back to Santa Fe. Will it be too big an inconvenience for me to cancel my appearance at your anniversary party? Have you already sent invitations with the names of the artists who will be present?"

"Actually, I have. But if you need to miss, you may be excused."

"I can wait until after the party and then go."

"Is there an emergency?" Edgar asked, looking at her closely.

"No, not at all. I just wanted to get away."

"Taking Garrett Cantrell with you?" Edgar asked and she sucked in her breath.

"No, I'm not," she snapped and then wished she had

not answered so abruptly. "It's over with him, Edgar. He's from Dallas and he was sent by the Delaneys."

"So how did you learn this bit of information?"

"He told me. He was sent to get me to talk to them. I told him how I felt about the Delaneys, particularly my father. I don't want the inheritance. I don't want to meet my half brothers. Garrett tricked me and I never want to see him again," she said.

"Seems as if he didn't trick you if he told you that they sent him."

Just as she opened her mouth to answer, their waiter appeared with lunches. She had no appetite for her tossed salad. She sipped water as she watched the waiter place chicken salad in front of Edgar.

"Edgar," she said as soon as they were alone, her curiosity growing. "You don't sound offended and you don't sound surprised."

Edgar sighed. "Garrett told me, Sophia. I knew why he was here."

"Why on earth didn't you warn me?" she asked, aghast at another betrayal from a man she had trusted all her life.

"You know why, Sophia," Edgar stated, putting down his fork and gazing at her intently. "You and I have been over this and I dropped it because it is your decision, but since it has come up again, I'll make another plea. I hate to see you hurt yourself. And you will be hurting yourself in a huge, lifelong manner that I think you will come to regret. You may be hurting yourself terribly in losing Garrett. He seemed like a good man, Sophia."

"Edgar, I'm shocked. You're my friend. Why did you side with the Delaneys on this? When did you turn against me?"

"Far from 'turning against you,' I want what's in

your best interests and I was thankful when Garrett told me why he was here. Sophia, stop being a wounded child about this."

Edgar's words stung. He had always been a mentor, her champion, always supportive and helpful until this argument about the Delaneys and even then, until now, he had backed off and kept quiet.

"Edgar, you know how Argus Delaney hurt Mom and me."

"That has nothing to do with your brothers."

"They're grown men and probably just like their father. They're half brothers, and they're strangers to me."

"You know there is a grandchild. A little girl who looks very much like you."

"Edgar, these people are worth billions. They're all going to be just fine."

"You don't really enjoy money the way some people do. But you do know how to help others with it. You could put it to so much good use. And what did you do—send Garrett packing?"

"Yes, I did. And he deserved it."

"Sophia, I got the impression that he cares for you deeply. Don't throw everything away because of his mistake. Someday, you might look back with enormous regrets that you may not be able to live with. You can take this inheritance and help so many others who have never been as fortunate as you."

"Edgar, I'm shocked that you and Garrett talked and you didn't tell me. I'm finished here. I don't want to argue this with you. I've had enough arguing with Garrett." She stood, tossed her napkin into her chair, grabbed up her purse and left. She couldn't believe Edgar had known why Garrett was here. Another betrayal that cut deeply.

Tears stung her eyes, adding to her anger. She rushed outside the restaurant.

"Sophia—"

She turned as Edgar appeared. Startled he had caught up with her, she stopped. "Leave me alone, Edgar," she snapped, wiping her eyes.

His blue eyes narrowed. "I daresay those tears are not over me. We've known each other too long. You're crying over Garrett."

"I am not," she blurted, knowing as she said the words that Edgar was right.

Edgar bent down slightly to look into her eyes. "I think you're in love with him."

"Edgar, you're not making me feel any better."

"That's what I'm trying to tell you. You're making a mistake and you'll be miserable. Sophia, don't mess up your life this way. Life can be harsh, cold and lonely. You're tossing away opportunities and family with both hands. And maybe tossing away love."

"I have to go and I don't want to hear this."

"You may not want to hear it, but you know I'm right," he said gently. "I told Garrett that I hoped he succeeded not just because you need to accept your legacy, but because it's time you let someone love you."

"Goodbye," she said, turning away.

"Sophia." Edgar's commanding tone was so unusual she stopped instantly and turned to face him.

"I'll be here if you want me. I suspect Garrett would be, too, if you let him."

She rushed to her car, climbing in and locking the door while tears poured down her cheeks. She couldn't stop her crying. It took several minutes, but finally when her emotions were more under control, she started the car and drove carefully.

When she got home, she changed and went to her studio, losing herself in paints, brushstrokes, colors. As she worked, she thought of the things both Garrett and Edgar had said to her about the Delaneys. *You're harming yourself as much as you're hurting them.... You can't select your parents and you didn't pick Argus.... Why are you doing this to the brothers?*

Garrett's gray eyes had been dark as he'd spoken. His words had cut, yet she couldn't deny that there was truth in them. Was she making mistakes she would regret the rest of her life? Should she take the inheritance and then distribute it to worthwhile causes?

Should she let these brothers—these Delaney men— into her life?

She stopped painting to clean her brushes and then continued cleaning tables and doing housekeeping tasks she had put off. It was all she was suited for at the moment. Her concentration on her painting was poor with her thoughts continually returning to her conversation with Garrett. His words rang in her ears. *I don't want to lose you....*

But he had lost her. She didn't think there was any way she could forgive him for not telling her his purpose from the start. He had been as intimate as a man could be without revealing the truth about himself. That was what hurt most of all. It was the first time she had trusted totally, let go of her caution and doubts, and then found that the whole time she hadn't known the truth about him or why he had wanted to meet her.

Take the money and give it to charity. Do some good with it. You don't have to keep it or live on it.

Edgar had said the same in his own way. But she couldn't see that she was hurting herself— She had no real need of the money.

You're being stubborn and unreasonable about this—spiteful and hurtful for no reason.

Stubborn and unreasonable, spiteful and hurtful. Both Garrett and Edgar had accused her of being self-ish.

She washed her hands and put away her brushes, going to her room to look at the letter from the Delaneys' attorney.

You are not getting back at your father.

Was she wrong and both men were right? Would she have huge regrets?

She rubbed her forehead, feeling the beginnings of a headache coming on. Everything had seemed so clear to her when it had first come up, but now she was beginning to wonder.

"Garrett," she whispered, angry with him and missing him all at the same time. Garrett had caused her to rethink her feelings about relationships. Was she about to rethink the whole Delaney situation because of him? She rubbed her hands together in anguish.

Had Garrett gone back to Dallas now, to his life there?

Had there been a woman in his life already? Had his declaration that there wasn't a woman been the truth— or another deceitful statement?

She spent a miserable, restless evening with little sleep that night. The next day, she got out the information from the Delaneys and their attorneys, and the copy of her father's will, which told of the bequest and the conditions.

She sat at her desk and read, studying the legal documents in her quiet house, weighing possibilities that she thought she never would have considered.

Edgar always had her best interests at heart. He had

backed Garrett, hoping Garrett could persuade her to take her legacy.

What she longed to do was see Garrett and talk to him. Facing the truth, she was shocked by her wish. When had Garrett become so important in her life? Could she forgive him? At the moment, she felt no inclination to do so. And even if she did, was he still angry with her? Garrett might not be forgiving. Her spirits sank lower. The pain of her argument with him was not only monumental, it kept growing.

She had never felt so lost in her entire life.

Friday night, for Edgar's anniversary celebration at his gallery, Sophia dressed in a plain, long-sleeved black dress. The neckline dipped to her waist in the back and the skirt ended above her knees. Her hair was looped and piled on her head, held in place with combs. She remembered what Edgar had said about when she wore her hair knotted on her head, but she didn't care. Tonight she felt better with her hair secured and fastened high.

Feeling numb, barely aware of what she was saying or the people present, she greeted old friends, talked briefly with people about different paintings and was pleased for Edgar that he had a good turnout.

Edgar appeared at her elbow in a gray suit with a pale blue tie that brought out the blue in his eyes. He looked his usual friendly self, as if their last conversation had never occurred.

"To anyone who doesn't know you, you look as if you're having a good time," he said. "To me, you look as if you're hurting. Sophia, you've made an appearance. You don't have to stay."

"I'm fine, Edgar. Thanks, though, for telling me I can go."

"Have you thought over what I said to you?"

"Of course."

"I won't ask your conclusions. Have you seen Garrett?"

"Not at all. I haven't talked to him or seen him this past week, which is what I told him I wanted. Whatever I do, Edgar, I do not intend to pursue a relationship with Garrett," she said, thinking her words sounded hollow and false to her own ears.

"That decision is solely yours and I have no comments to make. I don't usually interfere in your life."

"No, you don't, and I appreciate that as much as I appreciate the comments you make concerning my paintings and the art world."

"Good. We're getting another good turnout tonight."

"You are. The flowers are beautiful," she said, glancing around the room at baskets of flowers that held anniversary cards.

"Lots of people accepted my invitations and responded. We've sold two of your paintings and the evening is quite early."

"That's gratifying."

"Are you still going to Santa Fe?"

"Probably, but I haven't made arrangements yet."

"Good. I think you should stay here this time of year." He glanced around. "The crowd is growing. I'll go greet the new arrivals." He moved away and she walked along, greeting people she knew.

As she made her way through the gallery, she glanced toward the front door and her heart skipped. She looked into Garrett's gray eyes and it was as if they were alone in the gallery. All noise, surroundings, people—everything faded from her awareness except him.

Seven

Without breaking eye contact, Garrett walked through the crowd toward her. In a dark suit and tie, he looked as handsome as ever and every inch the part of the wealthy, commanding executive. The closer he came, the more her heart pounded. With an effort she looked away, turning to gaze at a painting and keeping her back to him.

Her emotions seesawed from joy at the very sight of him to the familiar anger she had borne for nearly a week.

"Sophia."

His deep voice sent electricity racing over her nerves. She turned to face him.

"Why are you here?" she asked. In spite of her simmering anger, her voice held a softer tone she couldn't hide.

"I knew you'd be here. I received an invitation a while back from Edgar."

"We have nothing to say," she said stiffly and turned her back. Garrett stayed beside her.

"I have something to say. Have you thought about our conversation?"

"Of course I have. I've thought constantly about all of it, about what you said and what you did."

"You can't blame the Delaneys for trying to meet you. All they ask is a chance to talk with you. Frankly, they're curious, too, about their half sister."

"I have no curiosity whatsoever about meeting them. Particularly if any of them would remind me of my father," she said, yet her words sounded hollow and empty. She clung to her old argument out of habit, but it was beginning to lose strength. Garrett had stepped in and changed her life.

"They'll all remind you of him, just as you'll remind them of him."

She shot him a look as anger welled up. "That wasn't what I wanted to hear."

"Sophia, let go of your grudges and just give them a chance. You can give yours away and after a year on the Delaney board, if you still feel the way you do now and don't like them, you can go on your way and never see them again. But if you give them a chance, I think you'll find a family that you will grow to love." He stepped closer and she turned away slightly.

"I sent you some brochures and annual reports. You'll see all the good the Delaney Foundation is doing. That all started when Will stepped in. Argus built that fortune, but Will and his brothers are the ones who have put Delaney money to many good uses. If you cooperate, more wealth can be poured into charitable causes, good causes that Argus never gave a dime to. That is sweet revenge right there, Sophia."

She looked up to meet his gaze.

"Spend Argus's money in a manner he never did," he urged.

Without commenting, she moved on to look at another grouping of pictures and was aware that Garrett followed, moving close beside her. She detected his aftershave, a scent that triggered unwanted, painful memories of being with him. Memories that tormented her.

"I'm glad you've thought about our conversation. If you change your mind, let me set up a meeting. I'll fly you to Dallas and back whenever you want. Or if you prefer, any or all of them will come to Houston and meet whenever and wherever you want."

"Garrett," she said, her voice so low it was almost a whisper. "If I decide to see them, I will not go through you. As I already said, I don't want to see you or talk to you again," she said. Even as the words left her mouth, she remembered Edgar's warning that she was letting go of a good man.

"Have you once thought about if our situations had been reversed? What would you have done?"

Startled again, she glanced up and looked away, clamping her jaw closed and refusing to answer.

"I didn't think so," he stated. "I didn't have to tell you who I work for or anything else when I did. I voluntarily told you when you knew nothing about it."

"That doesn't win you any points. I still feel deceived. I trusted you in the ultimate way, which I wish I could undo or at least forget."

A muscle worked in his jaw and his gray eyes seemed to consume her. Her pulse raced and even as she was lashing out at him because she hurt, she remembered his kisses too well.

"I'm sorry you feel that way. I don't. I can't forget

and I'd never want to undo the moments we spent together."

She should stop him or walk away—anything to reject him—but she couldn't move, trapped in his compelling gaze. His focus shifted to her mouth and she couldn't get her breath. In spite of her anger with him, there was no way to forget his kisses. She grew hotter with fury because she could not stop reacting to him physically.

Taking a deep breath, she turned away, breaking the mesmerizing spell. She moved on, no longer seeing him in her peripheral vision. Finally, she couldn't keep from looking. When she glanced around he was gone.

Her first reaction of disappointment stirred a surge of anger. She should be glad he had left. She tried to forget him, but it was impossible. Feeling unhappy and forlorn, she gathered her things and left without interrupting Edgar, who was talking to people.

At home, she sank in a chair. Her unhappiness grew, settling on her like a dense fog that shut out everything else. Garrett had looked so handsome tonight. She thought of being in his arms, the shared laughter and the passionate moments. She reminded herself that she was not in love with him, but she still felt betrayed. Impatiently, she changed clothes and went to her studio, pouring herself into her work, trying to shut out memories and longing. But once again, she had to stop because she was doing a poor job, ruining what had started as a satisfactory painting.

She spent the weekend in misery, with Garrett's arguments constantly nagging her. Everything he had said, Edgar had echoed. She had always tied the Delaney sons to their father, but they'd simply ended up with him, too, through no fault of their own, just as Garrett had pointed out.

Monday morning the brochures and reports Garrett had sent arrived in the mail. Clipped to the annual report was an envelope. She opened it to shake out the contents.

Snapshots fell on the table. She couldn't keep from looking at them as they tumbled out of the envelope and she saw the Delaney brothers. And there were pictures of the little girl, Caroline.

Sophia's insides clutched and she drew a deep breath. She picked up each picture, starting with one of Caroline. In a pink sundress, she had a huge smile and held a furry white dog in her arms. Sophia set aside the picture and picked up one of four men smiling at the camera. She recognized Will from the picture Garrett had showed her.

She stared at all of them. She bore the most resemblance to the two older brothers, Will and his deceased brother, Adam. For a while she pored over them before setting them aside and pulling out an annual report to start reading. A lot of money was going to help Dallas schools and parks, autistic children, medical research, various university scholarships. There was a long list.

Next, Sophia pulled out the will and read, seeing what would occur if they did not claim their legacies. It was a clear paragraph in which Argus stated that each inheritance would go to the church Argus attended and to the city for art projects—both worthy charities, but that money could do so much more if she cooperated with the Delaneys.

Rubbing her forehead, Sophia continued to think. When she considered meeting with them, should it be one or all of them? Would she feel overwhelmed by them? She could request they meet in Houston where she was at home. When the possibility began to overwhelm her, she went to her studio to inventory her paints and repair a broken chair, trying to think about something else, but she kept seeing the picture of Will and Caroline—the two people who looked the most like her.

Would it hurt to fly to Dallas and meet them? In spite of her anger with Garrett and what she had said to him, she imagined telling Garrett she would go with him. Even though she didn't want to go back to the relationship she'd had with Garrett, she knew she would feel better if he was with her.

She shook her head. She couldn't do it and she wanted to spend more time thinking about it.

In the late afternoon Edgar called to ask her to dinner.

"Thank you," she replied, smiling faintly. "But I don't want another lecture on why I should see the Delaneys. I think I'll pass, Edgar."

"Sophia, you and I go way back. I feel like a father to you. Whatever you decide, I do not want it to come between us."

"It won't as far as I'm concerned. But you may be unhappy with my decision."

"I'll live with whatever you decide. I really have your best interests at heart, though."

"I know you do," she replied with a sigh. "I've been giving it consideration today."

"Excellent news. Somehow I thought you would eventually let reason take charge. Usually you're quite levelheaded and sensible, and I expected the moment to come when you could stand back and see what you're doing here."

"Edgar, I'm getting the lecture again."

"All right, I apologize. If you don't want dinner, I'll try again another time. But don't go flying off to Santa Fe. Running isn't going to help on this one."

"All right, I'll bear your suggestion in mind."

"'Bye, Sophia."

She put away her phone and gazed into space. She didn't feel like eating. The sun slanted in the western sky and in another hour twilight fell. With it her spirits sank and nothing could get her mind off the Delaneys—and Garrett. She thought about the time she had spent with him, going back over their moments together, their lovemaking. Had he really cared about her? Or had it been a tactic he used while he tried to get close to her for his own purposes?

Even though his deception hurt badly, she missed him and his dynamic personality. Her life had been different with him, more exciting even through the most ordinary moments.

Have you once thought about if our situations had been reversed? What would you have done? His words had echoed continually in her memory. If she had been the one to try to get to know him with secret intentions, would she have had the same kind of reaction?

Had Edgar been right—was she making a mistake she would regret forever? Worse, had her anger with Garrett been misplaced? Had he been working toward a solution that would help them all, including her?

Garrett flew home Monday morning and went to see Will in the afternoon. Entering Will's office, Garrett carried a wrapped package under his arm. He crossed the room to place it on Will's desk.

"What's that?"

"It's for you, from me."

Will gave Garrett a puzzled, searching look and picked up the package to open it while Garrett settled in a leather chair across from the desk.

He tossed aside wrappings and paper and lifted out a painting in a simple wooden frame. "Garrett, this is excellent."

"It's one of hers. Now I don't have to tell you that she is truly talented—you can see for yourself."

"Damn, I'll say. This is a great picture. Looks like Santa Fe."

"It probably is."

"I'll put it here in the office. Give me a sales slip and you don't need to bear the expense."

"Forget it. It's a gift. Of course, she knows nothing about it."

"Yeah, too bad," Will said. His smile faded as he set the picture on a nearby table and then picked up the wrapping to dispose of it in the trash. He sat and faced Garrett.

"I did my best, Will. Sorry I didn't come back with Sophia."

"We all know you did what you could. What do you think? Any chance she'll appear?"

"I don't think there is, but she *was* taken aback when I showed her your picture with Caroline and told her this was Caroline's future inheritance, too."

"She must have really hated the old man. He didn't abuse any of us, he just ignored us until we were young adults. Even then, it was never a deep relationship. But once I started in this business that all changed."

"From what I could glean her anger toward him came mostly from him ignoring her. And she's angry over how much he hurt her mother. He merely liked her mother, but her mother always loved him."

"I don't know where we go from here."

"I'll think about it. In the meantime, keep hope alive because I sent her annual reports and brochures about the companies. I sent a few family pictures. I've said a lot to her that she can't keep from thinking about."

"Good. Maybe your efforts will pay off."

"It may be Caroline who does it."

"I don't care how it comes about, but we'd all like to know her. We'd like to have her in the family, which is where she belongs. Give her time and then you can try again."

"Next time, Will, get someone else. She's made it clear she doesn't want to deal with me."

"Garrett, sorry if this job assignment interfered—" Will started.

Garrett shook his head. "I'm ready to start catching up here. If you want me, I'll be in my office."

As Garrett stood, Will came to his feet. "Garrett, we all appreciate what you did for us. Time will tell. It may be too soon to judge."

"Even though she hasn't yielded on this, she's a great person. She's a very talented artist. I bought five paintings, including yours. I liked her."

"Evidently you had something going with her and this killed it. I'm sorry for that."

Garrett shrugged. "She was happy to tell me goodbye."

He walked out, feeling as if his story with Sophia was now officially over. He went back to his office in long strides and closed the door, crossing to his desk to start on the backlog of email. He only got through two before he stopped to pull out his phone and retrieve the picture of Sophia in the snow. His insides clenched as he looked at her picture. Memories engulfed him of that night and that moment when he could not resist kissing her.

He ached for her. Realizing where his thoughts were going, he put away his phone and concentrated on trying to catch up on work that had piled up while he had been away. But all through the day, memories of Sophia were distractions. His thoughts would drift to her and then when he realized he was lost in reminiscence and forgetting his work, he would try to focus.

Wednesday night, when he returned home from work, Garrett swam laps and worked out before going to his room to shower. As he dressed, he pulled on sweatpants and a sweatshirt. Glancing at a bedside table, he picked up the delicate gold bracelet he had given Sophia. He turned it in his hand, remembering it on her wrist. He recalled the moment she had thrown it at him. With a sigh, he laid it back on the table.

He wasn't hungry so he skipped dinner and went to his workshop to start building a rocking chair, sawing and losing himself in the labor, finding a respite from memories for a short time only to stop working to think about her.

He shook his head and returned to building the chair, a task that at any other time in his life would have given him real pleasure. But not now, not tonight.

Thursday came and he hadn't talked to Will about Sophia since Monday. She apparently had held to her original decisions and his disappointment was heavy. As he sat in his office, his cell phone beeped. He glanced at the number and frowned, growing nervous and curious. He touched it to say hello and heard Sophia's voice.

"Good morning," he said cautiously, hope flaring.

He struggled to keep from speculating on the reason for her call.

"You win, Garrett," she said, and he closed his eyes. Just her voice made his heart thud. He wanted to see her and be with her to such an extent it took a second for her message to register. His eyes flew open.

"How's that?" he asked, holding his breath.

"I've decided that I will meet with the Delaneys."

Relief swamped him, and along with it, his yearning to be with her intensified. "Sophia, you won't regret it," he said. "I'll arrange the meeting wherever you want."

There was silence and his heart drummed as she hesitated. "I'd like you to come with me. This is not something I expected to be doing and I don't want to meet them alone."

"Of course I'll go with you if that's what you want. How about Saturday evening for dinner, if that gives Zach time to get back from wherever he is?"

"Whatever you work out," she said in a quiet, forlorn voice that didn't sound like her. "I haven't decided what I'll do, but I will talk to them. I would prefer to avoid having attorneys present for this meeting. This is just to meet and get acquainted."

"That's all I asked. Then it will be between you and the Delaneys. I don't think you'll be sorry. You're doing the right thing—the unselfish thing."

"We'll see."

"You can stay at my house. We can keep out of each other's way. If that doesn't suit you, I know you can stay at Will's."

"I'll stay at your house," she replied, surprising him.

"Excellent. How about flying Saturday early afternoon?"

"That's fine."

"I'll pick you up at one. It'll take little more than an hour to get here."

"I know."

"Sophia, thanks," he said, meaning it, his heart racing with joy, relief and longing. He would see her in two days. "I'll be glad to see you."

"I'll see you Saturday," she said. Noncommittal words spoken in a noncommittal tone. Was she still angry? Or did staying with him mean she might give him another chance? He had no idea what to make of her tone or her plans. "My house at one."

"That's great. The Delaneys will be overjoyed that you've agreed to meet them. And, Sophia, I'll be glad to see you. I've missed you."

"We'll see each other Saturday," she said in the same noncommittal tone.

"I can't wait," he said. "See you soon."

"'Bye, Garrett."

She was gone. His pulse raced. He tried to curb his excitement because it was a baby step in the right direction, but not a commitment.

Saturday. Eagerness lifted his spirits.

He called Will on his cell. Before Will could even say hello, Garrett spoke. "I just had a call from Sophia, Will. I'm picking her up Saturday afternoon at one, and you all can meet with her Saturday night. I figured it would be easiest to do this over a dinner because it will be more relaxed than meeting in an office."

"You did it, Garrett!" Will exclaimed. "I knew you could. You got her to agree to meet with us. We couldn't get along without you. Thank you beyond words. I'll call Zach and Ryan and get them here. Saturday night we'll have dinner at my place. Fantastic, Garrett. Way to go. Talk to you later."

Will was gone and Garrett had to laugh and shake his head. He thought about Sophia and his laughter faded. He wanted more than just to see her, fly with her, go to Will's with her. Saturday night she would stay at his house. He couldn't wait to see her and wished he had asked if she wanted to come tonight. Saturday seemed far too distant in the future.

Eight

On the sunny Saturday afternoon, Sophia heard a car motor and looked out to see Garrett park in front and hurry to the front door. With a final touch of her hair that was tied back by a white scarf, she glanced briefly at her image. Her gaze ran over her white crepe dress and high-heeled white pumps,

When she opened the door, Garrett smiled. "Hi."

When Sophia told Garrett hello, her heart missed beats. She still had mixed feelings about what Garrett had done, about seeing the Delaneys, about accepting her legacy. But she had the same intense, instant reaction to him, stronger now than ever. She ached to be in his arms.

An uncustomary nervousness disturbed her over meeting the Delaney sons. She was glad to have Garrett at her side even though she continued to deal with her smoldering anger at his betrayal. However, she had to finally agree he was right. The Delaneys could not help who fathered them any more than she could. And she had never knowingly hurt anyone in her life the way she had been about to hurt all the Delaney principal heirs.

"I'm glad you agreed to come with me," she said quietly. "I don't expect to be in Dallas beyond this weekend, so I only have this bag."

"I'll carry it," he said, taking it from her to put it on his shoulder. His fingers brushed hers and a tingle sizzled through her. She continued to have the same volatile physical reactions to him, maybe more so because of being away from him.

He drove to the airport where they boarded a waiting private jet. Even though she was intensely aware of him beside her, she sat quietly looking out the window below at a long bayou lined on one side by tall pines. When they were at cruising altitude, she turned to find him watching her.

"You're doing the right thing."

"I suppose, Garrett. I'm nervous about it," she admitted, looking into his fascinating gray eyes. In spite of all that had happened, she still thought he would be incredibly interesting as a subject for a portrait. She had to struggle to keep her mind from imaging what it would be like to paint him, how intimate it would be...

"Why?" he asked, his eyes widening. "There's no earthly reason for you to be nervous."

"I suppose it's another carryover from childhood. My father also intimidated me. If and when he paid any attention to me, he would fire questions at me about how I was doing in school. I never seemed to give him the right answer."

A faint smile played on Garrett's face. "Argus De-

laney could be intimidating. I know what you're talking about—I was grilled in the same manner. 'What are
your grades this semester, Garrett? Why did you just
make a 98 on a test instead of a perfect score? Your dad
tells me you don't want to take a third year of Latin.
Why not?'" Garrett said, imitating her father in what
seemed an accurate portrayal. She had to smile.

"You sound the way I remember him. Didn't your
dad work for him?"

"Oh, yes. So why did Argus quiz me about grades?
He took an interest in my dad, therefore he took an interest in my life. My dad was happy to have Argus on
my case as well as himself, so I was caught between
the two of them, which I viewed as totally unfair. My
dad never quizzed Will or gave him a hard time and
I resented Argus for working me over when I wasn't
his son."

"That sounds like him," she said, finding it difficult to imagine the commanding, decisive man seated
by her as a boy who was intimidated by the same man
she had been. "Was he hard on his sons?"

"Yes. If he was around. Frankly, a good deal of the
years they were young, he probably ignored them as
much as he did you. They went to boarding schools
and Argus traveled."

"Yes, to see us," she said bitterly.

"Usually, Argus wasn't a lovable man—an exception
was your mother. Maybe with women he was lovable,
but in his other relationships, I doubt it. Intimidating,
domineering, he got people to do what he wanted them
to do."

"Are any of his sons like him in that manner? If so,
it would have been better to bring my attorney to this
meeting."

"I don't see it, but I've grown up knowing all of them. Will is my age, Zach and Ryan are younger. Will is as kind as can be with Caroline. She had a lot of problems after her father died. She shut herself off in her own world. She wouldn't talk to anyone. Will tried everything he could think of—doctors, counselors, tutors. Finally, he found a teacher who got through to Caroline and she opened up and became the child she was when her father was alive. Then Will married the teacher."

"Caroline looked like a happy little girl in the picture you showed me."

"She is now."

"I suppose I expected all three sons to be like Argus and my reaction to them to be the same. And I wasn't looking forward to encountering three carbon copies of my father."

"You won't, I can promise. The Delaney brothers are charming and delighted to meet you. They'll be as nice as they can be to you."

"My mother always said my father could be charming. I never saw that side to him."

"You'll see it in Will and that's what his dad was when he wanted to be. Frankly, I never found Argus to be charming. I was raised to call him Uncle Argus. I was quite delighted to learn that he was not my true uncle and that that was merely a title of respect. I didn't want to be related to him, probably any more than you."

"You surprise me. I wouldn't have guessed. If I had known that from the first—"

She broke off, remembering she had had no clue that Garrett had known her father, and that Garrett had had no intention of telling her.

"Do you understand yet why I did what I did?" he asked quietly.

"I suppose I do, because I wouldn't have seen you if you had told me you were sent by my half brothers," she said, looking into his gray eyes and trying to ignore the current of desire that simmered steadily. In spite of the division between them, she found him as appealing and sexy as ever. She had missed him and didn't want to look too intently at how strong her feelings ran for him. She was forgiving him easily, the same way her mother had always excused Argus and forgiven him. She was falling into the same trap her mother had, doing everything her mother had done—having an affair, forgiving the man, losing her heart to him no matter how he treated her. A chill ran down her spine. She was doing all the same things. Would she end up in the same situation as her mother—or worse?

He leaned close and she felt as if she were drowning in depths of misty gray. His fingers brushed her cheek. Tingles spun outward from the contact while she felt consumed in his direct study. She wondered whether he could hear her drumming pulse.

"Do you forgive me, Sophia?"

Her heart lurched. How easy it would be to say yes and go back to where they were before, but she couldn't do it. "Maybe. It isn't quite the same yet. That hurt, Garrett." The words came out sounding more sharp than she intended. Yearning showed in the depths of his eyes, stirring too many vivid memories.

Watching her, he slowly leaned closer. She couldn't get her breath. Her lips parted and her heart thudded. Garrett's gaze drifted down to her mouth, heightening her longing. He had to hear her heart pounding. He placed one hand on her knee and his other hand went behind her head to hold her as he continued to lean closer.

She could back off, tell him no, move away, refuse him. Instead, she leaned forward and closed her eyes.

His mouth covered hers, opening hers wider to give him access. He pulled her closer while her heart slammed against her ribs. Blazing with a need for so much more of him, she couldn't help but kiss him in return.

"When we get off this plane—" he whispered.

She shook her head. "I didn't intend for that to happen," she said. "Slow down. You're still going too fast."

"I missed you," he said. "Stay over longer to go out with me, even if it's only one evening."

She inhaled deeply, knowing she shouldn't while at the same time wanting to more than anything else.

"Sophia, I did what I had to. And it will give you an inheritance worth several billion dollars. That's not the same as deceiving you to hurt you. If you go through with this, you'll give the Delaney brothers what they want and set up money for Caroline so she will never have a worry. You saw the charities and how much they've given. So this is different—vastly different from deceiving you to do something underhanded or hurtful. I know you can see the difference whether you admit it or not."

"All right, Garrett, I can. It doesn't stop me from feeling deceived, or feeling my trust in you has been betrayed."

Her gaze lowered again to his mouth and she thought of his kisses. Her heart started pounding once more. She wanted to kiss him while at the same time she didn't want to see him again—it was confusing, overwhelming. With a deep breath, she leaned back.

"Garrett, we better stop this and get on a less personal note for now."

"I know what I want, Sophia. I want you in my arms and I want to make love to you again," he stated in a husky voice that made her shiver with anticipation. His gray eyes conveyed his desire, holding her mesmerized as he could so easily do. "We *will* make love again."

"You're so confident," she said.

He unbuckled his seat belt to lean forward and kiss her again, a hard, possessive kiss that made her heart pound until she longed to be alone with him. She ran her hands across his broad shoulders while she moaned softly.

He stopped abruptly and she opened her eyes to find him watching her with desire and satisfaction both clearly in his expression.

"I'm going to love you, Sophia. We'll finish what we've started."

She looked away, thinking about all that had happened between them. He was buckled back into his seat when she turned back. "Garrett, nothing has changed about my feelings concerning an affair and you have clearly convinced me you will not consider marriage for years. I don't want a casual affair. We had a night of passion. That's all. I will not get into a relationship like my mother had. You may have forgotten what I told you."

"I haven't forgotten," he said.

She looked outside again, her emotions stormy. She wanted him, wanted his loving, wanted to make love with him in every way, yet she still harbored anger over what he had done. She wondered if he thought her turnaround about the Delaneys meant she had changed her attitude about an affair with him, but she had not.

"How is the painting going?" he asked as if they had been separated months instead of days.

"I'm as busy as ever," she said. "How's the furniture?"

He smiled. "I've started a chair. Building something relieves tension. I'm enjoying the paintings I bought. They remind me of you."

"I'm glad. When I return home, I'm going to Santa Fe." He nodded. After a moment of silence, she said, "I told Edgar about this meeting and he was pleased. He agrees with you about this whole thing and he has my best interests at heart."

"I know he does."

"He's sort of a tie with my mom even though she's gone. Edgar is the father I wished I'd had in some ways."

"Remember, Sophia, this meeting isn't about Argus. It's about you and your brothers and the future."

"I've studied the Delaneys' pictures so I'll know which one is which."

"You won't have any difficulty with that. You'll know Will at once."

"Tell me about them again, please."

"With Adam gone, Will is the oldest surviving brother. He's always acted the oldest anyway. He's a decisive, take-charge person. Zach is forthright, practical, but at the same time, he's a renegade, the wanderer who never settles. Ryan is the youngest, outgoing, enthusiastic, an optimist, a cowboy at heart."

"They don't sound formidable when you talk about them. I'm so nervous about this, Garrett."

"Don't be. They're nice guys and they're going to like you. They're still in shock to discover a half sister."

"How could he have kept my mother and me from them all these years? Especially after they were grown."

"I don't think any of them were keenly interested in where he spent all his time as long as he stayed out of their lives and wasn't meddling. He's one of the reasons all of them have been so leery of marriage. The divorce was ugly. They fought and it upset his sons. Later, Adam married and she walked out early on. She was a party person. She wasn't interested in Caroline. It helped build a strong case against marriage."

"You said all that has had an influence on you."

"I guess it has. People change, though. Will fell in love and married, and he seems happier than I've ever seen him. Ava is great and so good with Caroline."

The pilot announced the descent into Love Field in Dallas. Sophia couldn't keep her nerves calm. Three half brothers she had never met. Argus's family. Garrett had been reassuring, but they were still Delaneys. Too clearly she could remember cold snubs or cutting remarks from her father.

Chilled, dreading the meeting in spite of Garrett's reassurances, she looked at Dallas spread out below. The sprawling city had long gray ribbons of freeways cutting through town. The aqua backyard pools were bright jewels set in green. Garrett's home was down there. All the Delaneys were there, waiting to meet her.

She was quiet on the ride to Garrett's home even though he kept up a cheerful running conversation. She suspected he was trying to put her at ease and he was succeeding to a certain extent.

As in Houston, they passed through a gated area and a gatekeeper waved. They wound up a long drive surrounded by oaks. When the mansion came into view, she was startled by his colossal home. "You're in a palace here," she said. "This is far more palatial than your Houston home."

"I spend a lot more time here," he said. "I'm in Houston only occasionally. This is where I call home."

"It's magnificent," she said, her gaze roaming over tile roofs above a mansion that had wings spreading on both sides and angling around out of her sight. A formal pond with three tiered fountains was flanked by tall oaks. "This is beautiful, Garrett. Far too fancy for my paintings here."

"Oh, no. I already have one of your paintings hanging here."

"When did you do that?"

"Earlier this week when I came back from Houston."

"You've been back here? Where were you when I called you to tell you that I would talk to the Delaneys?" she asked, realizing for the first time that he might have flown from Dallas to get her.

"I was in Dallas," he replied with a faint smile.

"Why didn't you tell me? I could have flown to Dallas by myself."

"This was infinitely more fun. I wanted to see you again and be with you." He picked up her hand to run his thumb over her knuckles. "I wanted to kiss you and hold you again. I was more than happy to fly to Houston and ride back with you."

"Thank you," she said, smiling and shaking her head. "When I called your cell phone, I never thought about you being in Dallas."

"I know you didn't and that's fine," he said as he parked at the front door. "Leave your bag. I'll get someone to bring it in," he said as he climbed out and came around.

At the top of wide steps they crossed a porch with a huge crystal-and-brass light hanging overhead. One of the massive twelve-foot double doors opened before they reached it and a man stepped out, smiling as he greeted them.

"Sophia, this is Roger, who has worked for my family for over thirty years now. Roger, this is Miss Delaney. She has a bag in the car."

"Yes, sir. Welcome to the house, Miss Delaney," he said.

"Thank you," Sophia replied as she entered a wide hallway with a staircase winding to the second floor and a twenty-foot ceiling.

"Garrett, Roger is older," she said. "I can get my bag or you can—"

"Forget it, Sophia. Roger works out every day. I've played tennis with him since I was a kid and I still can't beat him. If you saw him lift weights, you wouldn't be concerned. He worked for my folks and now he works for me. Actually, he's more like a relative to me than an employee. I grew up knowing him, which makes the relationship different from just employer and employee."

"That's nice, Garrett," she said, seeing another facet to Garrett in his relationships with the people in his life.

"I'll show you your room so you can change for dinner," he said while they climbed the stairs to the second floor and walked down a wide hall. They entered another wing. He continued, finally motioning toward an open door. She entered a beautiful suite with ornate fruitwood furniture.

"I hope I can find my way back where we came from."

"You will, and my room is down the hall. I won't let you get lost."

"Do you really live here alone?"

"On this floor. Roger has a large suite of rooms on the third floor. So does my chef, Larrier. There are two more suites where Andrea and Dena live. They're in charge of the cleaning crew. They have another entrance to that wing and we can all avoid getting in each other's way. There's an elevator farther along the main hall. I have a finished attic above the third level where luggage and various items are stored. I can give you a tour tomorrow."

She laughed. "Show me your studio and your furniture, but skip the tour. This place is far too big."

"Is there anything you need?"

"No, thank you."

He crossed the room to her to untie the ribbon holding her hair. She shook her head and her hair swung over her shoulders. Her pulse drummed now that she stood so close to him. She looked up at him, reminded again of how tall he was.

"Garrett, I can't keep from being nervous about this. The whole thing seems weird. I was six when my father divorced their mother. If he had married my mother then, as she wanted him to, I would have suddenly had four brothers. I would have grown up with them. Now I'm finally going to meet them. Suppose they don't like me?"

"They're going to love you. Are you kidding? Sophia, you're the key to them each inheriting four billion dollars. That will make them love anything you do."

"When you put it that way, it sounds ridiculous for me to worry. Also, it sounds as if money is the most important thing in their lives."

"It's not, I promise you. But what is this? You are so cool and poised in the art world and you're falling apart here?"

"This is entirely different. I've never had a close family except Mom. To suddenly know I'll be face-to-face with half brothers gives me the jitters."

"You can relax. Forget your father. His sons are very

nice guys. Ava is wonderful and Caroline is a little doll. The Delaneys are blood relatives, Sophia. You'll find they're like you."

She inhaled deeply as she gazed into Garrett's eyes. His words reassured her, but now that Garrett stood close and rested one hand casually on her shoulder, her attention shifted to him and she forgot her concerns about the Delaneys. Her nervousness vanished, replaced by awareness of Garrett and growing desire.

"Thanks for coming to get me and for sticking with me tonight."

"I missed you," he said solemnly and she could only nod. He slipped his hand in his pocket and picked up her wrist, turning her palm up. He placed the gold bracelet in her hand. "I want you to have this. Will you take it back?"

She looked down at the fine filigree gold in her hand before closing her fingers over it and looking back up at him. Her answer would mean forgiveness. She hesitated another second, knowing the path she was taking.

"Yes, I want it. Thank you, Garrett," she said. She was letting him back in her life and that would cause a whole different set of problems.

He slid his arm around her waist and pulled her to him as he leaned down to kiss her.

The instant his mouth touched hers, passion burst into flames. It was as if they had never been apart or had any angry words between them. Wrapping her arms around him, she clung tightly, kissing him with a fierce hunger.

While her heart pounded, she lost awareness of anything except Garrett, wanting him with all her being, holding him as if she feared losing him again. She let go of her anger and let her pent-up longing surface.

His hand drifted over her, sliding down her back and over her bottom, drifting up to her nape to caress her until she stopped him.

"Garrett, I need to get ready for tonight," she said, gasping for breath.

He looked at her a long moment and then he turned to go. "I'll come get you here when I'm ready." She nodded, watching as he walked out and closed the door behind him.

She turned to look at the elegant sitting room that looked like a formal living room. The floors were polished oak with furniture that looked antique, each piece a gem. She strolled to the bedroom, which was a beautiful room with a king-size canopied bed.

Turning her bracelet, she thought about Garrett. She could no longer deny it— She had fallen in love with him. She had never before felt this way about someone. No other man had ever been as important to her.

I'm not ready to get tied down. She could remember his words clearly yet it was impossible to resist Garrett. The struggle was growing. The more she wanted him, the more important commitment became.

She pulled off her sweater and gathered her things to head for the shower, hoping to clear her head before tonight.

When Garrett rapped lightly on her door, she was dressed and ready. Trying to be conservative, she wore a plain black dress with a high neck and long sleeves. The dress ended above her knees and she wore high-heeled black pumps. Her hands were cold and some of her nervousness had returned. She crossed the room to open the door, catching her breath at the sight of him in an open-necked shirt, a charcoal sports jacket and gray trousers.

When Garrett smiled, her nervousness dropped slightly. As his gaze took a slow inventory, his expression revealed his approval. "You're beautiful," he said.

"Thank you," she replied, feeling slightly better again.

"Shall we go?"

"If we have to," she answered.

"Stop worrying. You'll see."

"I hope you're right."

During the drive on the chilly fall night, Garrett kept up the cheerful chatter again. They didn't have far to go and soon she found herself at another palatial estate with lights ablaze and a party atmosphere already in the air.

Inside they were shown to a reception room that she barely noticed. Across the room stood a brown-eyed man with thick, wavy black hair. Handsome, he was slightly shorter than Garrett. Even she could see a family resemblance, realizing if she had seen him in a crowd on the street, she would have looked twice because he had the same bone structure she had, the same eyes.

As he smiled and crossed the room to her, she extended her hand. He accepted it, his hand closing around hers in a firm clasp. "Welcome to the Delaney family," he said and hugged her lightly. He released her and continued to smile. "We're strangers in a way, but one look at you and I know you're my sister. And we're not going to be strangers ever again. We're family."

"Thank you, William," she said, her nervousness and concern evaporating because he was as welcoming as Garrett said he would be.

"Please, call me Will. Everyone is coming, but I

wanted to meet you first. Sophia, thank you for meeting with us and giving us a chance here. I have to admit, we're all curious about our newly discovered sister. Unfortunately, we knew absolutely nothing about your existence. My dad kept things to himself."

"I didn't know that none of you knew about me, because I've always known about you. I never saw any pictures, though."

"That's enough about him. I want you to meet the family. They're waiting for us. One more thing—don't blame Garrett for what happened in Houston because we really pressured him. He's like a brother to all of us and we took advantage of that."

"I'll remember," she said, glancing at Garrett, wondering if she had been far too harsh with him.

"Everyone is in the family room," Will said, taking her arm lightly. "I'll show you."

They walked past various large rooms and then Will entered an open area with Corinthian columns and a glass wall giving a view of the veranda and pool area. Two handsome men stood talking to a tall, slender, sandy-haired blonde. To one side a little girl with black curly hair sat playing with a small brown bear. She glanced at Sophia and looked down quickly at her bear. She was even prettier than her picture had been.

Will introduced Sophia first to his wife, Ava, and they shook hands briefly. Ava had a welcoming smile as she greeted her. "We're all so happy to meet you."

"This is something I never expected to be doing," Sophia admitted.

"They've been eager to meet you," Ava said, smiling at Will. Sophia felt the current that passed between Ava and Will, realizing they were deeply in love. She ignored the twinge of longing she felt as she observed them.

Will turned to Sophia. "Ava, excuse us and I'll continue introducing Sophia."

"Of course," she said, giving Sophia's hand a squeeze. "We'll talk later. I've never met a famous artist before."

Sophia smiled, instantly relaxing a degree as she shook her head. "I don't know about fame," she said. "But thanks, Ava," she added, more for being nice than what she had said.

Will steered Sophia to the child. Caroline's brown eyes were filled with curiosity as she gazed at Sophia, who smiled.

"Sophia, this is Caroline," Will said. "I know you've heard about her. Caroline, meet your aunt Sophia Rivers."

"How do you do, Caroline," Sophia said, smiling at her. "You look very pretty, Caroline. How old are you?"

"I'm five."

"Is that your favorite bear?"

Caroline nodded. "Yes, ma'am," she answered, hugging the bear.

"I guess you sleep with your bear."

"Yes, ma'am," Caroline said, smiling at her.

"And you have a dog, don't you?"

"I have Muffy."

"I've seen your picture with Muffy who is a very cute dog. Sometime I'll meet Muffy, too."

Caroline nodded.

"Caroline looks like you," Will said. "Excuse us, Caroline, while I introduce your aunt Sophia to your other uncles."

They crossed the room. "Garrett showed me pictures

of all of you. Let me guess," she said, standing in front of the two remaining Delaney brothers. "You must be Zach," she said, extending her hand to a curly-haired man with startling crystal-blue eyes that were so unlike the rest of the brown-eyed family.

"The brother who does not look like a brother," she said. "I'm glad to meet you."

"It's about time. Welcome to the Delaney family."

"Thank you," she said, turning to the youngest brother, another handsome man with brown hair. "You have to be Ryan."

"Indeed, I am. Thanks for coming to meet us. We've looked forward to this since the moment the attorney read Dad's will. Let me get you something to drink. We have everything from beer to champagne to cocktails—whatever suits you."

"I'd love a piña colada," she said.

Garrett appeared at her elbow. "Zach, bring me a martini, would you?"

In a short time, Sophia felt drawn to all of them. They shared stories of childhood, which she guessed were being told for her benefit. They were at their best, she was certain. All of them were entertaining, polite, friendly. Garrett was relaxed and happy here with his lifelong friends.

It was almost eleven when she saw an opportunity to change the subject of the conversation. "I really should go soon, but before I leave I want to say something while I'm with all of you." She glanced at Garrett who gave her a faint smile.

"I'm thrilled to meet my half brothers and relieved that you've welcomed me into the family. I'm happy to discover that I like all of you," she said with a nervous laugh. "Even though he was very good to my mother,

I did not have a satisfactory relationship with your father. In financial matters, he was generous, I will give him that. But that's the past and really has little to do with the current situation. I know your legacies hinge on me accepting my inheritance. Well, after meeting all of you, I'm happy to cooperate with all of you."

She was drowned out by thanks and cheers.

"We really appreciate this, Sophia," Will said.

"I blamed all of you for things that none of you did or had any control over, and it was wrong. I'm sorry, but this should make up for it."

"Don't give all that another thought," Zach said, smiling at her. "We're glad to know you. We all had our problems with our dad, so we understand a bit about how you feel. We just say a giant thank-you for doing this."

"I stand to benefit, too, in a very big way," she said, smiling. "The most important thing is that I'm not alone any longer. I feel I have a family now. Thanks to each of you for being so nice and welcoming me. I'm really overwhelmed and owe you an apology for being so uncooperative." She was quickly drowned out by them telling her to forget the past.

She felt a knot in her throat. They were being incredibly nice to her and she hated to think how cold she had been to them, and how angry she'd been with Garrett when he had tried to get her to see their side.

"I think it's time I go home before I get really emotional over all this. The evening has been delightful."

The goodbyes were long and it was almost midnight before she was in the car with Garrett. He reached over to squeeze her hand. "You were fantastic tonight and you did the right thing, Sophia."

"You were right, Garrett. They were all charming.

Ava made me feel as if I've known her a long time and Caroline is an adorable little girl. It's hard to imagine her going through all she has."

"Ava has been the biggest blessing for Caroline and probably for Will, too."

"I had a wonderful time. I know they were at their best, trying every way possible to please me. Well, they succeeded. That was the most delightful dinner party I've ever attended."

"You know you can keep part of your money and do so many things you want to do—the house and gallery in Santa Fe, the gallery in Taos."

"I have my own money. The Delaney money will go to charities."

"You'll make a lot of people incredibly happy."

At his house, he walked in with his arm across her shoulders. "Sophia," he said in a husky voice that made her pulse jump before they'd barely closed the door.

Nine

As she wrapped her arms around him, her heart pounded. Longing swamped her, making her tremble while his kiss melted her. She clung to him tightly, yielding to mindless loving, swept away by desire.

He wound his fingers in her hair and tipped her head back. "I missed you and have dreamed about you, thought about you, wanted you constantly. Forgive me."

"Garrett, I do. I shouldn't have been so harsh—thank heavens you made me see that."

"Sophia, will you trust me again?" he asked. She gave him a searching look and slowly nodded.

"I missed you," he repeated.

"We haven't been apart that long, Garrett," she whispered, his words making her heart beat even faster. His gray eyes were dark, stormy with passion. He had faint stubble now on his jaw and his hair was in disarray on his forehead. Her gaze lowered to his mouth and she wanted to kiss him. She pulled his head down and his lips covered hers, hard and demanding. Her pulse thundered, shutting out other sounds.

She had missed him dreadfully, more than she had wanted to admit to herself. Now she was desperate to love and be loved, to kiss and caress him once again.

He drew the zipper down the back of her dress. As cool air rushed over her shoulders, she felt his hands moving on her. He peeled away the dress and it fell in a whisper around her ankles. She kicked off her shoes and he held her back to look at her.

"You're so beautiful," he whispered while she tugged free his buttons and pushed his shirt off.

His hands drifted over her. When her lace bra fell, he cupped her breasts, his hands warm, his fingers a torment.

Wanting to get rid of any barriers between them, she unfastened his belt and then his trousers, shoving them off. In seconds she was in his arms, naked, warm, feeling his solid, hard body. While he kissed her, he picked her up to carry her to a bedroom. She was not conscious of where he took her—just that he placed her on a bed, kneeling to shower kisses on her while he drank in the sight of her and caressed her.

She moaned and pleasure heightened until it was torment for her. She rolled over to kiss him, knowing that she did love him.

He rolled her gently on her stomach and knelt to continue trailing kisses on her legs as she writhed and whispered endearments. When he reached her back, she rolled over, reaching for him. He stepped away to get protection and then returned, ready.

Kneeling between her legs, he lowered himself to enter her. Crying out his name, she wrapped her legs around him. She held him tightly, turning her head to kiss him and he filled her and withdrew, moving slowly, a tantalizing loving that heightened her need.

Writhing with passion, she clung to him as she cried out. "Love me, Garrett," she gasped. "Love me now."

"You are fabulous, perfect," he whispered in her ear as he slowly filled her again. Trying to pleasure her, his control stretched. Sweat beaded his shoulders and chest. Finally his control went and he pumped furiously as she moved with him.

He shuddered with release when his climax came and she thrashed wildly, soaring over a brink, caught up in rapture. "Garrett," she cried, clinging to him, unaware of anything beyond his body and hers together.

She held him tightly as they slowed, finally growing quiet. Keeping her close, he rolled on his side.

"I want you in my arms every night."

"That's impossible."

"It's not." He kissed her with light, feathery kisses on her temple, her cheek, down to her throat, lower until she stopped him.

"Just hold me, Garrett. I want you close."

"I want to hold you constantly, to kiss you, to love you," he said, kissing her between words. "What I'd like right now is for you to agree to go back to Colorado with me again next weekend."

"Garrett, I don't want to think about schedules or weekends or anything else right now except you."

"Good enough. We'll put the Colorado discussion off until later. Want to go for a midnight swim? The pool is heated."

"I don't have the energy and I'm surprised you do," she said, laughing.

"How about a hot bath instead? Just sit and soak and hold each other."

"That sounds far more interesting." He led her to a bathroom with a large marble tub.

"Where are we? Are we in your room?"

"No. This is a downstairs guest bedroom. I didn't carry you up a long flight of stairs, if you remember."

"I don't remember. You could have been carrying me outside to the car and I wouldn't have noticed, which means your loving takes all my attention."

"That's good news." He ran water, taking her hand to walk down three steps into the bath. Hot water swirled around her, but she was barely aware of it. All of her attention was on Garrett and his marvelous body with muscles from shoulders to feet.

As the tub filled, she sat between Garrett's legs, pressed against his wet, warm body while he wrapped his arms around her and held her. Another weekend in Colorado with him tempted her—it was something she would love to do—but it went against her good judgment.

Everything was different now. Because she was in love.

Hours later Garrett stirred. Dawn's pale light filtered into the room. He turned his head to look at Sophia who was in his arms, her legs entangled with his. Soft and warm, she took his breath away.

His gaze roamed slowly over her, memorizing her features. She excited him more than any other woman he had known. He wanted her with him—the extent of how badly surprised him. His feelings for her had grown over the weekend. He had missed her when they had been separated, but now he didn't want her to go back to Houston. He wanted her to stay with him.

He had never asked a woman to move in with him, but he wanted Sophia to do so. He ran his fingers through her hair, remembering her stating vehemently that she never wanted an affair. He brushed aside her declaration because they were past that now. She had seemed as eager as he to make love.

He mulled over asking her to move in—a commitment of sorts that he'd never given anyone before Sophia. But the thought of her flying back to Houston and then to Santa Fe and being unavailable for long periods was unacceptable.

It had been far worse than he had expected when she had been out of his life. Which raised a very important question: Was he falling in love with her?

He couldn't answer that. His usual caution and weighing of pros and cons kicked in from a lifelong habit of thinking things through before he acted.

He kissed her so lightly, dropping feathery kisses over her face, finally kissing her on her mouth. Then he lay back beside her, staring into space while he thought about asking her to stay.

When Sophia awoke, sunlight streamed through the windows. She turned to find Garrett smiling at her as he drew her to him.

"I'll cook your breakfast. Are you hungry?"

"Yes. I'll guess it's afternoon?"

"Good guess. I can see my watch," he said, turning to look at his watch on a bedside table. "It's almost one. Explains why I thought of food. Let's go shower and then I'll cook."

"If we shower together, which I think is what you're suggesting, then you won't be cooking for a while," she said, smiling at him. He smiled in return, turning back to kiss her.

"You might be right. Let's try and see," he said, stepping out of bed, picking her up to carry her to the shower. "I don't want to let go of you."

"That's fine with me," she replied. She wished he meant exactly what he said to her. She had fallen in love with him and she wanted his love—his commitment—in return. She felt shut away in their own tiny corner of paradise, yet too soon the world would intrude on them.

He set her on her feet in the shower and turned on the water. He slipped his arm around her waist and pulled her to him. His body was hard, muscled, warm and wet against hers. He bent his head to kiss her and all conversation ended.

Over an hour later they were back in bed in each other's arms. "I told you so, about showering together."

"So you're one of those people who has to say, 'I told you so.'"

"I am in this case."

"You must be hungry."

"Sort of," she replied. "Maybe I should shower on my own."

"Nope. No fun at all. Let's just try again. At some point our hunger might overcome our lust."

She laughed as she stepped out of bed. They showered and he gave her a navy robe to wear. He pulled on jeans and they went to a large kitchen with an adjoining dining area on one side and a living area on another. The house was as elegant inside as outside.

"Your house is beautiful."

"Thanks. I enjoy it. I had it built five years ago."

"Five years—you were young to have a house like this."

He shrugged. "I was fortunate and then I stepped into a job with the Delaneys."

She watched him work, thinking about his past and how neither the Delaneys nor Garrett had even known she existed. "What can I do to help?" she asked.

"You can sit there on a barstool and talk to me. Want coffee? Orange juice? What would you like?"

Barely aware of the answer she gave, she watched him as he moved around, getting eggs and toast. He was shirtless, his chest covered with dark curls. His muscles rippled as he moved and desire ignited again in her.

Instead of yielding to it, she tried restraint, chatting with him while erotic images flashed in her mind.

After breakfast he took her hand. "Let me show you my shop."

They walked to another wing where he entered a workshop much larger than the one he had in his Houston home. There was a wide, overhead door and pieces of wood scattered around with tools on the wall and in cabinets.

"I assume the overhead door leads to a drive, so you can get furniture in and out?"

"Mostly out. You're right."

She walked over to look at pieces on the table. "Looks as if you're starting something."

"I am. It's a rocker for you. I hope you like to rock."

Surprised, she glanced at him. "You're building that for me? You must have expected to see me again—expected us to get back together. A rocker is a big project," she said, suddenly wondering how much he wanted her in his life. To build a piece of furniture took time and effort. Was Garrett falling in love with her?

"Building something for you made me feel closer to you and gave me hope that we'd be together again."

She walked to him to put her arms around him. "I'll love it. I don't know what to say. It's wonderful, Garrett."

"Wait until it's finished. You might not even like it."

"Now you have to let me paint your picture."

He laughed and shook his head. "That one—I can't imagine why you'd want to. Would I hang for sale in a gallery somewhere?"

"Never. Let me take your picture and I can paint from that. Oh, wait—I have one of you already from Colorado."

"If painting my picture gives you pleasure, then by all means, go ahead. You're easy to please."

"Thank you," she said, smiling at him.

"I just wanted you to see my studio. Now's a good time for a swim."

"I don't have a suit."

"You don't need a suit," he said, his gray eyes holding obvious lust.

"You don't live alone," she said, pointing upstairs. "You told me about all the staff who live here."

He shook his head. "Forget it. They are in another wing and we're locked away unless I let them know I'm here and need them. When I do need them, I give them as much advance notice as possible."

"That works, but if we swim without suits, I don't think we'll ever get in the pool," she said.

"I think you might be right," he said, picking her up and kissing her. She wound her arms around his neck and returned his kisses as he carried her back to bed.

* * *

Late Sunday afternoon she was in his arms in his king bed in the upstairs bedroom. He showered kisses on her. "This is paradise, Sophia."

"I agree," she murmured, combing her fingers through locks of his unruly hair. "Your hair has a mind of its own."

"I learned that at a very early age."

"I love it this way. It keeps you from looking so much the executive and in charge and more like someone approachable and fun."

He chuckled and wrapped his fingers in her hair. "And I love your hair loose. It's sexy and gorgeous and makes you look enticing." As she said thank you, he raised on an elbow to look at her.

"I don't want you to go back to Houston today."

"I have to. I planned on it and I have an appointment tomorrow. I'm painting a portrait."

"I can't talk you into breaking that appointment?"

"Sorry, I need to keep it."

He toyed with her hair and studied her. "Sophia, stay with me. Move in with me. I'll build you a studio and you can fly to Houston or Santa Fe or anywhere else anytime you want. You can open a gallery here in Dallas. A gallery should do as well in Dallas as in Houston."

Her eyes widened and her heart drummed. A part of her wanted to say yes. If she moved in, would he eventually love her enough to want to marry her?

He was quiet, patiently waiting while his gaze was intently focused on her. His gray eyes were unfathomable and she had no idea what he really was thinking.

She sat up, pulling the sheet to her chin and turning to face him. "Garrett, I've talked about this with you from the very beginning. I've told you I do not want to have an affair."

"What do you think we're doing now?" he asked. "But what I'm suggesting would be a whole lot better."

"I'm flying home shortly and I'll go to Santa Fe. We can see each other and go out, but we're not living together. Maybe we'll have occasional weekends together, but nothing intense. Not weeks at a time. I'm keeping my independence and hopefully, my heart intact. I'll not spend my life sitting around getting bits and pieces of a man. We each make our choices," she said, hurting as she said the words. "I want to be with you and you know I do. I haven't been able to resist you. But I need to be on my own."

"You're damn scared to live," he said. "You compare everything with the past. I'm not Argus Delaney and I'd never treat you the way he did your mother. I want a relationship with you. I don't want this to end, and you sure as hell act like you're enjoying it."

"I am, but I want more of a commitment than moving in together." As soon as the words left her mouth, she almost couldn't believe she'd said them.

His eyes narrowed. Sitting up, he stared intently at her. "You want me to marry you."

"I know you don't want that kind of commitment. And I don't want anything less. If I marry, I'll want a family."

"Marriage might happen if we have a good relationship, but I'm not ready for that now. I want to know someone long and well before I make a lifetime commitment."

"I agree that's the best way," she said, her gaze roaming over his bare shoulders and chest. "I think we're at an impasse and I also think it's time to get ready to return to Houston."

"I've never asked anyone to move in with me, Sophia."

Her heart raced and she hurt at the same time. Contradictory emotions clashed. "I'm flattered and part of me wants to say yes and throw aside logic, but I'm not going to. I'm very pleased you told me this is a first invitation from you."

"This is a commitment of sorts."

"It sounds to me like you want a mistress instead of a wife."

"I've never thought of you in terms of a mistress. This is different."

"I can't really see how."

"Think about my offer, Sophia. Don't give me a flat no."

She gazed back, wanting to say yes but fighting her own desire. She had to get away before she gave in. She wanted more from him— She wanted his total commitment, his love.

He reached out to pull her into his arms. His possessive kiss and his hands moving over her, taking away the sheet easily, made her forget their conversation and everything else. She was in his arms and he was kissing her senseless and nothing else existed.

Moaning softly with pleasure, she ran her hands over his smooth, muscled back and was lost to loving him. He was in her arms now and she could pour out her love and try to capture his heart completely so he couldn't let her go.

It was early evening before they were airborne. They were quiet on the flight and she could feel the underlying tension between them. When they were finally at her door, she turned to him. "Want to come in?"

"Yes," he said, watching her unlock and open her door. They walked inside and Garrett closed her door, turning to face her.

"Would you like a drink?"

"What I'd like most of all is to hold you," he answered in a husky voice, pulling her into his embrace.

Just as earlier in the day, she forgot everything else. But this time there was a running hurt that nagged. Because of her rejection, she suspected she was losing him and that he would soon go out of her life for good. She threw herself into loving him, feeling that their times together were numbered.

He stayed the night and she lay in his arms as he slept. She wanted more nights with him, more times for each of them to fall deeply in love. She already was wildly in love with him. Was she making a huge mistake by letting him go? She had almost made a huge mistake in refusing to talk to the Delaneys. Was she doing the same kind of thing here—only more disastrous?

She could imagine living with Garrett, hoping for a proposal, feeling the insecurity of an affair. She would not bring a child into that tenuous situation. With a sigh she tried to set aside her worries.

She turned on her side to run her fingers lightly through his chest hair and stroke him. He was sexy, delightful, exciting—and she was losing him. No matter what she decided to do, she would lose him. If she left for New Mexico, she would lose him now. If she moved in with him, she would lose him later.

What if she moved in with him? She could always move out again if it wasn't working, or they weren't drawing closer. The idea tempted her. Her gaze roamed over him, making her pulse race.

She fell asleep thinking about moving to Dallas and what it would entail. She thought ahead to living there, being with Garrett daily. No one, to her way of thinking, could possibly be as exciting as Garrett was. But then she thought about the years her mother had loved her father, hopelessly. Sophia couldn't move in now with Garrett. She was already doing so many things with him she had said she would never do. Moving in would be the last step, the most disastrous.

It was almost six when she awoke to Garrett showering kisses on her. He soon stepped out of bed and began to gather his clothing. "I have to shower and get back. You have appointments today and so do I."

He left for the shower without asking her to go with him and she felt a separation beginning.

When he was dressed to go, she stood just inside the front door with him while he held her in his arms.

"You've been wonderful all weekend. I think you're going to like knowing the Delaneys. Now you're part of a family."

"It's awesome and mind-boggling. Something I'll have to get accustomed to. I liked all of them. Thank you, Garrett, for getting me to that point."

"You might have gotten there on your own," he said lightly, pulling her closer. "The offer is still open. I want you to move in with me. Don't answer now. Think about it. And I want you to go to Colorado with me next weekend."

She nodded, standing on tiptoe and pulling his head down to kiss him.

Instantly his arms banded her tightly, holding her as close as possible. His kiss ignited passion, branded her as his, became embedded in memory. Shaking, she returned his kiss, trying to convey her feelings in their kisses as much as he had.

"If I had time, we'd be back in bed," he said gruffly. "I'll call you. Go with me next weekend."

"We'll talk," she said solemnly, feeling tears threaten. His gaze searched hers as if he could see her every thought. He turned and left in long, purposeful strides. In seconds he was gone.

"Goodbye, Garrett," she whispered, feeling that she was telling him a final goodbye. In her heart, she felt the budding relationship growing between them was over. Was she ending it? Or would there be this same ending a month or a year from now if she moved in? If that happened, logic indicated a break later, after a long relationship, would be far more devastating than having it happen now. But her heart said a later split with Garrett couldn't cut any deeper than it did now. She wasn't going to move in with him and she needed to make that clear to him.

She closed the door, certain she had ended their relationship. How fragile had it been? How deep did her feelings for him run? Time would tell. It was the first time in her life she had fallen in love. At the moment, she felt like it would be a forever love and that her regret might run incredibly deep.

In a surprising turn of events, she was beginning to have more empathy for her mother, to understand why she had been true to her father all through the years.

As one of his employees approached to park the car, Garrett's cell phone rang. His pulse raced as he answered and hoped it was Sophia with a change of heart.

Garrett tried to hide his disappointment when he heard Edgar's voice.

"Garrett, I haven't talked with Sophia, but I assume all went well in Dallas and her good judgment surfaced?"

"That's right. She's willing to cooperate fully. They all liked each other and got along well."

"She can thank you for getting all this to come about. Thank you for sticking with it when she gave you a difficult time."

"I wanted to for the Delaneys and after I got to know her, for Sophia, as well. She will benefit enormously and now she has a family that really likes her."

"Excellent. I'm glad you're in her life, Garrett. Sophia is a rare gem and deserves someone special. Take care and thanks. I'm greatly relieved."

"Thanks for calling, Edgar," he said.

As he headed for the plane with his thoughts totally on Sophia, he realized he already missed her. He wanted her to live with him. He wanted her where he could be with her daily. How could he entice her to accept his offer?

He flew to Dallas, missing her more with each mile of separation. He had never had a dilemma like this one before. Was he blowing it all out of proportion simply because he wanted her and she had turned him down? It was a first in his life with women.

He entered his Dallas home and for the first time it felt empty. Another first. Sophia had thrown his life into upheaval in too many ways. He swore and called until he found a friend who was free to catch the last half of the Cowboys game.

Twenty minutes into the game from his suite overlooking the field, Garrett realized Sophia had wrapped around his life and he could not shake her out of his thoughts by watching a ball game. He missed her and wanted to be with her. As soon as he got home, he planned to call her.

And say what? What could he say that might change everything for them?

Ten

She was in bed when she heard her cell phone. When she saw Garrett's number, she felt a familiar thrill. "Hi, Garrett," she said, trying to hide her excitement.

"I've been thinking about you constantly since I left you," he said gruffly and her pulse quickened.

"I'm glad you called."

"What have you been doing?"

"Actually, I concluded my appointment about the portrait, and then I haven't done much of anything except get ready for tomorrow." And think about you, she added silently. "What about you?"

"Went to a Cowboys game. They won."

"So you're a Dallas fan?"

"Yes. I barely saw the game. All I could think about was you and wanting to get home where I could call you in private."

Her heart skipped a beat with his answer. "I can't be unhappy with your answer. It's nice to hear your voice."

"This is frustrating. Talking to you causes me to want to be with you more than ever."

"Talking about it makes it even worse."

"I agree. I'll cancel my appointments and fly to Houston early tomorrow if you can cancel your day."

"I can't," she answered regretfully. "I'm leaving for New Mexico."

"Colorado next weekend?" he asked.

She took a deep breath. "Garrett, I'm not going. I'll be in New Mexico for an indefinite time," she said, wondering again if she was making the mistake of her life.

There was silence. "I miss you, Sophia. Really miss you," he repeated in a deeper voice.

"We'll talk when I get back," she said, suspecting that this could be goodbye.

When the call ended, she pulled his picture up on her phone and in minutes was in her studio sketching out a likeness of Garrett.

"I'll have this much of you anyway," she whispered.

She would miss Garrett. The nagging conviction that if she lived with him he might propose disturbed her. Each time she felt that way and succumbed to that belief, she remembered how her mother had felt that way for years, thinking if she did what Argus Delaney wanted, he would marry her. It never happened.

But was Sophia willing to risk losing the only man she had ever loved in order to protect her heart?

Tuesday she flew to New Mexico. She hurt badly over Garrett and missed him more than she had dreamed possible. He hadn't called and she assumed he was breaking things off with her now since she would not live with him.

Wednesday morning she drove to her isolated cabin outside Questa. The caretaker's two dogs came and stayed with her. The afternoons were warm, and the mountain air crisp. She set up her easel to paint outside with the two hounds coming to lie in the sun by her.

She tried to paint, but it was impossible to concentrate. She kept thinking of Garrett, knowing she still could change her mind about moving in with him.

He would soon go to Colorado. She missed him terribly and the nagging knowledge that she could have been with him for another wonderful weekend plagued her. Should she just take chances on life? She could compromise to a degree without moving in, instead of basically cutting him out of her life. Garrett wasn't Argus Delaney or anything like him. She should stop basing her life now on what happened when she was growing up.

She sat in the chair she had placed outside near a tall spruce. She loved Garrett with all her heart, so why not take a chance with him? Life was full of risks—maybe this one was worth taking.

It was worth it. Garrett was worth risking her heart.

Her cabin was out of cell phone range and she usually loved the peace and quiet, but this time, she was restless, steeped in memories of Garrett and missing him every minute until she packed up late Friday and hurried back to Santa Fe, anxious to hear from him.

She discovered she had no messages from him.

Taking off work Garrett flew to Colorado on Wednesday and spent Thursday on the slopes. That night he met friends at a pub, but his heart was not in the evening and he couldn't keep focused on conversations around him. There were women in the group he knew, but he had no interest in even talking to them.

Repeatedly, he reached for his telephone, only to drop it back into his pocket. He missed Sophia far more than he had expected to miss her. What was it about her that made her different from any other woman he had known?

She was beautiful, intelligent, sexy, fun to be with, talented—her own person. Garrett finally said farewell to his friends, grabbed his coat and went back to his place. He built a roaring fire, got a cold beer and sat looking at the flames as he sipped the beer. Was marriage totally out of the question with her?

He had planned to stay single until he was older, putting off a family until later. But why? He was already enormously wealthy as she had pointed out. He loved making furniture. What would happen if he changed his life? He had been a workaholic all his adult life. Will and the Delaneys would manage without him— There were other people capable of doing the job he did.

Sophia had made him look at his life in a different way, to consider the possibilities. The thought of change was exciting, but he could only think about it in terms of her. He wanted her with him if he changed.

Actually, he wanted her with him whatever he did. Marry Sophia whether he stayed at Delaney Enterprises or not. Marry Sophia and have her in his bed every night. Spend his time with her. Was it so impossible? Why not change his timetable? He loved her. He had known he did and tried to ignore how strongly he felt for her. For the first time in his life he was deeply in love.

This week had been pure hell and the thought of her going on her way, finding someone else who would ask her to marry—it was an intolerable notion that made his insides churn.

He grabbed his phone to call her and got nothing. He couldn't leave a message, couldn't even get a ring tone. He tossed his phone across the room and stood up to move closer to the fire while he took a drink of beer. If he had asked her to marry him, she would be with him here now. He drew a deep breath.

He retrieved his phone and called his pilot to see what the weather looked like to fly back to Dallas Friday morning. He couldn't enjoy Colorado and didn't care to stay another night.

After he made arrangements he tried Sophia again and had the same results. He hated being separated from her.

He sat in front of the fire again, thinking about his future and making plans to see her. How long would she be in New Mexico? He had no idea how to find her, but then he realized Edgar might know where the cabin near Questa was located.

Garrett couldn't wait for morning to come. He watched the flames, but saw only images of Sophia, memories spilling through his thoughts of their love-making, of being out with her, of dancing with her. He ached to hold her and be with her again and didn't want to spend another weekend like this one.

What was she doing? He couldn't stand to try to guess, hoping she wasn't out with friends the way he had been, meeting guys, seeing some she already knew.

He groaned and tried to think about something else.

He opened his phone and looked at her picture that he loved. That moment had been special, unforgettable. Her hair swirled around her head and she had a huge smile while she looked up with snowflakes on her lashes and cheeks. He wished he had never let her go to New Mexico. How long would she be where he couldn't contact her?

Friday morning he flew back to Dallas, getting in that afternoon. He spent one more night in deep thought about his future. One more night missing Sophia more than ever. During his time away from her, the hurt and loss were growing stronger instead of diminishing.

He had had time for a lot of thought. He wanted Sophia back in his life. Now if he could just convince her and do what he needed to do.

He left his home to drive to downtown Dallas. He had a list of things to do today and one of the first was to call Edgar and find the woman who would be his wife.

Sophia flew home Saturday, arriving in the afternoon. She had had time to think things over away from Garrett. She missed him dreadfully. She showered and changed and then called Garrett on his cell phone.

When he answered, she drew a deep breath. She closed her eyes and thought about him, seeing his gray eyes and locks of brown hair on his forehead.

"Garrett."

"I've tried to call you," he said.

"Sorry, but you can't get through where my cabin is. I'm home now in Houston."

"I'm glad," he said, sounding as if he really meant it.

"I've missed you," she said.

There was a long silence that made her heart lurch and wonder if she had waited too late to call him. "Garrett, I want to talk to you," she said. "And not on the phone. I want to talk in person. What plans do you have?"

"Nothing that can't wait."

"Can we meet somewhere?" she asked. "I can fly to Dallas tonight."

"I think we can find somewhere easier than that."

"I don't mind. I want to talk to you as soon as I can."

"You sound anxious, Sophia," he said.

"I want to see you," she repeated. "Where can we meet?"

"It's not too private, but how about your front door?" he asked, startling her. She leaped up and looked out the front window.

"Garrett!" she cried, dropping the phone and racing downstairs to the front door, throwing it open.

Patiently waiting, looking slightly amused, Garrett lounged against the door frame.

"Garrett," she cried again and grabbed his arm to pull him inside, throwing the door closed as she wrapped her arms around him to kiss him. His leather jacket was cold, but underneath he was warm.

For a fleeting moment he stood still. Frightened that she had waited too late to get back with him, she stilled. Then his arms wrapped tightly around her and he picked her up off her feet.

"Sophia, I've wanted you. I missed you incredibly."

She kissed him, holding him tightly, overjoyed he was in her arms. She leaned away slightly. "Garrett, I was wrong. I should take a chance on us. If you still want me, I'll move in with you and we'll try. I don't want to be alone like I was this week ever again."

"Ahh, Sophia. It's way too late for this moving in business," he said. "I've made my own plans."

"What?" she asked, wondering what he had done during their week apart to make him say such a thing.

Releasing her, he stepped back, reaching into his pocket. Her breath caught. Was he telling her goodbye?

How could he say goodbye and kiss her the way he had? Why was he here if he intended to tell her goodbye?

"Garrett, what—"

He grasped her hand. "Sophia, I love you. Will you marry me?" he asked and held out a dazzling ring.

Eleven

Her heart raced and excitement electrified her. She threw her arms around his neck, hugging him. "Yes, I will. I love you and yes, I will," she said, watching him slip the ring on her finger.

She turned to kiss him and he pulled back slightly. "You're crying."

"Tears of joy," she said, kissing him and ending their talk for a moment.

"Are you home alone?"

"I don't have a staff like you do," she laughed, pulling his head down to continue kissing him. Clothes were tossed aside and in minutes, Garrett picked her up. She locked her long legs around him as she kissed him and they made love passionately.

When she finally stood again, he picked her up and carried her upstairs to her bedroom. As he climbed, she looked at her ring. "I'm impressed with you for carrying me up the stairs. But I'm more impressed with my beautiful, gorgeous, perfect ring. It's wonderful and so are you." She tightened her arms around his neck and smiled at him. "This is paradise. I missed you beyond anything you can imagine."

"I missed you, too," he replied. "I want to marry as soon as possible and then I want to take you on a long honeymoon where I'll have you all to myself. You can't imagine how I missed you, Sophia. I don't want to let you out of my arms."

"Well, you'll have to do that eventually, but hopefully not for too long."

"When would you like to get married?" he asked with a smile.

"Soon. I don't have family to worry about, except the Delaneys, and they won't care what we do."

"They'll help. Let's pick a date. I want to rush this."

"I agree." She looked up at him. "Garrett, how did you know I was home?"

"I was going to fly to New Mexico and go to your cabin to propose. I called Edgar to get directions and he told me you were here."

"I was getting ready to fly to Dallas to see you."

"Then I'm glad we got together before you ended up in Dallas while I was here."

He placed her on her bed and lay beside her, pulling her into his embrace to kiss her again.

Minutes later she slipped off the bed, crossing the room to her closet to get a robe. Finding a calendar, she returned to sit on the bed. He pulled the sheet over his lap and propped himself up beside her.

"Now let's look at dates," she said.

"And then we'll call the Delaneys. I'll ask Will to be my best man."

"I just realized—you don't even know my close friends."

"I look forward to getting to know them. The big question is, how soon can we do this?"

She studied the calendar. "By spending a little more, I imagine I can have a hurry-up wedding. How's two weeks from yesterday? The second of November?"

"I don't want to wait that long, but I will because I want you to have the wedding you want."

"So now I'll live in that castle you call home. I'll need a map."

He laughed. "Tomorrow we can start making plans to build you a studio."

"We'll build me a studio while you think about retiring from Delaney Enterprises and building furniture so we can work at home together."

"We might not get much work done."

"Sure we will. Think about it."

"Actually, I have, a little. I might move it up on my timetable to a few years from now. In the meantime, it's a good hobby."

"If that's what you want. All I want is what makes you happy."

"You make me happy." She looked at him as he talked. His brown hair tumbled in a tangle. He looked fit, strong and handsome. He would soon be her husband—a forever marriage as long as they both would live. Love for him filled her and she placed her hand on his cheek. He stopped talking to focus on her.

"What?"

"I love you, Garrett Cantrell."

"I love you, Mrs. Garrett Cantrell-to-be."

"What happened to your plans to stay single?" she asked, studying him.

He smiled and caressed her cheek. "I met an incredibly beautiful, sexy woman and I had to have her in my life always, so—voilà—marriage."

She laughed and kissed him. When she sat back, she held out her hand to look at her ring, which reflected the light, sparkling brightly. "Garrett, this is the biggest diamond I've ever seen."

"I wanted something to impress you and to please you and to indicate how much you mean to me," he said.

She tossed the calendar on the floor and turned to straddle Garrett as she hugged and kissed him. He playfully shoved her on the bed and rolled over on top of her.

Their wedding plans were temporarily forgotten.

Epilogue

On the second day of November, Sophia stood in the lobby of a huge church filled with guests. The wedding was being held in Dallas since Garrett knew far more people in Dallas than she knew in Houston. The weeks since his proposal had been so busy, she had barely had a moment alone with him. There was a dreamlike quality to the morning. It was strange to think that this was her wedding day.

She carried a bouquet of white orchids and white roses that complemented her plain white satin wedding dress. Edgar had his arm linked with hers and would give the bride away. Before she started down the aisle, he leaned close to speak softly.

"You're ravishing, Sophia, so lovely. I know your mother would be delighted and happy for you."

"Thank you, Edgar," she said, smiling at him.

Trumpets blared and Mendelssohn's "Wedding

March" began. Her gaze went to her tall, handsome husband in his black tux. He took her breath away and she felt as if she were floating down the aisle.

Will was best man while Zach and Ryan, plus two close friends of Garrett's, were groomsmen. Her bridesmaids were all friends, and she had asked Ava to be matron of honor.

The bridesmaids and Ava wore simple pale yellow dresses with spaghetti straps and straight skirts. They carried bouquets of mixed fall flowers.

At the altar, Edgar placed her hand in Garrett's. His warm fingers closed around hers and his gray eyes held love.

They repeated their vows. He kissed her briefly and then they were introduced as man and wife, hurrying back up the aisle together. Her heart pounded with eagerness and joy. She was Garrett's wife, to have and to hold from this day forward. Happiness made her feel radiant.

They patiently posed for pictures and finally left for the country club and the reception. In the limo, Garrett pulled her into his arms to kiss her.

She kissed him, holding him tightly. "I love you, my handsome husband."

"I love you, Sophia. This is wonderful," he said, giving her a squeeze.

They kissed again and then she set about to straightening her dress, despite his best efforts to keep it askew. In minutes they climbed out and joined the reception.

Garrett had the first dance with Sophia. She still felt as if she were floating on air. "I can't stop smiling, Garrett. This is the happiest day of my life." He held her lightly, and she longed to touch his hair, brush it back in place, but she kept her hands to herself.

"I'm glad. I can say the same. You're stunning, So-phia. I have the most beautiful bride ever."

She laughed. "I know you're biased or blind, but I'm glad you feel that way."

"I wish my parents had known you, and known about our marriage. That would have pleased both of them. Dad would have been impressed by your business sense. Mom would have loved you."

"I'm sorry I didn't know them, too. And my mother would have been so happy because I'm happy."

"And very married. No danger of you being treated the way Argus treated her."

She smiled at her handsome husband and thought how wonderful to be married to the man she loved.

The music ended and she danced the next dance with Edgar.

"I'm happy for you, Sophia. This is truly wonderful and I like Garrett. I heartily approve."

"I'm glad, Edgar. I love him very much. How do you like my new family?"

"They're nice men and I think they are delighted to find you and have you marry their friend."

"I hope so."

She glanced across the room to see Garrett talking to the Delaneys. They were all handsome men. Zach had rugged looks, but his riveting blue eyes were as distinctive as Garrett's gray ones. Ryan was laughing at something one of them said. She was thankful that she had changed her mind— She had some wonderful half brothers now. The more she got to know them, the more she liked them, and Ava was quickly becoming a good friend.

Later, Will asked her to dance. As they began to move across the floor, he smiled at her. "We are all happy for you and for Garrett. We had to push and argue to get him to meet you for us, so this justifies our actions."

Smiling, she knew Will was teasing. "Now I'm glad you did. It's been wonderful to get to know all of you."

"Good. You're getting a great guy for a husband."

She glanced across the dance floor to see Garrett talking to Ava. "I know I am. I love him more than I thought possible."

"I wish you all the happiness in the world," Will said.

"Thank you," she replied, smiling at him.

"I see your new husband headed this way."

She danced with Garrett and then Ryan appeared at her elbow to ask her to dance. Unable to dance because of injuring his foot, Zach had given her a toast earlier. Now he sat on the sidelines while he talked to friends.

It was late in the afternoon when Garrett finally took her arm. "I've told the guys goodbye. If you're okay with Edgar, I'd say let's go."

"That's what I've been waiting to hear," she said, smiling at him, her heart racing at the thought of being alone with him.

"Come with me. I know the best escape route and we have a limo waiting." He took her arm and they left through the kitchen. Garrett spoke to each person they passed in the kitchen, calling them by name.

They rushed to the limo and soon were on their way to the airport. They flew in Garrett's private jet to New York City to spend the night. On board she changed to a tan suit and matching pumps. As soon as they were in their suite in New York, Garrett turned to take her into his arms.

"I love you, Mrs. Cantrell."

"I love you beyond measure, Garrett."

He nuzzled her neck. He raised his head to look at her, smiling with love filling his expression. She wrapped her arms around his neck and held him tightly while her joy was overwhelming. She loved her handsome husband with all her being and was ready to begin a life with Garrett that she expected to be filled with happiness.

* * * * *

NOTHING SHORT OF PERFECT

DAY LECLAIRE

To Rita Doerr.

Thank you so much for your assistance with the
Prologue of this book

and helping me keep it real.

And to the imperfect people in my life,

who make my life so perfect.

All my love.

Prologue

"Can you hear me, sir? Can you tell us your name?"

Pain exploded all around him. His head. His arm. His chest. Something had happened to him, but he didn't understand what. He sensed movement and heard a siren. What the hell? Was he in an ambulance?

"Sir? What's your name?"

"St. John. Jus— Jus—" The words escaped, sounding slurred and tinny to his ears. For some reason he couldn't coordinate tongue and mouth well enough to give his first name, forcing him to settle for the closest approximation. "Jus St. John. What…?"

The man seemed to understand the simple question. "You were in a car accident, Mr. St. John. I'm a paramedic. We're transporting you to the hospital where they'll treat your injuries."

"Wait," someone else said. A woman this time. Soothing voice. "Did he say St. John? Justice St. John? *The* Justice St. John."

"You know this guy?"

"Heard of him. He's some famous inventor. Robotics. Runs a company called Sinjin. A bit of a recluse. Worth billions."

The man swore. "Which means if he doesn't make it, guess who's going to get blamed? We'd better call this in to the supervisor and alert her we have a VIP. She'll want to get ahead of the media circus."

Someone asked another question. Endless questions. Why the hell wouldn't they leave him alone? "Do you have any allergies, Mr. St. John?" the voice persisted. Then louder, "Any medical conditions we should know about?"

"No. Can't move."

"We have you immobilized as a precaution, Mr. St. John." The soothing voice again. "That's why you can't move."

"BP is dropping. We need to get him stabilized. Mr. St. John, do you remember how the car accident occurred?"

Of course he remembered. An idiot driver was texting or yakking on a cell phone and lost control of the car. God, he hurt. Justice pried open one eye. His world appeared in a blur of color and movement. A harsh light struck him and he flinched from it.

"Stop it, damn you," he growled. Okay, that came out better.

"Pupils reactive. IV's in. Repeat vitals. Let the supervisor know we're gonna need a neurologist, just to be on the safe side. Request Forrest. No point in taking any chances. Mr. St. John, can you hear me?"

Justice swore again. "Shouting. Stop shouting."

"We're taking you to Lost Valley Memorial Hospital. Is there someone we can contact for you?"

Pretorius. His uncle. An image flashed across Justice's mind, of tawny St. John eyes set in a hound dog face and broad shoulders hunched over a computer keyboard. They could call his uncle. They'd need the phone number since it was unlisted and right now Justice couldn't think of it through the roar of pain. He tried to explain the problem and found his tongue refused to twist around the words.

And then Justice realized that even if he could explain, Pretorius wouldn't come. Oh, he'd want to, no question of that. He'd be desperate to. But like the impenetrable wall that prevented Justice from giving his rescuers the necessary phone number, an equally impenetrable wall prevented Pretorius from leaving their estate, his fear too great to overcome.

And that's when it struck him. He had no one. No one who gave a damn on an intimate level whether he lived or died. No one who could take care of his uncle if he didn't survive. No one to carry on his legacy or benefit from what he had to offer. How had it happened? Why had he allowed it to happen? When had he cut himself off so completely?

He'd lived in isolation these past years, keeping himself distant from emotional attachment, from the pain life had a habit of inflicting. And now he'd die alone and unmourned except by those who respected him in a professional capacity. He'd wanted to hold himself apart from the rest of the world, craved the solitude. Wanted desperately to just be left the hell alone. And he'd succeeded. But at what price? He could see it now, see so clearly how year after year, winter after winter, a fresh layer of ice had coated his heart and soul until now he didn't think he'd ever be warm again.

Once upon a time he'd known springtime, had known the warmth of a summer day and the love of a woman. Woman? Hell, she'd been nothing more than a girl. A girl whose name he'd attempted to bury so deep in the recesses of his mind that it would vanish from his memory, and yet who had branded herself on the very fiber of his being. Daisy. She'd been the one who'd proved to him once and for all that emotions were an unnecessary evil. And now what was he? What had he allowed himself to become?

"Mr. St. John? Is there someone we should notify?"

"No." He succumbed to the painful truth, allowing the blackness to carry him away. Allowing the painful memories to slip into some dark, nebulous place.

There was no one.

One

"What's the status of your latest computer run?" Justice asked.

Pretorius grimaced, peering at the screen from behind the same black-rimmed computer glasses he'd owned for the past twenty years. "Based on the parameters you've given me, I've found half a dozen possibilities that score at eighty percent probability or higher."

"Hell, is that all?"

"We're lucky to have found even that many women considering your list of requirements. I mean, no one with black hair? What was with that?"

Justice grimaced. He had no intention of explaining any of his prerequisites, especially that one. "Well, if my choice is limited to six, then I'll just have to make do."

"Make *do?*" Pretorius swiveled his computer chair in a swift one-eighty, eyes the same unique shade of gold as Justice's glittering in outrage. "Are you mad? You're talking about the future Mrs. Sinjin, Incorporated here."

Justice waved that aside. "Next issue. Are they a half dozen you can handle having here at the estate? There's no way you can avoid running into them on occasion. It's not like I can keep them locked up and out of sight. Something tells me they won't agree to that particular condition."

Pretorius shuddered. "Well, so long as it's one at a time and not all of them together in a horde. Can't handle a horde." His chair drifted closer, the casters skating freely across the wooden floor. "Justice, are you sure you want to go through with this?"

"I'm positive."

"It's because of that car wreck, isn't it? It caused more than memory glitches. It's changed you. Changed your long-term goals. Changed how you look at the world."

Justice retreated behind an icy facade, one that never failed to stop even the most pushy person dead in his tracks. Not that it intimidated his uncle. Damn it all. He'd do anything to avoid this conversation, perhaps because it sliced too close to the heart of the matter.

Without a word, he crossed the generous expanse of the computer room and picked up a silver sphere consisting of small interlocking sections, each one engraved with a mathematical symbol. It was one of his inventions, one he hadn't released to the general public. He called it Rumi, short for ruminate, since he played with it whenever he needed to work through a problem—which was basically most of the time.

Maybe he should have called it Obs for obsessive.

Pretorius pushed off with the toe of his sneaker and sent his computer chair shooting back toward his endless bank of computers and monitors. "You can't avoid the discussion, Justice. If you plan to go forward with your plan, I deserve the truth."

"I know." Justice's fingers moved restlessly across Rumi's surface, pushing and pulling the various sections until he'd transformed the sphere into a cylinder. Instead of smooth and flowing, it appeared jagged and disjointed, the symbols a chaotic jumble. These days the shapes were always a chaotic jumble. They'd been that way for over a year, a full six months before the accident.

He changed the topic, hoping it would distract his uncle. "Will all the women be at the symposium for Engineering into the Next Millennium?"

"Ridiculous title," Pretorius muttered.

"Agreed. Stay on target. Will they be there?"

"I made sure of it. Two weren't planning to attend, but I—" He hesitated. "Let's just say I arranged for them to change their mind."

Justice knew better than to request specifics. "Excellent."

"Talk to me, boy. Why? Why are you doing this?"

Justice shook his head, not certain he could put it into words. He attempted to coax the cylinder into a double helix while struggling to give voice to the realization he'd made after his accident. How did he explain the nothingness that had become his life over the past few years? Hell, he couldn't remember the last time he'd felt any emotion, whether anger or happiness or something—*anything*—in between.

With each passing day his feelings, the drive to invent, even his ambition had slowly iced over. While each minute ticked relentlessly by, everything that made him a "normal"— and he used the word in its loosest possible context—living, breathing human eked away. Soon only a cold, hard shell of a man would remain. He tossed Rumi aside, frustrated by its refusal to assume a clean-cut functional shape.

"It's just something I need you to accept," Justice finally said. "For my sake."

"Call and cancel," Pretorius urged. "Before you do something we both regret."

"I can't do that. I'm the keynote speaker."

Pretorius switched gears. "What in the bloody hell are you

supposed to say about engineering into the next millennia? That's a thousand damn years. It's impossible to predict whether there will even be a human race in a thousand years, let alone the status of engineering over that period of time."

"And you claim I swear a lot."

"What can I say? Your vices are rubbing off on me. Justice, you haven't made a public appearance in five years. This isn't the time to change that."

"I haven't made a public appearance in five years because I haven't had a damn thing worth saying for five years. When I do have a damn thing worth saying, I'll start making public appearances again. Until then, I can manage one little symposium without falling flat on my face."

"The media will be all over this one little symposium now that your name is connected with it. After such a lengthy absence they'll expect you to offer something of vital significance. I don't suppose you have something of vital significance to say to them?"

Justice waved that aside. "Don't worry about my speech, old man. I'll make something up. The ironic part is, if I claim it's possible, some fool in the audience will believe me and go out there and invent it. Win, win."

"But why? Just give me one good reason why you're doing this."

Justice dropped a hand to his uncle's shoulder with a sigh. He knew going into this would be hard on Pretorius, but something had to change. Now. Before time overcame opportunity. "I haven't invented anything in a solid year."

"Your creativity is just blocked. We can find a way to unblock it without going to such extremes."

"I don't see how it's possible for my creativity to be blocked since I don't possess any. I'm an engineer."

This time Pretorius sighed. "Inventors are creative people, Justice."

"That's a damn lie and you know it. Now take it back."

It was a running joke between them, but for some reason it lacked its usual humor. Maybe because he found it more and more difficult to laugh about his current situation.

"I understand that you need a woman. I don't object to that. Go...go find someone." To Justice's amusement the tips of Pretorius's ears turned bright red. "Let nature take its course. Once it has, you can come back all refreshed and revitalized."

"It's not that simple. I need—"

How did he explain? Ever since the accident he realized he needed more than just some temporary woman. More than a single night, or even a month of single nights. He longed for something permanent. Something enduring. Something that he could count on today and tomorrow and next month and next year. Someone who gave a damn. Someone he could call when...if—

"Mr. St. John? Is there someone we should notify?" Those words continued to haunt him, even after all these months. As did his answer, *"No." There was no one.*

"I need more," Justice whispered.

His uncle fell silent, then nodded, reading between the lines. He understood the subtext, even if he was reluctant to accept it. "It means you'll have to stop swearing so much. Granted, it would make for a nice change."

Justice's mouth twitched. "I'll work on that," he assured gravely.

"It would also mean we'd have some decent food around here." Pretorius warmed to the idea. "And a clean house."

"Somehow I don't think the woman I marry would appreciate knowing I picked her because I needed a housekeeper with privileges." Justice leaned over his uncle's shoulder and pushed a button. The laser printer sprang to life, shooting out sheet after sheet of material. "Which brings me back to my main concern. If I marry, you'll have to put up with her, too. You've read the information on these women. Can you handle one of them living here permanently?"

Pretorius frowned. "Is that why you haven't married before this? Were you worried about how I'd react to having our home invaded?"

Invaded. Justice suppressed a sigh. This was going to be a tough sell. "No, I haven't married because I've never found someone I could tolerate for longer than a week."

His uncle nodded morosely. "That's where my computer program comes in, I assume? I've done my best to transform the Pretorius Program from a business application to a more personal one. The parameters remain similar. Finding the perfect wife isn't all that different from finding the perfect employee."

"Exactly. It just requires inputting different data." He ran through his requirements. "An engineer, therefore rational and in control of her emotions. Brilliant, of course. I can't handle foolish women. Physically attractive would be a bonus. But she must be logical. Kind. Someone who won't make waves. And she must be able to handle isolation."

"I thought we were talking about a woman."

"If she's an engineer, chances are she'll already possess most of those qualities. More important, she'll fit in around here."

"Okay, fine." Pretorius straightened, assuming a professional attitude. "If you're determined to go through with this, I've narrowed the choices down to a half-dozen women, all of whom will be attending the symposium."

"With a little help from you."

"That was the easy part," Pretorius said grimly.

He picked up the stack of papers the printer had coughed out and fanned through them. Justice caught a glimpse of charts and graphs, photos, as well as curricula vitae, and— dear God—what appeared to be reports from a private investigator. Never let it be said his uncle wasn't thorough.

"And the hard part?"

"Women are odd creatures, Justice. They tend to have a

negative reaction when you invite them for a cup of coffee in one breath and in the next tell them you want a wife."

"Well, hell." He hadn't thought about that.

"You could always make up an excuse for needing a bride so quickly. I'm sure they'll buy it. After all, you are The Great Justice St. John. Or so all the scientific journals claim."

"Oh, for—"

"Or you can listen to the not-quite-as-great Pretorius St. John, who's actually considered that small detail."

"And?"

"And you're not attending the symposium in order to find a wife. You're there to find an apprentice."

His uncle caught him off guard with an abrupt left onto an unmarked road. It took Justice a moment to brake, make a swift U-turn and input the new course. "I don't need an apprentice."

"Yes, you do. At least, that's what you're going to tell these women. It's the only way to get them in your clutches. Once you settle on someone you think you can stand for longer than a month, get her to move out here. Work with her for a bit. Get her to fall in love with you and then marry her. That way she won't think you're some sort of kook. Or with luck, once she realizes you are, it'll be too late. She'll be wedded and bedded, with possibly a TGJSJ, Jr. on the way. And maybe she'll even cook and clean just because that's what women do." Pretorius shoved the stack of papers into Justice's hands. "In the meantime, study these. The symposium lasts three days which divides out to two candidates a day. You have that long to come back with an apprentice/wife we both can live with."

"And if it doesn't work out?"

His uncle folded his arms across his chest. "I've been thinking about this. And even though I don't want a strange woman wandering around here, poking her nose in where it doesn't belong, I've realized something."

"Which is?" Justice asked warily.

Pretorius stabbed a stubby finger in his direction. "You have a lot of knowledge and ability going to waste. You have an obligation to share it with others. Even if she doesn't work out as a wife, you'll have invested in the future either by providing inspiration for some brilliant young thing or, if you get lucky, you'll pass on your genetic code to another generation."

"That's a hell of a way to put it."

"Don't forget this was your idea, boy. Whether you realize it or not, that genius label you carry around comes with a price tag attached. You owe a debt to the universe."

"I gather the universe sent a bill?" Justice asked dryly.

"And you neglected to pay. That's why you're blocked. You've hoarded your knowledge instead of spreading it around. If the wife thing doesn't work out at least you'll have passed along your know-how to a worthy successor. And *that* I can live with since it'll only be temporary."

"And if she happens to fall in love and it's not temporary?"

Pretorius narrowed his eyes. "You think she's the only one who'll fall in love? Not the both of you?"

Justice knew better than to expect that. He doubted he was capable of love any longer. "Just her," he confirmed.

"In that case, I like my dinner served at six."

Justice St. John.

Daisy Marcellus stopped dead in her tracks the instant she caught sight of the familiar name centered on the Coronation Hotel's advertisement placard. Late-afternoon sunlight cascaded across the stunning black-and-white photo of him, threatening to bring her to her knees. Her bright fuchsia carryall slipped from her grasp and tumbled to the floor, pens and stickers and trinkets for toddlers spilling at her feet.

It was him.

Granted, a much different him than the one she'd known

a full decade ago. This man appeared harder, far fiercer than the version she'd known. Oh, his eyes were the same, betraying that heartbreaking wariness she remembered so vividly, like an animal constantly on the alert for danger. But that wariness seemed more intense now, and shaded with cynicism.

She studied each line of the revealing photograph, searching for other changes and finding them all too easily. Time had weathered creases into strong masculine features, the deepest ones bracketing a mouth set in far too severe a line. He'd acquired a grim edge over the years, a hardness that she could only hope was at the instigation of the photographer for overall effect, rather than a true reflection of the man.

Despite the worrisome changes, desire vied with a bottomless longing, while desperate joy cascaded through her. She reached out to trace his image, a shaky smile slipping across her face. After all these years, they'd found each other again. Well, okay. So they hadn't found each other. *She* had found *him*. But what did that matter?

Would he be equally delighted to see her? Would he even remember her? Considering how much she'd changed, possibly not. But she remembered him, and she also remembered every incredible summery moment of those short three months they'd spent together. She laughed out loud, drawing attention to herself. Not that she cared. Not when today meant she'd get to see Justice again.

Daisy stooped and shoved her belongings back into her carryall while she read the information on the placard. It would seem Justice had made a name for himself in the engineering world. Well, good for him. Even better, in just five short minutes his keynote speech would start. Excellent. She had nothing else scheduled for this late in the afternoon. Surely no one would object if she crashed the party, considering she and Justice were old friends—not to mention old lovers.

In fact, he'd been her first lover, the most special of them all, and she'd never forgotten him. Never known a love as wonderful or carefree as what she'd shared with him. Never found a man who quite equaled him. Generous. Patient. Kind. Someone who embraced life despite the turmoil of his past. Oh, she couldn't wait to see him again!

A pair of men stood outside the conference room, checking the badges the attendees all wore before allowing them entry. She waited until they were distracted to slip past and into the jam-packed room. People already lined the back wall, having given up on finding a vacant seat. Others milled in the aisles. Finally, she spotted an empty spot near the front row. She didn't really want to sit that close to the stage, but she'd feel even more uncomfortable standing in the back with the masses of engineers when she considered herself as far from being one of them as a butterfly was from a calculator.

For one thing, she'd dressed for a book signing, not a conference. Most of the attendees wore suits and ties, though she considered it a more casual, absentminded professor version than strict Wall Street "businessman" attire. Her breezy slacks and blousy red shirt—perfect for autographing children's storybooks—might as well have come with a sign that said: Alien being here. Give her the hairy eyeball until she makes a break for it.

For another, she hadn't understood a single word anyone had spoken since she walked into the place. She'd overheard any number of conversations, but she didn't understand Basic Geek, even though once upon a time Justice had attempted to teach her.

And finally, with the exception of a few women, the place reeked of testosterone. Not that she had anything against testosterone, but the sheer overwhelming number of men made her feel like a plump pigeon dropped among a roomful of cats.

Slipping into the vacant seat, she smiled at the men on

either side of her. They didn't smile back. Instead they seemed to dissect her with their gaze, and not in a sexual way. It was almost as though she represented an equation they couldn't solve. And maybe she did.

Right when she was on the verge of bolting, the lights dimmed and a portly man approached the podium. Whispered comments filtered through the room while everyone settled into their seats. The man didn't waste any time, but got right to his introduction of Justice St. John. He ran through an impressive list of credentials and accomplishments, told a brief, dry story that, based on the chuckles peppering the auditorium, was meant to be funny. Maybe it was an engineering thing, but she didn't get it. Finished, he stepped aside and glanced expectantly toward the left side of the stage.

Silence drenched the auditorium and people strained forward, watching eagerly for the keynote speaker. And then he appeared, sweeping across the stage with a feline grace that she remembered from their youth. Memories crashed over her. That day he'd stepped into her parents' home, a feral panther waiting to attack or be attacked. The lines he'd drawn to keep himself neatly boxed in and everyone else boxed out. "Respect the line," he'd ordered. A line she'd taken such delight in pushing. Erasing. Redrawing. The amazing night at the lake where their clothes had slipped away and their bodies had melded with such perfection. That blissful innocence that had tumbled into passionate knowledge.

Justice's gaze brushed the audience with impatient disdain and then he launched into incomprehensible Engineering Geek, which was clearly several levels up from Basic Geek. Despite understanding only one word in twenty, the deep, rough tones of his voice held her as mesmerized as everyone else in the audience.

He'd changed in the years since they'd last been together, changed beyond belief. But then, so had she. Would she have recognized him if they'd passed on the street? She frowned.

Possibly. If she looked hard she could just make out the boy overwhelmed by the man he'd become.

"Why didn't I think of that?" the man beside her muttered. A whisper of consensus swept around him.

"Think of what?" Daisy asked.

The man turned to look at her, outrage flashing behind thick glasses. "His suggestions for future inventions. Weren't you listening?"

"Not really," she admitted. "I was too preoccupied looking." A few snickers greeted her comment.

"I swear, when it comes to creating robotic sensors and actuators St. John is the best on the planet," an awestruck whisper came from the row in front of her.

"Especially robotics in relationship to autonomous cooperation with humans," an answering mutter drifted from behind, one equally awestruck.

Interesting. She returned her attention to Justice...and her self-appointed task of looking. She hadn't a clue what all that meant, but color her impressed if he was considered the best on the entire planet. But at what cost? She studied him more carefully.

His features were harder and more defined than they'd been at eighteen. Okay, nearly eighteen. Seriously, what difference did a few weeks make? His eyes were still that dangerous blaze of tawny gold, just like a jungle cat. His hair stopped a shade shy of ebony, the texture rich and dark. He wore it nearly as long now as he did all those years ago, as though far more weighty matters occupied his mind than something so insignificant as getting a haircut. He'd disdained wearing a suit and settled instead on a black shirt and slacks which seemed to swallow all the light on the stage leaving him shrouded in shadows.

He was Hades escaped from the Underworld and everything feminine within her shivered in response to the threat he posed.

Where had the Justice she remembered gone and who was this creature who'd taken his place? He'd changed in some ineffable way that defied her ability to identify. He'd always possessed a logical nature, governed by exquisite self-control. Before, that control hadn't been so reserved or icy. There'd been an openness to him that had allowed her to break through his barriers and lose herself in all that made him the remarkable person he'd been. Laughter had come easily to him, delight in their world a natural part of his personality, his attitude as brilliant as the spill of hot, golden sunshine that had encased them that long-ago summer.

Looking at him now, she realized that had all changed. He wasn't open, but locked up tight. She suspected he rarely laughed. And far from being delighted with the world, he regarded it with a cynical edge that eclipsed that hot, golden sunshine, leaving behind a cold, impenetrable darkness.

What had happened to him? It crushed her to see that he didn't resemble the character she'd created for her storybooks, the one based on her memories of him. How could she have gotten it so wrong? When she'd imagined what sort of metamorphosis he'd undergo transitioning from youth to adult, she'd never, ever conceived *this*.

Just then his gaze settled on her and something odd passed between them. Did he recognize her? Did he remember, even after all this time? Not likely, since her appearance had changed so dramatically in the past decade. His eyes gleamed beneath the overhead lights, like tarnished gold, yet lit with the fire of want.

And that's when Daisy decided. No matter what, before she left here she'd find out what had happened to Justice. She'd take the opportunity, once and for all, to deal with that long-ago past, one she'd never been able to forget. One that she'd used as a measuring stick in every relationship she'd had since their time together. She'd prove to herself that what they'd experienced wasn't so special since, clearly, he was no longer that amazing person he'd once been.

And then, finally, she'd be able to put him back in the box from which she'd released him…and move on.

He didn't want to be here. Didn't want to deliver a speech he not only didn't believe in, but one that involved shoveling the most bull he'd ever attempted in his twenty-eight years. He'd been in Miami Beach for less than a day and already he'd reached the conclusion that it was an abysmal waste of his time.

The minute he arrived, he'd checked into his suite, unpacked his bag and then went after the first name on his list. Why waste time, right? Dorothy Salyer stood just a few inches shy of his own six-foot-three-inch frame and seemed quietly attractive. There was no questioning her intelligence. Knowing the requirements Pretorius had incorporated into his program, all the women would be brilliant. But Dorothy—or Dot, as she'd insisted he call her (shudder)—had been even more shy than his uncle and utterly incapable of stringing even a half-dozen words together.

Strike one.

The second woman on the list was neither tall nor attractive and she never shut up, at least not once she found herself in the presence of The. Great. Justice. St. *John!* She even put the little italic on the John every single frigging time she said his name, which was so often he was tempted to change it then and there. He didn't know if she hoped to impress with her unending staccato chatter, but she'd definitely succeeded in terrorizing. He barely made it through coffee.

Strike two.

Deciding not to waste any further time, he went after the third woman. She proved to be quite delightful (a pleasant change). Pretty (a plus). Normal (a big plus). Intelligent (of course). He almost offered her the position of apprentice then and there. He probably would have if she hadn't chosen that moment to mention that she considered herself a city girl at heart, adored the cultural opportunities Chicago provided and couldn't imagine living anywhere other than the Windy City and—worst of all—she survived on takeout since she couldn't cook.

Third strike and he was almost ready to call it quits. Or he would have if not for a few salient points.

A. He liked women.

B. He liked sitting and having a quiet, adult conversation with a woman.

C. His uncle, damn him to hell and back, was right. He'd hoarded his knowledge instead of spreading it around. Worse, the level of isolation to which he'd dedicated himself had caused a certain stagnation in his intellectual processes, thus his inability to work.

D. The computer program wasn't working.

And that damnable E. Nothing had changed since his accident. He still needed…more. Wanted to take a passing shot at normalcy. To have a life. To feel again, even if he wasn't capable of the sort of depths of emotion romantics ascribed to. To have a family. Children. A legacy.

Which brought him to the woman in the red blouse. For some reason, he couldn't take his eyes off her. She struck some odd note that resonated deep within him, something that tickled a memory, though he couldn't quite place it. All he knew for certain was that he wanted her with a gut-wrenching desire he hadn't experienced in ages. Maybe ever. Which begged a single, urgent question.

Why the hell wasn't she on the list of candidates?

There must be something wrong with her, something the computer defined as unacceptable. Not her looks. Coltishly slender and fine-boned, she epitomized the type of woman he found most appealing. Even better, she was a blonde, the ruler-straight length streaked with just about every permutation of that color. Her features fell somewhere between elegant and fey, except for her mouth, which he could only describe as sultry. So, if it wasn't her appearance, why had she been eliminated from consideration?

Not smart enough? She couldn't be lacking in intelligence, not considering her presence at the symposium. Possibly he had set the intellectual standard a shade on the high side. Perhaps he could lower the bar an IQ point or two if she fell outside the parameters he'd predetermined. He ran through the list he'd given Pretorius again. Physically attractive. Big red check. An engineer. She was here, wasn't she? Double check. That left logical, kind and someone who could handle isolation and wouldn't make waves.

Maybe the computer had deduced in its inimitable fashion that she wasn't logical. Well, hell. He'd be willing to settle for reasonable if she didn't quite qualify as full-blooded rational. Kind? She looked kind to him. So, let's make that a check with a question mark. Perhaps the isolation had caused her to be rejected. He mentally flagged that for future reference. If they put their minds to it, they could find a way around that particular problem. Which left someone who didn't make waves… A nonissue, really. He was a man, wasn't he? He'd simply subdue any waves she made.

Justice smiled in satisfaction. It looked like he might have just found his apprentice/wife, and without any help from the computer. Just went to show that his intellect was more than a match for Pretorius's program. And wouldn't he take great pleasure in rubbing that fact in the old man's face.

Two

Daisy remained in her seat and waited while the line snaking toward the stage diminished. It would seem that everyone wanted a piece of Justice St. John and she wondered why. What had he done to inspire such effusiveness and excitement in the engineering world? Maybe she'd better research him when she returned home because, clearly, she was missing some vital information about her former lover.

The last individual reluctantly turned away and headed for the exit and in one lithe movement, Justice leaped from the stage and came straight for her. She wasn't surprised. She'd known from the first moment their eyes had met that he'd pursue her. For now, she'd let him.

"Would you care for a cup of coffee?" he asked.

She tilted her head to one side. Interesting. No wasted time. No social niceties. "Hello," she said and held out her hand. "Daisy Marcellus. It's a pleasure to see you again."

To her amusement that stopped him dead in his tracks and she could practically see the gears turning. "We've met before."

It wasn't a question so she didn't bother treating it like one, though part of her felt a stab of disappointment that her name didn't elicit more of a reaction. Or any reaction whatsoever. "You don't remember me, do you?"

"No."

Ah, that was the Justice she remembered. Blunt and to the point. "Maybe it'll come to you over coffee."

He folded his arms across an impressive expanse of chest. "Why don't you save us both time and refresh my memory?"

"I don't think I will. It's more fun this way."

"Fun." He said the word as though it left a nasty taste in his mouth.

She stood, startled to realize he'd picked up several inches in height along the way. When she'd known him, he'd been barely over six feet. He'd packed on at least three more inches in the ensuing years. "Yes, fun. As a noun, an amusement or playful activity. Alternately, the source of merriment. As an adjective, to give pleasure or enjoyment. As an intransitive verb, to play or joke." She grinned. "The mixed blessings of a photographic memory."

For some reason the admission allowed him to relax and he even managed a smile. A small one, but a smile nonetheless. "Thank you for the explanation. I wasn't familiar with the word."

"I'm shocked. How about *work?* Are you familiar with that word?"

He held up a hand before she could launch into a new set of definitions. "Quite familiar."

"Somehow that doesn't surprise me," she murmured.

"*Surprise.* Something unexpected that causes wonder or astonishment."

She chuckled, filled with wonder and astonishment at the unexpected sight of his laughing along with her. Impulsively, she caught his hand in hers. "I believe you said something about joining you for a cup of coffee?"

He stared at their linked fingers for a long moment. Then

he looked at her. Banked fire stirred in the brilliance of his gaze, a hunger and longing she couldn't mistake. Warmth filled her, splashing like hot liquid over and through her, sinking deep into her very core where it generated a hunger and longing as powerful as the one reflected in his eyes. From the moment he'd walked into her parents' home, he'd had the exact same effect on her. At least that much hadn't changed.

"Coffee would be an excellent start," he stated.

An excellent *start?* "And the finish?" she dared to ask.

"I think we both know the answer to that."

And she did. They would end up the same place they had the last time they'd been together.

In bed.

Hoping they wouldn't be interrupted by other conference attendees, Justice requested the hotel's café hostess show them to one of the more private tables buried toward the back and surrounded by greenery. It also happened to provide an impressive view across Biscayne Bay toward downtown Miami. The late afternoon rapidly transitioned toward dusk and the lights of the city flickered to life, the glow reflected in the soft blue water.

Daisy slid into the seat opposite Justice and he took the opportunity to study her. She was quite stunning, he acknowledged from a purely analytical standpoint, possessing features that society deemed beautiful. It didn't seem to matter whether he considered them each individually or took them in combination, they possessed an elegance in the same way he considered a carefully crafted mathematical formula elegant.

Her hair swept back from her brow to fall in a thick, straight line to cup her shoulders. Perhaps her left eyebrow was a tad off center, no more than a millimeter or two, but it only served to draw attention to the unusual green of her eyes, a shade that made him think of spring growth. Even more interesting, he could see every thought and emotion reflected there, her expression as open and ingenuous as a child. It disconcerted him since most female engineers were more guarded, perhaps as a result of working in such a male-dominated field.

He continued his appraisal. Her nose was much as a nose should be, straight and neither too narrow, nor too broad. Her cheekbones arched high, adding to that overall quality of elegance. As for her mouth… There, his gaze lingered. If she deviated from true classic beauty, it might be here. Her mouth was far more lush than elegant, full and a delicate pink. For some odd reason the shape and color made him want to bite it. Well, hell. That wouldn't do.

He cleared his throat. "So are you going to give me a hint?" he asked.

"I assume you mean you want a hint about where we met before?" Daisy asked, then shook her head in response to her own question. A tantalizing smile flirted with the corners of her mouth. Did she have any idea what that smile did to a man? The urge to bite grew stronger. "Give it time. It'll come to you."

"It might not." He frowned at the menu the hostess handed him and set it aside, unopened. He pushed the scientist in him to the fore, sliding into the reserved, analytical side of his nature with frightening ease. More and more he tended to retreat behind the facade whenever he found himself in an emotionally charged situation. He found it…safer. "I was in an accident six months and three-and-three-quarter days ago. Sometimes I struggle to recall names and certain events from my past."

She stared, shocked. "Oh, Justice, I'm so sorry. I had no idea."

"There's no reason you should since I worked quite hard to keep the general public from finding out." He hesitated. Maybe he should clarify. Women tended to appreciate that characteristic in a man. "Although it's caused a few memory issues, it hasn't affected my intellect, if that's of concern."

She caught his hand in hers and squeezed. "Don't be ridiculous. That's the least of my concerns."

He realized then that she was a touchy-feely type of woman. Unusual in an engineer, but he could live with it. Live with it? Hell, he could get used to it damn fast. He shrugged. "It's just one of those things you learn to accept. Sort of like the scars."

To his utter astonishment, tears pricked her eyes. "Oh, Justice. Scars?" She leaned toward him, speaking in a fierce undertone, her hand tightening on his. "Those don't matter, either. All they mean is that you're a survivor."

Another thought occurred. "We have the option of making love in the dark if you think the scars might have an adverse impact on your libido."

To his surprise, she burst out laughing. "Oh, thank goodness. I was afraid you'd changed. But you still have that marvelous sense of humor."

Did she think he was making a joke? He'd been dead serious. "Does that mean you're not interested in making love?" Maybe he should have led into the subject more gradually. But it seemed a logical progression, one that sandwiched quite neatly between coffee and asking her to be his apprentice/wife. "There's no rush. We have sixty-one hours and thirty-four minutes."

She laughed again, a light, carefree sound that arrowed straight to the icy core of him and thawed it ever so slightly. For the first time in years he felt the budding tendrils of hope. Maybe he wasn't a lost cause. Maybe winter would end. Maybe Daisy could deliver him into the warming arms of spring.

"I'm very interested in making love to you," she informed him. Her amusement faded, replaced by a bittersweet longing.

"It's been so long, Justice. I wish I'd thought to look for you sooner."

"You wouldn't have found me. Pretorius keeps us well hidden."

"Pretorius?"

"My uncle. He's a computer expert, which comes in handy since he helps maintain my anonymity."

"Huh." She fixed him with her lovely eyes, giving him her full attention and he realized he liked being the center of her universe. He liked it a lot. "I didn't realize you had any family. At least, you never mentioned anyone."

The way she spoke suggested they'd shared a certain level of intimacy. His eyes narrowed. Damn that accident. How could he have possibly forgotten someone like her? "How do I know you?"

She smiled. "Tell you what. I'll give you a hint. My appearance has changed quite a bit since we last met."

Aw, hell. Why did women always do that to a man? Normally, he was quite observant. But he rarely felt his observational abilities reached the level expected by women in male-female dynamics, particularly those of a romantic nature. "For instance?"

"My hair."

"Longer? Shorter?" He hazarded a guess, though guessing didn't come naturally to him.

She shook her head. "Lighter. It was a lot darker before. But I've gone back to my natural coloring."

Relief flowed over him like a comforting blanket. Okay, that explained it. No doubt the computer program disqualified her based on that minor detail. He'd have to speak to Pretorius about tweaking the parameters. Maybe he'd been a shade too rigid in his requirements.

"I could live with dark hair." Especially if it meant Daisy agreeing to become his apprentice/wife.

She tilted her head to one side, clearly puzzled by his comment. "Could you?"

Perhaps that sounded a trifle odd. Hadn't Pretorius warned him about inviting a woman for a cup of coffee in one breath and proposing to her in the next? Time to slow things down. After coffee he'd settle for propositioning her. She'd indicated a level of interest in pursuing that angle of their acquaintance, at least he hoped he'd made a correct interpretation of her interest. And if he were strictly honest with himself, if he didn't get her into bed soon he might give in to the temptation to bite more than just those lush lips of hers. He suspected such an action would be frowned upon given their current venue.

"Did we meet at a previous engineering conference?" he asked.

"Oh, I'm not—"

Their waitress appeared at his elbow and offered them a wide smile. "Good afternoon. My name is Anita and I'll be your waitress." She stated the obvious considering that she wore a uniform that clearly identified her occupation and her name tag had "Anita" written in bold black lettering. "Would you care for a drink from the bar?"

"I'll pass," Daisy said. "Though I'd love some iced tea, extra lemon please."

A sense of familiarity swept through Justice. Something about the extra lemon. And then it passed. The sensation happened all too frequently since the accident. Sometimes he couldn't summon the memory no matter how hard he tried. On other occasions—more and more often to his profound relief—the memory exploded into his mind in full vivid color, as though his brain had forged a new pathway through the neural wetware that held that precious information, avoiding the congestion and confusion left behind by his accident. But not this time. No matter how hard he tried to avoid it, he found himself square in the middle of a mental traffic jam, unable to maneuver his way to the coordinates that contained that particular node of memory.

He accepted the failure with his usual stoicism and switched his attention to the waitress. "Coffee. Black."

"I'll be right back with your drinks and to take your order."

The instant Anita left, Justice returned his attention to Daisy, homing in on her with laser-sharp focus. "Are you ready to give me another hint?"

She waved that aside. "I have a better suggestion. Why don't you tell me what you've been up to in the past few years? After all, you are the best in the business when it comes to creating robotic sensors and actuators."

They were on more familiar ground now. "Yes, I am."

"No false modesty, I see," she commented.

The observation made no sense. "What would be the point?"

He'd never met a woman who enjoyed laughing more than this one. He should find it annoying. Instead, it arrowed straight through him, bringing an unexpected surge of desire. "You crack me up, Justice. Still logical to the end."

He hesitated. "Is there something wrong with being logical?"

Everything about her seemed to soften, even her voice. "No, of course not. So long as you also remember to feel."

Feel? He didn't quite know how to respond to that, a rare occurrence and one that threw him off stride. He reached for Rumi, only to realize he'd left the sphere in his room. It also brought home to him how much he'd come to depend on his creation whenever he found himself in a quandary. And Daisy certainly left him in a quandary.

With most engineers, he knew exactly what to expect and how to speak to them. But not with this woman. Even her name seemed wrong, and yet... Right somehow. She had the same appeal as her namesake, a splash of color that brightened even the plainest, most barren landscape. She made him hesitate along his appointed path, encouraged him to pause in order to admire and while away the hours in ridiculous pursuits rather than the business of…well… business.

But it was more than that. She roused feelings in him he thought long dead, a want that eclipsed everything else. Right now sitting with her, he didn't give a damn about the conference, or the work he'd been unable to complete for the past year, or asking the necessary questions to ensure he'd found the perfect apprentice/wife. All he cared about was allowing spring to thaw the ice encasing his heart. To heat the blood flowing through his veins. To find the man lost in an endless winter and breathe new meaning into his life.

Daisy could do that for him. If he believed in intuition, he'd have blamed the abrupt, blazing certainty he experienced on that. But since he didn't, he decided his brain had been subconsciously working the problem and just now reached a rational and inescapable conclusion.

This woman was the answer to his problem.

He didn't question the newfound knowledge since he'd experienced something similar whenever he came up with a new idea in robotics. He'd learned to trust those moments of sudden enlightenment and proceed to the next step without delay.

She waited patiently for him to speak again, content with the silence. He found that an unusual attribute in a person, regardless of gender. While she waited, she smiled with what he interpreted as contentment and cupped her chin in the palm of her hand. She had pretty hands, he realized, the fingers long and supple. For an instant his brain short-circuited, and not as a result of his accident.

He flashed on an image of how Daisy's hands would look and feel on his body. Good God, where the hell had that come from? He wasn't normally the imaginative sort, and yet that one stunning picture caused an unmistakable physiological response, one far beyond his ability to control. No doubt because it had been so long since he'd been with a woman.

Something in his expression must have given him away. Daisy straightened in her chair. "Justice? What's wrong?"

He cleared his throat. "You'll have to forgive me. This hasn't happened since I was a teenager, but perhaps because of my recent isolation, I'm receiving an unusual amount of visually stimulating input which is having an adverse affect on my central nervous system. If you could strive to be a little less visually stimulating, my body will release an appropriate amount of nitric oxide to the *corpora cavernosa* which should cause my muscles to relax." Dear God, could he sound any geekier?

Sure enough, she blinked at him. "Excuse me?"

"You're giving me a hard-on."

The waitress chose that moment to return with their drinks and based on the unusual clumsiness with which she juggled her tray, he had a sneaking suspicion she'd overheard his final comment. Damn.

"Are you ready to order?" she asked, struggling in vain to maintain an impassive expression.

Justice didn't hesitate, but took the only reasonable course of action. "No. The check, please."

She handed it over, throwing a cynical look in Daisy's direction. For some reason that look stirred a fierce, protective instinct in Justice. Odd, since he didn't believe in instinct. The only explanation was some sort of genetic anomaly that had arbitrarily managed to survive the transition from an earlier, more primitive, intuitive state of man and been somehow included in his genetic coding.

Not that it mattered whether or not Daisy noticed Anita's reaction. Justice didn't want anyone looking at Daisy like that, thinking what the waitress was undoubtedly thinking, regardless of its veracity. Not that his soon-to-be-apprentice/wife noticed. She seemed totally oblivious to the byplay, probably because she was busy staring at him with undisguised shock. Maybe he should have been less blunt about his physiological problem.

Struggling to temper his reaction, he took the bill, added in a generous tip and slashed his signature across the ticket without his usual meticulous care. Then he shoved back his chair, relieved to discover that the nitric oxide had done its job.

Daisy's brows shot upward, a smile still playing at the corners of her mouth. "I gather we're leaving?"

"Yes. We're leaving."

She shrugged. "Okay."

She stood, snagged her carryall and slung the strap over her shoulder all in one fluid motion. The fuchsia of her bag should have clashed with the brilliant red of her blouse. Instead it made him think of the sunset that rapidly turned the Miami sky a similar color. Even the golden wheat shade of her hair seemed to add to the blend, intensifying his reaction to her.

Interesting. Perhaps he should consider researching the response of the human male's libido to the plumage choices of the female. He didn't know how he'd combine the results of the study in robotic design, but no doubt something would come to him in time. Until then, the only color he wanted to see was whatever shade Daisy turned when she was naked.

Before they'd progressed more than two feet, an elderly gentleman waylaid them. "Excellent speech, Mr. St. John. I particularly found your insights into future robotics and human interfacing quite fascinating."

Justice paused, taking the man's proffered hand. "Thank you. If you'll excuse me, we—"

Before he could whisk Daisy away, she spoke up, "He is the best on the planet when it comes to autonomous cooperation with humans."

"Very astute observation, young lady." His attention

returned to Justice. "I wonder if you'd have time to discuss an idea I had?"

Justice knew what would happen if he didn't get out of here and fast. It was the same thing that happened whenever engineers got together. They'd spend the entire night talking shop. Any other time, he'd have been happy to do just that. But not now. Not this night. Not when he hoped to spend it getting better acquainted with the woman he intended to transition into his apprentice/wife. Already he noticed surrounding ears and eyes perking up, could picture the gears turning, processors humming to life at the thought of an impromptu robotics discussion. Not a chance in hell.

"I have an appointment in precisely three minutes and forty-two seconds and it will take me exactly three minutes and thirty-three seconds to get there," he announced in a carrying voice. "If you'll excuse us?"

"Say no more." The man stepped hastily aside, as did the others who'd been in the process of approaching.

With the path clear, Justice settled his hand in the small of Daisy's back and ushered her through the crowd choosing a vector that afforded them the most direct route between their current location and the exit. The instant they stepped from the café, Daisy turned to confront him. She planted a hand square in the center of his chest, halting his forward momentum.

"What's going on?" she demanded.

Had he missed a step somewhere? "I thought you understood that part. Has there been a miscommunication?"

"You could say that. I probably wouldn't. Say it, I mean. I'd probably say something like, did we get our wires crossed?" She wrinkled her elegant nose. "Although even that sounds entirely too engineeringish."

Engineeringish? He folded his arms across his chest. "Would you prefer I be more direct?"

"No, you've been quite direct enough. I thought you invited me for coffee. What changed?"

He blew out a sigh. "I gather I should have allowed you to finish your iced tea before we proceeded to the next step?"

"Or maybe even have a single sip?" she teased. Instead of pushing against his chest, her hand lightened, shifted, driving him insane by making tiny, circular strokes. He had a sneaking suspicion that if she didn't stop—and soon—his body would use up its supply of nitric oxide. "I know we're attracted to each other. We always have been."

There it was again. That reminder that they knew each other from another time and place, a memory his accident must have stolen from him. "Have you changed your mind?"

"About making love to you?" She shook her head. "I just thought maybe we should slow down a little."

Yup. That nitric oxide needle was definitely shifting from *F* for Full to *E* for Empty. "I'm not sure I can," he confessed.

And it *was* a confession, since he found it difficult to admit to such a thing, and even more stunning to be experiencing what he regarded as a serious failing. Ever since he'd been in charge of his own life, he'd maintained ironclad control of his world and everything in it. Until then, he'd had no choice, no options, all decisions made around and to him regardless of the severity of their impact on him. The day he'd turned eighteen, he'd sworn that his life, how he spent it and who he allowed into it would be his decision and his alone.

Her eyes darkened, the spring green draped in deep forest shadow. "I can live without tea. How much time did you say we had until your next appointment?"

"There's ninety-four seconds left. But I lied about the appointment."

"Yes, I know. It's called a joke," she said gently. "In this particular use of the word, a noun. Meaning to cause laughter or amusement with one's words or actions."

"I'm not feeling laughter or amusement."

"No? What are you feeling?"

Feeling? He closed his eyes, a rush of adrenaline streaming through him. Heaven help him, she was right. After all this time, he was finally feeling. He struggled to identify the peculiar sensation.

"Hope," he whispered in a low, rough voice. "A verb used with or without attachment to an object. The anticipation, belief or trust that something greatly desired may at long last occur."

Daisy stared at Justice, her heart threatening to break. Did he have any idea how devastating she found his words? What had happened in those years they'd been apart that had altered him to the point where he'd gone so long without hope? Her hand fisted in his shirt and she tugged, drawing him closer.

"Take me to your room, Justice."

After all, what did it matter if she made love to him now or later? She'd known from the moment he'd swept onstage and their gazes had met and locked that this moment would come. They could sit in the trendy little café and drink coffee or tea until the sun set and stars spilled like fireflies across the velvety carpet of night sky. And it would only delay the inevitable.

She wanted him. She'd always wanted him. And despite the accident which had robbed him of some portion of his memory, part of him still knew her, still remembered how it had been between them. Because clearly, he wanted her, too. Spinning on her heel, she kept her hand anchored in his shirt and towed him toward the elevators.

"I gather we're leaving?" he asked in a dry voice, throwing her own words back at her.

"Yes. We're leaving."

He shrugged. "Okay. But just so you know, the elevators are in the opposite direction."

She didn't break stride, but simply reversed course. Was

that an actual smile she saw flash across his face? "And it didn't even crack," she informed him.

"Excuse me?"

"Your face when you smiled. I'm sure you'll be relieved to know that it didn't crack." This time when the smile came it was far broader and lingered longer. The sight filled her with intense satisfaction.

They arrived at the bank of elevators at the same moment that a set of doors opened, spilling passengers from its gilded innards. Entering the car, they stood in silence during the ride skyward, but Daisy could sense the growing tension between them, the bubble and simmer of it barely held in check, an explosion primed and ready to blow. The doors parted and Justice gestured to the right.

"Twenty-five-oh-one."

She waited by the door while he used his key card, then stepped inside, impressed by the size and beauty of his suite. "Wow."

"I like having both space and privacy. Since I was afforded neither during my formative years, I've found it holds greater value and appeal now."

"That doesn't surprise me." Daisy crossed to the expansive living area, one that looked out over a stunning view of the beach and ocean. "Who would have imagined we'd end up where we are now?" she murmured.

"I did. At least, in regard to my own future endeavors." His voice came from directly behind. Even though the comment sounded calm and prosaic—well, okay, and a trifle geeky— she could sense the desire seething just beneath the surface. "I had my life all planned."

"Yes, I suppose you did. You always were good at planning."

"It merely took determination combined with the right doors opening at the right time."

She threw him a smile over her shoulder. "Luck, Justice?"

He shook his head. "I don't believe in luck. I prefer to think of it as chance colliding with opportunity."

She chuckled, turning fully around to face him. "In other words...luck."

He lifted an eyebrow in inquiry. "Is it luck that you're here today?"

"Yes. Absolutely. If I hadn't seen your name advertised as the keynote speaker for the conference, I wouldn't be here now."

"But you did see it." He took a step in her direction, just one. But it was enough to kick her heart rate up a notch. "A door opened."

"And I decided to step through it." She spared a glance around. "Literally."

"As I said, chance combined with the right doors opening at the right time."

She gave a brisk nod and released her breath on a sigh. "So, tell me something, Justice. Now that you have me here, whatever will you do with me?"

He didn't answer right away, instead studying her with unnerving intensity. Had his expression always been so grave? He'd been quiet as a teen, studious, focused. But he'd also had the capacity to laugh. Where had that gone and how did she find it again?

He must have figured out what he intended to do with her because he took a final step in her direction. Hooking his index finger in the deep V of her blouse, he propelled her into his arms. She tumbled, just as she had all those long years ago, captured in an unbreakable hold.

"I believe I'm going to take off your clothes and make love to you," he informed her quite seriously.

And then he kissed her.

Three

Daisy slid her arms around Justice's neck and clung for all she was worth. She'd never appreciated methodical until this moment. But Justice managed to change her mind.

The first touch of his lips against hers came as an easy, tender caress. It stayed that way for a brief moment, just long enough for her to react. The instant she threw herself into the embrace, the tenor changed, became harder, more insistent. She sighed in delight, opening to him without hesitation or caution. He breached the seam of her lips, his tongue teasing hers, edging her hunger ever higher.

His control was exquisite, his taking decimating her. And then his teeth closed over her lower lip and tugged, threatening to drive her straight over the edge.

"You have no idea how long I've wanted to do that," he informed her.

It took Daisy a long moment to gather her wits sufficiently to respond to Justice's comment. "Not a clue. But I'm willing to bet you could tell me to the minute."

"To the nanosecond."

He cupped her face and practically inhaled her, his kiss the most thorough she'd ever received, his mouth firm and assured and potent. "Tell me what you want and I'll spend the rest of the night giving it to you."

It was all she could do to keep from moaning in response. "I was hoping you'd say that."

He smiled again, more easily this time. "Do you want the lights on or off when I remove your clothes?"

"Oh, yes."

Now he grinned. "Maybe I'll leave them off and see you wearing nothing but the sunset."

It was the most poetic comment he'd made since they'd become reacquainted and a cold place deep inside thawed, melted, warmed her, inside and out. "Then you'd better hurry because it's almost gone."

"I don't hurry. Not when it comes to something as important as this."

Daisy could only stare at him, helpless, a shaft of raw desire shooting through her. "Oh, Justice. I was so afraid."

"Afraid?" A frown creased his brow. "Of me?"

"In a way." She lifted a shoulder in a shrug and heard the happy clatter of children's toys rattling around in her carryall. The sound reassured her as nothing else could have. "Of how you'd be when I met you again. Whether you'd have changed. At first, I thought…"

"That I had?"

"How did you know?"

"It seemed the logical conclusion."

"Yes. I thought you'd changed." She swept the strap of her carryall from her shoulder and tossed the bag carelessly to the carpet. Fortunately, the contents stayed put, though they did jangle in protest. "And you have changed. It's natural, I suppose, since change is inevitable over time."

"An astute observation."

She couldn't help but laugh. "And yet, you're still the same. Underneath all the scientific jargon and aloofness, you're still the Justice I remember."

"I assume that's good?"

"It's…" For some reason tears pricked her eyes and she hastened to lower them, praying he hadn't noticed. She couldn't seem to contain her energy and plucked at one of the buttons on his black shirt. "It's fantastic," she admitted in a husky voice.

"Let's see if we can't make it even more fantastic."

Daisy had to admit, one of the qualities she'd always admired about Justice was his intense focus. He didn't waste further time talking, but applied his superb intelligence to shoving the buttons of her blouse through the corresponding holes. Sliding it from her shoulders, he neatly removed her bra with an experienced flick of his fingers.

What little remained of the setting sun bathed her in soft purpling shadows. His gaze followed the final traces of sunlight, while his hands painted her in heat. He cupped the weight of her breasts and slid his thumbs across the tips. His hands surprised her with their power and strength. They weren't the soft hands of a pencil pusher, but those of a laborer, callused and hard. Whatever sort of engineering and robotic work he did involved the use of those hands, his efforts strengthening and defining their shape and texture. She moaned at the delicious abrasiveness, her knees threatening to give out beneath her.

"Justice, please."

"Don't ask me to rush this. I can't. I won't. I want to enjoy every moment."

Despite his demand, his hands reluctantly slid from her breasts across her quivering abdomen. The sound of the zipper of her slacks being lowered sounded as harsh as their breathing. He skinned the last of her clothing from her body, leaving her cloaked in nudity.

It was Daisy's turn to return the favor. She didn't have

Justice's patience, nor his attention to methodical process. She yanked and tugged whatever came to hand, whether trousers or shirt or shoes and socks. While darkness enclosed them in a soft fist, she allowed her hands to be her eyes while she reacquainted herself with every inch of him.

So much had changed. Not only was he taller, but broader. More heavily muscled. Deliciously ridged and toned. She'd love to paint him like this, to capture not only the incredible maleness of him, but that essence of intellect combined with potent masculinity.

Her hand glanced off a ridge that wasn't muscle, a long slashing tear across smooth skin. "Oh, Justice. You weren't kidding about the scars, were you?"

He stiffened. "It should be too dark for you to see."

"Well, yes. But I can feel it."

"Do you find it offensive? Would you prefer to terminate our lovemaking?"

"Termin—" Daisy smothered a laugh. "Honestly, Justice. You're so funny. I can always tell when you're upset. You start talking in Basic Geek."

"I'm not upset."

"Then what are you?"

"I'm…" He released his breath in a long sigh. "I'm emotionally compromised."

"It would be a little surprising if you weren't," she informed him gently. He didn't reply, but remained still and quiet beneath her tentative touch. Did he think she'd walk away because of a few scars? He didn't know her very well anymore, but he'd soon learn. "Let me show you how offensive I find your scars."

Ever so gently, her touch as soft and light as the sweep of butterfly wings, she pressed her lips to the first, tracing it from end to end. She located the next one and kissed that one, as well. And the next, until she'd found each and every one, created a road map of lingering caresses across his body.

"No more." His harsh voice split the silence, as twisted and tortured as his scars.

He swept her into his arms and carried her through the living area into the bedroom. A single light burned a pathway through the darkness, chasing away the shadows and haloing the bed in a ring of gold. He came down beside her and the warm glow skated over his work-hardened muscles and sank into the crevices lining his face. Pain lingered there, a pain she'd have given anything to ease. And maybe she could.

Daisy reached for him, pulled him into the warmth of her embrace and adjusted her curves to accommodate his lean, graceful form. No question, Justice had become the panther she'd long considered him, sleek and trim, with an edge of tough, masculine danger. His skin rippled beneath her touch, the sweep of warm, taut sinew as appealing to the artist within her as the faint golden hue of his skin tones. His hardness pitted against all that made her yielding and feminine, creating an interesting dichotomy, one she could lose herself in. So why resist?

This time when she mapped the pathway of scars, she did it within that merciless glare of light. She wished her kisses had the power to heal, that she could give ease and comfort to the rips and tears that had damaged not just his body, but somehow his heart and soul, as well. She anointed each and every one while he lay rigid beneath her, his jaw rigid and eyes squeezed shut.

She had an instant's warning before he moved, the quick clench and flex of toned muscle. And then he had her flat on her back, his arms planted on either side of her head, caging her. He held himself above her, his gaze marking her like a hot branding touch.

"My turn," he said.

Not giving her an opportunity to reply, his mouth closed over hers, hungry with demand and intent. Sheer pleasure swamped her and she wrapped her arms around his neck, tugging him down until all of him blanketed her in endless masculinity. With a husky laugh that turned her insides molten, he slid his hands between them and traced her breasts, exploring every inch, shaping them, dragging those delicious calluses over and around before lowering his head to catch one taut tip between his teeth. Her breath escaped, sharp as an explosion while pleasure ripped through her.

"Justice..." His name escaped on a cry, blurred with passion. "Do that again."

The last time she'd been held in his arms, had known his possession, it had been gentle and sweetly tender. Tentative. They'd been little more than children, filled with an insatiable curiosity and delight in the physical, yet cautious in that exploration.

This time, it was so much more, their knowledge deeper, their desires fine-tuned. And they were far from children. In all the years that separated the two occasions, one thing hadn't changed. The magic still existed between them. At his first touch, he revived some inexplicable connection between them that strengthened and intensified with each passing moment.

Justice's hand slid from her breasts and drifted ever lower until he'd found the welcoming warmth at the apex of her thighs. He dipped inward, a stroking touch, easing her legs apart until she lay spread beneath him, fully open to his gaze. The muscles of her belly and thighs rippled with pleasure, the feeling intensifying with each slow movement of his fingers. He took his time, driving her insane with his thoroughness. Heaven help her, but she adored thorough men.

"Please, Justice. I can't take any more."

"I hope you can take more, since I have plenty to give you." Again, he treated her to that soft, husky laugh. So deep. So dark and delicious. So intimate. She heard the slide of a bedside table drawer followed by the muted rip and crackle of a wrapper. With swift, economical movements, he protected himself. "Let me give you everything I have, Daisy."

She groaned, her breath quickening, just as her body quickened, tightening with a desire so intense she thought she'd die from it. He levered himself above her, cupping her bottom and lifting her. He came down heavily, dipping into her liquid heat.

With one slow stroke, he surged into her, filling her with steely power. She wrapped her arms and legs around him, angled her hips to take him more deeply. She wanted it to last forever, to cling to this moment and revel in it. Never had she experienced anything like this, not with anyone other than him. She didn't understand it, didn't need to understand. She simply embraced it and rejoiced.

And then she couldn't think, could only crack and splinter while she rode the storm with him, fragmenting into endless pieces as she embraced the wildness that exploded from beneath his impeccable control. With every thrust he sent her flying toward ecstasy, driven higher and further than she'd ever been driven before.

It was a transcendent moment she'd only experienced once before and with only one man. This man. These arms. This same joining, even if years apart. Did he feel it? Did he sense the connection they'd forged once again? Did he realize what she did? She'd thought by having this night together that she'd finally be able to let her memories of him go. Instead, she'd discovered something far different.

Somehow, despite all odds, they'd become one, and there would be no going back. From this moment on, she belonged to him, just as he belonged to her. And they always would.

Nighttime wheeled by. Justice ordered food that remained uneaten. Started sentences that broke off, unfinished. Drew a bath that turned cold, forgotten. Instead, they tumbled into each other's arms, insatiable. At some point they slept.

He only knew it with any certainty because somehow night became day.

He woke with a slow smile and a bone-deep certainty that his life had taken a turn, had shifted from one plane to another, and there'd be no going back. Not that he had any interest in going back.

He glanced down at Daisy where she slept like the dead, curled against him so tightly they practically shared the same skin. She'd pillowed her head on his shoulder, her hair a tormenting sweep of silk against his chest. Her hand was splayed there, as well, her palm dead center over his heart, as though she gathered up every beat, absorbing it until it became one with her own.

So what next? How did he convince her to become his apprentice/wife? Because he had no intention of letting her go.

Gently, lovingly, he eased out from beneath her. Lifting up on one elbow, he traced the velvety length of her from shoulder to breast, waist to hip to the pert curve of her bottom. And that's when he saw it, resting right behind her left hip. A tattoo peeked out at him, a pair of golden eyes gleaming from behind deep green leaves.

The memory exploded in his head, so ripe with pain it might have occurred only minutes ago. His foster home. What should have been his last placement. For the first time since he'd been orphaned, this one had been a real home, not like the endless stream of residences where he'd been one of a pack. The unwanted. The forgotten. The neglected. The rejected.

This was a true home with loving parents, his own room... and Daisy. Her name scorched his brain with tongues of fire, ripping through the misty veil of forgetfulness caused by his accident and he remembered, remembered it all. The Marcellus residence had been a summertime way station between his senior year in high school and his first semester at Harvard. He wasn't the only foster child, and yet the Marcelluses had somehow juggled family interests with work with caring for the needs of those they took in. It would have been perfect, except…

Except for Daisy.

The moment he'd walked into his new home and seen her at the bottom of a pile of foster rugrats, he'd wanted her. He shouldn't have, not considering she'd sported spiky Goth-black hair, kohl-rimmed green eyes and purple-tipped finger- and toenails. He'd been so used to people judging without knowing him, that he tried never to make the same mistake. And it only took one look to see straight through to the sweetness beneath the outer craziness. Or what he thought was sweetness.

Instead, she'd lied to him from beginning to end.

Justice escaped the bed in one fluid movement and crossed the room. Ripping open the closet, he snagged the first pair of slacks that came to hand and yanked them on, struggling for control. Damn it to hell, where had his control gone? It had always been like that with her. She possessed an uncanny knack for pushing the exact right buttons guaranteed to turn his carefully laid plans inside out and upside down.

"Justice?" Her sleepy voice came from the warmth of the bed, slow and sweet and contented. And oh, so false.

He snatched a deep breath. Then another. His temper might be held by a tenuous thread, but at least it held. He turned and faced her. "Good morning."

She blinked the sleep from jade-green eyes, focusing in on him. "What's wrong?"

"Nothing. I'd like you to leave now."

She sat up in bed. Her hair should have been snarled and knotted with snakes, like Medusa's head. Instead, the wheat-blond length tumbled straight as a waterfall to her shoulders. The sheet dipped toward her waist exposing the lovely apple-breasts he'd found so unbearably sweet last night. In the morning light, he could see the nipples were rosy pink, the same rosy pink as the color sweeping across her cheekbones.

It didn't make sense to him. She was a snake in the grass. An asp posed to strike. And yet, he didn't think he'd ever seen a more beautiful sight. How was that possible?

She blinked those impossibly green eyes at him. "I'm sorry. Did...did you just ask me to leave?"

"Yes."

Good. Short and to the point. No mistaking the response, either. She was a woman. They tended to take longer to dress and do whatever it was women did in the morning. He ran a fast calculation. Chances were excellent that she'd be gone in just under nine-point-four minutes.

"There is something wrong. What is it?"

She shot from the bed and seeing her in the sunlight, every inch of her on full display, nearly brought Justice to his knees. No question. If he survived the next nine-point-three minutes it would be a miracle. And he didn't believe in miracles.

"I remember who you are."

"You do?" She smiled in delight. "That's great. How did you figure it out?"

"Your tattoo." That damnable tattoo. "Seeing it has somehow forged a connection between my consciousness and that particular set of memories."

"Was that all it took?" She had the nerve to laugh. "I'm surprised your own tattoo didn't do that."

"I don't have a tattoo."

"Sure you do. A panther's paw with claw marks to match my cat's eyes." She pointed. "It's there on your hip—" She broke off, distress causing her to catch her lower lip between her teeth, a lip he'd taken great delight in catching between his own teeth only hours earlier. "Oh, Justice. There's only a scar there now. I'm so sorry."

"Stop it, Daisy." He cut her off with a slice of his hand.

"Your tattoo is merely a catalyst. I don't just remember who you are. I also remember what you did."

"What I did?"

A tiny line formed between her brows. Excellent. Maybe it would encourage wrinkles to form and she'd be less appealing. Of course, that might take thirty years. Or even fifty, depending on her genetics. He didn't think he could wait that long. He needed her out *now*.

"You lied about your age that summer. You told me you were seventeen. You told me you would be a high school senior to my college freshman, just one year behind me. Instead, you were a fifteen-year-old child."

"Almost sixteen," she retorted, stung. "And I lied because I knew you wouldn't kiss me if I told you the truth."

"Kiss you?" The thread holding his temper snapped. He literally heard it, the sound as loud and sharp as the crack of a whip. He came at her, not even realizing he moved until he caught her shoulders in his hands and yanked her onto her toes. "I made love to you. You were a damn virgin. You were…untouchable and I touched you. The one true home I'd had since my parents died and you ruined it for me. Took it from me. I lost my scholarship because of you because I was no longer of 'good character.'" Dear God that had hurt. Devastated. "Because of you Harvard wouldn't touch me."

"What?" He couldn't mistake the shock on her face. Nor could she have faked the way every scrap of color drained from her face and the pupils of her eyes narrowed to pinpricks. "Oh, Justice. I'm so sorry. They told me you'd left early for college… I never realized…"

He released her and stepped away. "Put on your clothes."

That brought color back to her face. Without a word, she snatched up the various bits and pieces scattered across the suite and dressed. Even that she did with grace and elegance, and Justice turned his back, unable to watch without— Without wanting her again. Without touching her again.

Without snatching her into his arms, carrying her to that bed and making love to her until they were both too exhausted to move. How the hell could he still want her after what she'd done?

"Justice?"

He hadn't heard her approach, but he sure as hell felt her tentative touch on his bare arm. He almost broke, catching himself at the last instant. He turned on her, wanting her to understand just how much she'd cost him. How he'd never forgive her duplicity.

"That final home, that *place*—" he practically spit out the word "—they put me those final months was the worst of them all. They knew what I'd done and treated me…" He broke off, shaking his head, his back teeth clamping as he fought back the blistering spill of emotions. Emotions he refused to acknowledge. Refused to allow to touch him ever again. "When I turned eighteen, they kicked me loose. I had nowhere to go, no one to help me. No job or money and no chance of acquiring either."

Her breath hitched throughout his recital, disbelief warring with… It took him a moment to identify the emotion. Pain? Heartbreak? "I didn't know. I swear I didn't."

Tears came then, sliding down her cheeks and reddening her eyes and nose. She wasn't a pretty crier. Instead of pleasing him, the discovery bothered him on some deep, visceral level, perhaps because it suggested that her tears were sincere. He should have taken pleasure in her distress, felt some sort of redemption. Once upon a time he might have. But not now. Not after all these years. He struggled to ignore the tears, using her emotion to lock away his own. To distance himself from that long-ago time.

"Are you even an engineer?" he demanded.

"No, of course not."

Of course not? God save him from illogical women. "You are at an engineering conference. Only engineers were permitted to attend the keynote speech. No guests. No media. No—" He made an impatient gesture. "Whatever you are."

"I write and illustrate children's storybooks."

It was so far out of expectation that it took him a split second to adjust his thinking. "Then, what the hell were you doing at my speech?"

"I saw your name and photograph on one of the hotel placards and recognized you. I slipped in on impulse."

"You told me you were an engineer."

She scrubbed impatiently at her cheeks before planting her hands on her hips. "I most certainly did not. In fact, I told you I wasn't."

He sorted through their time together and came up empty. "No, you didn't."

"It was when we had tea. Or rather, didn't have tea." She drove that point home with pinpoint accuracy. "You asked if we'd met at an engineering conference and I said I wasn't an engineer." She hesitated. Blushed. "Well, to be honest—"

"Yes, please. I'm sure it would make a nice change for you."

Anger flickered to life in her gaze. "I never lied to you. I told you we'd met before. I never claimed to be an engineer. In fact, I started to explain what I did for a living when the waitress arrived. If she hadn't interrupted, I'd have been able to finish my sentence. By the time she left, the conversation switched gears." She folded her arms across her chest. "As I recall, you asked me for another hint."

"Maybe you should have told me you were the woman who ruined my chance to attend Harvard. That would have been an excellent hint."

"I'm sorry. I had no idea." Her apology sounded sincere, not that it helped.

Even so, he caught the distress and pain. Not on her own account, but for him. Not that he wanted it. "They could have pressed charges against me. Your parents threatened to."

"If they'd pressed charges I would have told the authorities the truth. That I lied to you about my age and what happened between us was consensual. Quite consensual," she made a point of adding, then released a sigh heavy with regret. "I swear to you, Justice, I didn't know they'd found out. They never told me. I just woke up one day and you were gone."

"And that would have made everything all right? Damn it to hell, Daisy. I took you to a tattoo parlor—" Another thought struck him and he groped on the dresser for Rumi, his fingers fumbling across the smooth surface. "Son of a bitch. I let you drive to the tattoo parlor."

She reddened. "I was a bit…precocious back then."

"Precocious?" he roared. "You were a walking, talking bundle of rampaging hormones intent on getting into as much trouble as possible, while dragging me along for the ride."

"That, too." Her expression turned wistful. "But it was fun while it lasted, wasn't it?"

"Out." He couldn't take another minute without totally losing his temper. What was it about her that drove him so close to the edge? "I want you to leave. Now."

"For what it's worth, Justice, I really am sorry. I never realized you paid such a steep price for something so wonderful."

"It wasn't wonderful for me."

"No," she whispered. "I guess not. Just like last night wasn't wonderful, either."

"It was sex."

She flinched and he realized he'd hurt her. Really hurt her. She moistened her lips and gave a curt nod. "Of course. Well, thanks for the amazing sex, Justice."

Without another word, she turned and left the bedroom and his only thought was that she considered their sexual encounter amazing. He wasn't sure any of his previous partners had ever called it amazing. It shouldn't matter, and yet somehow it did. He heard her rummage around in her carryall for endless moments, the contents clashing and chattering in agitation. Then silence. What the hell was she doing? Because he knew damn well she hadn't left. He could still *feel* her. And that alone threatened to drive him insane. Finally, finally, finally, the suite door opened and closed behind her.

He released his breath in a long sigh. Okay, she was gone, this time for good. It might have taken fourteen-point-six minutes instead of the nine plus he'd originally calculated, but at least the confrontation was behind him. He headed for the living area and crossed to the phone, intent on alerting the front desk of his early departure. Sitting on the desk he found a book that hadn't been there before. A children's storybook. He set Rumi aside and reached for the book, hesitating at the last minute.

The cover exploded with color, teeming with plants and flowers that seemed to overrun the jacket. It took his eyes a moment to adjust to the chaotic riot of shape and shade. Then the analytical side of his brain kicked in and he began to separate the various objects, leaf from bud, fruit from flower, until finally he caught the intense gold eyes peering through the jungle foliage, their appearance almost identical to her tattoo.

The eyes were also eerily familiar, maybe because he looked at them every damn day in the mirror.

He touched the cover, tracing the bit of black panther she'd buried within the scene. Unable to help himself, he opened the book. She'd autographed it with her first name and a swift sketch of a flower—a daisy, of course. *"To Justice,"* she wrote. *"I got it wrong. You're not Cat."*

The words didn't make any sense to him until he leafed through the pages and discovered that she'd named the panther Cat. Beside the huge jungle cat romped a domesticated kitten named Kit. She was a tabby, one with green eyes and wheat-blond stripes, identical in name and appearance to the kitten he'd given Daisy the day they'd made love. He'd chosen the silly creature because it reminded him of her. He'd even tied a huge floppy green bow around its neck, one that had been half-shredded by the time he'd presented Daisy with the kitten.

Unable to resist, Justice flipped the book to the beginning and read more carefully this time. He quickly realized this was the first in a series of books about the adventures of Kit and Cat, and told the tale of a kitten lost in the jungle who meets a panther cub. The two became best friends. Kit caused nothing but trouble and Justice found himself smiling since it was so similar to the sort of escapades Daisy used to get into. But Cat was always there to rescue her, to protect her from the dangers of the jungle. Even when it meant choosing between her and his pride, Cat faithfully remained by Kit's side.

He flipped the book closed and his glance fell on Rumi. Somehow, at some point during his argument with Daisy, he'd transformed the sphere. It sat on the desk, its ebony pieces gleaming in the sunlight, the mathematical symbols flowing symmetrically across the metallic petals of the flower he'd created.

A daisy.

Justice's hands balled into fists and he took a step back, rejecting both creations—book and flower. He wasn't Cat any more than she was Kit. Even more telling, she'd made a mistake in the book. Didn't she know? Hadn't she researched her facts? Panthers didn't have prides.

Panthers were loners.

Four

Nineteen months, fifteen days, five hours,
nineteen minutes and forty-three seconds later...

Daisy jiggled the tiny earbud that never seemed willing to fit properly in her ear. "Are you sure you have the directions right, Jett?" she asked the girl she'd agreed to foster nearly a year earlier.

"Positive," came the breezy retort.

With an exclamation of disgust, Daisy pulled off the pavement and onto the narrow shoulder. A harsh November wind swept by, causing the small compact rental to shudder from the blast. This time of year never failed to depress her. It was an in-between season that offered neither the crisp and glorious richness of fall, nor the deep, frosty slumber of full winter. Instead, it hovered somewhere in the middle, a twilight that was neither a beginning nor an end, not a becoming nor a final metamorphosis.

She snagged the map from the passenger seat and fought

through the various fanlike folds to spread it open across the steering wheel, even though she could picture every road and turn in perfect detail from the last time she'd checked it. Sure enough, her memory hadn't failed her. None of the various lines and squiggles included the turnoff for the homestead Jett had described.

"Listen up, Jett," Daisy announced. "I'm lost in the wilds of Colorado. This place isn't on the map and your stupid GPS is demanding I make a U-turn at my earliest convenience and leave. I'm inclined to do what she suggests."

"Dora is an idiot," Jett announced cheerfully.

"I believe I told you that when you insisted I take her."

"She's still young. Give her time to mature."

Daisy choked on a laugh. "*She's* young? That's rich, coming from you."

"I'm sixteen and eight months, or I will be tomorrow. Dora is eleven months and three days, the exact same age as Noelle."

Daisy flinched at Jett's precision. Even though there was no biological relationship, her comment was so like Justice. When would she get over it? When would those little reminders finally stop bothering her? Never. That's when.

As impossible as it seemed, she'd fallen in love with Justice when she'd been little more than a child and had been devastated when he'd disappeared without a word of explanation. Without even saying goodbye. She'd mourned for years, searched for him for years, the constant hope dancing in her heart that he'd somehow find his way back to her. So strong was the hope that she refused to form any other attachments until her junior year at college. To her intense disappointment that relationship had never matched what she'd experienced with Justice.

And then a miracle had happened and she'd found him again. Despite the fact that they'd only shared a single night together, this latest parting had been far worse, perhaps because they'd bonded on an adult level. Or so she'd thought. For those few short hours she'd opened herself completely to him, just as she had as a teenager. Allowed herself to believe that he'd connected as deeply and utterly as she had.

If it hadn't been for her daughter, she didn't know how she'd have gotten through the past year and a half. And now that it had become apparent that Noelle shared her father's brilliance, Daisy had tracked Justice down to the bitter ends of the earth. Though Jett didn't realize it, the brazen teen reminded her of him, as well, possessing both his keen intellect in addition to his meticulous nature. Of course, she also reminded Daisy of herself at that age—creative, a bit outrageous, brash, and pure trouble waiting to happen.

Daisy set her jaw, thinking about the coming confrontation with Justice. Somehow, someway, she needed to harden herself against her emotions. To shut them off as cleanly as he had. She couldn't risk tumbling a third time. She didn't think she'd survive it.

"Okay, Jett. Let's get this done," Daisy announced. "Now where am I and how do I get to Justice? Because from what I can see, there's nothing out here for a billion miles."

"That's quite a feat considering the circumference of the earth is only 24,901.55 miles. That's at the equator. If you're referring to the circumference from pole to pole—"

Daisy's back teeth clamped together. "You know what I mean."

Jett had initially been her parents' foster child. She'd still be one, if the Marcelluses hadn't withdrawn from the program due to her father's heart attack. When he'd become ill, Jett begged Daisy to take the required steps necessary to foster her since the two had struck up a firm friendship. Fortunately, Daisy's storybook series had been a huge hit, one that provided the sort of royalty checks enjoyed by only an elite few, enabling her to live her life as she saw fit, including fostering a precocious teenager. That had been ten months ago and they'd discovered to their mutual delight that the arrangement worked well for them both.

"Okay, listen and obey," Jett instructed. "Drive precisely three-point-two miles south from your current location. There will be a dirt road on your left. Turn down it. Continue on for another ten-point-nine miles. If you still don't see anything, call me."

"And one more thing... How do you know where I am?"

"Dora told me."

Daisy sighed. "Tattletale."

"Noelle and I are following your GPS signal, aren't we, Red?"

Daisy caught the happy babble of her daughter's voice slipping across the airwaves and found herself missing her baby more than she thought possible. It was the first time she'd left Noelle for an extended period of time and she found the separation beyond distressing.

She put the car in gear and pulled out onto the pavement. "I'll call you when I get there."

"We'll be waiting."

An undercurrent of excitement threaded through Jett's voice. Ever since she discovered Daisy actually knew The. Great. Justice. St. John. and more impressive, he was Noelle's father, Jett had worked nonstop to uncover his lair. At least, that's how Daisy thought of it, considering he kept his location so well hidden. Heaven knew, she'd never been successful at locating him. And she had tried.

The minute she'd discovered she was pregnant, she'd spent a full year and a half attempting to track him down with zero success. She'd sent endless letters through every engineering source she could think of, again with zero success. It had taken Jett precisely one month. Okay, twenty-nine days, eleven hours, fourteen minutes and a handful of seconds. The teenager had noted the exact time in her final progress report.

Which brought Daisy to her current location and task…to snare the elusive panther in his equally elusive den.

The fourteen-point-whatever mile drive took nearly an hour. Daisy couldn't help but think the rutted road, one that threatened to break both axles, as well as shake loose most of her teeth, was a deliberate attempt on Justice's part to keep unwanted visitors from accidentally stumbling across him. Because, sure enough, the instant Dora's mileage indicator hit the combined distance of surface and dirt roads Jett had decreed, Daisy crested a hill and found a huge complex sprawled beneath her, blending so beautifully into the surrounding meadow that it almost looked like a mirage.

Brigadoon rising from the mists of time.

She put through a call to Jett. "I'm here."

"I found it? For real?" Jett practically squealed in excitement, sounding for the first time in a long time like a typical teenager, something she definitely was not. *"Yes!"*

"You're pumping your fist, aren't you?"

"Yes!"

"I'll call you after my meeting."

"I want it word for word."

"I have a photographic memory, not audiographic, but I'll do my best."

Daisy removed the earbud and switched it off. Shoving the car in gear, she rolled down the hillside toward what appeared to be a ranch complex, complete with barn, paddock, pastures, homestead and even a windmill. Despite that, a vague sensation of emptiness hung over the place, as though time held its breath. Rolling to a stop in front of the sprawling house, she switched off the engine and sat, fighting for calm.

All during the lengthy process of tracking Justice down, she'd shied away from considering how she'd deal with "the moment" when they finally came face-to-face. What would she say? How would he react? Would he even care that she'd given birth to their daughter?

Or would he say something clever like, "Fascinating," and then go invent more robotic whatzit sensors and cooperating actuators with autonomous humans, or whatever he was the best on the planet at doing. Not that it mattered. So long as he acknowledged his daughter, acknowledged his responsibility in her creation and supplied their baby with what she needed, Daisy didn't really care what he did or where he did it.

So. This was it.

She eyed the wide front porch and gnawed on her lower lip. No more procrastinating. Time to beard the mad scientist in his secret lab. Smacking her palm against the steering wheel for emphasis, she shoved open the door to the rental car, climbed out and slammed it closed. Marching up the steps to the front porch, she crossed to the entryway. Something about it struck her as odd and it took a moment to realize what.

No windows in or around the door.

No handle.

No doorbell or knocker.

Damn.

Balling up her fist, she pounded on the thick oak barricade. "Justice? Justice St. John? I want to talk to you."

Nothing.

She gave the door a swift kick for extra emphasis. "I'm not leaving, Justice. Not until we talk."

Not a sound. Not a reaction of any kind. It was as though the house slept. Daisy shivered. Almost like it was caught in some other moment in time or an alternate universe. Another dimension, maybe, like Brigadoon. Maybe it wasn't time for them to wake up, yet.

Or maybe he simply wasn't home.

She paced in front of the door, wondering what she should do next. And that's when she noticed another oddity about the doorway, a reflective gleam buried in the trim work. She paused in her pacing and studied the anomaly. Son of a gun.

A camera. Someone was watching and she'd bet her next four impressively large royalty checks she knew who it was.

Well, now. Wasn't that interesting? She might stink at math, but she could solve this particular equation. She'd found the God of Geekdom hiding in an unmarked valley in Colorado, buried behind thick walls with a door but no handle, the place as unwelcoming as he could make it. Oh, she could add up those numbers to equal…

She marched straight up to the camera and tilted her face so she could glare directly at the tiny circle of glass. "Justice? You either open this door or I'm going to get on the phone and call every media source I can think of and tell them where you live. And then I'm going to get on the internet and post the location on every geek-site I can find."

An instant later the front door emitted a persnickety click and eased inward a fraction. Daisy gave it a shove, not the least surprised when it opened to her touch. She stepped across the threshold into a chilly gloom that left her squinting. The door swung closed behind her and the dead bolt slammed home with a rifle-sharp retort, locking her inside.

"If that's meant to scare me, you didn't succeed," she announced. Then in an undertone, "Intimidated me a little bit, maybe, but you didn't scare me."

Daisy glanced around the foyer, struggling to get a good look at her surroundings. Difficult, considering the lack of natural light. What was the deal with windows around here? The cold air contained a stale, dusty quality, as though the area was rarely used. Justice certainly hadn't wasted any of his trillions heating this section of his homestead and she shivered in the confines of her thin coat, missing the Florida warmth and sunshine.

She took another step into the dimness. Without any carpeting to absorb the sound, the impact of her shoes against the slate flooring bounced in noisy protest off the featureless walls. She looked around, curiosity combining with nervousness. The huge entranceway lacked the usual bits and pieces most foyers contained. No tables or racks or mirrors or pictures or freestanding artwork. Just…emptiness. Well, and dust. She turned in a slow circle looking for a light switch and coming up empty. Okay, that was just weird.

What little she could see through the gloom of the surrounding rooms spoke of huge expanses of space as stark and empty as the foyer, though she could see their potential in the flow and symmetry of the overall structure. She particularly liked the liberal use of wood, not to mention the fact that the other rooms had honest-to-goodness windows, even if they were shuttered. Why in the world would he live in such a magnificent home and keep it closed up and empty? It didn't make any sense.

Before she could work up the nerve to explore, she caught the hard clip of boots ringing against floorboards, the sound echoing through the painful emptiness. The footsteps moved in her direction at a steady, unhurried pace. For some reason that firm, deliberate tread added to the intimidation factor, his coming an inescapable certainty.

No turning back now.

A moment later his impressive form filled a doorway to her right, one draped in dense shadow. Everything inside of her blossomed to life, responding to the man instinct told her was Justice, even though she couldn't see him clearly. She closed her eyes, fighting against an almost overpowering urge to race toward him and throw herself into his arms. To allow all she kept bottled inside to burst free, like spring sunshine burning away the ice damming a river's reckless flow.

"How did you find me, Daisy?" His cold voice cut through the darkness with knifelike sharpness, confirming his identity. Not that she had any doubt.

She sighed. How like him to skip over the social niceties. "Hello, Justice. I'm fine, thanks. Yes, it's been a long drive. Why, yes, I'd love something to drink."

He didn't respond immediately. And then, "You threatened to expose me to the media."

"You wouldn't let me in. It was the only leverage I had." This was ridiculous. She crossed the foyer toward him, feeling the bond between them tighten and ensnare her with each step she took. "Come on, Justice. Get us something to drink and let's sit down and talk. It's important."

The closer she came the more clearly she could see him. Dear heaven, but he'd changed during the months they'd been apart. An icy remoteness cascaded off of him in frosty waves. He'd become harder, more self-contained than ever. What had happened to cause such a change?

She didn't dare touch him. No point in risking frostbite, though part of her longed to. "Are you all right?" she asked in concern.

"No."

Another thought occurred, a horrifying thought. "Oh, Justice, are you ill?"

"My health is perfect, thank you."

Then what in the world had happened to him? She stiffened. He couldn't have turned into this glacial, winter-bound man as a result of their encounter at the engineering conference. In order for that to be the case, their night together would have had to mean something to him, impacted his life in some way. And though it broke her heart to admit it, she'd long ago come to the conclusion that those glorious hours had meant nothing to him. Less than nothing. Otherwise he'd have tracked her down. At the very least he'd have responded to the endless letters she'd sent him.

He lifted an eyebrow. "You wanted something to drink before you left?"

Daisy released her breath in a sigh. This was going to be even harder than she'd anticipated. "I would, yes."

Justice led the way down a wide hall into a huge, impressive kitchen that looked like something out of a futuristic movie, though it seemed to be missing the normal collection of appliances. "Lights," he requested and instantly a bank of recessed lighting flared to life.

She stared in wonder, impressed. "Is that how you turn on the lights around here?"

"Yes, if your voice is coded for computer authorization." He paused a beat, his smile set well below frigid. "Which, yours is not. Water, tea, pop or something stronger?"

"Water's fine." She swiped her hands along the sides of her jeans, fighting nerves. "I wouldn't have told, you know. Where you live, I mean," she added for clarification.

He tapped a swift code onto a black glass plate affixed to the wall. With a soft hiss a pair of bottles slid out from a slot in the wood paneling. He handed her one, the temperature so cold her fingers went instantly numb. Twisting off the lid of the other, he stared at her while he took a long swallow. "I know you wouldn't have told anyone," he said.

"Really?" For some reason his certainty pleased her and she relaxed enough to smile. "How do you know?"

"Because Pretorius has jammed your cell signal. And he'll continue to jam it until I tell him otherwise."

Her smile faded. "When do you intend to tell him otherwise?" she asked warily.

"As soon as my uncle and I relocate. Until then, you'll remain here as our guest."

She paused with the bottle halfway to her mouth. "Excuse me?"

"You heard me."

"But…but you can't do that," she sputtered.

"Watch me."

Dear heavens, he was serious. She could see it in the hard glitter of his eyes and intractable set of his jaw. She'd never seen him look tougher or more formidable, cloaked with a dark, dangerous edge. She would have panicked if she hadn't also seen something else. Something that actually gave her hope.

There in the tawny gold of his eyes, she caught the unmistakable flame of desire. He might fight it, he might deny it, he might have attempted to bury it beneath endless layers of ice, but she didn't doubt for a minute he felt it.

Daisy decided to test the possibility. "What am I supposed to do while you're keeping me here?" She caught it again, just the merest flash. But it answered her question without his having to say a word. "You can't be serious."

"You chose to come here. By doing so you assume the risk and consequences of your actions."

She invaded his personal space until they were only inches apart. Not that he backed down. "And making love is the risk and consequence I assumed by showing up on your doorstep? Oh, excuse me. According to you we've never made love, have we?" She wrapped air quotes around the words, "made love." "I seem to recall your telling me it was just sex."

A cool smile snagged the corners of his mouth. "According to *you,* amazing sex."

Her temper shot straight through the roof. "Oh! How dare you throw that in my face after all this time. And how dare you decide to keep me here against my will. Just because you haven't gotten any in a while and I conveniently appear on your doorstep, you think you can toss me in your bed and have your wicked way with me?"

"Yes."

Her mouth opened and closed, but she couldn't seem to do more than make odd little choking noises. Finally, her vocal cords kicked in. "Yes? That's all you have to say? *Yes?* Have you lost your mind?"

He went nose-to-nose with her. "Once again, yes! I lost my mind nineteen months, fifteen days, six hours, twenty-eight minutes and twelve seconds ago. And I want it back, which is precisely what you're going to do. Having you here in my bed should return some modicum of sanity to me. It's a perfectly logical solution to an utterly illogical problem."

Daisy couldn't recall Justice ever coming so close to losing his temper. Not to this extent. Always in the past he'd shown impressive self-control and restraint. Whereas she'd fly off in a thousand different directions, spewing emotional lava like a human volcano, he would pull tighter, deeper, one by one shutting off all those hot, torrid outlets until he had everything tamped down and safely buried.

Well, not this time. Not now. She knew that if she pushed so much as one more button, she could stand back and watch him blow. Her finger itched to try it, and yet, she hesitated. What would be the cost if she tipped him over the edge? What would it do to him to have that control ripped away? He'd hate it. Despise himself. And she simply couldn't do that to him. If he ever opened to her, actually expressed those emotions and revealed his vulnerability, it would be his choice. She wouldn't force it on him.

Daisy allowed the seconds to slip by, allowed the simmer and boil to cool. Allowed the volcano to slip back into dormancy. "You have a lot of nerve, Justice," she told him quietly.

"You're correct." He wrapped control around himself like a blanket of snow. Even so, she could sense the heat of desire lingering beneath the ice. "That doesn't change the fact that you'll do whatever I tell you."

For some reason his comment made her smile. "Anything?"

"Anything and everything," he confirmed.

Her amusement faded and she lowered her gaze so she wouldn't betray her reaction. She doubted she could conceal the intense longing that gripped her. The underpinning of desperation and want. It wasn't fair. Not after what he'd done. Not after all the time and distance separating them. "I thought you didn't want me."

To her relief, Justice didn't deny it. "Apparently, I was wrong. I guess we both were."

"An affair, is that what you're proposing?" She looked at him again, allowing a hint of her own yearning to slip through. "I stay here for however long it takes you to find a new place to hide—"

"I'm not hiding."

Daisy couldn't help herself. She laughed, the sound almost painful. "Oh, please."

"I'm protecting my privacy. If the general public knew where I lived—"

"The general public couldn't care less. Maybe the media would express some interest. But I suspect the only ones you need to worry about are other mad scientist wannabes." She leaned her hip against the kitchen table. "So, what's the real reason, Justice?"

He took a slow drink of his water, no doubt to give himself time to consider the most logical response to her question. He must have come up empty, because he asked instead, "How did you find me?"

She'd been waiting for that, wondering when he'd get around to it. "I had help, which is another reason you can't keep me here against my will. Jett will eventually grow concerned and alert the authorities."

"Jett." His eyes flamed before he regained control. "Boyfriend? Husband? Lover?"

Two could play this game. She folded her arms across her chest and lifted an eyebrow. And waited.

"How did this Jett person find us, Pretorius?" Justice asked while his heated gaze remained locked with hers.

To Daisy's shock, a disembodied voice responded. "I'm working on it."

"Work harder. I want him traced and shut down."

"You think I don't know that? I know that. This Jett is good. Real good."

"I thought you were the best."

"Go to hell, Justice."

Much to Daisy's relief, a peeved tone rippled through Pretorius's voice, confirming his status as a living, breathing human versus a machine. Even though Justice had claimed Pretorius was his uncle, she wouldn't have put it past him to have considered that some sort of private joke. Of course, that would mean Justice would need to possess a sense of humor, something he'd probably worked long and hard to eradicate, along with every other emotion.

Well, except desire. That remained fully operational.

"I think I found how he traced us. Shutting him down. Okay, he's cut off."

Justice offered a wintry smile that perfectly matched the raw November day. "Is that it?" she asked. "We're now invisible to Jett? You do realize that I got here with a GPS. I was tracked every step of the way."

"It won't take long to relocate."

"I find that difficult to believe unless you already have a backup site ready to go." The glitter in his tawny gaze confirmed her guess. "Okay, fine. You know something, Justice? You go right ahead. Keep me here until you and your uncle are ready to run to wherever your new cave is located. Then you can hang from the rafters in the privacy of your latest den of doom and gloom. Frankly, I don't give a damn."

"I already told you we're not in hiding. And mad scientists hide in basements not in rafters."

Okay, that was definitely a joke. Who knew? Not that it mattered. She brushed the comment aside with a sweep of her hand. "Whatever. That's not why I'm here. You're so worried about the hows and whys of my finding you that you've totally ignored the main question."

"Such as the reason you wrote twenty-six letters and requested they be forwarded to me? Not to mention why, after all this time, you've gone to so much trouble to track me down? Those main questions?"

He'd received her letters and *still* never got in touch? Fury ripped through her. "Yes, those main questions," she said through gritted teeth.

"Don't keep me in suspense. What could you possibly have to say that we didn't cover nineteen months and fifteen days ago?"

He wanted it straight? Fine. She'd give it to him straight. "You have a daughter."

Five

Justice had always considered himself a rational man. Intelligent. Sensible. Calm and collected. His emotions firmly within his control. But with those four simple words he discovered just how mistaken he could be. Only one other time had he experienced this severe a brain disconnect—the hours following his accident. He opened his mouth to say something, only to discover that every last word had emptied from his mind.

"Wha—"

"What's her name? It's Noelle."

"Whe—"

"When was she born? Eleven months and a handful of days ago. Christmas morning, to be exact. If you need further exactitude, which I'm sure you do, they recorded the precise time on her birth certificate. I'll arrange for you to receive a copy."

"Ho—"

"How do I know you're the father? Because you're the

only man I've slept with in the past three years. No doubt you'll want a DNA test and I have no objection. I thought you should know about Noelle, so I've spent the past year and a half trying to track you down without success. But then, since you received all my letters, you already know that, don't you?" She paused for a beat. "Are you listening, Pretorius?"

"Uh—" came his uncle's disembodied voice.

"I thought so. I can hear the family resemblance. It only took Jett a few short weeks to find you." She shot Justice a steely look. "I think that means my computer expert outcomputes your computer expert. Now. What were you saying about keeping me here?"

The logjam clogging Justice's vocal cords cleared. "Son of a *bitch!*"

Daisy planted her hands on her hips, glorious in her outrage. "I trust you won't use that sort of language around our daughter. She's quite verbal for so young an age. She tries to parrot everything you say."

"I want her."

Something very much like hurt flashed across Daisy's expression and her eyes darkened to the deep green of a mountain forest. For some reason it shredded his defenses and arrowed straight to the emotional core of him. How was that possible? How could a single look possess the power to stir a combination of guilt and defensiveness? He'd worked diligently for over a year and half to eradicate any and all reactions to her from his emotional makeup. And yet from the instant she appeared on his doorstep he'd discovered that he hadn't eradicated anything at all. One glimpse of her elegant face glaring up at the camera and desire came storming back, eclipsing logic and self-determination.

It defied comprehension.

He hastened to amend his earlier statement. "I want both of you."

He hadn't helped his cause. Her chin shot up and her eyes

flashed with green fire, full of feminine fury, mingled with a gut-wrenching anguish. "I don't think you deserve me. And I know you don't deserve Noelle."

"If that's what you believe, why are you here?"

He caught her wariness before she wiped every thought and emotion from her face, closing down and shutting him out. She'd never done that before. He suspected she'd never been capable of it until recently. When they'd last been together she'd been open and forthcoming, her opinions and feelings out there for everyone to see. Was he responsible for so dramatic a change? Had their night together caused her to regard the world with such caution? He flinched from the thought, from the idea he was capable of inflicting that level of pain on anyone, though for reasons he couldn't bring himself to analyze, Daisy in particular.

"You deserved to know about your daughter. Now that you do, I'm finished here."

She was keeping something from him, he could tell. "It's more than that, isn't it?" He could also tell she had zero intention of explaining herself. "Never mind. Considering how guarded I am about my own privacy, I won't intrude on yours."

"Thank you."

"But if I can help, I will." He had no idea where the words came from. He certainly hadn't planned to say them, an unfathomable lapse on his part, but they caught her attention.

She studied his face for a long, tense moment. Then her head jerked in a nod. "Thanks. I appreciate it."

Whether she realized it or not, Daisy's announcement offered him the perfect opportunity to achieve the goals he'd set more than two years ago—to create a family. To have someone in his life who mattered. Who cared. Though she didn't and couldn't meet his conditions for an engineering apprentice, any more than those for the perfect wife, the potential existed to shape her to fit many of the same param-

eters. Hell, he'd even be willing to alter his lifestyle somewhat to suit her requirements for a husband. Within reason,
of course.

And then there was Noelle. He struggled to draw air into
his lungs at the thought of his progeny. *A daughter.* He had
a child! It stunned him how much that simple fact changed
the means by which he processed information. He found he
craved her, sight unseen. Wanted and needed them both in
ways he found inexplicable. No matter what it took, he'd give
Daisy whatever she required in order to have his ready-made
family part of his life.

He crossed to a sturdy wooden table and pulled out a chair,
formulating a swift game plan. "Let's sit and talk about this.
Are you hungry?"

Annoyance flashed. "Let me get this straight. Now that
you know about Noelle you're willing to feed me?"

"No," he responded mildly. "Since I planned to keep you
here until we relocated, I would have gotten around to feeding
you. Eventually."

That provoked a smile. A tiny one, but a smile nonetheless.
The impact of it far exceeded what it should have, based on
all rational consideration. And yet, just as at the engineering
conference, it drew him in, put thoughts and ideas in his
head he'd spent every day since their night together working
to eradicate. How many potential apprentice/wives had he
interviewed since Daisy? How many times had Pretorius
tweaked his Pretorius Program in an effort to find the
"perfect" woman? How many failures had there been?

And all because none of them were Daisy, he now realized.

Oh, they'd suited his conditions to a T. Every last miserable one of them had engineering credentials. Were brilliant, rational, sensible women in complete control of their
emotions. A few were even more attractive than Daisy, though
for some inexplicable reason their beauty left him cold. To
be fair, none of them revealed any true meanness that he'd

noticed, still he wouldn't call them kind. Perhaps their very lack of emotional depth prevented them from exhibiting the qualities Daisy possessed in distressing excess.

Regardless, his search had ultimately resulted in only one serious candidate...along with the indelible memory of Daisy. Now he had the ideal opportunity to mold the woman he actually wanted into the perfect wife.

"I thought we were going to talk," she prompted with another of her irresistible smiles.

"Talking is the easy part."

Again, the wariness. "And the not-so easy part?" she asked.

"I don't cook and neither does Pretorius."

She glanced around. "Maybe that explains the lack of appliances."

"There's a fully stocked refrigerator and freezer in the cabinet behind me, as well as a full complement of appliances." He took a seat beside her. "I also have someone stop in once a day and prepare our meals, so you can cross that concern off your list."

She blinked. "I didn't realize I had a list."

"I'm making one for you."

Daisy's eyes narrowed. "And why would you do that? And why should it matter whether or not you can cook, or whether or not you have someone fixing your meals? It has nothing to do with me."

Now for the hard part. No point in delaying the inevitable. Better to get right to it. "It's about to have a lot to do with you, because I want you and Noelle to move in here with me and I'll do whatever it takes to make that happen."

She shook her head before he even finished speaking. "Forget it, Justice. I'm not interested in having you in my life any more than you're interested in being in mine."

He lifted an eyebrow. "You'd rather share custody of Noelle?"

The breath left Daisy's lungs in a rush. "What?"

"You said she's mine. Now that I know about her existence, I'm willing and able to be a father to her. There's only two ways that'll work. Either we live together or we shuttle her back and forth between us. I'm thinking it's in our daughter's best interest for her to live with both of us. Together."

Her gaze swept the room and he struggled to see it through her eyes. Despite the state-of-the-art equipment and electronics tucked neatly behind warm oak cabinets, it came up lacking. Empty. Cold. Aw, hell. Dark and dusty, even with the lights.

"You want us to live out here, in the middle of nowhere?" she asked in disbelief. "What sort of life is that for a child?"

"We can work around any of your objections," he insisted doggedly. "There are reasons I choose to live in the middle of nowhere."

"Such as?"

"Pretorius? Permission, please."

There was a momentary silence, then, "Tell her."

"My uncle has a social anxiety disorder. It's one of the reasons I was put in foster care after the death of my parents. The courts didn't consider Pretorius an acceptable guardian."

Compassion swept across Daisy's expression and he realized that it was an innate part of her character. It always had been. "Agoraphobia?" She hazarded a guess.

"That's probably part of it. More, it's people in general he has difficulty handling."

"Huh. I have that same problem…with certain people."

He acknowledged the hit with a cool smile. "Whereas he needs the isolation, I value my privacy. When I turned eighteen and had nowhere to go, my uncle opened his home to me, even though he found it a very difficult adjustment. Since then, it's worked for us. Or rather, it did."

"Should I assume something changed?"

Time to be honest with her. Totally honest. "Yes. It changed a couple of years ago."

"What happened a couple of years—" He caught her dawning comprehension and again that deep flash of compassion. How did she do it? How did she open herself up like that and let everyone in? Especially when it guaranteed she would be hurt in the process. "Oh, Justice. The car wreck?"

He nodded. "It made me realize what I had wasn't enough."

"And…?"

He chose his words with care. It felt like tiptoeing through a minefield. "I asked Pretorius to rewrite a business program he marketed a few years ago. I gave him a set of parameters combining qualities important to me, with characteristics that would also be compatible with my uncle."

She stared blankly. "You just lost me."

"He asked me to find him a wife," Pretorius interrupted. "One that we'd both like."

Justice swore. "I'm telling this story, old man."

"And I'm just filling in the parts you seem to be skipping over."

"I was getting to them. I just wanted to do this in a logical order."

Pretorius snorted. "Right. And E-equals-MC-you're-full-of-crap."

Damn it to hell. "Computer, close circuit to kitchen and keep it closed until I say otherwise."

"No, I want to hear—" Pretorius's voice was cut off midsentence.

Justice took a deep, steadying breath. "Now, where was I?"

He could see the laughter in Daisy's eyes before gold-tipped lashes swept downward, concealing her expression. "I believe you were explaining how you used a computer program to find a wife." The merest hint of amusement threaded through her words.

"It made perfect sense at the time."

"Of course it did."

"The Pretorius Program has been quite successful at choosing the perfect employee in the business sector." He heard the defensive edge slashing through his comment and took a moment to gather himself. What was it about Daisy that caused him to lose his composure with such ease and frequency? "I had more specific requirements to take into consideration for a wife, so Pretorius tweaked the parameters."

"What sort of specific requirements and what parameters?"

Hell, no. He would not walk down that road. "That's not important."

Unfortunately, she seemed unusually adept at adding two and two together, squaring it and leaping to a completely illogical, though accurate, conclusion. "You were looking for a wife at that engineering conference, weren't you? That's why you were so mad when you discovered I wasn't an engineer."

"That's a distinct possibility," he admitted.

She leaned forward, staring intently, her spring-green eyes disturbing in the extreme. "Are you telling me that Pretorius devised a computer program to find you the perfect woman and she was supposed to be at that conference?"

Damn, damn, damn. "Yes."

"Are you seriously going to sit there and admit that you thought you could waltz into that conference, check out the women your uncle's program selected and convince one of them to marry you?"

He gritted his teeth. "Engineers are very logical. The women involved would have seen that we were an excellent match."

Her mouth dropped open. "And agreed to marry you right then and there?"

"That would have been helpful, though unlikely."

"You *think?*"

He suspected from her tone that the question was both rhetorical and a bit sarcastic. Just in case he was mistaken, he gave her a straight answer. "Yes. But Pretorius suggested a way around that."

"Oh, this I have to hear."

"He suggested I offer her a position as my apprentice. That would allow us an opportunity to get to know each other better before committing to marriage. It would also allow me to determine whether she was acceptable to Pretorius."

"Huh." Daisy mulled that over. "Okay, that's not such a bad plan. So explain something to me. It's been almost two years. Why don't you have an apprentice/wife by now?"

He would have given anything to avoid this conversation. But he suspected that unless he put all his cards on the table, he'd lose any chance at having a family. A real family. And over the past two years he'd discovered he wanted that more than anything else. Needed the connection before the ice crystallizing in his veins won and he lost all ability to feel. "It would seem the computer program contained a flaw."

"Remarkable."

"Agreed." He frowned. "In retrospect, I realize that there are some indefinable qualities that prove difficult to adapt to a computer program."

"Wow. Who would have thought. Enlighten me. What sort of indefinable qualities are we talking about?"

Justice had given it a lot of thought over the ensuing months and as irrational and unscientific as it was, there'd been only one inescapable conclusion. "I believe it must have been chemical in nature and therefore extremely difficult to quantify."

"In English, please?"

He stood and crossed the room to give himself some breathing space. "I didn't want them. I wanted you." The words hung in the air, frank and inescapable. And completely, painfully honest. "It's not logical. I can't explain it. It just is."

She shook her head and to his alarm he saw tears gleam in her too-expressive eyes. "Don't, Justice. I can't go there again. Not when I know how you really feel about me. That you still hold me responsible for losing your scholarship and being sent to some hideous foster home."

He leaned his hip against the counter and folded his arms across his chest. "The truth?"

She forced out a watery smile. "Will it hurt?"

He weighed the possibility. "I don't believe so."

"In that case, I guess I can handle it."

"Six months, three days, twenty-two hours and nine minutes ago I came to a conclusion."

"And what conclusion is that?"

"That even if I'd known before we made love that I'd lose my scholarship, I'm not positive I could have resisted. I would have tried due to your age, but to be perfectly frank, at seventeen I lacked the maturity to make decisions based on intellect rather than hormonal imperative."

Her smile wobbled, grew. "Does that mean you forgive me?"

"It wouldn't be rational to continue to hold a grudge." He frowned, picking through his words. "Though I no longer feel any anger in association with what occurred, I still possess a certain level of resentment. But considering that my success in the field of robotics hasn't been negatively impacted by those events, even resentment is an unreasonable response."

"Yes, it is," she agreed.

"I also never asked whether our relationship had a negative impact on your life," he found himself saying, much to his surprise. "Were you negatively impacted?"

"Yes."

He frowned in concern. "How?" A sudden thought struck and he froze. "You didn't get pregnant, did you?"

"No, nothing like that. I was hurt because you left without a word. Of course, now I understand why. But at the time it broke my heart." Her chin quivered ever so slightly. "I missed you so much."

An odd feeling raced through him, a yearning combined with an almost forgotten pain. "I missed you, too," he confessed. "I didn't want to, since I blamed you for what happened. But you were the first real friend I'd ever had."

"Oh, Justice."

She escaped her chair and threw herself into his arms. At the first touch of her soft form colliding against his hard angles, he discovered he'd made a serious miscalculation. Whatever they'd experienced all those months ago hadn't dissipated over time as he'd anticipated. If anything, the craving had grown progressively worse. It might not be logical, but it was unquestionably true. He took the only action he deemed reasonable.

He kissed her.

Alice down the rabbit hole.

Only in this case Daisy tumbled head over heels down the hole and landed in a crazy, new world. Or maybe it wasn't all that new. She'd worked so hard to forget what it had been like to lose herself in his arms. To know his kiss and have it sweep her away. To reach for something she thought long lost to her. He took his time reminding her of every moment of those lost memories.

Pleasure erupted, a tidal wave of sparkling joy, rushing through her without rhyme or reason. Not that it was love. She couldn't love him. Refused to allow it. Passion. Lust. Sexual attraction. All those things she could accept, but not love. And she'd do everything within her power to avoid feeling an emotional attachment to a man who spent a lifetime suppressing them. She couldn't deal with the despair and disillusionment again. It was too painful.

His mouth shifted across hers, deepening the kiss—a kiss that shouldn't have improved since the last time they were together, but somehow had. She didn't know whether it came from a growing familiarity or nearly two months of longing. She could only acknowledge the truth of it before going under, drowning beneath the cascade of sensations swamping her.

How did he do it? How did he stir such a helpless reaction? Her lips parted beneath his delicious invasion, opening to the heat. He was a man of logic and control, and yet she felt the instant that control slipped and shattered. He demanded, then tempted. Teased, then seduced. He touched her, kissed her, shifted his body against hers in a rhythm they'd both perfected that long-ago night. And yet, it might have been yesterday, the movements as familiar to her as they were arousing, and she found herself surrendering to the raw power of that primal song that played whenever they came together.

His hands cupped her face, tilting her head so he could more fully explore her mouth. She lost herself in the kiss while the sweetest of memories slid over and through her. Memories of their last night together when he'd taken her countless times, the final one sweet and tender beyond bearing. She suspected it had been then that she'd conceived Noelle, then that passion had caused them to forget a bedside table drawer full of caution. Then that he'd forever branded himself on her, heart and body and soul.

No! Oh, no, no, no. How could she be so foolish?

Daisy ripped free of his embrace and put the width of the table between them. She'd come here, dead certain in her ability to hold Justice at arm's length, and instead all he'd had to do was touch her and she tumbled into his arms and surrendered. Did she think that everything that had gone so dramatically wrong twenty endless months ago, a single kiss could set right?

Swearing silently, she snatched up her bottle of water and hastily unscrewed the lid and took a long swallow while she struggled to gather her thoughts. "When you said you wanted me and Noelle to move in and you'll do whatever it takes to make that happen—"

"I have always found that positive reinforcement works best."

"You'd bribe me to live with you, Justice?" She took her time recapping the bottle. "Or perhaps that kiss was part of your positive reinforcement."

"Only if it worked. Otherwise, what can I offer that will convince you to do as I request?"

"Do you realize that you sound like a computer whenever you get tense?" Based on the blank look he gave her, he didn't. "Bribery won't work, Justice. Nor will kissing me."

"What will?"

She stood and crossed the kitchen to the shuttered window. "Is there any way to open this?"

"Computer, open window at Kitchen, Station 1A."

A soft hum sounded and the shutters parted. This side of the house faced a long, rolling valley that must be stunning in the spring. Right now, with winter on the verge of overtaking them, it offered a raw, unforgiving beauty. Without the green of spring to cloak it, or flowers to add bright color and texture, only the bare bones remained. Nature at its most stark, without the pretty artifice to soften the harsh truth.

And the harsh truth was that she hadn't been completely honest with Justice about why she'd tracked him down. Their daughter, Noelle, had been a huge part of it—the main part. But there was another reason, one she kept from him, one she found difficult to admit, even to herself. Ever since their night together she'd been unable to paint. She'd attempted countless times, without success. But, whatever creative spark, whatever gift or talent she'd been given, had evaporated as though it never existed. It had driven her to extreme measures, to allowing Jett to use every means at her disposal to find Justice's hideaway in the hope that she could set right something that had gone hideously wrong—both for Noelle's sake, as well as her own.

He'd asked her to stay and she wanted to, wanted with all her heart to be with him and discover if they couldn't recapture some part of what they'd shared once upon a time. Why was she hesitating, when he offered to give her just that?

Because he wasn't offering her love.

Well, too bad. She could move in and take her chances, or she could share custody of Noelle. She released her breath in a sigh and turned to face him. "No bribery, Justice. And I can't commit to staying with you permanently. But I am willing to come for a visit as your guest. We'll try it out for a few months and see how it goes. Sort of like what you intended with your apprentice/wife program. Will that do?"

"For now." His gaze strayed to the window. "I wouldn't wait too long, though. Winter's coming."

"It shouldn't take longer than a week to organize. Is there enough room for all of us?"

"This place has a dozen bedrooms. I'll get them ready and you can pick whichever ones you want."

"And Pretorius? How will he handle having visitors?"

Justice frowned. "He has his own section of the house. So long as you don't intrude, he should be fine."

Daisy nodded. "Then I'll see you in a week." She turned and started from the kitchen, pausing at the last minute. And that's when she accepted the heartrending truth. "Our lives will never be the same again. Everything changed twenty months ago, and there's no going back now, is there? Not for either of us."

And without a backward look, she fled.

Justice stood unmoving while the house settled into

silence, returning to its cold air of detachment. Always a house, never a home. Always cold, never filled with light and laughter and warmth.

"You're right. There's no going back," he whispered. "But what you don't realize is…I don't want to go back. I can't live like that anymore."

Daisy gritted her teeth, zigging to avoid driving through yet another pothole, this one the size of a large crater. If she ended up staying with Justice for any length of time, she and Justice were going to have words about this road.

"Almost there." Excitement ricocheted through Jett's voice, making her sound far younger than sixteen. "Just another one-point-four miles and we should be able to see it."

"See it?" Noelle parroted. Only it came out more like "feet?"

Dear heavens, if it wasn't Dora the GPS keeping track of every inch of every mile, it was Jett. And Daisy was willing to bet her last tube of Old Holland Viridian Green oil paint that when Noelle was a few years older she'd be every bit as bad.

"We're surrounded," she muttered to Aggie, her house-keeper. "Better get used to it now. There's worse and you're about to meet him."

"I can handle it," came the calm, seasoned response.

Years ago Aggie had been an elementary school teacher. She'd taken early retirement in order to nurse her husband through a lengthy illness, only to discover their savings exhausted by the time he died. The realization that she had no choice but to return to work coincided with Noelle's birth and Daisy's decision that she needed help with cooking and general housekeeping chores, especially after she'd assumed guardianship of Jett. She'd hired Aggie on the spot. To their mutual delight, the four of them had cemented into a cozy little family, one Justice would have to accept—if he wanted them to remain in Colorado.

"Are you sure Mr. St. John won't mind that you brought all of us along?" Aggie asked with a hint of nervousness.

Daisy started to say she didn't give a hot damn whether Mr. St. John minded, but aware of a backseat full of big ears, she modified her reply. "The four of us are a family. That means we're a package deal. Don't worry. Justice will be cool with it."

A tiny sigh of relief issued from behind her, making Daisy aware that Jett was also feeling apprehensive. She always appeared so self-assured, it came as a bit of a shock the few times she reverted to the nervous, suspicious girl she'd been when Daisy's parents had first taken her in as a foster child.

"I can't believe I'm about to meet the man behind Sinjin," Jett said.

"Finfin?"

"That's your daddy, Red."

"Daddy."

That word came out clear as a bell. For some reason it caused Daisy to flinch and Aggie shot her a sympathetic look. "I'm sure he'll make a wonderful father."

"There's no question Noelle needs him." Her own inadequacies threatened to overwhelm her. "Lord knows, I can't meet all of her needs."

"No parent can give their child everything they require. It's not possible," Aggie was quick to reassure. "If you're very lucky, you can cover most of it between the two of you and hope that friends and family and teachers cover the rest. Just loving them goes a long way."

But was Justice capable of love? Was it programmed into his software or had that particular upgrade been wiped from his hard drive? Only time would tell. At long last the car crested the final hill and they coasted down to the sprawling homestead. She parked near the steps leading to the main house and cut the engine.

"Okay, everyone grab something and let's get inside." Together they tromped up the steps. She gave the door a tentative shove, relieved when it opened to her touch. At least she wouldn't have to threaten her way in like last time. That would have been a tad embarrassing. "See?" she said with a reassuring smile. "Let's head for the kitchen and get something to drink while we wait for Justice."

It didn't take long. Within a minute he stepped into the kitchen, his tawny gaze sweeping the group. One look warned Daisy he hadn't taken the unexpected guests well. He reminded her of the panther she'd immortalized in her storybooks, stalking into the room, looking sleek and predatory and incredibly dangerous. For a man so proud of his restraint and emotional detachment, he certainly gave a fine imitation of someone who'd gotten his tail in a twist.

For a long, almost painful moment, his gaze lingered on his daughter. Tears pricked Daisy's eyes at the intense longing that ripped apart his expression. It tarnished his eyes and crept deep into the crevices bracketing his mouth. Then his lashes dipped downward, concealing his expression, and he deliberately turned away. She suspected he didn't have a choice, not if he hoped to maintain even a modicum of self-control.

"You said a week," he all but growled. "It's been ten days, three hours and fourteen minutes."

"Sorry about that. It took longer than I expected to get everyone organized. I did email you about the change in dates." He swept the assembled group with a look that probably would have decimated everyone on the spot if Daisy hadn't stepped between Justice and her family to intercept the full blast of it. "Problem?" she asked sweetly.

"A moment of your time?"

His voice had lowered to a threatening rumble, forcing

Daisy to spare her family a reassuring smile. "If you'd wait here," she requested, easing Noelle into Aggie's arms. "There are drinks in the refrigerator, assuming you can figure out where it's hidden."

"I'm on it," Jett announced brightly, her gaze practically eating Justice alive.

"Behave," Daisy mouthed to the teen. Though why she bothered, she couldn't say. She might as well tell a mouse to stay away from the cheese.

Not giving Daisy a chance to issue any further instructions, Justice snagged her arm and drew her from the room. They retraced the path to the front door and continued on in the opposite direction to a large office with a spectacular view of the Rockies. She didn't think he used this room any more often than any of the others on this level. The same feeling of neglect hung over the few furnishings it contained. But at least the shutters were open.

The early afternoon burned across the mountains, coating them in every shade from deep royal blue to the dense purple of eggplant. Trees, bare and stark, slept beside stands of conifers, the green rich with the promise that life would one day return to the windswept landscape. In the distance snowcapped peaks shoved upward against a remote sky, the pale blue expanse winter-hard and slashed with high streaks of gray cirrus clouds. It made her itch to grab her sketchbook and pencils and have at it. But ever since she'd lost her creative spark, she'd been afraid to do even that much, afraid she'd be forced to concede, once and for all, that she'd lost all artistic ability.

Releasing a sigh, Daisy turned from the view and discovered Justice pacing the room in perfect imitation of a sleek jungle cat. Or, to be precise, an infuriated jungle cat ready to attack at the least provocation. He also held the odd spherical device he'd played with the night Noelle had been conceived, twisting and turning it into shape after shape.

"All right," Justice announced, bringing her to earth with a thud. "Let's hear it."

"What do you want to hear?" she asked. As if she didn't know.

He regarded her with burning, narrowed eyes. "You know damn well, Daisy. Who the hell are all those people?"

Six

"One of 'those people' was your daughter," Daisy retorted calmly. "And if you'd given me a moment to introduce the others, you'd know who the hell they are."

Anger flared and the sleek sphere stuttered in Justice's hands. "Damn it, woman!"

Did he just call her "woman"? She approached, her anger rising to meet his. "Now that I'm here, I think it's time to discuss my conditions for staying."

That stopped him dead in his tracks. "Conditions? You never mentioned conditions to me."

"Well, now I am." She didn't give him time to debate the issue. "Condition One. If you want us here for longer than the next five minutes, you're going to have to adjust your language. Noelle is unbelievably verbal and tries to repeat just about everything she hears. I won't have her swearing before she even turns one."

"Hel—" He broke off and then swore again. "Fair enough. I'll do my best. I can't promise I'll be perfect."

"Condition Two. My name is Daisy. Call me 'woman' in that tone of voice or swear at me again, and I'm out the door. And so is your daughter. Got it?"

He clenched his teeth together so tightly it was a wonder they didn't crack. Even so, he conceded the point with an abrupt nod. "Any other conditions?"

She simply smiled. "Third, Aggie and Jett are members of my household, and where I go, they go."

He must have picked up on her determination. She could practically see him adjusting his mental paradigm or thought processes or whatever the heck went on inside that amazing brain of his. "Who is Aggie?" he asked, the question so prosaic Daisy almost laughed.

"Aggie's a former elementary school teacher and currently my cook and housekeeper. Since I'm a disaster in the kitchen and since the four of us need to eat, I hired her to take care of all things domestic."

He perked up a little over that. "She cooks?"

"And cleans," Daisy stressed. She eyed the room in open displeasure. "Seriously, Justice, this place is a disaster. I can't believe you're comfortable living like this."

He glanced around, though she suspected he didn't see the office and surrounding rooms the same way she did. "It's just a bit of dust, and I don't live in this section of the house."

It didn't take much thought to figure out where he did live. "Mad scientist plus secret location equals mysterious, hidden lab?"

"Something like that," he conceded.

"A spotless mysterious, hidden lab?"

"Of course."

"Well, since you now have guests who will be living in this section of the house, we'll need our accommodations to be as spotless as your lab."

He examined the room again, this time really looking— this time finally seeing. She could tell from his gathering frown that until that moment he'd been oblivious to the full extent of the problem. "I've been focused on a project and didn't realize how bad..." He blew out a sigh. "I apologize. I should have done more to prepare for your arrival."

"We'll handle it."

The "we" succeeded in returning his attention to his unexpected guests. "You've explained Aggie. Who's the scary Goth girl?" he asked.

Daisy couldn't help but smile. "That's Jett."

"Jett." He froze. "Not *that* Jett. Not your computer expert."

"That's the one," she took delight in confirming. "She was my parents' foster child. After Dad suffered a heart attack, it became clear she'd have to move to a new home. Jett decided she didn't want to start over somewhere else and asked me to become her foster parent instead."

"This is November. Shouldn't she be in school?"

"She received her GED at sixteen. She's currently considering colleges."

Justice's brows shot upward. "How old is she? She looks about twelve."

"She'll turn seventeen in a few months. Jett can give you the days, hours and minutes, right down to the seconds if you want a more exact number."

"She's smart."

"Scary smart. Like you, scary smart." Daisy hesitated. "Like Noelle."

His gaze sharpened. It didn't take him long to process her comment and come up with the correct explanation. "That's why you're here."

"One of the reasons, yes." No point in going into any of the others. Those would become apparent over time. "It's clear she requires someone who's going to understand the way she thinks. Right now she has Jett, which is a huge help. But, Jett won't be around forever. Plus, there's no male figure in

Noelle's life other than my father and now that he has health issues…"

At the mention of her parents, his expression closed over, turning as cold and bleak as the mountains at his back. "I don't want them anywhere near Noelle. Not after what they did to me."

Daisy stared in disbelief. "You can't keep them out of her life."

"Watch me."

"Condition Five."

"Four."

"Whatever. My parents are part of my life, the same way Jett and Aggie are. Deal with it."

A muscle jerked in his jaw and his eyes burned like liquid gold. "Any other conditions?" He bit off each word as though they scorched his tongue.

"You haven't agreed to my last one."

"Why don't we leave that one open for future discussion."

She refused to allow it. "Why don't we put that one to rest right now, because if you think for one little minute I'm going to deny my parents access to their only grandchild, you can think again." She held up her hand. "And before you decide to break Condition One again—"

"Too damn late!"

"I suggest you put yourself in my place. In Noelle's place. You're the one who walked away, Justice." She struggled to conceal her hurt with limited success. "My parents have been with me every step of the way. You haven't."

"Only because I didn't know."

"You're a brilliant man. You should have considered that possibility and made sure. At the very least, you should have contacted me after the first dozen letters." Could he hear the pain bleeding through her words? "Instead, you went out of your way to make certain I couldn't find you again. That we'd never see each other again."

"That's not true. I would have—" He broke off and swung around to face the picture window. "Any other conditions?"

"Do you agree to my last one?"

"Yes."

He sounded so bleak it almost unnerved her. She took a moment to gather her thoughts before pressing forward. "Condition Ten."

"Five."

"I'm holding the others in reserve." She didn't give him time to argue the point. "I need a room for a studio. One with windows." She had no idea whether she'd actually use the studio. She considered it more of a last-ditch effort. Because deep inside she secretly wondered whether she'd ever paint again. And the thought flat-out terrified her. "Unshuttered windows, if you don't mind."

He shrugged. "You can take a look around and see if anything suits. Make sure it's on this level or upstairs. The basement is off-limits to everyone."

"Is that where your uncle lives?"

"Yes. It's also where my lab is located."

Justice faced her once again. The sphere flowed through his fingers, assuming one shape after another. First a cylinder, then a pyramid, then something that twisted in on itself, making her dizzy. "What is that thing?" she asked.

"I call it Rumi. It helps me think." He'd regained his self-control and regarded her with a calm, icy expression that seemed to lower the temperature in the room by several degrees. She shivered, waiting for snowflakes to start drifting from the ceiling. "My turn," he announced.

Uh-oh. She hadn't anticipated this and should have. "You have conditions?"

"You thought you'd be the only one?"

She retreated a pace, even knowing it portrayed a certain defensiveness. "Okay, fine. What are your conditions?"

He took a step in her direction, following in the path of

her retreat, all the while the sphere twisted, twisted, twisted. "One. It is your responsibility to keep everyone out of the basement. That includes you. Having you and Noelle here is tough enough for Pretorius. The addition of two more people will be extremely difficult for him. He needs to know that he's safe in his area of the house. Am I clear on this point?"

"Crystal."

"Two." Another step closer. "I have a routine. Disruptions to that routine are unacceptable."

He couldn't be serious. "Get real, Justice. We're talking about a baby. Babies disrupt routines. It's their nature."

"In that case, I'll expect you to keep the disruptions to a minimum."

She planted her hands on her hips and faced him down. "You're the one who insisted we come here, remember? If you can't handle the occasional disruption we'll leave."

"It's too late. We're about to get snow. A lot of it."

"I'm sure we can stay ahead of any incoming storms."

Justice jerked his head toward the window and Daisy's mouth dropped open. In the short time they'd been talking, ominous clouds had built up, sweeping over the mountain peaks and tumbling down the craggy slopes toward the ranch complex at an unbelievably rapid clip. Where in the world had that gorgeous expanse of pale blue sky gone?

He set Rumi on the table and took a final step toward her. Snagging her collar, he gave a swift tug, propelling her into his arms. "Three. I want to attempt to create a bond with you. To see if we can't form a family unit."

A bond. Family unit. How like him to describe something so intimate in such remote terms. "For Noelle's sake?"

He started to agree, but must have changed his mind at the last moment. "For all our sakes," he said instead.

"Even though I don't fit the parameters you created for a perfect apprentice/wife?"

"I suspect we'll both need to adjust our expectations since

I'm certain I don't fit your parameters, either. I'm willing to make the attempt if you are."

"And by 'bond' I assume that would include—" She started to say "making love" and took a quick verbal detour at the last instant. "Sex?"

Fire kindled in his golden gaze like wildfire. "Sex will be involved since it's one of the few places we seem able to communicate with perfect accord."

"Willing or not?" she dared to ask.

"Oh, you'll be willing. I guarantee it."

He cupped her face and lifted it for his kiss. She didn't resist. In truth, she didn't want to. He'd given her a delicious sample one short week ago, a sample that had reignited a passionate longing, as undeniable as it was overwhelming. She thought it had died long ago, but she'd been mistaken. Every time he reentered her life, he brought with him a want so intense, she didn't know how she'd survive if he didn't make her his again.

Beneath the icy exterior a fire burned, one fierce enough to melt any and all resistance. Did he realize what a dichotomy he represented with that ice-cold logical exterior and that white-hot inner blaze? He reminded her of a distant star, an inferno of heat within the cold vacuum of the space it occupied.

His mouth came down on hers and she sighed, opening to him with bottomless enthusiasm. His fingers tightened in her hair as he sank inward and she heard a faint rumble, almost like a cat's purr. Maybe she hadn't gotten it wrong in her books. Maybe at heart he really was like her jungle panther creation, Cat. While Cat hid behind a wall of protective foliage, Justice hid behind his icy demeanor and the isolated walls of his compound. Were they truly so different?

"What do you want from me?" Her question was smothered beneath his mouth.

But he caught the words. And he understood. Reluctantly,

he pulled back, pressing a searing kiss to the dampness of her lashes before taking her mouth a final time, a bittersweet tribute to the emotions he denied.

His thumbs traced the swollen contours of her mouth. "I want you."

"It's not that simple," she protested. "You treat whatever this is like it's a simple sexual equation. You plus me equals sex."

"It's just that simple."

She fought free of his hold, some of his iciness invading her own veins. "Is this really how you regard people in your life? Like simple equations? While you skate across the surface, never daring to plumb the depths?"

He turned away from her and reached for Rumi, freezing at the last instant. And that's when she saw it. Somehow, at some point during their earlier conversation, he'd transformed the device into a flower, one that looked remarkably like a daisy. She started to comment, then stopped, something warning her to tread carefully.

"I didn't realize it could do that," she commented, striving to sound casual and offhand.

"It's only happened once before." He spoke so quietly she almost didn't catch the words.

Before she could press him about it, Pretorius's voice erupted from hidden speakers. "Justice, who are those people in the kitchen?" He sounded almost frantic. "They're doing things in there. You need to stop them. Now."

"Take it easy," Justice replied. "I'll deal with it."

"You'll make them leave?"

"I'll deal with it."

At a guess, probably not the answer his uncle was looking for. "Cut communication," Justice ordered. He took a second to lock gazes with her. "This isn't over."

She lifted an eyebrow. "You're just figuring that out? Well, let's see if I can put this in terms that your computer-like brain will process…" She fisted her hand in his shirt and yanked until they were practically nose-to-nose. "I've known it wasn't over between us for nineteen months and twenty-five days. You didn't manage to figure it out until ten days ago and only when I showed up here to draw you a picture. Try to keep up from this point forward, okay?"

With that, she released him and swept from the room, though she could have sworn she heard a snort of laughter. Must have been the wind. Lord knew, it couldn't have been Justice. Together they returned to the kitchen…and walked in on sheer chaos.

"Son of a—"

She elbowed him. "Condition One alert."

"Look at what they've done to my kitchen!"

She couldn't blame him for being upset. She would have been, if it had been her home. Aggie had pulled everything out of the huge, walk-in pantry and stacked the contents on every available surface. A bucket of hot soapy water rested on the floor while she swabbed every shelf and cubbyhole.

Jett sat with her back to the doorway, earbuds plugged in and no doubt rocking out music at full blast. She pounded away at her laptop. Next to the laptop sat the cat, Kit, the other half of the inspiration for Daisy's storybook creations. She'd been freed from her carrier and reclined on the table, busily grooming herself, accepting the craziness around her with her usual equanimity. A computer's disembodied voice gave incomprehensible updates in a hiccuping voice, competing with Pretorius's shouted demands, demands that were interspaced with some truly creative obscenities.

And then there was Noelle. Daisy sighed.

All of the cupboard doors stood ajar. And her precious daughter sat buck naked in the middle of the floor surrounded by articles of baby clothing, along with every last pot and pan the kitchen possessed. She busily banged lids against pots adding to the noise level.

For an instant, Daisy thought Justice would explode. "Computer, disengage!"

"Disengaged."

Abruptly, silence reigned. Noelle paused in her banging, Jett in her typing. Aggie poked her head out of the pantry. One look at Justice and she flinched, knocking over her bucket of soapy water. It swirled in an ever-expanding puddle of suds heading toward Noelle.

Jett's fingers hovered over her laptop, mid-keystroke and her head jerked around. Her inky dark eyes widened in dismay when she saw Justice standing there. "Uh-oh."

Daisy hastened to pluck her daughter off the floor before the surge of dirty water reached her. "Darn it, Jett. You promised to behave."

Jett cleared her throat. "Actually, I didn't. You told me to. But since I didn't answer, technically I didn't promise anything."

"How many times have I warned you not to get technical with me?"

"Nineteen hundred and fifty-two."

"Enough!" Justice broke in, glaring around the room. "Someone tell me what the bloody *hell* is going on and I mean now."

Noelle beamed from the safety of her mother's arms and spoke her very first words to her father. "Hell!" she said, clear as a bell.

Daisy groaned. "Oh, that's just great. Which part of Condition One didn't you understand?"

"I possess perfect comprehension. This, however—" He swept his arm in a wide arc to encompass the disaster that had previously been his kitchen. "This defies even my ability to comprehend. But it's not beyond my ability to correct. First things first."

He waded through the water to the one drawer that had so far escaped Noelle's detection and remained intact. He upended the stack of dishtowels it contained onto the floor. Then he crossed to Jett's computer and with a few swift keystrokes disconnected her from his computer system.

"Full control returned to you, Pretorius."

"They're leaving now, right?"

"I'll be down shortly to discuss it."

"Discussing implies 'not leaving.' I don't want to discuss." A hint of panic crept into his voice. "I want them to leave."

"Give me five minutes. Computer disengage."

Then he turned his attention to his daughter and Daisy flinched. He'd allowed himself a quick look earlier, when they'd first arrived. A look, she didn't doubt, that had just about destroyed him. At a guess, he hadn't realized until that moment what sort of effect such a tiny human being could have on him. Well, he'd found out, and then some. He teetered on the edge of losing it, something she wouldn't allow to happen in front of so many witnesses.

"Aggie?" Daisy murmured. "Why don't you and Jett go on upstairs and pick out rooms."

"Would you like me to fix you a cup of hot tea before I go?" She spared Justice a warm smile. "I consider it the perfect restorative. No matter how upset I am, hot tea always makes me feel better."

"Later, perhaps."

The housekeeper's gaze shifted from Justice to Noelle and she gave a brisk nod of understanding. That quick comprehension was one of the qualities Daisy most admired about the former schoolteacher. Without another word, she gathered up Jett, and the two slipped from the room. Justice continued to stand, rooted in place, unable to take his eyes off his daughter. He started toward her and then hesitated. His usual forcefulness deserted him, exposing an unsettling vulnerability.

"May I?" he asked with painful formality.

Daisy swallowed against the tightness in her throat. "Of course. She's your daughter, too."

He approached Noelle and held out his hand. The move was so tentative and cautious it threatened to break Daisy's heart. Noelle grabbed his hand with her usual impulsiveness and yanked it to her mouth for a taste. Not giving him time to withdraw, Daisy transferred their daughter from her own arms to his. And then she stepped back, watching a connection form that no computer interface could duplicate.

Ever so gently, Justice settled his daughter into his arms, cradling her as though she might shatter, his grip a trifle awkward. She responded by touching everything within reach. If she could grab it, it went into her mouth for a taste. If she couldn't, her nimble fingers explored it as though attempting to discern how and why, where and what. And most important, whether she could take it apart.

"She's beautiful," he murmured.

"Thanks. I'd say it was the luck of the draw. Somehow I suspect you'd say something about the expression of genetic information and the role of dominant versus recessive versus blending genes," she dared to tease.

He glanced up, his eyes glittering with a hunger that threatened to bring her to her knees. How quickly it happened, that unbreakable bond that connected hearts and souls, parent to child. She caught the stamp of possession. The want. And even more, the need.

"Actually, I was about to say that she takes after you," he said.

Simple and sincere and utterly unlike Justice. It could only be Noelle's influence, and Daisy wished with all her heart that it wouldn't stop there. "I'd say she was a perfect blend. Look at her, Justice. Her eye color is somewhere between yours and mine. Her hair is more strawberry than blond or ebony. She's as extroverted as I am and as brilliant as you are."

As though in response to the comment, Noelle beamed at her father, showing off eight pearly nubs.

"She has teeth already." A slight frown creased Justice's brow. "And you said she's verbal. Can she walk?"

"Yes. She's still a little unsteady on her feet, but that doesn't stop her from getting to where she wants to go."

"So much," he murmured. "I've missed so much." He passed a hand over her curls, stroked a creamy cheek with his fingertip. She crowed in delight, grabbing his finger and tugging it back to her face. "She's not the least reticent."

"No, she has a very outgoing personality. She's never been at all clingy."

"Is she naked for a reason?"

Daisy wondered when he'd get around to that. "I'm afraid your daughter doesn't like wearing clothes. I don't know how she does it, but she's a little escape artist. I'll turn my back for no more than two seconds and she's wriggled out of whatever I've dressed her in. Cribs and high chairs don't hold her. And forget about a playpen."

"Huh."

"What does 'huh' mean?" she asked suspiciously.

He ignored her question. "And the cupboards?" he asked. "Was that your housekeeper or our daughter?"

Daisy sighed. "Noelle," she admitted.

"Huh."

She planted her hands on her hips. "That's twice you've 'huhed' your daughter and you still haven't explained the first one, let alone the second. What do you know that I don't?"

He hesitated, his eyes guarded, intensifying her level of concern. "My 'huh'—both of them—indicate a familiarity and understanding of Noelle's methods and thought processes."

She didn't bother to conceal her relief. "That didn't take long."

"No," he murmured. "But then, there's a reason for that."

"Please," she encouraged in a polite voice. "Don't keep it to yourself or I might just grab one of the pots Noelle was banging and beat it out of you."

Justice eyed her almost defensively. "I believe this might be the appropriate time to admit to a certain genetic propensity, one that I hope you'll learn to accept over time."

Her maternal instincts went on red alert. "You're making me very, very nervous. Are you suggesting there's something wrong with our daughter?"

"Not exactly."

"Then what? And I do mean exactly."

"It's not Noelle's fault. It's mine. It's part of the genetic makeup she inherited from me. How her brain is wired." He cradled Noelle tight against his body, very hard, the sweeping line of his posture telegraphing a clear protective impulse, one he'd no doubt deny if she dared point it out to him. "I would appreciate it if you wouldn't hold it against her."

"Hold it…" Daisy trailed off, stunned. "Dear God, Justice. Do you think I'd ever criticize our daughter for something as natural and basic as human curiosity? That I'd ever punish her for exploring her world and trying to figure out how it works?"

"Some people would. Some people would consider her flawed."

Hurt ripped through her, catching in her throat and bleeding through her words. "I'm not some people. I'm Noelle's mother. I adore her. I'd do anything for her. Sacrifice anything."

Justice closed his eyes and drew in a deep breath. "I apologize. It's just…" He looked at her again, direct and unflinching, his eyes the color of tarnished gold. "I've seen it happen before."

He made the statement so simply and resolutely, and yet with such unspeakable pain and vulnerability. Her heart ached for him. "Who did you see it happen to, Justice?" she asked gently. "You?"

He nodded. Once. "Noelle is processing her world by dismantling it," he explained. He paused a beat. Gathered himself. "That particular characteristic got me kicked out of my first half-dozen foster homes."

She didn't know what she'd expected, but it wasn't that. "Let me get this straight. Some of your earlier foster parents made you leave because you took things apart? Are you serious?"

"Quite." He clenched his jaw. "I tried not to. I did. But I couldn't seem to help myself. I imagine it became annoying when they'd get up in the morning, only to discover the coffeepot or toaster disassembled."

"Then, why did you do it?"

"I needed to take things apart and study them in order to understand how they worked." He made the statement as though it should have been obvious. "It was perfectly logical."

Daisy hid a smile. "Of course it was. Assuming you could then put them back together."

"That took a bit longer to master. Now that I think about it, your parents were the first to understand that." A small frown creased his brow, as though the memory were an unwelcome one. "I'd forgotten until now. Your father actually encouraged my curiosity by finding broken-down lawn mowers and computers and car engines and letting me tinker."

"I remember you had all these mechanical parts spread out over our entire garage," she murmured. "Everything organized just so on counters and tarps and in jars. And heaven help anyone who dared move so much as a single nut or bolt."

"And yet, you moved them all the time."

Her mouth tugged into a mischievous smile. "Only because it made you react. You were always so self-contained. My parents constantly told me to leave you alone. To respect your privacy."

"Not that you ever did."

"I couldn't," she admitted with a shrug. "While you were busy tinkering with mechanical puzzles, I couldn't resist deciphering a far more human one."

"My mistake with your parents was that I didn't confine my tinkering to the lawn mowers and computers and car engines." Unmistakable want burned a path across his face. "I had to take you apart, too."

Daisy sighed. "And some things, once taken apart, can't be put together again."

"Not the way they were before," he agreed.

She approached like a moth to a flame, drawn to the circle of heat and light formed by Justice and their daughter. "I swear to you, I didn't know they found out about us. I didn't know that's why you left. Why you were forced to go. I would have stood up for you if I had. I would have stopped them. Explained. Something."

He shook his head. "You were fifteen. There was nothing else to explain. Nor would standing up to them have changed anything. What we did was wrong and I paid the price for dismantling you."

"You shouldn't have had to."

"Yes, I should have. I realize that now." He glanced down at his daughter. "What would we do if it were Noelle at fifteen? If someone dismantled her at that age?"

Her breath caught. Shivered in her lungs. She couldn't begin to find the words to express what she felt and she could only stare at Justice in dismay.

"I agree," he said softly.

"Oh, Justice." Helpless. Hopeless. "What are we going to do?"

As usual, he had a plan. "First, I need to go downstairs and talk to Pretorius. He's going to have difficulty with the changes." Reluctantly, he handed over Noelle. "Afterward, I'd like to spend more time with our daughter, assuming that's acceptable to you."

"You don't need my permission." The fact that he felt he did distressed her. "You're her father. I'm here because it's important to me that you two bond."

He stared at his daughter and all expression winked from his face. "She's walking and talking, already. She has teeth. Are you certain it's not too late?"

Tears pricked Daisy's eyes. "No, Justice. It's not too late. Not if you don't let it be."

His gaze locked with hers and he gave a quick nod. "Then I won't let it be."

Seven

Daisy supposed she shouldn't be surprised that she couldn't sleep. It had been a long day, full of emotion. She'd seen Justice again after what felt like an endless separation. And Justice had finally met his daughter. That first tentative moment the two shared still brought tears to her eyes whenever she thought about it. It was far too early to determine whether she and Justice could live together on a permanent basis, though considering his third condition she hoped they stood a chance. But, she didn't have a single doubt he'd do everything within his power to be a father to Noelle. The bond she'd witnessed forming had been as immediate as it had been enduring.

She squirmed beneath the covers in an attempt to get more comfortable, but the glint of eyes from the corner of the nearly barren room snagged her attention. Kit was on the prowl. The cat slunk over to the bed and rumbled out a purr before leaping onto the mattress and giving Daisy a gentle head butt.

She scratched the cat behind the ears and was rewarded

with another thunderous purr. "So, what do you think of the new digs?" she whispered.

Not that she'd disturb anyone, even speaking in a normal voice. Justice had built a sturdy, solid house, and she couldn't help wonder if the impressive size stemmed from a subconscious imperative to fill it with a large family. Regardless, the walls and oak doors were heavy and thick enough that she could belt out Lady Gaga and they'd never hear her. Plus, Jett and Noelle had elected to "camp out" together in one of the massive bedrooms on the opposite side of the house, a room that overlooked a large pond, currently iced over and glittering with fresh fallen snow.

Instead of settling down at the end of the bed in her customary position, Kit's ears pricked up and her head swiveled toward the door. Tension swept through her sleek body and she went into predator mode. Slipping off the mattress, she made a beeline from the room.

Curious, Daisy gathered up the ankle-length cotton nightgown she wore, the warmest of her options, and followed the cat. The chill of oak flooring beneath her feet caused her to shiver. She reached the main level in time to catch a glimpse of Kit darting into forbidden territory.

Uh-oh. Did Justice's first condition—to keep everyone out of the basement—include the cat?

She hesitated at the top of the stairs leading to Justice's bat cave, debating whether or not to sneak down after Kit. She doubted the cat would come to any harm. Still... Who knew what Justice kept down there? There could be automated vacuums that might suck up a poor, defenseless cat. Electrified fences. Even killer robots.

Admit it, she silently scolded herself. Just admit that she couldn't sleep and wanted to talk to Justice to see if they had any chance at creating a lasting relationship. That she half hoped he would insist on giving her an intimate and thorough demonstration of Condition Three. Or she could confess she was dying of curiosity to take a peek at the forbidden. Concede the fact that she just couldn't resist stepping over whatever lines he drew in the figurative sand and never had been able to.

She surrendered to the inevitable, knowing full well she wouldn't sleep until she'd put a toe over that darned line of his.

Daisy reached the bottom step, that no-man's land between her territory and his, and stood there. Though she suspected the lower level occupied the same space as the floor above it, the setup was vastly different. Much more high-tech. The overhead lights were off, while low wattage lighting along the floor reflected off blindingly white walls and a crisp, almost sterile corridor. Leaning forward from the safety of the bottom step, she peered down a dimly lit hall to her right. Doorways sealed tightly shut led to mysterious rooms that she itched to explore.

"Now how did I know you'd break Condition One before the day was even over?"

Daisy jumped and her head jerked to the left. She wobbled on the step, catching her balance at the last possible second. "I haven't broken your condition." She offered an abashed grin. "Not yet."

He'd approached so silently she hadn't heard him. The subdued lighting of his underworld lair cast interesting shadows across his face, giving him a forbidding appearance. Okay, a more forbidding appearance. And yet for all that she found him appealing in the extreme. But then, she always had. She'd never understood it, never been able to adequately explain it. She just knew from the moment she first set eyes on the man he'd been the only one who did it for her on every possible level.

When Justice had left to go to college—or not to college, as she now knew—it had taken her years to get over what she'd assumed was an infatuation, that indelible mark left by her first love and lover. There had been other men in her life since, a select few. But they'd never stirred her the way Justice had. Never ignited that fierce fire that had quieted over the years, but never quite been doused. And since the night Noelle had been conceived, it had only grown worse. Intensified. Made her realize what they had was special and unique. More, she realized she wanted to be with him for as long as he'd allow it.

"What are you doing here?" he asked, the prosaic question making her smile.

"I'm on a rescue mission. Our cat came down here and I didn't know what sort of trouble Kit might get into."

"Kit?" He stilled, an odd expression shifting across his face. "As I recall, you named the kitten I gave you Kit. It was the night we made—"

He broke off, but she knew what he'd been about to say. The night they made love. Not "had sex" as he'd been so careful to label it since. Daisy let the silence stretch a moment before responding. "You said you chose Kit because we both had green eyes and were pure trouble."

"This can't be the same cat."

His adamant statement confused her, pricked her for some reason. She planted her hands on her hips and fixed him with a look of exasperation. "Of course it's the same cat, Justice. Didn't you recognize her?"

"I didn't even realize you brought a cat," he confessed. "I guess my focus was elsewhere."

She softened, feeling a tug on her heartstrings. "Yes, of course it was. You couldn't take your eyes off your daughter."

"Or you."

He approached with the silent grace she'd always associated with him. Thanks to her position on the step, they stood eye-to-eye, the odd dark gold of his gaze gathering up the light and hinting at wonders and mysteries and delicious depths to be plumbed. They also glimmered with an odd emotion, one she couldn't quite pinpoint.

"You kept the cat I gave you for all these years?" He phrased the question almost like an accusation, as though determined to force her to deny it.

Indignation swept through Daisy. "Did you think I'd throw her out?" she asked. "I adore her."

Adored her in part because he'd given her the cat, though she didn't dare admit as much. But also because she'd formed an immediate attachment to the mischievous little beast, one that continued to this day. Kit was part of her family. Part of her life. And a lifeline that remained to this day, connecting the two of them through all the years stretching between them.

"I thought your parents might get rid of her." He shrugged. "All things considered."

"You mean because they threw you out, they'd throw your cat out, too?"

His expression closed down. "Something like that."

"Well, they didn't," Daisy retorted. "She's been with me for ten years now. If I'm lucky, she'll be with me for another ten. Didn't you notice I used her in my storybooks?"

Clearly, he hadn't made the connection. "So, she really is Kit, both in reality and in fiction," he murmured.

"Yes, she is. And in case you didn't catch it… You're Cat."

"The panther?" His eyes darkened. "That's me?"

"It seemed fitting at the time." She smiled, daring to tease. "So are you going to let me use Kit as an excuse for a tour of the forbidden?"

"If I satisfy your curiosity, will you stay out?"

"I'll try."

He released a sigh and held out his hand. "Come on."

She stepped into the hallway, the tile even icier than the wood flooring. She suppressed a shiver, not wanting to give

Justice any excuse to send her away. "What's down that way?" She pointed to the right.

"That's my uncle's section. You don't get a tour of that area without his express invitation." He paused, capturing her chin within the warmth of his palm and tipping it up. "I'm serious, Daisy. You have to allow him his privacy. No stray cats. No sneaking down in the middle of the night. No excuses. Got it?"

"I wouldn't do that," she assured him. "Honestly, I wouldn't. I might give you a hard time because I know you can take it. But not Pretorius."

Her sincerity must have come through loud and clear. He gave a single sharp nod, then gestured to the left. "I have a number of labs down this way, as well as my private quarters."

Good Lord. "A *number* of labs?"

He shrugged. "For measurement and instrumentation. Another for research and development. A computer lab. A test lab. It isn't as specialized as the Sinjin complex, but it works well enough for tinkering."

"I want to see the robot lab."

He actually grinned. "Okay. I'll let you see the nonsterile one."

"You have sterile labs?"

"Yes, but you have to be naked and sterilized before you can go in."

One look assured he was kidding. Excellent. She'd only been here a few hours and she'd already infected him with a sense of humor. "It must not do a very good job sterilizing," she retorted. "Otherwise you wouldn't have a daughter."

He placed his palm against a plate outside one of the doors and then requested admittance. "Maybe we don't have to be sterilized," he admitted while they waited for his security system to run his palm and voiceprint.

"And maybe we don't have to be naked, either?"

The door to the lab slid silently open. "No, I'm pretty much going to insist on nudity."

She stepped into a huge room that looked very much like a workshop. Long tables spanned one half of the room and lined the walls. Predictably, they were a crisp, painful white. Instrumentation—none of which she recognized—clustered in a half-dozen stations perched on top of various tables. Each station also possessed its own computer system. At the opposite end of the room were endless cabinets and shelves and banks of drawers, most on rollers. Supplies, at a guess. Everything was ruthlessly organized which didn't come as much of a surprise considering Justice's propensity for neatness.

Dead center in the middle of the room stood a huge, sturdy workbench, possibly the messiest section of the room, not that Daisy found it all that messy. To her amusement, one of his Rumi spheres had been left there, and like the one in the office, this one had been transformed into a daisy, as well. She started to comment on that fact, then thought better of it, something in his expression warning her to tiptoe around that particular subject. Instead, she turned her attention to his work project.

Resting on the table squatted two odd devices on treads, presumably to give them mobility. She studied the first which combined dark metal and light gray plastic in a round shape the approximate size of a canister vacuum cleaner. Specialized arms spoked the device and what looked like a ring of aquamarine eyes dotted the circumference. A small helmet capped it, the helmet studded with lights and buttons and a display screen. Beside it squatted its more sophisticated twin.

"What are they?" she asked, fascinated.

"That's Emo X-14 and X-15. Short for Emotibot, X for the tenth generation, fourteenth and fifteenth versions." Justice frowned. "At least, that's what they're supposed to be. Right now they aren't much of anything."

"What are you hoping they'll become?" She shot him a questioning look. "Is that a better way to phrase it?"

"Much better, I'm afraid." He blew out a sigh. "Eventually I'm hoping Emo will be the next generation lie detector. A feeling detector, I suppose."

She stared at the robots, intrigued by the idea. "Why would you want to create a feeling detector?"

"I'm attempting to design a robotic that can anticipate and respond to human needs, not just based on what is requested verbally, but also to nonverbal cues. In fact, I'd like to use the in-house videos and cameras to photograph everyone's various emotion responses to stimuli over the next several weeks in order to help teach it. Assuming none of you objects."

"Huh." Intriguing. "I'll check with the others, but I have no objection. So, let me get this straight. By using photos and videos of us coming unhinged, or whatever, Emo will figure out when we're happy or sad or hungry or thirsty and do something about it?"

"Exactly." A smile danced across his mouth. "Although it isn't necessary for you to come unhinged in order to teach it appropriate emotional responses."

Daisy waved that aside. "That is *so* cool." For some reason she was drawn to the less sophisticated model, perhaps because the haphazard appearance gave it a bit more personality than its starkly streamlined big brother. "And this little guy can do some of that already? He can process emotional responses?"

Justice grimaced. "No, this little guy cannot do that, which is the current problem. Emo 14 hasn't been as successful at reading emotions as 15. I may have to scrap this particular model and repurpose its parts."

"Oh, no," Daisy protested. "He's too adorable to scrap."

One look warned he'd shifted into remote, logical scientist mode. "Adorable or not, sometimes when there's a catastrophic failure and what you're attempting to produce isn't working on any level, you just have to scrap it and start over."

Logical, as always, but still… "I hope you won't do that with 14."

Justice lifted an eyebrow. "Why not?"

She caught her lip between her teeth. "I don't know. He's so cute…it seems mean, somehow."

"Mean," he repeated. "Daisy, Emo is a machine, not a 'he.' It's not sentient. It'll never be sentient. If I anthropomorphized every one of my creations, I'd never get anything accomplished."

"I guess. Although you did name it. What's that if not anthropomorphizing a machine?" To her private amusement, he winced, her point finding its mark. Satisfied, she continued. "I know Emo isn't alive. It's just that he reminds me of something you were working on ten years ago."

He stilled. "You remember that?"

"Of course, I remember it. I found all your creations fascinating." She pulled out one of the stools tucked under the workbench and perched on the padded seat. Anything to get her poor abused feet off the cold floor. "But my favorite was the one that reminds me of Emo. The spaceship on rollers."

"It wasn't a spaceship."

"Yes, I know." She didn't know whether to laugh or roll her eyes. "You told me that a thousand times. But it looked like one and it somewhat resembles this little guy."

"Actually, it's the other way around. This little guy resembles the spaceship, as you call it. That's because it's the prototype for Emo. I work on the project in my spare time."

"I'm surprised you haven't finished it after so many years." His expression closed over and she wondered what she'd said to upset him. Because there wasn't a doubt in her mind that she'd struck a nerve. "But I guess you have to give the paying projects priority," she hastened to add.

"Yes." A hint of bleakness crept into his voice.

Somehow she'd opened a door she shouldn't have and she didn't have a clue how to close it again. "What's wrong, Justice?"

He turned away. How did she do it? How did she slip beneath his guard with such ease? For as long as he'd known her, she'd possessed that uncanny knack. And for as long as he'd known her, it had thrown him off-kilter. With that glorious fall of wheat-blond hair and those sparkling green eyes, she could short-circuit his brain with a single smile. In all the years he'd known her, he'd never figured out why the hell he didn't affect her the way he did every other person in existence, why she chased instead of ran.

He'd discovered at a young age that his appearance and intellect intimidated people, even his parents to a certain extent. They'd never understood the cuckoo who had appeared in their nest, though he'd later learned that he took after his father's brother, Pretorius, another strike against him considering his uncle's social anxiety issues. His parents' death in the car accident when he'd been all of ten had thrown him into foster care and prompted him to use that knowledge to hold people at a safe distance, often with a single, dark look.

But not Daisy. Never Daisy. No matter how many black looks he gave her, she remained impervious. No matter how many lines he drew, whether virtual or actual, she wriggled that potent little body across them as though they didn't exist. Even now, sitting in his workshop in a nearly transparent nightgown she managed to fit in when she should have been as out of place as an ice sculpture in the fiery bowels of hell.

He remembered when he'd first moved in with the Marcellus family, Daisy had invaded his room and his life like a dizzying spring breeze, both relentlessly determined and passionately warm. He hadn't wanted to be invaded, so he set boundaries, literal ones. He'd taped lines on the rug, blocking off his personal sections of the house, lines she'd taken great delight in yanking up and moving until he'd discover his personal space encompassing smaller and smaller areas. In the end, he'd been left with tiny boxes that would barely contain a mouse. Daisy simply refused to be shut out.

She still refused to be shut out, whether from his thoughts or his emotions or even his career. Somehow she managed to sweep into his life and lock herself around him with all the brilliance and delightful joie de vivre that was such an innate part of her. As a callow teenager, he'd been unable to defend or resist. And now...

Now, nothing had changed.

Surrendering to the inevitable, Justice joined her at the workbench and touched the panel on the robot's helmet. Instantly, Emo 14 hummed to life, a series of lights twinkling gaily. "Emo, this is Daisy."

"Hello, Daisy," a sweetly youthful male voice said.

She was instantly enchanted. "Hello, Emo."

"How are you feeling today?"

To his amusement, she gave the question serious consideration. She shot Justice a glance from beneath a sweep of lashes. "I'm feeling a little nervous and a bit upset at the idea that your creator might dismantle you."

"Perhaps you simply require a restorative cup of Aggie's hot tea," Justice suggested.

She narrowed her magnificent eyes in clear displeasure. "Perhaps I do."

Emo's lights twinkled and she caught a muted hum, somewhat similar to the sound Jett's laptop made when it accessed a program. "Processing," Emo informed her, his voice giving a little hiccup.

Daisy frowned. "Or perhaps Emo needs some tea. What's with his hiccup?"

Justice grimaced. "It happens sometimes when he—*it*—is running multiple functions."

A quick, appealing smile winged free. "He can't walk, talk and process at the same time?"

"Not very well."

She patted the robot's helmet. "He's still young. Give him time." A small frown formed between her brows. "You're not going to kill him off just because he's a little slow, are you?"

Kill him? Justice scrubbed his hands across his face. "I'm going to say this one more time, Daisy. I would appreciate it if you would pay close attention. Emo is a machine. You can't kill a machine."

At the sound of its name, Emo perked up. "How do you feel?" he chirped.

She shot Justice a look of supreme indignation. "I'm very, very sad, Emo. Sad enough that I may just have to wake Aggie and ask her to fix me a cup of tea. And it's all your maker's fault."

Justice held up his hands in surrender. "Okay, okay. I won't dismantle Emo. Instead of giving his parts to a future sibling, I'll keep him for the sake of posterity. Happy now?" Dear God, now she had him calling Emo "he" and "him." How did she do it? And how the hell did he fight against it?

"Yes, I'm happy now. Thank you."

She hesitated and he waited her out. "There's something I've been meaning to discuss with you."

"I'm not going to like this discussion, am I?"

"Doubtful." Not that that stopped her. "We need to hire some people to come in and scrub the upper two floors. It's not fair to dump this level of cleaning on Aggie, Jett and me." Then she got really nasty. "More importantly, having the house in this condition isn't healthy for Noelle."

"Son of a—"

"Condition One."

"Gun." He glared at her. "You are the most irritating woman—"

"Condition Two."

"—I have ever met. And if you don't stop spouting conditions at me, we'll go elsewhere and have a thorough and comprehensive discussion of my third condition. Are we clear?"

To his satisfaction, bright color burned a path across her elegant cheekbones. "Crystal."

"Excellent." He made an adjustment to Emo's control panel while he considered. "As for the cleaning problem, of course you can hire anyone you need to help. It's important you be comfortable here."

"What about your uncle?"

He gave it a moment's consideration. "I'll have Pretorius run a comprehensive system diagnostic scan during the cleaning process. That will take us offline for almost half a day, which knocks out his eyes and ears, and should prevent him from realizing anyone has been in the house until they've already left. Will that be sufficient, do you think?"

"Thank you. That should be perfect."

One quick glance warned she wasn't finished. "Another issue?" he asked mildly.

Daisy cleared her throat. "Not an issue, exactly."

"Please. Let's be exact."

"It's about your house."

"Is there something wrong with my house other than the level of cleanliness?"

"Yes. There isn't any place to sit."

Justice frowned. His one foray into the apprentice/wife waters had been with Pamela, a huge mistake, riddled with compatibility issues. Far from being the perfect fit the Pretorius Program assured him they'd be, they were perfectly imperfect for one another. After Pamela's departure, he'd cleared out the upper levels she'd furnished and decorated. With the exception of his office, he rarely visited them and hadn't bothered to replace any of the furniture. "No, I guess there isn't."

"We'd like to sit," Daisy said gently. "And, oh, I don't know, a few extra beds and dressers wouldn't go amiss."

"Would you be willing to order the necessary furniture?"

"You don't object? Considering the size of this place, it could get pricey."

"Will it cost more than nine-point-seven-three billion?"

To his amusement, she thought it through before replying. "I'm pretty sure I can keep the expenses under that."

"Then I don't object."

"Thank you."

Escaping her perch, she approached, her nightgown swirling around her, clinging to intriguing curves just long enough to give him a visual taste before billowing free, leaving him longing for another glimpse. Longing for a touch. Longing to have her in his arms and in his bed one more time and discover if what they'd experienced those previous occasions had been fluke or the norm. Although, he readily conceded, there'd been nothing in the least normal about Daisy or what happened between them whenever they made love.

Finally, she spoke. "There's something else bothering me."

"Other than the cleaning and furnishings?"

"Yes." She caught her lower lip between her teeth. "Do you really believe that when you experience a catastrophic failure and what you're attempting to produce isn't working on any level, you just have to throw it away and start over?"

"Yes."

She spared him a brief, hesitant look. "You could say that our relationship experienced a catastrophic failure."

Huh. He hadn't considered it that way. "I would consider that an accurate description."

"So would I," she confessed. "And the morning after we made love you did throw our relationship away, at least the potential for a relationship."

She was killing him, bit by bit. "I tried."

"Maybe now we can start over, dig beneath our surface attraction. Maybe we could repurpose the good parts and get it right this time. Because there were good parts, occasions when we communicated quite brilliantly."

He didn't pretend to misunderstand. "I believe you called it amazing."

"I believe I did." She moistened her lips, the only sign of her uncertainty. "What do you say, Justice?"

He couldn't resist her now any more than he could ten years ago. Or even nineteen months, twenty-six days, seven hours and two minutes ago. For the first time in his entire life he didn't hesitate. Didn't ponder and consider. He simply jumped, grabbed. Held on for all he was worth.

"I'd like that," he said gruffly. He pulled her into his arms. She walked into the embrace and enclosed him in softness and warmth. "How are you feeling?" he whispered against her mouth.

"Hungry. Very, very hungry."

Justice swept Daisy into his arms and carried her from the lab. The sheer cotton of her nightgown fluttered around them as though dancing beneath a wayward breeze. It clung to the shape of her, allowing the sheen of pearly skin to seep through the material while obscuring the details. Not for long. He intended to have her in his bed and naked within the next thirty seconds. Less, if at all possible.

He shouldered open the door to his bedroom. "Lights," he ordered. "Low wattage."

The bedside table lights flickered to life, sending a soft glow across her features. She was so beautiful, her eyes a deep, shadowed green, reflecting an unstinting passion. So open. So generous. So giving.

He realized in that endless moment that he didn't want to rush. Time no longer held any meaning, which he found vaguely bewildering. All that mattered was giving her pleasure. He set her on the bed and came down beside her. Cupping her face, he lifted it to his. And then he took her mouth. He held himself back, intent on making each second as memorable as possible. A quiet sigh escaped her, one of sheer joy, and in that moment he felt a happiness and contentment he hadn't experienced since the last time he had her in his arms and in his bed.

Maybe it was because of the extent of his own satisfaction that he realized he couldn't make love with her under the current circumstances. When they came together it wouldn't be due to conditions or obligation, but because it was what they both wanted.

Even so, that didn't keep him from stroking the curve of her cheek before drawing back. "You don't have to stay, if you'd rather not. I rescind my third condition."

Laughter glittered in her eyes. "I really wish you wouldn't."

She'd taken him by surprise. "No?"

"Definitely not. Because then I won't be forced to sacrifice my virtue and might feel obligated to leave."

Her clear amusement drew a smile from him. "I gather you don't want to leave?"

"Not in the least."

"You're willing to sacrifice your virtue?"

"Well…if you insist." She drew him into the soft heat of her embrace. "Please insist," she whispered against his mouth.

"In that case, I rescind my rescission and insist that you let me have my wicked way with you." He nibbled at her lower lip. "Most definitely insist."

She released her breath in an exaggerated sigh. "Since I have no other choice, I'm all yours. But I expect you to keep your promise and be wicked with me. Very, very wicked."

He swept a hand along her cheek again, then lower. God, her skin was like satin. "Whatever I want?"

"If you need a few suggestions, I'm happy to provide them."

"I think I have it covered," he informed her gravely. "But if there's anything that will make your sacrifice more bearable, don't hesitate to let me know."

She slanted him a sparkling look. "Perhaps another kiss will help me tolerate it a little better?"

"A kiss like this…?"

He took her mouth again, allowing his passion to slip his control ever so slightly. She sighed in appreciation and her lips parted, surrendering to him, before matching him kiss for kiss.

"It's different this time, isn't it?" she asked him.

He tucked a silky swathe of hair behind her ear. "Different how?"

She regarded him with unusual gravity and all the while her hands fluttered across him like butterflies. They constantly touched and stroked, anchoring him to her in some indefinable, yet permanent manner. "The first time we made love we were children and I was pretending to be someone I wasn't," she explained. "The second time you thought I was someone I wasn't. But this time…"

He understood then. "It's real. It's honest. You know who I am and I know who you are."

She nodded. "I like it better this way."

"So do I."

And he did. It added a deeper dimension to their love-making. Strengthened the connection between them. Unable to resist, he eased the soft cotton of her nightgown from her shoulders only to find even softer skin beneath, pliant and warm and responsive. He traced her curves, familiarizing himself with the subtle changes motherhood had wrought.

Even that bound them together, a deep, irreversible connection he couldn't break even if he felt so inclined. They'd created a child together, would always be linked through their daughter. For the rest of their lives they'd have that in common. And if they were fortunate, Noelle would only be the start.

Their mouths collided again, more urgently this time, and the mattress cushioned their tumble, their arms and legs entwining, clinging with a growing urgency. A prelude to what was to come. Without the least trace of uncertainty or artifice, she broke free and came up on her knees. With a grace she'd possessed even as an untried teen, she swept her nightgown up and over her head and allowed it to drift to the floor. She continued to kneel before him, utterly vulnerable in her nudity and in the unstinting way she gifted herself to him. That openness and generosity of spirit was such an innate part of her.

And it never failed to impress the hell out of him.

The bedside lamp cast a gentle glow across her, sweeping over the fullness of her breasts before sliding coyly into the shadowed juncture of her thighs. Her skin made him think of virginal snow, yet offered the vibrancy of new life. And he wanted her. All of what she offered. Wanted her more than he thought possible.

She represented everything he wasn't. Everything he lacked. She was the hope of an everlasting spring who'd somehow invaded the dark desolation of winter. She was Persephone, surrendering to Hades.

"Stop," she murmured. He jerked back, steeling himself to let her go, no matter how difficult. She sighed, reached for him, drew him closer and enclosed him in warmth. "I don't mean stop touching me. I mean stop thinking. Stop analyzing. Just let go and feel, Justice."

"I don't think I can do anything else," he admitted. Or maybe it was a confession. "Not with you."

Gently, tenderly, he wrapped himself around her and kissed her with a passion that left her gasping for breath.

Desire brought heat storming across her skin, tinting the paleness with the soft flush of need. He cupped her breast, took the tip in his mouth and anointed it with tongue and teeth. He could feel the pounding of her heart against his cheek and the soft moan that shuddered from her lungs, a moan that carried his name.

She shifted against him, her legs parting, hips lifting and meshing with his. He'd wanted to take his time, to reacquaint himself with every inch of her. "Next time," he promised, though he had no idea if she understood.

Or maybe she did because she laughed. "Okay, next time we'll go slow. But not now. Now I want all of you. Fast."

She flowed around him, gripping and stroking, taking, then giving. His hands tripped across trembling thighs, cupping the silky backs and angling them upward. Then he sank into her soft, fluid warmth. Her moans turned to sobs, frantic and pleading, and he drove into her, desperate to drive her to peak. To please her. Satisfy her in every way possible.

He saw it in her eyes an instant before she climaxed, right before he followed her over the top. The brilliant desire. The burgeoning. And he saw something else. Something that threatened to destroy him. In those stunning green eyes he saw the one thing he'd never trusted. Never dared believe in.

He saw love.

Eight

Oh, no. What had she done?

Daisy closed her eyes and burrowed against Justice, hiding her expression from him. Too fast and too soon, came the helpless thought.

This time round she'd planned to take their relationship at a slow, steady clip, instead of with her usual exuberance. This time she'd hoped to allow their feelings time to develop and mature slowly. Fully. To grow at a reasonable pace that encompassed the intellectual and rational, rather than just the emotional. To reach the point where they could make a commitment to one another on every level, not just a sexual one.

She suppressed a tearful laugh. So much for that plan. It hadn't even lasted twenty-four short hours before she'd flung herself into Justice's arms and bed, just as she had every other time she'd been within kissing distance of the man. And why? Because it was the one place where they'd always been in perfect accord. The place where she hoped their relationship could take seed and flower into something deeper and more meaningful.

But in order for that seed to flourish, it meant Justice would have to make an emotional commitment to her. And at this point, she didn't know whether he even recognized that he possessed emotions. She'd seen them, been stunned by the depths of them—when they'd made love. When he held his daughter. On rare, bittersweet occasions when she caught him looking at her.

But considering the depth of his disconnect, she doubted he'd made the connection. Maybe if he managed to get his robots up and running they could explain it to him. Of course, he probably wouldn't believe them. He'd probably think they still weren't working right, and dismantle them in order to repurpose the parts for an Emo model X-Trillion and Two.

"Daisy?" he murmured. "Are you all right?"

"Not really." She needed to distract him, find a way to disguise how fast and hard she'd tumbled. To give him the time he would need to consider and analyze and explain away the emotions that locked them together over time and circumstance, before surrendering to the inevitable. She forced a smile to her lips and peeked up at him, forcing a teasing tone to her voice. "I'm a little confused about one of the sub clauses to your third condition. Perhaps if you explained it to me in a bit more detail?"

To her delight, he chuckled, more relaxed than she'd ever seen him. "Which sub clause didn't you understand?" He slid his hand along her leg until he wandered onto territory blessed by soft, feminine warmth. "This clause…?"

"That's one." She returned the favor, stroking her hand along the length of him, a territory neither soft nor feminine. "And I do believe this is another."

"Ah. Now that particular clause I can explain in explicit detail."

She smiled, keeping her tone light, though her jumbled emotions spilled recklessly free, refusing any attempts at restraint. "I'd like that," she told him. "I'd like that very much."

First thing the next morning, Daisy made a firm promise to herself that she'd take her relationship with Justice at a slower, more decorous pace. That she'd hide her feelings from him until he'd had time to assimilate or analyze or cogitate or whatever mad scientists did in order to reach their ridiculous conclusions regarding issues that should be perfectly straightforward and obvious.

Like love.

Of course, her vow lasted right up until he took her into his arms the next night. This time he swept her off to her upstairs bedroom. Once there, clothed only in honesty, her true feelings escaped her ability to control. Unbidden and unhidden, they exploded from her, as clear and brilliant as sunlight, while Justice's remained cloaked in shadows. And over the subsequent nights they spent in her bed, Daisy continued to hope he'd eventually surrender to his feelings instead of hiding behind his rationality and logic and the darkness of past memories. But instead, he left her bed each morning to return to his underground lair before the first rays of daylight dared penetrate the room.

In the meantime, she arranged for the cleaning crew to scrub the house from top to bottom. As promised, Justice requested his uncle run a complete housewide diagnostic scan. Not that it worked as planned. No sooner had the cleaners departed than Pretorius came online, his voice booming through the speakers.

"Justice? Justice! Red alert. One of the units has gone off the grid. I need a head count right away."

"Everything's fine, Pretorius," came Justice's calm response. "I'm in the kitchen with Aggie, Daisy and Noelle."

"There's still one missing," Pretorius shot back, then couldn't prevent himself from dipping into sarcasm. "Or have you forgotten how to count?"

"Would you like a nice cup of hot tea?" Aggie asked in a motherly voice. "You sound upset."

"No, I would not like some hot tea," Pretorius snapped. "I want to know where the other one is. The troublemaker. She's missing."

"I'm not missing. I'm right here."

Pretorius erupted out of his chair and spun around. Jett sat curled like a cat on the counter behind him. Panic caused his heart to race and he fought to control his breathing. He tugged at the collar of his Metallica T-shirt, feeling cold sweat pool at the base of his spine. "What the hell are you doing down here?" he demanded tightly.

Only her eyes moved, a quick blink over intense, dark irises. "You and Justice sure swear a lot," she commented in such a cool, matter-of-fact voice that he felt some of his panic ease.

"You haven't answered my question, little girl. What are you doing here?"

"First, I'm not a little girl. I'm sixteen."

He snorted and shoved his glasses higher on the bridge of his nose. "Try twelve."

Her eyes narrowed, but she let that pass. "I figured since the computer was offline you'd lose your eyeballs and I could sneak down here and watch you for a change. Since you're always watching us, it only seemed fair."

To his utter shock, he felt a blush warm his cheeks. "Justice tell you not to come down here? That I don't like people, so you should stay away?"

"Yeah." Jett frowned. For the first time a hint of uncertainty crept across her pixielike features. "But I figured I wasn't exactly like real people."

"Well, you are." His frown matched hers, grew to a scowl.

"Why don't you think you're like real people?" he asked, driven despite himself to ask the question.

Jett shrugged. "Everybody always said so."

"Oh, yeah? I got news for you. Everybody's full of sh—" Pretorius broke off and he stabbed a stubby finger in her direction. "Take my word for it. You're real people. I should know. I can't abide real people and since I can't abide you, that makes you real."

His rudeness didn't faze her in the least. She simply nodded. For some reason her stoic acceptance of his remark bothered him more than he thought possible. "I was thinking since I bug you so much, you could pretend I was one of Justice's robotics or something." She focused on him, her expression carefully blank. "That's what they called me, you know. Faulty Chip. Like a computer chip because I was so smart and logical, but faulty because I didn't get all freaked and worked up like the rest of them over every little thing. Wasn't emotional enough to suit them."

"They really called you that?" Pretorius couldn't seem to get past her single, painfully composed statement.

"It's okay." She lifted a shoulder in a shrug that was meant to appear uncaring. Instead it made her seem unbearably young and vulnerable. "Anyway, I was thinking... Maybe if you thought of me like that, like a robot or something, you know? I could hang out down here sometimes and watch you work. Pick up a few pointers."

"Well, you can't. I don't like people. They make me nervous."

"You don't look nervous. You just look ticked." Jett tilted her head to one side. "Maybe if you let me come around every once in a while, you won't be so nervous or ticked anymore. Maybe you'd even learn to like me."

He'd spent years listening to people, observing them from a safe distance. The practice had honed his ears and eyes to the point that he caught the merest hint of nerves slipping through her voice. A desperate want. And though she tried to control it, he also saw the wistful hope that tumbled across the youthful planes of her face. He opened his mouth to reject her and found he couldn't speak the crushing words. Couldn't be one more person in her life to rebuff her. Didn't have the heart to send her away. Besides, for some reason she didn't make him quite as nervous as most people.

"Okay, you can stay for a bit," he grudgingly agreed. "But the minute I get nervous, you're out of here."

Her eyes lit with excitement, glittering like the semi-precious stone for which she'd been named. She fought to keep tight control over the explosion of emotions others had been foolish enough to believe she didn't experience. "Thanks, Uncle P. I'll just sit here real quiet and stay out of your way. You'll never know I'm here."

The "Uncle P." almost did him in. "Sit there? Not a chance. You hang down here, you gotta pull your weight."

"Really?" Her joy was so painfully intense that he had to look away before he did something unmanly. Like blubber.

"Yes, really." He kicked the spare office chair in her direction. It shot across the floor toward her, the castors rattling noisily. "Well? What are you waiting for. Get down here and show me some of your computer moves." He curled his lip in the best sneer he could manage. "Assuming you have any."

She erupted from the counter and bounced into the seat, scooting over beside him. "You're on."

The next week furniture showed up from a local manufacturer whose work Daisy admired. And she hired a huge mountain of a man, Cord, to oversee the various alterations. They were along the line of minor tweaks, since Justice had built an excellent house with fabulous bone structure. It just needed a few cosmetic touches to take it from a house to a home. Well, tweaks and furniture.

"That's all I'm trying to do," she explained to Justice when he confronted her about the "tweaks." "Create a home for all of us."

"Fine. I get that part. But does the creative process have to be so damn noisy?" Instantly a shrill *wheep* sounded from the speakers. His brows pulled together. "And what the bloody hell—" *Wheep!* "—was that?"

Daisy winced. "First, yes, the creative process of transforming a house into a home has to be noisy. I promise it won't be for much longer. And I think you'll be quite pleased with the results."

One look at her anxious expression and he caved. "I'm sure I will be pleased," he reluctantly agreed. "And that noise?"

Oh, dear. She twisted her hands together. "Jett is running an experimental program."

"Not any longer she isn't." Justice frowned, and she could practically see him rewinding her explanation and homing in on the one detail she hoped would escape his notice. She should have known better. "What sort of experimental program?"

Daisy cleared her throat. "I believe it's a behavioral modification program."

It only took him a single heartbeat to add two and two. But then, Justice had always been excellent at math. "Are you telling me she's created a program that emits that…that *noise* whenever I swear?"

Daisy flinched at the outrage in his voice. "I'll speak to her."

"You're damn—" *Wheep!* "—right you'll speak to her. I want that program terminated by the end of the day."

"And the other changes?" she dared to ask, gesturing toward the great room.

They'd made serious headway over the past few days. The great room, as well as the dining room, was beginning to assume the function and appearance for which they'd been intended. The walls were still a painful white, but she'd address those in short order.

Justice stepped into the great room and studied the huge high-ceilinged expanse. She'd opened the shutters covering the picture windows to allow in a glorious view of winter landscape. The furniture she'd ordered was solid, yet elegant. Simple, yet comfortable. The textures and colors practically cried out, "Sit on me. Relax. Enjoy a conversation with friends and neighbors."

Dead center in front of the picture window she'd put up a Christmas tree. Though Cord had strung it with colorful fairy lights that twinkled merrily, they'd yet to decorate it. She hoped to involve the entire family in the activity. Best of all, she'd found a mischievous cherubic angel to top the tree, the bright golden-red curls and beaming face uncannily similar to Noelle's.

"It's lovely, Daisy," Justice said gruffly.

"Really? You like it?"

He tugged her into his arms. Since her arrival—and their lovemaking—he'd been more open and demonstrative in his affections. He was trying, no question about that. They just needed time. Time to become accustomed to each other. Time to settle into a routine. Time to learn to open up and trust.

To love.

There in front of the Christmas tree he kissed her and in that perfect moment she realized she was vanquished. She'd lost her heart to him when she'd been little more than a child. And though her feelings had been those of a child, they'd been the wellspring for what she now felt. What she hoped he'd also feel, given time. She had no idea what wonderful fate had caused them to cross paths again, or what accident of nature had occurred that ended in Noelle's conception and birth, but she would be eternally grateful.

"I always have done everything backward," she murmured dreamily. "Jumping first and looking afterward when it was far too late."

He glanced at the tree, at the room, and smiled. "Funny. I would have said you did it perfectly."

Well, perfect or not, now that she'd gotten Justice on board, it was time to address a final serious imperfection. As one day flowed into the next, Daisy couldn't take it any longer. All these white walls were driving her insane. It was almost as though they taunted her. *You've lost it. You'll never paint again.* Even though she'd set up her studio, she still couldn't work. She wouldn't accept those heartbreaking whispers. She couldn't. If she started believing them, she'd go insane.

Besides, ever since coming here, something wondrous had happened. She'd felt a…a burgeoning. A stirring of new life not unlike what she'd experienced while pregnant with Noelle. Her hands itched to wrap around a brush. She longed for the messy mix and slide of paints. Of endless colors filling her palette. The scent of linseed oil. The texture, thick and rich and dense. The soft, wet skate of brush against canvas. The growth of a dream from first stroke to last.

She glared at the walls. Canvas. White wall. What was the difference? It didn't matter one bit so long as it gave birth to the dream.

It didn't take long to find the case containing her supplies. She selected a brush, stunned when that one simple action caused tears to fill her eyes. It had been so long. So unbelievably long. An endless winter of creative barrenness. Careful now, trying not to raise her expectations too high, she selected her paints while tears tracked her cheeks, a bewildering combination of joy and fear.

She'd start slow, she decided, swiping the dampness from her face. Small. Just something whimsical to get herself started. Something Justice would never notice…

* * *

Justice halted in his tracks and glared at a section of wall near where Noelle sat playing. "What the bloody he—*heck* is that?" he demanded.

"Hell," Noelle happily prattled.

"Please don't swear in front of our daughter," Daisy said automatically. She strove for Noelle-like innocence and fell somewhat short. "And what is what?"

"Da—*darn* it! It's practically winter. Pretorius?"

Noelle clapped her hands together and crowed. "P.P!"

The hidden speakers crackled to life. "Hey there, munchkin," the man who hated everyone practically cooed. "What can your uncle P.P. do for you?"

"Uncle P.P. can call the exterminators," Justice answered in a dry voice. "We have bugs."

Daisy sighed. "Pretorius?"

"Still here."

"Cancel the exterminators. You don't have bugs. You have…well…me."

Justice hunkered down on the floor and peered at the insect. Then he shot her a look that should have fried her on the spot. He spared Noelle a quick glance that told Daisy whom she had to thank for her reprieve. A temporary reprieve, no doubt.

"Are you an alien bug or a domestic one?" Pretorius asked Daisy. "I mean, do I need to worry about you turning into a giant cockroach and eating us, or are you the homegrown garden-variety type of bug that nibbles on leaves and such?"

Daisy's mouth twitched. "And such."

"Then quit bothering me. Jett and I are working on a new program."

Justice climbed to his feet and confronted her with eyes the color of sunshine, yet filled with the coldness of a subzero morning. "What have you done to my house?"

"I improved it. You said I could."

"I do not recall saying you could paint bugs on my wall. Nor do I consider bugs, even virtual ones, an improvement."

She glanced at the floorboard. "I've got news for you, Justice. Anything that covers up all that white is a definite improvement. And actually, it's not a bug. It's a caterpillar."

"Which technically is an insect. That, madam, makes it a bug."

She should have known better than try to outrationalize Mr. Rational, himself. Seizing a different tack, she offered a winning smile. "But a very pretty one, don't you think?"

He pointed at her artwork. "That is the larva of an *actias luna*. Based on its orange shading, I assume it's in its fifth instar." He frowned at the busy little caterpillar. "You do realize that luna moths aren't indigenous to Colorado? It isn't logical. How would it have gotten here?"

Oh, for the love of... Daisy glared at Justice. Enough was enough. "It got here when I painted it on your wall." She spared her daughter another glance. Noelle watched with far too much interest. "Could we discuss this in private? Your office, perhaps?"

"I don't know." He folded gorgeous arms roped with intriguing ripples and bulges across an equally gorgeous chest, also roped with intriguing ripples and bulges. "Are there any insects in there?"

Technically? "No."

"Fine. Come on, Red," he said, using Jett's nickname for his daughter. He scooped her up and settled her into the sling of his crooked arm. "I think we'll both find your mother's explanation highly interesting."

Daisy trailed behind him in the direction of his office. "What part of 'discuss this in private' didn't you understand?" she complained.

"My comprehension continues to be excellent, as I'm sure you're well aware. I simply enjoy having my daughter with me whenever possible."

Daisy released a sigh. How could she argue with that? With increasing regularity she'd catch Justice pausing in his various activities to describe what he was doing to Noelle. For a man who'd so unexpectedly discovered himself in possession of an instant family, he'd sure taken to it like a duck to water. Once she'd even caught him explaining he was about to go to work in his lab, refusing to leave until he'd satisfied himself that Noelle understood his departure was temporary, though Daisy had her doubts about how much their daughter grasped of his technical explanation. Still. It gave her hope for the future.

The instant Justice thrust open the door to his office, his gaze swept the walls. The absence of any *actias lunas* seemed to reassure him, and he relaxed. "Okay, what's going on, Daisy?"

She shrugged. "All the white was getting to me. You gave me permission to make improvements. I made a few."

"As I've already explained, painting bugs on my walls does not improve them." He instantly realized he'd hurt her, that fact reinforced by Noelle's indignant babble. He rubbed his daughter's back in a soothing motion. "You're right, Red. That was thoughtless. I didn't mean it that way. There's no questioning your talent, Daisy. You're a stunning artist."

"But you prefer I confine myself to canvas?" she asked tightly.

A frown creased his brow. "What's wrong, Daisy? What's going on?"

She couldn't bring herself to look at him, to tell him the truth. Instead, she crossed to the window to stare out across a snowy, windswept landscape. White-capped mountains rose in the distance, a fitting backdrop for both the man and his home. "Like I said. All the white around here is making me uncomfortable."

"Funny. I find it reassuring."

Daisy turned and grabbed the opening he'd unwittingly provided. "Why is that, Justice?" At his hesitation, she offered an encouraging smile. "I'm serious. Why is all that white reassuring?"

He gave it a moment's serious thought before replying. Noelle squirmed in his arms and he set her at his feet. Instantly, she tugged at her clothing. No doubt she'd be naked as a jaybird in thirty seconds flat. Or would have if Justice hadn't plucked a child's version of Rumi he'd specifically designed for Noelle from a pile of toys he kept on his desk. He offered it to his daughter. Diverted from her striptease, she plopped down on the floor. After tasting it, her clever little fingers went to work pulling and tugging at the device, delighted when the pieces turned and twisted into different shapes.

Satisfied that she was adequately distracted, Justice shrugged. "I guess I find white reassuring because it stands for possibility," he said. "I spend an inordinate amount of time sitting and thinking."

"Yes, it's part of the creative process."

"No, it's part of the analytical process."

This time she didn't bother to hide her amusement. "Heaven forbid anyone call you creative, huh, Justice?"

"I prefer you not."

"Okay, so staring at a blank wall is part of your analytical process. Would that analytical process be interrupted if the walls were painted?"

"With bugs?"

"Not necessarily. With whatever I wanted to paint."

He speared her with another look, one that struck her as far too perceptive. "I asked you this when we first walked in and I think I should ask again. What's going on, Daisy?"

She didn't want to answer the question. She really didn't.

It cut too close. Hurt too much. Still, he deserved an answer. She tiptoed to within splatter distance of the truth. "I just felt like painting."

He shifted closer, trapping her against his desk. He was so strong. So powerful. So intensely male. And those eyes of his... They glittered with a gold as sharp and brilliant as his intellect. He slid his hand along the sweep of her throat to cup the left side of her face. Unable to resist she turned into the caress, allowed his warmth to seep into her pores and heat her blood. Want stirred, leaving her utterly helpless to resist.

"Talk to me, Daisy," he murmured. "I know you've been keeping something from me. What is it?"

She debated for a long moment. What good did it do to hide the truth? Maybe if she explained, he'd understand. Blowing out a sigh, she closed her eyes and confessed. "That caterpillar? It's the first thing I've painted in a while."

He froze. "Define a while?"

She shrugged. "A longish string of days."

"Longish, as in twenty months, eight days, seventeen hours and twenty-nine minutes?"

She opened her eyes, hoping they didn't reflect the intensity of her misery, and nodded. "To the nanosecond."

Without a word, he drew her into his arms and held her. The delicious scent of him flooded her senses. So did his strength and determination. It was as though by being here with him, she'd absorbed bits and pieces of him. She couldn't explain it, certainly didn't understand it. She could only accept and revel in being with him again and experiencing the return of her creativity, even though she suspected it had a lot to do with the man who held her.

"Perhaps this is the appropriate time to make a confession of my own," he murmured.

"You can't paint, either?"

A chuckle escaped him. "No." His humor faded. "And I also can't work. In my case, it's been going on for longer than twenty months, eight days—"

"—seventeen hours and twenty-nine minutes?"

"Thirty-one," he corrected absently. "And I'd say it's been closer to two years, two months and thirteen days. I can provide you with the hours and minutes if you require."

"That's not necessary. I get the idea. So what happened two years—" Her breath escaped in a rush. "Oh, Justice. Your accident?"

"Yes. That's when I realized that, other than Pretorius, I had no one in my life. At least, no one who would miss me if I were gone."

"And you wanted someone?"

He swept her hair back from her face and smiled at her, something vaguely bittersweet clinging to the corners of his mouth. "Very much."

"No wonder you resorted to a computer program to find a wife." She caught her bottom lip between her teeth. "Instead, you're stuck with me."

"I guess that means we're stuck with each other."

She searched his face for a clue to his innermost feelings. "Are we, Justice?"

"Only if we want to be. And only if we can find a way to make our relationship work. With that in mind, I suggest it's time for another condition."

"Oh, great. One of yours or one of mine?"

"How about one that's ours," he suggested. "Joint Condition One. You have permission to paint on walls. Certain walls and *only* certain walls."

Everything inside softened and warmed. "Really?" she asked, delighted.

"I want this to be your home, too, and if that's what it takes to unblock your artistic talent and get you painting again, I'm more than willing to sacrifice a few white walls."

Daisy wrapped her arms around Justice's waist and hugged him tight. "Thank you. I promise you won't be sorry."

He wrapped her up in a snug embrace. "Before you get too excited, the labs downstairs and all of Pretorius's areas are strictly off-limits." She could feel his steady heartbeat against her cheek, while his voice rumbled in her ear. "You may paint down to the bottom of the steps leading to the basement area, but no farther. Understood?"

"Understood." She tilted back her head and smiled up at him. "You may even discover you like what I've done so much you want me to paint those walls, too."

He swore so softly Jett's behavior modification program didn't catch it. Nor did Noelle, thank goodness. "We're not kids anymore, Daisy. This isn't like the lines I used to draw, lines you took such delight in stepping over."

She had a sneaking suspicion it was exactly like the lines he'd drawn all those years ago, lines meant to box her out. Instead, she'd forced her way in, forced him to expand those lines to include her. Just as she was doing now. But he'd have to discover that for himself. "Thank you, Justice. Thank you for understanding."

"You're welcome." As though unable to resist, he kissed her, the moment one of the sweetest she'd experienced since her arrival. "Well? What are you waiting for? You have walls to paint."

"I'm on it, I'm on it."

Daisy bolted across the office and closed the door behind her. Then she waited. She knew the instant he saw what she'd done to his office wall—the painting of Emo X-14 peeking at him from behind the safety of the door, his electronic control helmet askew, processors twinkling, his row of aquamarine eyes glowing with mischief.

"Son of a—!" *Wheep!*

Daisy grinned. Whether Justice liked it or not, he now had people who cared about him. And with luck it would help him work again. With luck they'd find a way to blend their imperfect little group into the perfect family.

Nine

Perhaps it happened because Justice gave his permission to paint the walls. Perhaps it was because his analytical block mirrored her own creative one. Or perhaps happiness gave her the release she needed, but when Daisy woke the next day, it was with the overwhelming urge to paint. Not just caterpillars, but entire sweeps of lovely, blank wall.

And paint she did.

The floodgates opened and there weren't enough hours in the day to transpose all the ideas rampaging through her head into painted images. Little by little, the house transformed as furnishings arrived and lush jungles exploded to life. Exotic creatures peeked from corners or flitted along the ceiling or whimsically appeared in unexpected places, much to everyone's amusement and delight.

But the section that gave Daisy the most pleasure was the stairway leading to areas off-limits. There she painted an amusing rendition of Noelle creeping down the steps, a mischievous expression on her impish face, the little girl trailed by Kit, Cat and all manner of creatures. At the very bottom of the staircase, one naughty toe crossed over Justice's line and into forbidden territory.

Daisy knew the instant Justice spotted that single, defiant toe. His roar of laughter echoed up the stairwell, the sound so unexpected, so unrestrained and so painfully rare, that it had everyone in the household scurrying to see what had caused his amusement. Even Pretorius made an appearance, though he only stayed long enough to chuckle before darting the group a nervous glance and scampering back to his computer room. He'd actually relented later that day and gave her a brief, nervous tour, no doubt at Jett's insistence. But Daisy knew it was a start.

It gave her hope that they were all coming together as a family, and maybe, just maybe, she and Justice would be able to make a permanent commitment and…as he put it "bond" and "form a family unit." Or as she put it, fall in love. Maybe she'd have taken up permanent residence in her personal fantasyland if she hadn't had a conversation with Cord while working on the final home improvements.

"I'd like to create a better flow between these two rooms, maybe open up this section of wall." Daisy pointed to a long expanse of painful white. "I can't imagine what the architect was thinking to close it off."

"Wasn't the architect. Used to be open," the huge man informed her. "That Pamela woman…beg pardon…*Dr.* Randolph, as she insisted I call her, had it closed up and plastered over. Might have a bunch of fancy initials after her name, but I gotta tell you, Daisy. That woman was an idiot."

Daisy froze, thinking fast. She suspected if she expressed ignorance about Dr. Randolph, Cord would clam up. He was that sort of man. "I didn't realize the wall had been one of her decisions," she said in what she hoped was a casual manner. "I'm surprised Justice didn't have you change it back to the way it was."

"Nope. He was more concerned with getting all her fancy East Coast furniture cleared out right pronto. Never did suit the place. All stiff and formal and cold. Like her, if you know what I mean." His gaze swept the improvements Daisy had made and a satisfied smile settled on his broad, homely face. "Just like I can look at your changes and know what kind of person you are."

"I hope that's a good thing," she murmured.

"Very good." He slanted her a quick, curious look. "You one of his apprentices, too? You don't strike me as the type."

"No," she replied, hoping she didn't sound too forlorn. "I wouldn't qualify. I'm not an engineer." Or anything close.

After Cord left, Daisy thought long and hard about what he'd told her. Justice had never mentioned that he'd actually found an apprentice/wife. Or that it hadn't worked out. While part of her wondered why their relationship ended, another part couldn't contain her relief that it had. How would she have handled it if she'd arrived on Justice's doorstep only to be faced with a Mrs. Dr. St. John? Daisy flinched at the idea.

So, what did she do now? Confront him or keep the knowledge to herself? Pamela's existence and Justice's continued use of the apprentice/wife program hurt, she finally decided. Seriously hurt, even though they weren't together at the time. They would have to discuss it at some point. But not yet. Not when everything and everyone rested on a knife's edge. She'd give them time to grow closer, to see if he wouldn't open up on his own. And then she'd demand answers.

Her assessment proved sound when Aggie decided to throw her first bridge party. "They're just some people I met in town," the housekeeper explained. "Since socializing is difficult with everyone spread out, we decided to meet on a weekly basis to play cards. So, I was wondering…" She clutched her hands together. "Could we meet here?"

"I'm sure Justice won't mind," Daisy said. "Invite them over."

"Right now it's only two other people. But I'm confident we'll find another player before long. We'll play a dummy hand for our fourth until we do."

"I think it's a great idea. You can use the dining room, if you want. Or, better yet, we can set up a table in the great room in front of the fireplace."

Aggie beamed in delight. "That would be the perfect place for a lovely cup of tea, don't you think?"

"I can't imagine a better one," Daisy replied with an answering smile. "Bridge and tea. You can't improve on that."

"No, you can't."

Justice's only objection on the night of the bridge party related to Pretorius. "He's been dealing with a lot of changes these past couple of weeks." He shot a look toward the great room where Aggie's visitors had gathered. "I don't want him pushed too far."

"If it doesn't work out, we'll reconsider," Daisy replied. "Let's give it a try to see what happens."

"My trick, I believe," a voice boomed from the speakers just then.

Justice shot Daisy a look of utter bewilderment. "That sounds like Pretorius."

The two crept closer to the doorway, staring in fascination. Justice stood behind her, so close she could feel the warmth of his body and hear the give-and-take of her breath. The bridge group sat around a table in front of the fireplace, just as she'd suggested. A sparkling tea service perched on a cart closest to Aggie, dainty cups and saucers at the elbows of the three women gathered there. The fourth position at the table remained empty, although a holder full of cards occupied that portion of the table, facing the fireplace.

"This is delicious tea, Aggie," Pretorius continued from on high.

"Thank you, Pretorius. It's an English blend I order off the internet."

"I appreciate your sending Jett down with a tray so I could enjoy it with the rest of you ladies."

"And we appreciate your being our fourth," one of the women said, her laugh carrying a girlish, almost flirtatious ring. "Maybe, when you feel up to it, you'll consider joining us in person."

Dead silence met the offer. Then to Daisy's utter astonishment, Pretorius said, "Maybe I will."

"Are you having any trouble seeing your cards?" another of the ladies asked. "Do you need the holder moved?"

"An inch to the left would help. No, no, Grace. I should have said *my* left. Yes, that's better. The camera was having trouble focusing on that last card."

"He's playing with them," Daisy whispered. Tears gathered in her eyes and she turned, burying her face against Justice's broad chest. "He's actually interacting with people."

"I never thought he'd be able to change," Justice murmured in a husky voice. "You've only been here nineteen days, three hours and five minutes. And look at the difference you've made."

She could hear the emotion ripping apart his words. Pretorius wasn't the only one changing. She could sense the loosening of Justice's tight control, as well, where the events of the past had left a painful smear on his soul and encouraged a man who already tended to distrust emotions to suppress them entirely. Maybe he'd talk to her about Dr. Pamela, take her deeper into his confidence. Daisy could only hope.

Right now she sensed that he was becoming more the man she knew all those years ago. Allowing his heart—on rare occasions—to rule his intellect. Certainly at night he became that person, the intimacy of their lovemaking allowing him to open what he'd always kept so carefully closed and locked, giving them a place to relate…and grow from. Maybe, just maybe in this season of miracles, he'd learn to trust. To open his heart in the brilliance of daylight, as well as the shadow of night.

Maybe, instead of trying to teach a robot to feel, he'd learn how to do that for himself.

"The program's ready," Pretorius announced. "When you're done playing…?"

Ever so gently, Justice threaded Noelle's tiny hands with a thin band, while his daughter sat—for once still and silent—and watched in fascination while he strung a cat's cradle. "I'm not playing. I'm teaching," he corrected. "There now. We've just made a rectangle. Can you say *rectangle,* Noelle?"

She prattled happily and Justice nodded gravely. "Excellent."

"That wasn't *rectangle,*" Pretorius objected. "That was baby babble."

"Oh, and I suppose P.P. isn't baby babble?"

"P.P!" Noelle crowed, twisting around toward Pretorius.

"See? She associates P.P. with me."

"Not something I'd run around admitting to all and sundry," Justice muttered. He bent attentively over the criss-crossing laces entwined around his daughter's fingers and ever so gently restrung them. "And this, Noelle, is a triangle. Say, *triangle.*"

Pretorius snorted at the baby's laughing coos.

"And this…" He pulled gently on two of the strings. "This is a Christmas star for my Christmas baby."

The excited burst of gibberish came precariously close to the word *star* and left both men beaming in pride at her brilliance. But it was her final word that gutted Justice. A sweet, clear baby-voiced "Dada," followed by her holding out her arms imperiously, still entangled in the cat's cradle. He pulled her close and she mashed her face against his in an awkward, openmouthed kiss.

A cascade of emotion flowed through him, the sensory

input overwhelming. His arms tightened around his daughter and he literally inhaled her. The distinctive baby scent, the incredible softness of her warm skin, the silky strawberry-colored curls that brushed his face. The living, breathing essence of her filled him to overflowing and all he could do was hang on and ride the tidal wave of emotion that threatened to swamp him.

He had no idea how long he indulged in the irrational, before finding his way back to a more normal frame of mind. To his relief, Pretorius self-consciously occupied himself with banging away at his computer, giving Justice time to recover. He started to speak, then discovered he needed to clear his throat for some odd reason.

"Next time we'll work on trapezoids and equilateral parallelograms," he informed his daughter gruffly, holding out his hand for her to clutch. "If you work hard you'll have your geometric shapes mastered by Christmas. Eighteen months, tops."

Pretorius did some throat clearing of his own. "Hey. Dada. Can we get down to business? I don't know how much wall space is left to keep Daisy occupied. If you don't want her getting wind of what we're doing, I suggest you shake a leg."

The instant Justice removed the strings from her fingers Noelle began to wriggle, not pleased with the interruption to their game. "Damn it—" A siren sounded a discordant *wheep, wheep.* "*Darn it*—how am I supposed to get a measuring tape around her? She won't stop squirming."

Noelle stilled, grinned, then fluttered her pale green eyes at him. "Damn."

For some reason the siren didn't sound for the baby. Hell, no. Only when *he* slipped up. "I'm beginning to dislike your computer. A lot."

"Darn it, Justice—" *Wheep!* "It's not my computer. It's Jett's. But if you don't stop breaking Condition One, all heck—" *Wheep!* "—is going to break loose. Now, why the hell is it going off when I'm not even swearing?" *Wheep! Wheep!*

Noelle gurgled. "Damn. Hell." Dead silence.

"This is all your fault," the two men said in concert. They paused in their efforts long enough to glare at each other.

"It's not my fault," Pretorius protested. "That juvenile delinquent hacked in again and set up another Condition One Violation program. Every time I delete it, it pops back up."

"I'll give you one day. After that, I take matters into my own hands and I promise you, it won't be pretty."

"I'll speak to her."

They went back to work. All the while, Noelle fidgeted and burbled and jabbered nonstop, thoroughly enjoying the attention, as well as finally being rid of most of her clothes. Justice shook his head in amusement. If he didn't watch her like a hawk, she'd shed her diaper, too.

"Okay, I have the first measurement," Justice announced. "You ready?"

"Set." Pretorius spun his chair around and sent it shooting across the floor toward his computer banks. He jabbed his eyeglasses higher on the bridge of his nose. "And go."

"Height. 74.2936 centimeters."

"Wait, wait. The comparison chart is in inches, not centimeters."

"Who the hell—" *Wheep!* "—uses inches in scientific measurements?"

"A baby comparison chart."

"Well, convert my measurements from metric to imperial."

Pretorius thrust his hands through his hair, standing the graying tufts on end. "Do you know how long it's been since I…? Never mind." Snatching up his calculator, he banged in a series of numbers. "Okay, 29.2494 inches. Go."

"Weight. 9.0356 kilograms. Let me guess. You need it in pounds."

More banging. "Got it, got it. Go."

"Head circumference. 45.5930 centimeters. I might be a smidge off on that one. She won't stop squirming."

"Head circumference—17.95 inches. Entered." He stabbed a button and waited. "Okay. I have no idea whether this is good or bad, so don't kill the messenger. And for the love of Pete, don't break Condition One."

"Just get to it, old man."

"For height, she's in the 65.1 percentile."

Justice lifted his daughter into his arms and cuddled her close. Not that it was really cuddling. More like a sensible, protective hold with maybe a gentle tickle to distract her. "I am taller than average and height is a dominant gene. It's logical to think she received that particular genetic propensity from me. What about head circumference?"

"Seventy-one percentile." Pretorius spun around. "That mean she's gonna be smart?"

Justice swept his hand across his daughter's blaze of curls. "There have been studies done on the correlation between head size and intellect. Though the results aren't definitive, individuals with high IQ scores do tend to have larger than average heads."

"Literally or figuratively?" Pretorius asked dryly.

Justice refrained from responding since he suspected it would set off the siren again. "What about her weight?"

"Darn." *Wheep!*

Noelle clapped her hands. "Damn."

"Now, don't get upset, Justice, but Noelle is only in the 37.6 percentile."

"What? Run it again."

"I have. Three times. Thirty-seven-point-six." He spun around, a frown forming between thick dark brows. "You think Daisy isn't feeding her enough?" he whispered.

"Not deliberately. From what I've observed she's an excellent mother." Justice gave it some thought. "How much would Noelle have to weigh to be in the fiftieth percentile?"

"She'll need to hit 11.4543 kilograms by Christmas."

Justice nodded. "Then we'd better get busy. You have twenty-four hours to research the appropriate dietetic needs for a female infant of eleven months, twenty-five days and calculate how many additional calories it will require for her to achieve her goal weight."

"On it."

"I'll research potential health risks for underweight toddlers and request to see Noelle's medical records."

"Do you think Daisy will allow you access?"

"Allow you access to what?" Daisy asked, stepping into the lab. She spared Pretorius a quick, apologetic smile. "Sorry to trespass, but the computer said Noelle was down here and it's time for her nap." She returned her attention to Justice. "What do you want access to?"

"Noelle's medical records. She's underweight."

Daisy planted her hands on her hips. "She most certainly is not. She's a perfect weight given her bone structure and energy level."

"She's 3.11 grams off plumb," Pretorius offered helpfully.

One look at Daisy's expression had Justice doing some swift backpedaling. "Noelle does possess her mother's fine bone structure. Does the comparison chart take that into consideration?"

Daisy frowned. "Comparison chart? What comparison chart? And what are those black lines on Noelle?" She caught her breath and glared at Justice in disbelief. "Did you paint grid marks on our baby?"

"You painted flora and fauna on my walls," he retorted a shade defensively.

"That was different," she snapped. "They're walls. This is a baby."

"Correct. My marks have a scientific purpose. Yours are merely for decoration." He flinched at the intense hurt that flickered across her expression, hastening to add, "It's very attractive decoration. And you will recall that I have since given you permission to continue with your project. Joint Condition One, remember?"

"Well, I did not give you permission to turn our baby into a scientific experiment. Nor did I give you permission to cover her in grid marks." Daisy crossed to his side and snatched their daughter from his arms. "Is that all she means to you, Justice? Some sort of research project?"

"No, of course not."

Tears glittered in Daisy's eyes and the expression almost killed him. "I thought you were beginning to care. But I guess I was mistaken. Once a scientist, always a scientist?" With that, she turned on her heel and stalked toward the door.

"Damn, hell," Noelle cooed in farewell, waving her little hands as they exited the room.

"You said it," Justice muttered.

Pretorius released a slow breath. "What now?"

"Now we create our own comparison chart, taking into consideration a few more factors, such as bone structure."

"I can help with that," came a voice from on high.

The two men jumped and the computer let out a shrill *wheep, wheep!* Jett grinned down at them from where she sat curled up on top of the bookcase.

"Now that damn—" *Wheep!* "—siren is going off when I'm even thinking about swearing," Justice growled.

"Weren't you paying attention? It was going off even when we *didn't* swear."

"That was just me." She grinned and waggled a remote at them. "So, what do you say, Uncle P.? Want some help with that program? I'm not doing anything."

"Actually, I believe you're spying on us. Again. And…and *wheeping* us."

"True. But I can do all that while I help. I'm great at multitasking." She leaped nimbly from the bookcase to one of the long counters to the floor. "What are you planning to do if the program still shows Noelle's underweight even after you've altered the parameters?"

"Feed her," the two men said in unison.

"Can't have Justice's daughter off plumb," Pretorius muttered. He kicked a chair in Jett's direction. "Don't just stand there. We have work to do."

Justice didn't delay further, but went after Daisy and his daughter, knowing full well he had some serious groveling to do. He found Daisy in the bathroom, giving Noelle a bath.

"I'm sorry."

It seemed the safest thing to say. Of course, it helped that he meant it with the utmost sincerity. He hadn't intended to hurt her feelings, any more than he intended to treat their daughter like a scientific experiment. Well, not exactly. Daisy kept her back to him, gently rinsing away the water soluble lines crisscrossing Noelle.

"Do you resent my painting on your walls?" she asked, not pretending to misunderstand the apology.

"I did at first," he admitted. "I'm quite partial to white."

"I've noticed."

"But in the last few days I've noticed something odd."

"Something off plumb?" she asked dryly.

"Yes. Quite off plumb, at least for me."

He leaned against the doorjamb and watched her clever hands stroke the marks from Noelle's body. Daisy really did have lovely hands, both gentle and firm, graceful and tantalizing. More than anything he wanted her running those supple fingers over him, teasing and stroking as they chased a path across his body. Gripping him tight while he drove her to climax. Soothing him in that timeless aftermath. He closed his eyes in disbelief. Dear God, it was happening again. All he had to do was look at her and he lost all control. How was that possible?

Daisy shot him a questioning glance over her shoulder.

Fortunately, she didn't seem to notice anything amiss. "What have you noticed, Justice?" she prompted.

He forced himself to focus on the subject at hand. "Each day I find myself searching for any new changes or additions you might have added to the walls. On average I expend a minimum of forty-nine minutes a day on the activity."

Her shoulders tightened and her spine formed a rigid line. "Expend or waste?" she asked crisply.

He debated whether to give her an honest answer and decided he'd never been comfortable lying. With Daisy he found it almost impossible. "At first, I categorized it as a waste. One time I utilized in excess of one hundred and thirty-two minutes attempting to locate all the additions. I'm afraid I can't be more accurate since I—" He cleared his throat. "I lost track of time."

"You, Justice?" Was that a hint of irony he caught?

"I recognize that it's a serious anomaly, but…" He frowned. "I no longer consider it a waste of time."

"Really? You astonish me. Why is that?"

He took her comment at face value. "I've recently discovered the pursuit causes a positive sensory experience that's engaged me outside the realm of my scientific endeavors and altered the manner in which I prioritize various aspects of my life."

"Uh-huh." She lifted a wildly kicking Noelle from the tub and wrapped their daughter up in a fluffy yellow towel that contrasted quite delightfully with her bright strawberry-blond hair. He grinned. They really did have an adorable daughter. "Translation, please?" Daisy requested.

"It…it makes me happy."

Soft color suffused her face and she smiled. Hell, she beamed. "Really? My paintings make you happy?"

"They certainly cause a strong visceral reaction."

"That's one of the sweetest thing you've ever said to me."

He eyed her uncertainly. "Is that sarcasm?"

She carefully set their daughter on the floor, still wrapped in the bath towel. Approaching, she slid her arms around his neck and lifted her face to his. "It's Noelle's nap time. Why don't we put her down and then I'll show you exactly what I'm feeling. I'll even give you a hint." Her laughter sparkled up at him. "It's not sarcasm."

The next hour was one of the most enjoyable he'd ever spent in the middle of a workday. What was it about Daisy that she could so easily divert him? How was she able to decimate rational thought and rock-solid intent with one mischievous glance? And how could he have ever imagined he'd be satisfied with an apprentice/wife programmed to order? The one time he'd attempted it had proven to be an unmitigated disaster. He'd been bored to tears within twenty-four hours. Hell, he'd been bored to tears within twenty-two hours, fourteen minutes and fifty-one seconds.

But not with Daisy. Never with Daisy.

She rolled over and traced the contours of his face, tripped along the taut lines of his jaw. "That was amazing. But then, it always is." She rested her chin on his chest. "Why is that, do you suppose?"

"We're sexually compatible."

She released her breath in a sigh, warning that he hadn't given her the answer she'd hoped. Desperate for a hint, he asked, "Why do you think we're amazing together?"

"I guess there's some truth to that old adage opposites attract."

"It's more than an old adage, it's a scientific fact. At least, when it comes to magnetic properties and electrically charged particles." She laughed, but he caught a hint of wistfulness beneath the humor. "What's wrong, Daisy?"

She drew lazy circles across his chest, painting him with her fingertips. He couldn't help but wonder what colors she was imagining. Dark, passionless ones that glittered with the iciness of a dark winter? Or brilliant shades of springtime hope? "What do you want from our relationship, Justice?"

He wasn't stupid. He could see a trap when it yawned in front of him. He chose his words with extreme care. "I want marriage. I want a family."

"Yes, you explained that was your game plan when I first told you about Noelle. When you told me about your apprentice/wife program," she added with far too casual an air.

His gaze sharpened. "Nothing has changed since then."

"Funny. I'd say a lot has changed since then."

He stirred, uncomfortable with the direction of their conversation. "I meant, nothing about my game plan has changed. I still want marriage. I still want a family. I'm hoping, given time, that our relationship will progress in that direction."

"Like you were hoping it would with Pamela?"

The words hung in the afternoon air. Justice scrubbed his hands across his face and swore. Damn, damn, damn. He'd suspected something was up. Now she'd confirmed it. "I assume Cord told you?"

"You should have been the one to tell me." Then she let him off the hook. Somewhat. "Why don't you tell me now?"

Okay, fair enough. "She seemed like the best candidate for the job." He shrugged. "I was wrong."

"Why didn't you tell me about her when we first arrived?"

"We had enough to deal with. Plus, the relationship didn't work out, so it was no longer an issue."

"Why didn't it work out?"

"Damn it, Daisy. Do you need every last detail?"

She tilted her head to one side in consideration. "Yes."

"Fine." He considered carefully before speaking. "You know what we were saying about opposites attracting? Well, like objects don't. Pamela was too much like me. Hell, she was worse than me. She was logical and rational and brilliant."

"Beautiful, an engineer, kind, someone who won't make waves and who is able to handle the isolation of life in Nowhere, Colorado?"

"Apparently, Cord isn't the only one with a big mouth." When Daisy didn't answer, Justice blew out a sigh. "Yes, she met every single one of my criteria. Are you satisfied now?"

"Not really."

"She met every single one of my criteria, particularly the one about being in control of her emotions. In fact, I've never met a colder, more emotionless woman." He shuddered at the memory. "I have a feeling if I'd ever worked up the nerve to touch her, I'd have died from frostbite."

Daisy couldn't hide her smile. "Then what *do* you require in a wife?"

Damn it to hell. Why did women ask such impossible questions? Why did women get a man naked and in bed, wait until he was at his most vulnerable and incapable of escape, and then blindside him with questions guaranteed to initiate an argument. Okay, he knew why. They were women. Still…

"I want you," he said, hoping it would make a difference. "And although neither of us planned it, I couldn't ask for a better daughter than Noelle."

"Want." She tried out the word. It must not have been the flavor she'd hoped because she discarded it with a tiny wrinkle of her nose. "What about love?"

He closed his eyes and silently swore. He should have seen that one coming, especially with a woman like Daisy. "Is it one of your prerequisites to marriage?" he asked carefully.

"Yes."

He nodded, not surprised. "I wish I had it to offer." He cupped her face, locking gazes with her so she could read his sincerity. "Someone like you deserves love, deserves a husband capable of love. If we decide to marry, you need to know that I can't provide you with that."

Her lashes flickered downward to conceal her eyes, but not

before he saw the sheen of tears. "What *are* you offering?" she whispered.

She was killing him by inches, but he forced himself to be brutally honest. "I'll give you everything I have. My home. My intellect. My money. Sex." His mouth twisted in a parody of a smile. "According to you, amazing sex. I've even given you my walls. But I can't give you what I don't possess."

"And you don't think you possess the capacity to love?"

"No, Daisy. I don't think it," he stated ever so gently. "I know I don't."

He was going to lose her.

Justice woke to the knowledge while dawn's first light invaded Daisy's bedroom. His hold on her tightened convulsively and she stirred in her sleep, murmuring in protest. He didn't doubt for one tiny second that she was going to leave him and he fought a growing sense of panic as the certainty became stronger with each passing moment. He had to do something, anything, to keep her. Unfortunately, the three simple words guaranteed to make her his, were the only three he couldn't in all good conscience utter.

The irony didn't escape him. He'd always thought he possessed everything a woman could possibly want. He was worth billions. Owned a company respected around the world. Boasted a respectable intellect. Even better, he wanted marriage. A family. He frowned in bewilderment. Most women would be satisfied with that, wouldn't they?

Unfortunately, Daisy wasn't "most women." Rather than reveling at the idea of spending his money, she'd used a mere pittance of his billions. And for what? To transform his house into a home. She'd only made one serious demand of him, regardless of her ridiculous conditions—that he involve himself in their daughter's life. And wouldn't he have done everything within his power, given all that he possessed to be allowed that opportunity, even if she hadn't insisted? The only real request she'd made on her own behalf had been to paint his walls. And what had she done when he'd reluctantly agreed? Created magnificent murals that stunned the senses and delighted the eye.

With each passing minute, light eclipsed darkness, marching relentlessly across the mattress. It encompassed Daisy within a halo of radiance and yearning, pouring passion onto passion while he remained caught within night's lingering death. Gently, tenderly, he slipped from her embrace, and withdrew from the light and warmth aboveground to retreat to the darkness below.

No, there wasn't any question. Daisy was going to leave and he had to do something, find a way—any way that didn't involve lying to her—to convince her to stay.

She couldn't stay.

Daisy woke to the knowledge while dawn's first light streamed into her bedroom. Beside her, Justice's hold tightened protectively and she stirred against him, murmuring a reassurance. She didn't doubt for one tiny second the need to leave and she fought a growing sense of panic as the certainty became stronger with each passing moment. She would do almost anything if it meant she didn't have to go. Unfortunately, three simple words stood between them, creating a gulf that couldn't be bridged.

The irony didn't escape her. Justice possessed everything a woman could possibly want. He was worth billions. Owned a company respected around the world. Boasted a respectable intellect. Even better, he wanted marriage. A family. She struggled against tears. Most woman would be satisfied with that, wouldn't they?

Why couldn't she be like "most women"? Why couldn't she be satisfied with the material possessions he had to offer, the physical relationship that bordered on incandescent, the heart-wrenching way he'd taken to fatherhood? He loved, even if he didn't believe it. She saw it every time he looked at his daughter. But did he love her? Were the words that important? She closed her eyes and faced the painful truth. Without those words—and the emotions behind them—the rest held no real meaning. Not for her. She'd trade all the other trappings in a heartbeat if only Justice loved her.

With each passing minute, light eclipsed darkness, slipping effortlessly across the mattress. It encompassed her within a halo of radiance and yearning, pouring passion onto passion while Justice remained caught within night's lingering death. Gently, with unmistakable finality, he slipped from her embrace, and withdrew from the light and warmth aboveground to retreat to the darkness below.

No, there wasn't any question. She was going to have to leave, even though everything within her cried out to stay.

Ten

Daisy started to enter Justice's lab and hesitated at the sound of Noelle's voice. "Wuv you," she demanded, patting her father's cheek, her lashes fluttering flirtatiously.

"Yes, I love you very much," Justice assured her as he made an adjustment to Emo's helmet. The instant he finished, he leaned over and kissed his daughter, and Daisy caught the sheer, unadulterated love in his gaze when Noelle grabbed his ears and pulled him in for a second helping.

A worried frown darkened her brow. "Emo wuv you?"

"Yes, Emo loves you, too."

He grinned at the exuberant hug and kiss Noelle gave the X-14 model. "Now why is he your favorite? And don't try to tell me he isn't because I'd be forced to call you a teeny-tiny fibber." Noelle babbled in reply and he listened seriously. "Yes, maybe 15 is a bit too sleek, but then he is an upgrade." More babble and more serious consideration. "Huh. I hadn't considered painting the chassis. No doubt your mommy could design something bright and colorful, probably paint whimsical faces on them to give them personality. Hmm. Now that I think about it, that's not a bad idea."

Noelle babbled away, this time at Emo, and to Daisy's amusement, Emo emitted a series of beeps and hums that only served to encourage their daughter's efforts to communicate. She waved her hands, her piquant features scrunched into an intensely focused frown while she chattered away in her own private baby language. All the while, Justice watched and listened, his focus equally intense, as though attempting to decipher her meaning.

When the words wound down, he scooped Noelle into his arms and cradled her against his heart. She curled up there with a happy sigh and he closed his eyes, such an expression of undisguised love on his face, it was painful to witness. Daisy stared down at the stack of papers she held, blinking back tears. How could he believe himself incapable of love? How could he doubt it for even one tiny nanosecond? And how could she get him to see the truth?

Aggie appeared in the hallway just then and tossed a quick smile in Daisy's direction before hurrying into the lab. Daisy followed behind, relieved that the interruption gave her a moment to regain control of her emotions. "It's time for Noelle's lunch," the housekeeper announced. "Would you like me to bring her back down here after her nap?"

"If you wouldn't mind." Justice reluctantly handed over the baby and turned his attention to Daisy. "Perfect timing. I have an idea I want to run by you."

"Giving Emo a paint job?" she guessed.

He stared in surprise. "How did you know?"

"I overheard you discussing it with Noelle." Before she could ask him about the papers she held—the reason for her visit—she was distracted by endless images of herself cycling across the computer screens around the room. "Good Lord. What are these pictures for?"

"They're photos of your emotional responses to various

stimuli. I have videos, too." He lifted a sooty eyebrow. "You may recall I did ask."

The memory clicked. They'd been right here in his lab, the day he'd first introduced her to Emo. "Oh, right. You want to teach Emo to read our expressions." For some reason all those photos made her uncomfortable, perhaps because they showed her expressing such a range of emotions, some of them downright painful. "You have videos, too?"

"Yes. They're excellent teaching tools."

"Can you show me?"

Justice picked up a remote control and aimed it at one of the computers. Instantly, the screen switched from slide show to video and exhibited an image of her walking toward the kitchen. She remembered that day. It had been weeks ago, not long after she'd arrived and before she'd begun to paint the walls. It had been an unusually bad afternoon and she watched in dismay, forced to relive her misery.

The camera switched angles, revealing Aggie puttering at the kitchen table, chopping vegetables for a salad. At the sound of the door opening, she glanced up, a hint of concern drifting across her expression. Daisy dragged herself to the table, took a seat beside the housekeeper and buried her head in her arms.

"I gather the painting didn't go well?" Aggie asked sympathetically. She reached out, her hand skimming across Daisy's head in a motherly caress.

"You could say that." Daisy lifted her face, her expression miserable. "I don't understand, Aggie. I should be over it by now. But every time I see that blank canvas..." The breath shuddered from her lungs and her voice escaped, low and desperate. "I don't think I'll ever paint again."

Aggie tutted, worry pulling at the lines bracketing her mouth. "Of course you will. It's only a matter of when," she said, her encouraging comment ripe with sympathy.

"How long a when, Aggie? It's been nearly two years. It's

like the desire to paint has drained right out of me. I lost it right after Justice and I…" She trailed off and shook her head. "Anyway, I thought maybe I'd find it here."

For an instant Aggie appeared at a loss, then she said bracingly, "Now that you're with Justice again, I'm betting it'll come storming back. You wait and see."

"I love…" Tears filled her eyes and she shook her head, the words bottling in her throat.

Daisy remembered she'd been about to admit she loved Justice, that her hopelessness on that front had infected her creative ability, and had ever since they'd parted nearly two years before. But she'd been unable—or unwilling—to admit the painful truth and had altered what she'd ultimately said. She slid a sideways look at Justice. Did he know? Had he picked up on the subtext at all?

"I love painting so much," the video continued, her true feelings for Justice left unstated. "You have no idea how much I miss it."

"There, there, sweetheart. You've gone and gotten yourself all upset." Setting aside her vegetable peeler, Aggie bustled to the stove and turned on the burner beneath a copper kettle. "How about a nice cup of tea to cheer you up?"

"Thanks, Aggie." Daisy forced out a smile. "I don't know what I'd do without you and your tea. I'm feeling better already."

The clip ended and Daisy fought against that old sense of panic and fear and helplessness. Before she could say anything, Justice was there. He tugged the papers from her hand, tossed them aside and pulled her tight into his arms.

"I'm sorry. In all honesty, I'd forgotten that particular video was the next one in the queue. That was thoughtless of me. There are times I think I could use the sort of emotion chip I'm attempting to design for Emo." He held her, offering his strength and compassion, while she struggled to regain some distance from the events he'd taped. "Are you all right?"

"I'll survive." She pulled back, determined to stand on her own. "I don't understand. Why would you keep that video, Justice, when you must know how painful it is?"

"Precisely because it is so emotional. You four are rarely sad. I have several of Noelle crying, but it's not quite the same. Adults aren't as open as children. I want Emo capable of spotting more subtle cues."

"That was hardly subtle," she pointed out.

"True. I thought if I started with more obvious emotions, we could refine his program over time." He picked up the remote. "I can delete it if you prefer. I have other videos of Jett, Pretorius and Aggie. Granted, none of them are sad, but they cover a sufficient emotional range."

That stopped her. "Jett, Pretorius and Aggie. And me." She shot him an odd look. "What about you, Justice? Do you also have teaching videos of your emotional range?"

A muscle jerked in his jaw. "No."

"Is that because you aren't expressive?" She paused a beat, her heart aching for him. "Or is it because you don't believe you experience those emotions?"

He flinched. It was barely perceptible, but it was there. And she caught it. "I experience certain emotions. Just none that will benefit Emo." Pain filled his gaze and she knew beyond a shadow of a doubt he wasn't talking about sharing his emotions with the robot, but about sharing them with her. "I can't give Emo what I don't possess."

"You're wrong, Justice," she dared to argue. "You do possess those emotions. Granted, you've safeguarded them behind locked doors and thrown away the key. But if you'd just let me in—"

"What if you discover there's nothing behind the locked doors?" he cut in. "That I'm emotionless. Lacking in empathy."

Her eyes narrowed. "You're quoting someone. Who?"

He shrugged. "Any number of foster parents and counselors. Hell, even my own mother and father never understood me."

"Oh, Justice. You were a ten-year-old child when they died. I'm sure that's not true."

He simply stared at her, his glorious eyes blank and empty of all expression. "You're wrong. I overheard my mother say just that, not long before her death. She was talking to my father about me. She said she thought I was incapable of love. That I took after Pretorius and would turn out just like him."

Daisy's mouth dropped open. "You're not incapable of love, any more than Pretorius is," she retorted fiercely. "He may have a social anxiety disorder, but he's one of the most caring, loving people I've ever met. And damn it, so are you. Is that why you refuse to say the words? Because someone was foolish enough to believe you incapable of love and you bought into their ridiculous assumptions?"

"Enough." He stepped away, turning his back on her. "Why are you here, Daisy?"

She debated pressing the issue. But the coldness in his voice, along with the stiffness of his stance warned of the futility of making the attempt. Instead, her gaze settled on the stack of papers he'd tossed aside. A timely reminder. She crossed to his workbench and fanned through the pages before tidying the stack.

"Justice, are you still looking for an apprentice/wife?"

"No. After Pamela…" He shrugged. "The program needs further modification. Besides, I no longer have any use for an apprentice. In a few years Noelle will fill that role nicely. Now I'm just interested in acquiring a wife."

The matter-of-fact statement nearly brought her to her knees. She opened her mouth to say something, anything, but couldn't get the words past the knot in her throat. She shoved the stack of papers in his direction. "You're interested in acquiring one of these women for your future wife?" she managed to ask.

Puzzled, he picked up the first several pages and scanned them. "These are from my apprentice/wife program. How did you get hold of them?"

"The printer was spitting out women when I walked past."

"Huh. I guess the program is still running."

"I read the bios on these women. I'm nothing like them, am I, Justice?"

"No. You're nothing like these women." He flipped through a few pages. "This one has a PhD in Biological Systems Engineering. Useless to me as an apprentice. This next one appears perfect on paper, but so did Pamela. Besides, she looks mean." He showed her the photo. "Doesn't she look mean to you? This one's got *city girl* written all over her. This next one with the glasses has a crazed look about the eyes. No, none of them fit my parameters."

"Your parameters for the perfect wife." When he didn't immediately reply, she added, "These women aren't perfect, Justice. No one is. There's no such thing."

"I know that."

"Do you?" She stepped closer, fixing her gaze on him. "Why do you want me, Justice? Is it because I'm Noelle's mother or because I'm me? I'm not just a body, you know, not just someone to warm your bed." She gestured in the direction of the printouts. "Nor am I a list of parameters some program has spit out. I'm *me,* damn it. And my list of parameters for the right husband—not the perfect husband, but the *right* husband—includes an emotional connection."

He closed his eyes. "We discussed this. I explained—"

"Why are you building a robot that can interpret emotions? Is it so Emo can tell you what you can't figure out for yourself...how people feel? How many versions of Emo have there been? How many Emos have been dismantled and their parts repurposed?" She hammered the questions at him. "Is that what's going to happen to me if you're dissatisfied with the way I function? When you realize you can't mold me into your idea of perfection? I'll be scrapped so you can start over?"

If she'd hoped for an emotional reaction, she finally got one. "Have I ever said any of those things to you?" he demanded. "Have I ever demanded perfection from you?"

"Not exactly."

Fierce anger glittered to life, turning his tawny gaze from cool and remote to incandescent. "Oh, please. Please do be exact. And allow me to repeat… Have I ever said anything along those lines?"

"No," she grudgingly admitted.

"No." The satisfaction sweeping through that single word set her teeth on edge. "I've never said it. And, for your information, I've never even thought it."

"You must have at some point," she snapped back. "Since I have a mile-high stack of women specifically tailored for the role of Mrs. Sinjin, Incorporated, all somewhat short of perfect because you haven't fine-tuned the program."

"If I'd wanted one of those women in that stack, she'd be here right now instead of you. I'd have chosen Pamela. Or I would have picked someone at that engineering conference twenty months, twenty-five days, twenty…twenty—" He heaved the remote against the wall where it shattered. "Damn it to *hell,* Daisy! I can't even tell you the hours and minutes, you have me so pissed off with your endless pushing, pushing, pushing."

She stared, stunned. "Twenty-one hours and twelve minutes ago," she whispered.

He closed his eyes, exhaustion carving deep lines alongside his mouth. "Let me make myself perfectly clear. The only woman I want is you."

That simple statement had the anger draining right out of her. She went to him, wrapped herself up in him. His arms closed around her, pulling her tight. "What are we going to do, Justice?"

"Keep trying. We have to keep trying." He lifted her face to his, took her mouth in an endless kiss. "Please, Daisy. Please, don't give up on me."

But she did. He discovered that painful fact the very next day.

"Phone call from Cord O'Malley," the computer announced.

"Put him through," Justice ordered. He waited until the computer made the connection, before asking, "Yes, Cord, what can I do for you?"

"I just wanted to confirm a work order."

Impatient with the interruption, Justice returned his focus to Emo and settled his magnifying headset over his face. "Daisy is in charge of all work orders. I thought I made that clear."

"You did. But since you're the one paying the bills, I thought I'd better check before we hopped on this particular job."

"Fine. What does the job entail? More furniture? Plumbing or electrical alterations?" He touched the tip of his tool to one of Emo's circuits and a brief smile slipped across his mouth. "Or maybe she's run out of walls to paint and wants you to add a few."

"Actually, this does have to do with painting walls. Only she wants me doing the painting."

"Don't be ridiculous," Justice responded absently. "They're already painted."

"Yeah, that's the thing. I thought those pictures she drew were real pretty, but she wants us to whitewash over them. And take out all that nice furniture she bought. Even the Christmas tree. Strip it post-Pamela clean. Her exact words."

Justice's attention snapped to the conversation with laser-sharp focus. Straightening, he yanked off his headset and tossed it to his workbench. "What the hell are you talking about?" He bit out the words.

The sound of a hand slapping paper came through the speakers. "I'm talking about this work order I have right here that says I'm supposed to come the day after Christmas and yank out all that furniture we dragged in there and paint every last wall white. I'm talking about this work order that says we're supposed to... Hang on and I'll read it like she wrote it. We're to, quote, return the house to the exact same condition it was before our advent. Strip it post-Pamela clean. End quote. Now unless my dictionary is mistaken, that means put everything back the way it was before she came."

Justice fought to breathe. "Your dictionary isn't mistaken, but the work order is. You will ignore it. Is that clear?"

"She's put an after-Christmas rush on it."

"I'm canceling the rush. I will, of course, send you a cancellation fee for your trouble."

"Aw, Justice, you know that's not necessary. I figured there had to be some sort of mistake. I gotta tell you, I'm glad to get it cleared up. I think I'd've cried like a baby if she made me paint those walls."

"Agreed. Please check with me if any further work orders are issued."

"Will do. Hope you have a Merry Christmas."

But Justice wouldn't have a Christmas, merry or otherwise. Not if Daisy left. Not if she took his daughter with her. He couldn't bear the thought of Aggie and Jett leaving, either. They'd become too important to him. Vital to his happiness and well-being. Just as he was willing to bet he and Pretorius had become vital to their happiness. They were a family, damn it, and no matter what it took, he had to find a way to stop her. To convince her to stay. To convince her that they belonged together. All of them.

For the next three days, as the calendar crept steadily closer to Christmas, Justice vacillated between confronting

Daisy over the work order and waiting until after the twenty-fifth. Concern that a confrontation might convince her to leave before the holiday was all that kept him silent. During the day he worked like a man possessed, hoping that even if he couldn't love, maybe his robot's ability to sense emotion would help him analyze the problem and come up with a logical solution. And with each passing night their lovemaking took on an element of desperation, as though they both sensed their time together would soon end.

On Christmas Eve she slipped from his bed and returned to her own room, and he knew he'd lost. Silently, he paced through the house, picturing it without the noise and laughter and joy that had permeated each and every room since Daisy and her household had arrived.

He paused in front of the Christmas tree, one they'd all decorated together. It had been Pretorius's first visit above stairs. Justice tapped an ornament, a miniature laptop with ho-ho-ho scrawled across the tiny screen. Pretorius had given it to Jett to symbolize the bond the two of them had cemented. And he'd given Daisy one of a cradle with Baby's First Christmas inscribed on it.

Finally, he returned downstairs to the lab. He still had a few more hours in which to complete the Emo X-15 model and he intended to use each and every precious minute remaining to him in the hope that he'd finally succeed at getting the upgrade fully operational. He booted up the computer and accessed the list of "emotion" files Pretorius had put together. His uncle had labeled one of them Love, and Justice couldn't remember ever viewing those.

There were still photos as well as videos and he clicked on them at random. The first were a series of Daisy and Noelle and he smiled at the stream of images. Blowing kisses. Snuggling. Bath time. Story time. Bedtime. There were even a few of Jett, curled up with Noelle like a pair of exhausted kittens.

And then he hit an endless cascade of photos of himself with his daughter and his breath stopped. They were pictures he hadn't even known existed, and as he scrutinized one after another he couldn't mistake the look on his face, any more than he'd been able to mistake it on Daisy's.

But it was the final photo that threatened to utterly destroy him. He'd just come from the outside and was still in his coat while he held his sleeping daughter in his arms, his embrace as gentle as it was protective. But he wasn't looking at his daughter in this photo. He was looking at Daisy, who busily painted a picture of Emo, oblivious beneath his watchful gaze. And there, written in his own face, he saw the truth.

He saw love.

Who the hell had he been fooling? All this time he'd been using science and logic as a buffer, refusing to see what was right in front of his eyes. Afraid to take that leap of faith in case he found empty air beneath his feet instead of solid ground. But here he stood, rooted by what he saw. There in stark relief was an undeniable love, from the small, tender way his mouth curved, to the adoring gleam in his eyes, to the hunger written into every line and crevice of his face.

He loved her.

He shot to his feet, intent on telling her just that, but froze at the last moment. Would she believe him? Or would she think it was desperation speaking, a last-ditch effort to convince her to stay. How the hell could he hope to prove to her that he genuinely loved her, especially considering how slow he'd been figuring it out?

There was only one possible way. He needed proof. He needed… His attention shifted to Emo X-15's sleek form. He needed a robot capable of detecting emotion. "There's a chance. There's still a chance," he muttered.

"Where's Justice?" Jett whispered to Pretorius, though Daisy overheard. Overheard and could have wept.

"Where he always is these days," Pretorius answered glumly. "In his lab."

"But it's Christmas. Even you're up here."

Pretorius shrugged uneasily and straightened the bow on one of the presents before tucking it under the gaily lit tree. Instantly, Kit pounced on it, and proceeded to shred the bow. "Maybe he's forgotten. We never did a full-blown Christmas before. It could have slipped his mind."

"Maybe someone should remind him," Jett replied and pulled a remote control from her pocket. With a casual air, she fiddled with the buttons.

Daisy snatched a deep breath. Enough was enough. She'd hoped having Cord call about the work order would give Justice the nudge he needed. That facing the loss of all the improvements she'd made over the past month would be sufficient to force him to his senses. She should have known better. He'd always been in full possession of his senses. Which could only mean one thing.

Clearly she'd misjudged him. Misjudged what he wanted. Misjudged his intentions. Misjudged how he felt. That he could somehow come to love her.

"Okay, everyone," she said with a determined smile. "Time to open presents."

Justice didn't remember how long he worked into the night. Until three? Four? A determined *wheep! wheep!* woke him from a sound sleep. Damn Jett and that blasted...

He shot to his feet, looking around in confusion. What? When? Where? For the second time in recent memory his inner clock failed him. "Computer, date and time?" he demanded in a rusty voice.

"December twenty-fifth, 11:02:12 a.m.," came the dispassionate response.

He swore, then thrust his hands through his hair in an attempt to comb it into some semblance of neatness. Not that it helped. Between the beginnings of the sandpaper beard shadowing his jaw, eyes he didn't doubt were rimmed in sleepless red, and wrinkles pressed into his face from conking out at his workbench, he looked like someone who'd been ridden hard and put away wet.

He glanced at the robot and groaned. He'd tried. He'd worked so long and hard, worked like a maniac, in flat-out desperation. It hadn't changed a damn thing. Emo X-15 still didn't work, any more than its predecessor. He'd failed. Sinking into his chair, he scrubbed his hands across his face. He was so tired. So drained. For the first time in his life he was at a loss, uncertain how or where to move from here, longing for something he couldn't name. Didn't dare name. And yet, the names came to him, anyway.

Daisy. Noelle. Even Aggie and Jett had become part of his life. Part of what made his house a home. And he'd blown it. Failed at every turn.

"You look tired," a cool, remote voice announced.

Justice froze. Slowly he looked up. X-15 hummed with electronic life. "What did you say?"

"You look tired," X-15 repeated.

"Would you like a cup of tea?" came another hesitant voice, the voice of a robot he should have repurposed long ago… and hadn't had the heart to.

Maybe he'd kept it because Noelle adored the older robot. Maybe it was because of Daisy's softhearted attitude toward it. Or maybe it was his own reluctant affection for the silly thing. He fought for control, struggled to remain calm and rational. "Why are you asking me that question?" he asked X-14.

Emo emitted a tiny, nervous beep, as though afraid it had done something wrong. Then it spoke. "You feel sad. Tea will make you feel better."

And that's when he saw his two choices stretching before him. On one hand, the cold logic that had been his close companion for most of his life. On the other, sheer emotion.

And he smiled as he reached for Emo. For the *perfect* Emo. Because he'd just discovered an amazing truth.

Logic wouldn't get him a cup of tea.

Justice raced up the stairs, his hastily wrapped Christmas gifts overflowing his arms. He hit the top step at the same moment Daisy announced, "Okay, everyone. Time to open presents."

"Hang on," he called. "I have a few more to put under the tree." He stepped into the great room and caught Daisy's expression, a heartbreaking gaze full of pain and hope. "Sorry to keep everyone waiting. I was putting the finishing touches on my gifts."

"What did you get me?" Jett demanded greedily.

He selected hers and placed the remaining packages under the tree, rescuing them from Kit's eager claws. "This is a joint gift from Pretorius and me."

Jett ripped open the long, narrow box without hesitation and peered inside. Papers were nestled beneath tissue paper. She used more caution now, lifting them out and carefully unfolding them. Her breath caught. "These…these are letters of recommendation."

"For college," Justice confirmed.

She clutched them to her chest. "From The. Great. Justice. St. John."

"And from me," Pretorius groused. "I'm not exactly chopped liver, you know. It so happens I'm a highly respected member of the computer community."

"Thanks, Uncle P."

She raced to his side and gave him an exuberant hug, one that should have sent him into an immediate panic. Instead he turned a deep shade of red and patted her awkwardly on her back. "Now, now. That's quite enough of the mushy stuff. You haven't even seen the real present."

"There's more?"

She pulled free of the embrace and gently refolded the letters of recommendation as though they were made of spun gold before opening the envelope that accompanied them. She read the note inside, her face crumpling.

"Jett?" Daisy asked uneasily.

"It's…it's a full scholarship, all expenses paid, from Sinjin, Incorporated for the college of my choice, anywhere in the world." She buried her face in her hands.

"Of course, you have to get accepted first," Justice warned.

This time she flew into his arms and wrapped him up in a tight, teary hug. "Thank you. You couldn't have given me a better present."

"Well, now," Aggie said, dabbing at her eyes. "I do believe this calls for a nice cup of tea."

Pretorius selected another gift from under the tree, a large square box, and offered it to the housekeeper. "In that case, you'll need this."

Unlike Jett, Aggie opened her present with care, removing the ribbons and sliding a fingernail beneath the tape. Neatly unfolding the wrapping paper, she set it aside "to add to my scrapbook." Finally, she lifted the top from the box. "Oh, Pretorius. You couldn't have picked a better gift." She eased the dainty teapot from its protective paper. "It's Spode, isn't it?"

"Their Christmas tea set," he confirmed. "And Justice is giving you a selection of teas from around the world. You'll get a new one every week."

She gave the men a misty smile. "Well, then, we'll just have to try out a lovely cup of tea in my new teapot, won't we?"

Jett emerged from beneath the tree, carrying one of Justice's haphazardly wrapped presents. "I found this for Noelle." She handed it to the toddler and helped with the wrapping paper. "Check it out! It's a baby Emo. Does it work any better than the other ones?"

"Nowhere near as well," he admitted with a sly grin, then gestured toward the tree. "Any more presents under there?"

"Something for you," Daisy announced. She handed him a large, sketch pad-size gift, as well as an envelope. "I suggest you start with the envelope."

He had a sneaking suspicion he knew what it contained and hoped against hope he was wrong. Unfortunately, he confirmed his guess the instant he read the work order Cord had called about. "What if I don't want this gift?" he asked tightly.

"Then you can have the other one. It's sort of an either/or proposition. You can have whichever one you want, but not both."

He cautiously removed the gift wrapping on the second gift, surprised to discover that it really was a sketchpad. He flipped open the cover. To his delight he realized she'd drawn a mockup for a new storybook, the futuristic adventures of a mischievous preschooler who bore a striking resemblance to Noelle, and a broken-down robot the image of Emo, whose function was to read and respond to human emotion. But because he got everything wrong, he'd been sent to the junkyard, where the little girl found him and carted him home.

The storyline was adorable, funny and poignant, and he savored each and every page. Toward the end of the story, the two were discovered by the authorities and the robot had to either get his emotion reader to work or the little girl would be forced to return him to the scrap heap.

The final test came in front of a stern-faced tribunal. "What do I feel?" the little girl asked her robot, her heart in her eyes.

Justice gently flipped the page. But instead of a conclusion he found himself staring at a blank sheet of paper. He looked at Daisy in bewilderment. "I don't understand. There's no ending."

"That's because I can't end it…until you tell me how. If you can't, you'll have to accept the work order. Either/or, Justice."

He closed his eyes. He knew how this story concluded. He'd known all along. Until today, he hadn't believed himself capable of the emotion. But not anymore. Not when everything he wanted was on the line…a line he'd drawn and dared Daisy to step over. She hadn't stepped over it, she'd leaped over it, kicking his line into nonexistence.

He closed the sketch pad and picked up his gift to her, setting it down in front of her. It didn't take much imagination to guess what he'd so awkwardly wrapped. Without a word she stripped away the wrapping paper to reveal Emo.

"Turn it on," he encouraged.

She pressed the appropriate button on the robot's control panel helmet. Emo hummed to life. "Hello, Emo," she said.

The head turned in circles, the bright aquamarine eyes scanning the room, scanning the people one by one. "I love you. I'm hungry. Would you like a nice cup of tea?"

Jett burst out laughing and Noelle clapped her hands, babbling in excitement. "Emo," Justice said. "How do I feel?"

"You would like a nice cup of tea," Emo chirped.

It was all Justice could do to keep from yanking his hair out by the roots. "Damn it, you good for nothing bucket of bolts! You were supposed to tell Daisy I love her!"

For a split second no one moved. No one even drew breath. Then Daisy flew into his arms. "I believe you just did tell me. And to be honest, I'd much rather hear it from you than from Emo." She gazed up at him, her own love spilling out like rays of sunshine on a cloudless day. "And that was exactly the line I hoped to use to end the story I wrote."

Justice blew out a sigh. "I'm sorry, Daisy. I worked all night on him. I thought…" He trailed off, shaking his head.

"That he could tell me what you couldn't?"

"No!" He took a deep breath. "No. I do love you, Daisy. I

love you with all my heart. But I didn't think you'd believe me, not after I resisted saying the words for so long."

"You figured if Emo said them for you, if he read your emotions, I'd believe you?"

"Yes." He dropped his forehead to hers. "I've spent twenty-seven years, two months and twenty-six days believing I couldn't feel. It was easier to believe. Less painful."

She gave him a tremulous smile. "And now?"

"Now it's more painful not to say the words," he admitted. "I can't bear the thought of losing you and the rest of our family. Please don't let the story end with a blank page. Please be the one who'll give me a real family, not an apprentice family. Who'll always be there for me if I'm ever hurt again. Take a chance. Marry me, Daisy."

Her smile grew, blinding him with its brilliance. "I'll marry you, on two conditions."

Aw, hell. "Which are?"

"First, Joint Condition Two. I'm allowed downstairs whenever I want."

His tawny gaze grew brighter than the Christmas tree lights. "I'll agree to that if you'll agree to Joint Condition Three," he bargained.

"Which is?"

"You create a room upstairs just for the two of us. One on the south side of the house."

"But…" Uncertainty filled her expression. "That's the sunny side."

"So it is." Warmth filled his eyes. "It's time to leave the darkness behind and step out into the sunlight, don't you think?" He pulled her closer. "Now will you marry me?"

She nodded, hope springing to life and filling her expression with joy. "If you can answer just one more tiny question."

"And what question is that?"

"How do you feel, Justice?" she whispered.

He could hear the collective inhale as everyone waited for his response. When he spoke, he spoke from the heart. "I feel…happy. Like our story is just beginning."

"Oh, Justice." Tears of delight filled her eyes. "And what a story it will be."

"One for the books," he agreed and feathered a kiss across her mouth. "After all, you taught a robot to feel."

"No, Justice." She returned his kiss, their first real kiss. "I taught a man to love."

* * * * *

LET'S TALK
Romance

For exclusive extracts, competitions
and special offers, find us online:

- facebook.com/millsandboon
- @MillsandBoon
- @MillsandBoonUK

Get in touch on 01413 063232

For all the latest titles coming soon, visit
millsandboon.co.uk/nextmonth

MILLS & BOON

THE HEART OF ROMANCE

A ROMANCE FOR EVERY KIND OF READER

MODERN

Prepare to be swept off your feet by sophisticated, sexy and seductive heroes, in some of the world's most glamourous and romantic locations, where power and passion collide.
8 stories per month.

HISTORICAL

Escape with historical heroes from time gone by. Whether your passion is for wicked Regency Rakes, muscled Vikings or rugged Highlanders, awaken the romance of the past.
6 stories per month.

MEDICAL

Set your pulse racing with dedicated, delectable doctors in the high-pressure world of medicine, where emotions run high and passion, comfort and love are the best medicine.
6 stories per month.

True Love

Celebrate true love with tender stories of heartfelt romance, from the rush of falling in love to the joy a new baby can bring, and a focus on the emotional heart of a relationship.
8 stories per month.

Desire

Indulge in secrets and scandal, intense drama and plenty of sizzling hot action with powerful and passionate heroes who have it all: wealth, status, good looks…everything but the right woman.
6 stories per month.

HEROES

Experience all the excitement of a gripping thriller, with an intense romance at its heart. Resourceful, true-to-life women and strong, fearless men face danger and desire - a killer combination!
8 stories per month.

DARE

Sensual love stories featuring smart, sassy heroines you'd want as a best friend, and compelling intense heroes who are worthy of them.
4 stories per month.

To see which titles are coming soon, please visit

millsandboon.co.uk/nextmonth

MILLS & BOON
True Love

Romance from the Heart

Celebrate true love with tender stories of
heartfelt romance, from the rush of falling
in love to the joy a new baby can bring,
and a focus on the emotional
heart of a relationship.

MILLS & BOON

HEROES

At Your Service

Experience all the excitement of a gripping thriller, with an intense romance at its heart. Resourceful, true-to-life women and strong, fearless men face danger and desire - a killer combination!